RED

D0051788

'difficult to put
down... a thoroughly
entertaining novel that
I would recommend
to those looking for a
summer blockbuster'
Sacramento Book Review
on *Age of Odin*

New York Times Best Selling Author
JAMES LOVEGROVE

SOLARIS

US $7.99
CAN $9.99

ISBN 978-1-907992-05-6

First published 2011 by Solaris
an imprint of Rebellion Publishing Ltd,
Riverside House, Osney Mead,
Oxford, OX2 0ES, UK

www.solarisbooks.com

ISBN: 978 1 907992 05 6

10 9 8 7 6 5 4 3 2 1

A CIP catalogue record for this book is available from the
British Library.

Designed & typeset by Rebellion Publishing

Printed in the US

JAMES LOVEGROVE
REDLAW

WITHDRAWN

SOLARIS

LONDON AT NIGHT.

The city's veins throb with light, with life. Traffic pulses to and fro, white one way, red the other. Signs glare. Windows flare. The massed glow from neon and incandescent bulbs burnishes the sky.

But there are dark areas down there in the urban sprawl, like cancer growths on an X-ray. Places where no lights shine. Black spots.

See them?

There in Harringay. In Southall. In Deptford and Stoke Newington, Hounslow and Beckenham, Kilburn and Peckham Rye.

They stand out, black amongst the brilliance. The opposite of beacons. Not beckoning—repelling.

Shall we descend towards one of them? Why not? That one there to the east, say, in Mile End.

Well, what are you waiting for? An invitation? You don't have to have one. Still, if it'll make you happy...

Come on. Come on down with me. Enter London from above. Enter freely and of your own will.

The traffic growl grows as we get lower. The vehicles of the night—what music they make.

Few drivers, however, choose to go where we are going, and so we sink into a kind of bubble of hush as we near our destination. London's twenty-four-hour grumble is muted, and here amid the bleak concrete geometry of a high-rise housing estate we hear only the softest of sounds. A scurry. A snarl. A whisper that could be a voice, or the rustle of a scrap of newspaper blown across cracked tarmac.

All that moves is the wind, clawing over waste ground and round the gigantic tombstone tower blocks. The rest is stillness.

You can feel it, though, can't you? The sense—the certainty—of being watched. Eyes, staring at you from broken windows, from behind that gutted car, from within that patch of head-high knotweed. Deep red eyes.

The estate looks unlived-in, abandoned, deserted.

Yet there are residents.

Everywhere.

Watching.

So let's depart, if it unnerves you. We don't have to stay. Let's rise and travel, away from the dark, towards the light.

But not far. Not too far.

Because there's activity, just outside the decrepit but still tenanted housing estate. A street or so beyond its boundaries, beyond the tall, wire mesh fence with its thorny crown of barbed wire...

...someone is running.

A boy.

In terror.

Running for his life.

CHAPTER ONE

NIKOLA, AS HE ran, wished many things.

He wished he was faster. He wished he had wings. Above all he wished he had never strayed beyond the fence. They had warned him against it. Everyone had. Countless times. The fence, they had told him, is there for a reason. Not to keep us in. To keep *them* out. So do not go over it. Stay this side. It is dangerous out there for our kind.

Nikola had listened. But he hadn't *listened*. He'd seen little of London since arriving on the ferry from mainland Europe. In fact, once he'd been discovered stowed away in the back of the articulated goods lorry, all he'd seen was a detention centre, the inside of a van, then the housing estate. He was sixteen, and he did not care for being confined.

So tonight he had scaled the fence. All but vaulted over it, in fact. It was not that high, four metres or thereabouts. The barbed wire had scraped his hands but drawn no blood. An easy escape. Everyone was right: the fence was a deterrent to the rest of the world, not to those inside it.

Tentatively, curiously, Nikola had begun to explore.

In the immediate vicinity of the estate there was nothing much. Dead shops, hollow houses, pavements latticed with weeds. Nobody wanted to live here, so close to a Sunless Residential Area. Local Londoners had decanted themselves elsewhere.

Nikola startled a stray cat, which yowled and spat at him like a demented thing before scurrying away. A short while later he had to hide as a SHADE patrol car rolled by, sweeping its searchlight. Emerging from the basement stairwell down which he'd ducked, he carried on his voyage of discovery warily. He hugged the street shadows, of which there were plenty, as he moved out towards where the city was alive and humming.

He only wanted to take a look, that was all. Just to see what it was like, this English capital, this fabled metropolis that was now, by default, his home. He was certainly not on the prowl, hunting for victims. He could smell them from afar, and the smell was unbelievably exotic and intoxicating, but he had no intention of taking one of them for himself. He knew how insanely unwise that would be, how it could have dire repercussions for his whole community. A little curiosity, though, a little sightseeing—that was allowed, wasn't it?

His attackers came out of nowhere. There was no warning. They were quick, and they were wrapped head to toe in thick clothing which masked their scent. This, more than anything, told Nikola that they were specialists. They'd been lying in ambush, hoping for precisely this opportunity, waiting for someone like him to happen along. Someone rash. Someone reckless.

There were four of them, all in motorcycle helmets with leather neck guards. Two were on rollerblades, leading the attack, hurtling unexpectedly around a corner, keeping low as they kick-thrusted themselves towards Nikola, arms pumping. He started to move, but they were on him in no time. A blow from a chainmail-gloved fist caught him on the side of the head and sent him reeling.

Nikola staggered to his feet, only to see the two rollerbladers arc around each other in the middle of the street and veer at him again. As he turned to run, he came face to face with the other two members of the gang. They stood with their legs apart, braced, each carrying an ash-wood stake.

Nikola felt fear then like he had never felt before. The stakes' sharpened points were bright white in the darkness. The visors on the helmets of the men wielding them were implacably black and blank.

He sprang sideways. It was all he could do. He collided with a set of railings, which he hurdled clumsily. Within seconds he was scaling the face of a three-storey terraced house. He heard shouts behind him, below him. He scuttled up the brickwork as fast as he could, finding finger purchase in the narrowest of crevices. Height. If he gained height, surely he would be safe. These men could not follow him up onto the rooftops, could they?

But they could. While the two rollerbladers raced off in opposite directions, heading for the ends of the terrace to cut off Nikola's escape that way, the other two men lodged their stakes in their belts and went in pursuit of him on foot, propelling themselves up the front of the house much as he had, if not quite so straightforwardly. Drainpipe, window ledge, door lintel, anything that projected outwards, however slightly, was of use to them. They were free runners. Vertical, horizontal, diagonal, it made no difference—it was just a surface to be negotiated, just a series of handholds and toeholds they could employ to get to where they were going.

Nikola reached the roof, moments ahead of his pursuers. He darted along the vertex, doing his best to keep his balance on the rounded tiles. The two men thundered after him. Nikola swung round a chimney stack. A second afterwards, so did they. Only a couple of houses lay between him and the end of the street. One of the rollerbladers was waiting for him there, at the corner. Nikola jinked right and slithered down the angle of the roof towards the houses' backyards and the alley that furrowed in between. He leapt off the gutter, landing lightly on a wall below. Then he was in the alley, skirting overturned dustbins and upended shopping trolleys. The pair of free runners weren't far behind.

The rollerblader intercepted him at the alley's mouth. Nikola, however, sprinting with all his might, barged straight into the man, his shoulder low. The rollerblader was shunted backwards, went scooting across the street, and whacked into a lamppost, letting out a loud grunt of pain. He recovered and joined the two runners in chasing after Nikola; soon all three of them were at Nikola's heels. Nikola pounded on, praying that he was going the right way. The tower blocks of the Residential Area loomed ahead, but the street he was on seemed to be curving away from them. He had no idea whether to take a right or a left at the next junction. If he could get to the Residential Area he would surely be okay. The men would not dare follow him over the fence. But he felt that he was in a maze, and any wrong turn he made would be the end of him. He was strong, stronger than any of the four men, but they outnumbered him, and they had weapons.

Then Nikola slammed face first into the ground. He didn't know how it had happened. Had he tripped? He tried to get up but couldn't. His legs were stuck fast together. Ropes entwined his ankles, attached to weighted steel spheres. A bolas. Frantically Nikola began to unpick the ropes, but the three attackers now had him surrounded. The other rollerblader appeared, skidding to a halt. Nikola looked up at them all, baring his teeth and hissing in rage. He swiped at the nearest of them, raking talons across the man's leg, but his trousers were made of Kevlar or something. Some fabric that talons couldn't penetrate.

Knees pinned Nikola's wrists roughly to the road. He struggled with all his might, but the men bore down, holding him in place. A stake was brandished. Nikola writhed and spat. All he could think of, even as he lay there helpless and apparently doomed, was tearing open the throats of his four attackers and feasting on the delicious warmth within. His thirst, spurred by anger, was a feral thing. He despised them all. They were nothing but cattle. Prey. Given the chance, he would drain every last drop of life from them.

The stake hovered, poised above his chest. The fist around it tightened its grip.

"Drop it."

The voice was deep, calm. Its tone did not expect refusal.

"I'll give you to the count of three. Drop it, or I drop you."

Nikola's English was not good, but he knew enough to tell that the person speaking was threatening his four attackers, not him. He twisted his head round on the tarmac to look. He saw boots, a long overcoat, a tall man with moon-white hair and a face as craggy and imperturbable as a chalk cliff. He saw, too, a high shirt collar like a priest's, one that went all the way up to the jawline, and a gun, a weighty, long-barrelled handweapon of the type he knew was called a Cindermaker.

Which meant SHADE. The Night Brigade.

Which in turn meant Nikola was no less doomed than he had been a few seconds ago.

"ONE LAST CHANCE," said the SHADE officer. "Put down the stake or be put down. A bullet's a bullet. Wooden or not, it'll still put a damn great hole in you."

"Fuck off, fangbanger," said one of Nikola's attackers. "This here's a vamp and it's out of its nest. If we weren't about to dust it, you'd be doing the same yourself."

"Maybe," came the reply. "The difference is that I'm a servant of the law. You, you're nothing but vigilantes. Stokers, right?"

"Yeah. So?"

"So, drop the stake and move away from the Sunless." The SHADE officer advanced, Cindermaker to the fore. "One. Two..."

"Wait," said another of the Stokers, one of the rollerbladers. "Wait just a second. Let us poke a hole in the bloodsucker"—he gestured at Nikola—"and we'll be gone. No one will know we were ever here, and you can claim the dusting as your own. Come on, what do you say, shady? That's reasonable, isn't it? Everybody wins."

"Do you know who I am?"

The Stokers shook their heads.

"The name 'John Redlaw' ring a bell?"

Not with three of them, but the fourth man stiffened. "Yeah, I've heard of this geezer all right. Tough bastard, they say."

As for Nikola, he was truly terrified. He might not have been in this country long but even he had heard of John Redlaw. The man was spoken of among his kind often and only ever in hushed tones, the name rarely uttered louder than a whisper.

"Then," said Redlaw to the man, "you'll know I can't be dissuaded and I can't be bargained with." He halted less than five paces from the Stokers and Nikola. "I'll happily blow each and every one of you out of your socks, and to hell with the paperwork. The 'Less is mine. Leave now, and you leave intact. My best and final offer."

The Stokers looked at one another. Then the one with the stake said, "Fuck it," and flung it at Redlaw. As Redlaw twisted to evade it, the Stoker pounced on him. He punched Redlaw's gun hand, sending the Cindermaker flying, then he punched Redlaw himself, full in the face. Blood spurted from the SHADE officer's nose.

"Fuck's sake, come on!" the Stoker yelled to his cohorts as Redlaw went down. "There's just one of him, and he's old. Let's have some fun here."

The other three needed little encouragement. They relinquished Nikola and dived in to beat up Redlaw.

"Wave a gun at us, will you?" one cried.

"Ash-wood fucking bullets?" snarled another. "Ash-wood? On *people*?"

Kicks and punches flew. Nikola could no longer see Redlaw. The SHADE officer was buried beneath the Stokers, the hidden eye of a storm of violence. He didn't appear to be fighting back. Why not? Was he really not as fearsome as his reputation suggested? Was he, in fact, nothing without a gun in his hand?

Then there was a loud crunch, and one of the rollerblader Stokers whirled to the ground, clutching a broken knee.

A snap, and a second Stoker sank down, shrieking, his left arm skewed hideously at the elbow.

Suddenly Redlaw was on his feet, and he was gripping the other rollerblader by the jacket, swinging him into the fourth Stoker, and sending them both crashing onto the road in a heap. Redlaw straddled them, grabbed the uppermost by his neck guard, and began pounding his head against the man below's. The helmet visors shattered; splinters of black polycarbonate were hammered into skin. Redlaw didn't relent until both Stokers were half senseless and their features were like bloody maps of hell. Then he went over to the rollerblader Stoker with the crippled knee and, almost clinically, stamped on his good knee until it was crippled too. Finally he turned to the man with the broken arm, who was hobbling away, whimpering. He yanked the man's helmet off, exposing a pain-wracked, tear-streaked face.

"If there's one thing lower than vampires," he said, "it's people who prey on vampires. I want you to carry a message to your cronies, all those other Stokers who think they're so self-righteous and clever. A personal message. Will you do that for me?"

Desperately the Stoker nodded.

"Tell them this, from Captain John Redlaw of the Sunless Housing And Disclosure Executive..."

Headbutt.

The Stoker toppled backwards with a ghastly yelp. His skull cracked on the road surface, and he lay still.

Redlaw straightened out his shirt collar, smoothed down his overcoat, and went to retrieve his Cindermaker.

THROUGHOUT THE FIGHT Nikola did nothing but gawp. He knew he should flee while Redlaw was busy with the Stokers, but he was still badly shaken from the attack. He'd been moments away from getting staked, his immortality over almost as soon as it had begun. He was hollowed with fear, and besides, once the tide of the fight turned and Redlaw started taking the four men apart, he had wanted to watch. It was an awesome sight, Redlaw despatching the Stokers with such ruthless, savage precision. Gratifying, too, to Nikola. They deserved what they were getting. Every bit of it and more.

In hindsight, he realised he had made something of an error. For now Redlaw was striding towards him, Cindermaker in hand, its barrel levelled at Nikola's heart. Nikola started scrabbling to free himself from the bolas ropes.

"*Bun seara.*" Redlaw said. "*Labvakar. Blaho ve er. Jó estét.*"

The last one, Nikola recognised. "*Jó estét,*" he replied. *Good evening.*

"Ah," said Redlaw. "Hungarian. *Magyar?*"

Nikola nodded. "*Igen.*"

"You speak English?"

"A little. Please, not shoot."

Redlaw glanced at his gun, then back at Nikola. "Don't give me a reason to shoot and I won't. You understand?"

Nikola did, just about. The SHADE officer's expression was, if not gentle, then marginally less severe than when he'd been addressing the Stokers. His face's solidity had softened just a fraction, though his eyes remained hard and watchful.

"It would help if you stopped staring at the blood from my nose."

Nikola averted his gaze guiltily. The fresh blood sang to him. Its sweet ferrous smell was unbearably enticing. As a boy—a human boy—back in Miskolc, the most wonderful aroma he'd ever known was his grandmother's hot chocolate, warming on the stove, and the most wonderful flavour he'd ever known was the drink itself, laced with spices and a dash of apricot *palinka*. But blood was a hundred, a thousand times more wonderful than even that.

Redlaw dabbed at his upper lip with a linen handkerchief. "Lucky shot. I should never have let the idiot catch me unawares like that, or get so close. Old man. Losing my edge. Although, having said that, I did fancy a bit of a scrap. Listen, sonny."

Dark eyes bored into Nikola's.

"From the looks of you—incompletely emerged fangs, still a trace of pink in your complexion, only the faintest reddening of the sclera—it wasn't so long ago that you were turned. My guess is you don't just look young, you *are* young. So I'm going to give you the benefit of the doubt. It's not something I often do. Ever do, actually. But I'm prepared to make an exception. You wanted to see the outside world. I get that. Don't. Don't ever want that. You can see why." He indicated the four Stokers strewn in their various poses of agony and semi-consciousness. "You don't belong out here. No one wants you out here. The Sunless Residential Area is your home. Your only home. Forever. Clear?"

More or less. His tone, if not his words. Nikola nodded.

"Then go. Get back behind the fence. Before I change my mind."

The Cindermaker continued to point, unwaveringly, at Nikola's beatless heart.

Ropes loosened, Nikola ran no longer in an ecstasy of dread, but suffused with relief and joy.

LEARNED HIS LESSON, thought Redlaw as the boy vanished from view.

The four Stokers had doubtless learned theirs too.

Redlaw pulled out the crucifix that hung round his neck. The wood was warm against his lips as he kissed it briefly. He murmured a prayer of thanks—for victory, for deliverance from his enemies. The prayer was perfunctory and low, so much so that even the Almighty might have missed it.

As he was returning the crucifix to its rightful place next to his sternum, Redlaw's phone sounded. His ringtone was the opening chords of 'Jerusalem' played on a thunderous cathedral organ.

"John." The throaty, no-nonsense tones of Commodore Gail Macarthur.

"What can I do for you, Commodore?"

"GPS puts you down Mile End way."

"That I am."

"But your car's not moving and you're not in it."

"How do you know I'm not in it?"

"Well, if you were you'd have heard the bulletin from dispatch and be en route already. There's a disturbance at the Hackney SRA."

"What a surprise."

"Local units have responded, but they need backup. Someone with some seniority."

"Me."

"Anything better to be doing?"

Redlaw scanned the street; eyed the Stokers. "Not much, marm."

"Right, then. Off you go."

Redlaw ended the call with a sigh.

It was going to be a long night.

But then weren't they all?

CHAPTER TWO

THE HACKNEY SUNLESS Residential Area was the largest SRA in all of Greater London and the most densely populated. It consisted of forty hectares of former local authority property plus an additional ten hectares of buildings wrested from private ownership by compulsory purchase order. Within its boundary lay architecture spanning a century and a half, from Victorian semi-detached villas to modern brutalist blocks, all now forming one large convoluted warren where Sunless roamed freely in their thousands.

It was a notorious trouble spot. Had been since the start, but more so now than ever. There was always *something* going on in the Hackney SRA. That, along with its sprawling size, made it a blight on the entire borough. Hackney was now considered all but uninhabitable to anyone with a heartbeat. A few hardy Somali and Eritrean refugees lived here, deeming it safer than their war-torn, drought-blighted homelands, but that was all.

Redlaw arrived to find a half-dozen SHADE patrol cars stationed outside the Residential Area's main entrance and twice that number of officers standing around seemingly at a loss to know what to do. From beyond the fence could be heard a chorus of howls and gibbering, shrill and loathsome, echoing up to the bronze-tinged night sky.

The highest-ranking person on site, until Redlaw turned up, was Sergeant Ibrahim Khalid. He gave Redlaw a token salute, more than a little glad to be able to hand over responsibility for the situation. More than a little glad, too, that it was Redlaw who would now be carrying the can for this one. There was no love lost between these two men.

"What's going on here?" Redlaw demanded.

"As you can hear," said Khalid, "we have some very unhappy campers. Details are sketchy, but the gist of it is, a regular consignment of cattle blood went in at twenty-three hundred hours, as scheduled. That was forty-five minutes ago, and the truck hasn't come back out. Thirty minutes ago the drivers—standard two-man unit—radioed in a mayday to base. Since then there's been no further contact from them. Judging by all that caterwaul, it'd be sensible to expect the worst."

"The hauliers?"

"BovPlas Logistics, of course. Their guys are pros. Trained for all outcomes."

"Training isn't always enough. Why haven't you mounted a rescue attempt yet?"

Khalid's eyes flicked downwards briefly. "As I said, no one's heard from the truck for half an hour. Closer on thirty-five minutes now. It would be unreasonable to expect—"

"Unreasonable, sergeant?" snapped Redlaw. "I'll tell you what's unreasonable. A dozen fully-armed officers hanging around with their thumbs up their fundaments while two human beings are trapped inside an SRA surrounded by God knows how many vampires. *That's* unreasonable."

"Sir, with all due respect..."

"Don't 'with all due respect' me, Khalid. You damn well should have gone in, and you know it."

Redlaw swung away from Khalid and strode towards the Residential Area entrance.

"Captain!" Khalid called out after him. "The 'Lesses are in bloodlust mode. They'll tear anyone who goes in there apart."

"Much though I appreciate the concern, sergeant," Redlaw replied, holding his crucifix up above his shoulder for Khalid to see, "I have this to protect me. And failing that, I have this." With his other hand he waved his Cindermaker. "What the Good Lord doesn't provide, gunpowder and the laws of physics will."

THE STEEL ARCH surmounting the entranceway bore the SRA's name and the SHADE logo along with the legend "Working For A Safer Community For All." Over this someone had spray-painted the words:

UNDEAD ZONE

And under, in loopy tag lettering that dripped like blood:

THERES A SUCKA BORN EVERY MINUTE

The gates stood wide open. No reason for the BovPlas Logistics drivers to have bothered closing them. Had this been a routine run, the truck would have made its delivery and been back out, ten minutes flat. Nobody was likely to saunter in through the entrance in the interim. At least, nobody with any sense.

As Redlaw passed through, he made a quick mental inventory of his weapons. Ash-wood stakes—six. *Allium sativum* extract smoke bombs—two. *Aqua sancta* grenades—five. All clipped to the standard-issue field deployment vest he wore under his overcoat. Plus, of course, his Cindermaker, for which he was carrying an extra twenty-one rounds in three magazines.

His crucifix was better than any of these, his ultimate deterrent.

Or so he had always used to think.

He trod a street littered with trash and detritus. Sunless were anything but proud about the state of their accommodation; badly boarded-up windows, sagging roofs, holes in floorboards, filth lying everywhere, none of it bothered them. The copious vermin the squalor attracted—rats, foxes, pigeons—didn't bother them either. In fact, vermin were welcome in an SRA. Handy free range snacks.

A trio of Sunless emerged from the shadows of an overgrown front garden—youths in trainers and hooded tops, sentries whose job it was to see off intruders. Redlaw clocked their presence and kept on walking. They took up position alongside him, matching their pace to his, murmuring taunts in their native language (Romanian, if he didn't miss his guess). Framed by the hoods, scarlet eyes and sharp white teeth glinted.

The three kept their distance, though. The unholstered Cindermaker and Redlaw's evident lack of fear saw to that.

He headed on towards the noise. It was the kind of racket that could drive an ordinary person to the edge of sanity, a bedlam of inhuman voices wailing sounds that were almost but not quite words. It was shot through with fury, and indignation, and above all a dreadful, aching hunger. A jail full of starving prisoners, slowly losing their minds, might well set up a cacophony like this.

"The Lord is my shepherd," Redlaw intoned under his breath. "I shall not want. He maketh me to lie down in green pastures..."

He entered a square, still with his three-strong escort. This would have been a highly desirable address once, large old houses on all sides and a small rectangular park in the middle. The houses' façades were now leprous with pitted plasterwork and peeled paint, while the park was bald earth dotted with the odd clump of grass and a few neglected, wilting trees and shrubs.

Here stood the BovPlas Logistics refrigerated truck. Like the square, it was in a sorry state. Its tyres were burst. Its radiator grille had been torn off and the engine eviscerated. Its rear doors hung askew, and the cattle blood it had been transporting for the Sunless to distribute among themselves, several hundred plastic pouches of the stuff, was everywhere. Pavements were slick with it. Walls dripped with it. The pouches themselves lay scattered about, deflated, shredded, like so many dead jellyfish washed up by some crimson tide.

Of the two drivers, Redlaw could see no immediate sign, but the truck's cab had been broken into, which did not bode well. BovPlas Logistics armoured its fleet. Every vehicle came fitted with heavy-duty dual-layer plexiglass and a tungsten-and-ceramic composite shell. Tough, but nothing that would hold up to a horde of frenzied Sunless.

And "frenzied" was the only word for it. Vampires thronged the square, scores of them, a mob, surging here and there with looks on their faces that ranged from baleful to deranged. Some were fighting among themselves, engaged in a tug of war over the last few blood pouches still intact. Others were vandalising the already dilapidated houses, ripping off roof slates and kicking in gables and fascia boards, or denuding the trees of the scant branches they had left. Redlaw thought of zoo animals, maddened by captivity, wantonly destroying their cages. Their massed banshee cries reverberated in his ears, deafening.

The sensible option would have been to retreat. The trio of Sunless behind him were an obstacle to that, but not one that couldn't be overcome.

Instead, Redlaw raised his Cindermaker and fired into the air.

Once.

Again.

A third time.

That got everyone's attention. The rioting subsided. Heads turned his way. Shortly, Redlaw was the focus of countless crimson, blood-gorged gazes. Vampires began moving towards him. They crawled down from the houses. They crept along the road, some of them on all fours. They clustered and closed around him in a large circle, like the pupil of an eye contracting. He was surrounded by pallid, contorted faces and gnarled, clawlike hands. Noses sniffed greedily at the odour he exuded, the raw thick throb of *life*. The creatures' own stench was unfathomably foul—partly decomposed flesh mixed with fresh blood.

Redlaw stood erect, refusing to be intimidated.

"I shall say this only once," he announced, loud. "You will disperse. This kind of conduct will not be tolerated. Leave the square immediately and in an orderly manner. Return to your homes."

Nobody obeyed. The circle tightened, narrowing the gap between Redlaw and the throng of Sunless around him.

"You will also," Redlaw said, "surrender the drivers of that vehicle to me. Whether they are alive or dead, I want them now."

Sniggers and cackles.

Redlaw aimed his Cindermaker at a random vampire and cocked the hammer.

"You," he said to the creature, a female. "Do you want to die—again? It won't be instantaneous, either. No head shot or heart shot. A flesh wound." He pointed the gun at her leg. "Fraxinus round, ash wood carbonised to steel hardness. Fragmenting on impact. Toxic splinters slowly poisoning you. Your body crumbling away bit by bit. It could take hours. Days, even. And nothing you can do about it. A vile way to go. Is that what you'd like?"

The Sunless woman cringed and backed away.

Another vampire, feeling bold, said, "We are many, you are one. We will feast on you, Night Brigade man. We will drink your veins dry, and when that is done we will break you open and crack your bones and suck out the marrow."

There was a smattering of agreement among the crowd.

"Sounds delicious," Redlaw said. "And no doubt that might happen. But not before I dust a dozen of you, maybe more. So which of you are prepared to sacrifice yourselves so that the rest can have a piece of me? Come on. Who's up first? Any volunteers?"

He swivelled the gun round. "You?"

He swivelled again. "You?"

And again. "How about you? One of you's got to make the first move. Who's it going to be?"

The Sunless stayed put. Several of them bowed their heads, looking at the ground. Others shuffled their feet. Mouths which had opened wide to expose rows of fangs now closed.

"Exactly." Redlaw gave a quick, satisfied nod. "So, to reiterate. Disperse. Now. And give me the two drivers."

For a few seconds nobody moved. Then the Sunless began, almost sheepishly, to leave. The circle broke apart, the crowd drifting away, casting the odd sullen look back at Redlaw, the odd resentful glare.

Redlaw grabbed one of the departing vampires by the arm.

"Not so fast."

The man was a squat, shabby little individual, hunched and pinched, wearing an aged leather blouson jacket splotched with unnameable stains and peeling in flakes along the seams. The spark of bloodlust was still in his eyes, but dwindling.

"Maybe you can tell me where those two men are."

"They were dragged off," the Sunless said.

"That much I could work out for myself. Where to? Did you see?"

"I think... I do not know... Possibly to..."

"To...?"

The man was about to reply when all at once a transparent sphere the size of a tennis ball came spiralling through the air and detonated in the midst of the departing crowd. Vaporised liquid burst in a mist, and every Sunless it touched recoiled in distress. There was the sizzle of burning skin, an outbreak of screams and shouts. Another three spheres followed the first, all with identical results. The crowd panicked. Suddenly there were vampires bolting in every direction, stampeding.

Into the square charged SHADE officers, led by Sergeant Khalid. He barked orders, and more *aqua sancta* grenades flew. Allium sativum smoke bombs were lobbed too; clouds of pungent yellow garlic gas erupted, billowing outwards. Sunless ran from them, spluttering and choking.

"Go! Go!" yelled Khalid. "Fan out! I want the place cleared. I don't want to see a single 'Less within a hundred yards of this spot. Flush them out, shoot or stake any stragglers."

Redlaw stormed towards Khalid through the chaos, dragging with him the man he'd been interrogating.

"Sergeant! What the hell are you doing? What is the meaning of all this?"

"No need to thank me, captain," Khalid replied. "Just saving your skin, that's all."

"I had everything under control. They were calm. They were leaving."

"Didn't look that way to me. And you're the one who said we should go in. So that's what we've done."

"I'm trying to retrieve the truck drivers, or at least their bodies. You've just made that ten times more difficult. It's a good thing I've got this fellow here to—"

At that moment Redlaw felt a tug. He looked round to find that, instead of a vampire, all he was holding onto was the tatty blouson jacket. The man had wormed out of his grasp and was haring off across the square, in his shirtsleeves, as fast as his stubby little legs could carry him.

"Sir," said Khalid, a hint of a smile peeping through his beard.

"We're going to have words about this later, you and I," Redlaw said, jabbing a finger at the sergeant.

Then, tossing the jacket aside, he raced off after the Sunless.

GARLIC SMOKE STUNG his eyes, and he skidded on discarded blood pouches. Frantic vampires blundered into his path and had to be skirted around or shoved aside.

Redlaw forged on regardless, intent on his quarry, determined not to lose sight of him. The fellow had seemed to have some idea where the truck drivers had been taken. It was a slender lead but it was better than nothing.

For all his stumpiness, the creature could certainly shift. He had the preternatural strength and speed common to his kind, and Redlaw, going flat out, could only just keep up. The vampire had stamina, too. Five minutes into the pursuit, Redlaw's lungs were heaving and he was starting to flag, whereas his quarry was still bounding along like an Olympic athlete, pace undiminished.

"Stop," Redlaw called out raggedly. "I just want to talk. I'm not going to hurt you."

The Sunless only ran faster.

The chase took Redlaw deep into the Hackney SRA, deeper than he'd gone before or had ever wished to go. Relatively genteel surroundings gave way to a 1970s-built planned community, an agglomeration of blocks of flats connected to one another by overpasses and walkways. The flats rose in shelving tiers, beetle-browed and hulking, like the superstructures of semi-submerged warships.

The vampire continued to increase the distance between him and Redlaw. Every instinct Redlaw had—not to mention the blaze in his lungs and the ache in his leg muscles—told him to abandon the pursuit. He'd ventured far too far into Sunless territory. He wasn't even sure he knew the way back out. He was on his own, and the blocks of flats offered potential hiding places by the hundred. His quarry could go to earth here and he would never find him.

Dogged persistence, however, was one of Redlaw's great virtues. Or great failings. He could never decide which.

The Sunless man plunged into a thicket of buddleia, brambles and nettles, and Redlaw followed unhesitatingly. He emerged the other side, scratched and stung, to find himself in a children's recreation ground. Part of it was skate ramps and bowls, the rest rusty play apparatus—a collapsing climbing frame, a swing set without swings, a roundabout that had come off its axis. Pads of velvety moss bulged from the seams between paving slabs and the cracks in concrete, like some kind of gluey lymph being squeezed out from beneath.

The man, predictably, was nowhere to be seen.

If Redlaw had been the swearing type, he would have sworn.

He paused to catch his breath, bent double, fists planted on thighs. Well the wrong side of his half-century. Old, old man. His knees would be a nightmare tomorrow. Why did he do this to himself? What was he trying to prove?

Straightening up, he set off across the recreation ground. The building beyond seemed the likeliest place to go looking for the fugitive. It was asking for trouble, he knew, heading in there. Indoors, inside a Sunless lair, you were more than vulnerable. You were dead meat. SHADE training had drummed into Redlaw that this was a Thing You Never Do, especially alone, even more especially at night. Experience, however, had taught him that if you never did any of the Things You Never Do, you never made any progress.

He entered a lobby through a door that had once been glassed and was now patched over with plywood. Outside, there'd been just enough ambient light to see by. Inside, once the door creaked shut, the darkness was all but impenetrable. Regulation image-intensification goggles remedied that. Redlaw peered around at a glowing, fuzzy green night-vision world. There was a pair of lifts, or rather two sets of sliding steel doors that gaped ajar to reveal empty lift shafts. There were lockable mailboxes, not one of them in a fit state to keep anyone's correspondence private any more. There were a couple of vending machines, cobwebbed inside and out, still loaded with packets of crisps and cans of soft drink that were years past their sell-by dates.

Something scurried at the periphery of the goggles' visual field. Redlaw spun, aiming his Cindermaker. Just a mouse, whiskering along the wainscot.

He nudged open a door to a stairwell. The stench that poured out almost bowled him over. The Sunless were using the stairwell as a kind of communal open-plan latrine. Covering his nose, he listened for footfalls; heard none. His quarry had not gone up there. Thank God.

He checked the lift shafts. These would be how the residents chose to get from floor to floor, rather than the foetid, faeces-spattered stairs. Vampires loved a climb, the sheerer the better. All Redlaw could see, as he craned his neck upwards, were slack cables and jammed-open doors, rising into dimness. No movement.

That left the ground floor itself. A corridor tunnelled away from the lobby, leading to flats. Redlaw ventured down it, reckoning this a futile action but unwilling to admit defeat just yet. Wearing the night-vision goggles, he felt as though he were in a murky, fluorescent cave. He hunched under a length of duct pipe, dangling loose from the ceiling, and squeezed past a wingback chair that had been thrown out of one of the flats and lay on its side across the corridor. He brushed aside some loose-hanging electrical wiring, and cat-stepped over a smashed vacuum cleaner, a computer monitor with a punctured screen, and a twelve-string guitar whose neck had been brusquely snapped. These items symbolised everything Sunless rejected. They were too comfortable, too practical, too materialistic. Too human.

The corridor right-angled at the end. Redlaw took the turn, leading with his gun. The adjoining corridor was empty apart from more domestic debris. He counted six doors, all firmly shut. If Sunless were lurking behind them—and some undoubtedly were—they already knew he was there. He could tread as softly as he liked, but they could still detect his footfalls with their ultrasensitive ears. Moreover, they could smell him.

The opening lines of the Lord's Prayer helped steady

his nerves, but only because it always had. The response was ingrained. Had reciting a limerick done the same trick, Redlaw would have recited a limerick.

Try a door handle? He could, were it not unwise. A startled vampire, cornered in a room, confined, would react unpredictably. It might cower, but equally it might go on the offensive. Redlaw wished to avoid further violence tonight if possible. He definitely didn't want to be obliged to dust a Sunless and then have a score or more of them come down on him, alerted by the gunshot, screaming vengeance.

The corridor dead-ended. Redlaw began to retrace his footsteps, accepting that the man he'd been chasing was lost to him.

When he reached the lobby, he halted.

Had to.

It was full of vampires, blocking his path to the exit.

They'd been waiting for him.

REDLAW DIDN'T HAVE time to count heads. Seven, maybe eight, maybe more. He straight away dropped to one knee, Cindermaker levelled. His free hand went to his vest, unclipping an *aqua sancta* grenade.

But the Sunless swarmed him, a wave of swift shadows. He felt claws and the rough, clammy touch of dead skin. His Cindermaker was slammed from his grasp. He threw the grenade, but he hadn't had a chance to pull the pin beforehand. Its explosive not primed, the device was just a ball of near unbreakable Perspex which bounced harmlessly off a vampire's shoulder and rolled away into a corner, priest-blessed holy water sloshing inside.

His attackers pinned him up against a wall. One of

them yanked off his night vision goggles, leaving him in darkness, benighted. Redlaw squirmed, struggled, but he knew it was useless.

Foolish old man. Careless. Overconfident.

"Make it quick," he told the Sunless. "All of you at once."

That was the best he could hope for, under the circumstances. Multiple bites, simultaneous draining, and a relatively speedy escape to his eternal reward. The vampires could stretch the process out, if they were in the mood. Take it in turns, tap off a little at a time from the jugular, keep their victim lingering half faint with blood loss, hovering in a continuum of nausea and pain that could last up to three hours and no doubt feel like forever. If Redlaw was lucky, this lot would go for all his major veins and arteries as a pack, and it would take less than five minutes. If he was lucky.

"No," said a voice from the dark. "I don't think that will be happening."

It was a woman's voice, East European accent—Albanian?—with the usual slight sibilant lisp that came with having sharp fangs instead of teeth, the usual slurring of the dental consonants. It was, too, a surprisingly mellifluous voice, far from the harsh, grating growl that usually issued from a Sunless throat.

"Redlaw, is it not?"

"You have me at a disadvantage," Redlaw said. "You can see me, I can't see you. Who are you?"

"Yes, without those goggles of yours you're blind as a bat in the dark. Whereas we see as clearly as if it were day."

"Why not give them back? Let's level the playing field."

"I think not, old bean."

Old bean? "Then I'll ask again: who are you?"

"I'm..." A soft laugh. "Well, at this precise moment you might call me your saviour."

"I have only one Saviour," Redlaw said, "and He isn't you."

"Ah, faith," the owner of the voice said, drawing closer. "Is that still an essential requirement for SHADE recruitment? Or have they done away with it, along with the minimum height restriction?"

"If it isn't still essential, it ought to be."

"For, without faith, those crucifixes and those stars of David and all the other religious tokens you people wear won't work, will they? They're just so much tawdry costume jewellery."

"If it makes you happy pouring scorn on my beliefs, 'Less, then go ahead. Far greater men than me have suffered far worse persecution in the name of God. It would save everyone a lot of hassle, though, myself included, if you simply got on with the bloodletting."

"Eager to sit at the right hand of the Lord, eh, shady? Heaven can't wait, is that it?"

"Spare me the cheap jokes."

"You are John Redlaw." The Sunless woman was talking almost directly into his ear now, in an insinuating purr. He had the feeling this was all a piece of play-acting, a knowing, self-mocking parody. "You are considered the scourge of our kind, a holy terror. Possibly that is how you see yourself. And now here you are, your precious life in our hands. Delivering yourself to us like a Christmas present, ready to be unwrapped. We could kill you, yes. Quaff your lifestuff like a fine wine until not even the dregs remain. Or... one of us could turn you. How would that be for irony? John

Redlaw, vampire slayer, become vampire himself."

"I am not a 'vampire slayer.' I am a SHADE officer charged with keeping the peace between humans and Sunless. And were I ever turned, rest assured that at the first opportunity I would drive a stake through my own heart."

"So you say. You would, I suspect, feel differently once you discovered how joyous it is to be Sunless, as you non-vampires insist on calling us. The power, the freedom, the senses, newly awakened..."

"The cannibalistic thirst."

"The world opening up around you like a night-blooming flower. The darkness breathing its secret consolations over you. The realisation that there is so much more to life than, well, mere life."

"Very witty."

"Redlaw."

He could feel cold lips butterfly-brushing his cheek.

"Oh, Redlaw, there is so much I could offer you," she sighed. "So much you could *be*."

She pulled away.

"But," she said briskly, "why waste such a gift on so undeserving a recipient? You came here chasing Grigori. You've scared the poor blighter half out of his wits. What has he done? What is his crime? Grigori is not one to misbehave. I know him well. Meek as can be."

"Are any of you meek when the bloodlust's on you?" Redlaw retorted.

"True. No. Has he killed, then?"

"Not to my knowledge. But there's been a riot. You must have heard it."

"The blood dropoff."

"Havoc. I've seen it happen before but never this

bad. The delivery drivers have been taken. Your Grigori seemed to have some idea where they might be."

"This is all you're after? The drivers?"

"Yes."

"If I promise to find them for you, will you leave?"

"Gladly. *Can* you find them?"

"It shouldn't be too difficult. I can't guarantee their... health."

"I'm not expecting you to. Bodies for their families to bury, the assurance that they haven't been turned—if they're not alive, that's the next best outcome."

"Very well, Redlaw," said the voice. Then she issued an order, and the many hands holding him let go. He was chaperoned outside, and his goggles and Cindermaker were returned to him. Redlaw scanned the vampires, but they were all male. The owner of the voice had stayed indoors.

Anonymous.

Well, if that was how she wanted to play it, then fine. No sweat. As long as she made good on her promise.

AN HOUR LATER, two corpses were brought to the entrance of the SRA and deposited there.

By then, Redlaw had obtained copies of the two drivers' personnel files from BovPlas's human resources department. He compared the faces on the ID photos, flushed with life, to the white, shrivelled faces of the bodies. A match. Trevor Martin and Derek Bannerman. Both married men, with a total of five kids between them.

Then came the grisly business of post mortem neutralisation—decapitating the corpses. It had to be done on-site, as soon as possible after discovery of a drained body, regardless of whether the victim had been fully bled or only partially. Standard procedure. While even just a few fluid ounces of blood remained in a corpse's venous system, the potential for reanimation existed. The next of kin would rather have their loved ones back in two pieces, definitely deceased, than as a handful of ashes or, worse, not at all.

Redlaw volunteered for the task, and the other officers were only too happy to let him. TV news crews had arrived on the scene, but a cordon tape held the reporters well back. All the camera operators were able to film was distant footage of a white tent and a man going into it carrying a surgical steel saw.

Ten minutes later Redlaw reappeared, nodded curtly to a fellow SHADE officer waiting outside the tent, said the bodies were ready now for the morgue, got into his car and drove off into the night.

CHAPTER THREE

GILES SLOCOCK, CONSERVATIVE Member of Parliament for Chesham and Amersham, awoke in his constituency home with a cocaine hangover and a prostitute snoring next to him in bed. He dealt with the former by means of a quick hair-of-the-dog toot from the stash in his bedside drawer, and the latter by means of a kick in the ribs, a thick wad of cash, and a taxi. He gave the girl a little more than the agreed-upon fee, mostly because she had consented to bum sex (bareback, too, a double bonus) but also to ensure her silence. He had hired her from a reputable escort agency which prided itself both on the exclusivity of its client list and the discretion of its employees, but still, one could never be too careful. Slocock had been burned a couple of times in the past by tattletales flogging their stories to the scandal sheets. His career had survived, but he was aware that the public's tolerance for misbehaviour from its elected representatives was not infinitely elastic.

It stretched only so far before it snapped, with often painful consequences.

A shower rinsed the smell of the girl's cloying perfume from Slocock's body and the smears of shit from beneath his foreskin. Then he dressed and went downstairs to breakfast and the morning papers.

More interesting than anything to be found in the pages of the print media was an item on *BBC Breakfast* about trouble the previous night at the Hackney SRA. Slocock, eating the first of three boiled eggs, watched with detached curiosity as a reporter spoke of a bloodlust riot and the deaths of two BovPlas delivery drivers. The twin brother of one of the dead men was interviewed.

"Derek, he was, like, a decent bloke who did his job," said Keith Bannerman, fighting back tears. "He knew it was dangerous work, like, but the money was good and he was always a bit of a night owl anyway, so the hours, y'know, suited."

"And what are your feelings about his killers?" the reporter asked, somehow managing to flutter her eyelashes even as she put on a concerned and solicitous frown.

"Scum," Keith Bannerman spat. "It's the only word for 'em. Bloodsucking scum. Come over here, make everyone's lives a misery, we bend over backwards to help them, and this is how they thank us? Send them back home, that's what I say. I mean, who invited them? Ruddy parasites. Send them back home—if we can't stake the lot of them, that is..."

SIX HOURS LATER, Slocock stood up in the House of Commons in his role as Shadow Spokesman for Sunless

Affairs and quoted the grief-stricken Keith Bannerman verbatim.

"'I mean, who invited them? Ruddy parasites. Send them back home—if we can't stake the lot of them, that is...'"

Slocock let the words ring round the chamber, before continuing: "The view, Mister Speaker, of a man who has just lost his brother, his *twin* brother, in the most tragic and dreadful circumstances imaginable. A man whose closest relative fell prey to a crazed mob and was brutally, viciously attacked and exsanguinated by them. A man struggling to come to terms with the appalling knowledge that the very individuals whom his brother was helping turned on him and subjected him, along with his colleague, to the most cruel and barbaric form of murder that we currently know of. And Keith Bannerman is far from alone in holding the opinions he does. Rather, he speaks for a broad swathe of British citizenry. I put it to you, Mister Speaker, that the right honourable gentleman before me, the Secretary of State for Sunless Affairs, barely comprehends the level of public disquiet and disgust that his policies evoke."

There was braying from across the floor of the House, cheering from Slocock's own side.

Slocock raised his voice to make himself heard. "Furthermore, does the Secretary of State not realise— *does he not realise*—that to continue to pursue those policies is simply to invite repetition of the events of last night? Were it an isolated incident, I could perhaps understand the right honourable gentleman's apparent lack of concern. However, as we all know, these so-called bloodlust riots have shown a marked increase in recent months, both in frequency and severity. The

Sunless, if we must use that word for them, are getting noticeably more restive and aggressive. On behalf of the Great British public, those who rightfully belong here, those with pulses and a dietary appetite that doesn't extend to haemoglobin, I ask him what is the Department of Sunless Affairs going to do about these uninvited, unwanted immigrants? Their numbers are growing day by day, or should that be night by night? What is the government's response to a situation which, no one is in any doubt, is becoming more and more untenable?"

Slocock sat down. From the Labour front benches his opposite number rose to his feet.

Maurice Wax, the Secretary of State for Sunless Affairs, was a gloomy-looking man with a sharp widow's peak and a sallow, greyish complexion. The political cartoonists regularly depicted him with fangs and a black cape, often hanging upside down from the rafters of the debating chamber. More than one stand-up comedian had made the joke that the man with ultimate political responsibility for the Sunless could do with a little sun himself.

Wax had been chosen for the post because he was widely regarded as a safe pair of hands, someone workmanlike and imperturbable who wouldn't court controversy or fumble what was an exceptionally tricky brief. He lacked flash, but he knew his way around a set of statistics, and nobody could argue that he did not take his job, or himself, very seriously.

"Mister Speaker," Wax began, "at best reckoning there are a little over thirty thousand Sunless present in the UK. That is to say, one Sunless per two thousand humans. Or, to put it another way, the Sunless currently comprise zero-point-zero-five per cent of the overall population."

Slocock yawned elaborately for the benefit of the BBC Parliament cameras and the sketch writers in the public gallery.

"In those countries where Sunless are a longer-established feature," Wax went on, consulting his notes, "it has been calculated that the Sunless-to-human ratio needs to rise to one per thousand before the balance becomes unsustainable. In other words, before they become an active menace. We are, I would submit, a considerable way from that, and indeed this government's programme of robust, proactive identification and containment will ensure the United Kingdom does not go the way of Romania, Bulgaria, Slovakia, Hungary and their ilk in finding itself burdened with Sunless superabundance—the cause, of course, of the Sunless's initial westward drift some two decades ago. For the record, new SRAs have been established just this month in Liverpool's Toxteth and Moss Side in Manchester, and we're consulting with the Scottish Government and the Welsh National Assembly with a view to rolling out further SRAs in..."

By that point Slocock didn't need to pretend to look bored. He was. He tuned out Wax's drone, his mind turning to his meeting at eight tonight with Nathaniel Lambourne.

Knowing Lambourne, the restaurant would be an expensive one. But expensive didn't automatically equate with good.

SLOCOCK ARRIVED PUNCTUALLY at the Flaming Aubergine on Greek Street. He was mildly impressed to learn that the place had a Michelin star. What mattered, though, was that, judging by other diners' meals, it served proper-sized portions, not namby-pamby little strips of this and that draped crosswise on a plate and drizzled with a few drops of sauce.

"You look hot," Lambourne observed dryly as he and Slocock shook hands. "Run here all the way from Whitehall, did you?"

Slocock's face still carried a sheen of perspiration from his session with his *muay thai* trainer, Khun Sarawong, at the nearby Soho Dojo. "Been working out. Absolutely famished. Shall we order?"

The *maître d'* danced attendance around Lambourne like a drone bee around the queen. There were plenty of the rich and powerful dining this evening at the Flaming Aubergine. None, though, was quite as prestigious, nor as apt to tip good service so liberally, as the CEO of Dependable Chemicals PLC.

"May Ah *rah*commend ze oyster of steer stuffed wiz oysters, M'sieur Lambourne," the *maître d'* said. He was a bilingual Lyonnais who could speak English almost without a trace of an accent, but when at work he laid the Frenchness on thick. It was what people expected.

"Oyster of steer?" Slocock enquired.

"Testicles," said Lambourne. "Bull's balls."

"Ah. Maybe not. You know what I fancy? A nice fat steak."

"A steak. *Oui*, eet iz posseebluh, m'sieur. Ah sink chef can rustle up that." The *maître d'* made no attempt to hide his scorn. This, too, was expected. "Wiz ze tomato ketchup, *non*? An 'ow would m'sieur like eet cooked?"

"Rare. Very rare."

"*Bleu.*"

"Very *bleu*. True *bleu*."

"*Formidable*, m'sieur."

The steak arrived pink and oozing watery blood, and Slocock tucked in avidly. Lambourne, who'd chosen the *à la carte* special of duck breast in a pistachio marinade on a bed of wilted dandelion leaves, eyed the young MP with a lofty amusement in an avarice marinade on a bed of wilted fondness.

"Can't stomach blood," he said.

Slocock looked up from his food. "What?"

"Human beings. Can't actually drink blood in any quantity. Makes you physically sick. You throw it right back up."

"Oh." Slocock dabbed steak juice from his mouth with a linen napkin. "Your point being?"

"It's not natural, what the vampires do. None of it natural."

"They are, are they not, *super*natural creatures? Clue's right there."

"Don't get snarky with me, Giles," said Lambourne. He brushed back his wavy mane of silver hair. It may have lost its colour but he still had a full head of it, unlike the majority of men his age. "I'm merely saying anyone who even considers a Sunless a person is an idiot. A dangerous idiot. Your pal Wax, for example."

"He's not my pal. And I don't know if he particularly approves of vamps or not. He's just toeing the party line on them. 'We must be fair. We mustn't judge. We have to treat them as if they were human, different but equal'—which they're clearly not." Slocock sheared off another glossy sliver of steak and forked it into his mouth. "What are you complaining about anyway? You're raking in a fortune off them."

Dependable Chemicals, from relatively humble beginnings as a minor player in the pharmaceuticals industry, had grown under Lambourne's aegis into an immense umbrella corporation sheltering numerous smaller firms, one of which was BovPlas Logistics. Lambourne had zeroed in on the cattle blood market at the earliest opportunity, when the first SRAs were being set up, and had created BovPlas by buying up a medical supplies transportation company and a chain of abattoirs and splicing the two together. BovPlas had further benefited from the Private Finance Initiative scheme, a brilliant wheeze whereby private companies working in the public sector were able to charge the government usurious rates of interest on their initial outlay. The Treasury, a seemingly bottomless well, never failed to meet the repayments however extortionate they became and, should the business fail, would invariably bail it out or write off its losses. This meant responsibility without accountability and profit without risk, which for a magnate like Lambourne was something akin to the Holy Grail: as close to a no-lose deal as you could get. BovPlas had undeniably, these past few years, prospered, and Lambourne had personally creamed off the rewards.

"I never complain," Lambourne corrected firmly. "What you need to appreciate, Giles, is that the public mood is turning against Wax and his softly-softly approach."

"I do appreciate that, Nathaniel, I do. Did you not hear me in the Commons this afternoon? I said just that. I was sticking it to Wax like you wouldn't believe."

"So I gather. Wax, now, may sound like he's talking tough, but it's mealy-mouthed stuff. Weasel words. And the public can see through that. The *electorate* can see through that."

Slocock didn't miss the emphasis. The deadline for an election loomed less than six months hence, and if the opinion polls were anything to go by, the government was in for a massacre. The constituency map of Britain, now predominantly red, was about to turn an apoplectic shade of blue.

"And if—when—his lot get turfed out on their ear," Lambourne went on, "it'll be principally because they haven't managed to get a handle on the Sunless situation. They're not prepared to take radical steps. They're not willing to do what really needs to be done."

"And I am," said Slocock. He leaned across the table, lowering his voice. "You know I am."

"Of course you are, my boy. I know it because a seat on the board of Dep Chem awaits you at the end of all this, with the promise of a salary ten times what you can earn as an MP, even as a Cabinet minister. The reason you're on-side is you think the right way but also, more importantly, you put your own self-interest first. Don't pretend to pout, Giles. You know it's true. Hence I'm perfectly assured that when the times comes you'll be happy to institute the measures we're busy putting in place. There's just one small snag."

"What, you think I might not get returned?"

Lambourne chuckled. "To the safest Tory seat in Buckinghamshire, which is to say one of the safest Tory seats in the country? Oh, there's no danger of that. No, the snag I'm talking about isn't anything to do with you. It's our timetable. We're going to have to accelerate it somewhat."

"Eh? Accelerate? Why?"

"Never you mind why. All you need to know is that what I thought could wait until after the election, can't. We're going to have to get cracking sooner rather than later."

"How much sooner?"

"Right away."

Slocock took a few moments to digest this.

"What you're saying is you want me to get to work on Maurice Wax," he said. "Bring him round. Change his mind."

Lambourne looked pleasantly surprised, like a huntsman whose Springer spaniel pup has just broken its first game bird from cover. "That's precisely what I mean. Not just a pretty face, Giles."

"I don't know if it's feasible. Don't you have lobbyists to do this sort of thing for you?"

"None of them has the same level of access. None of them could be nearly as influential on Wax as his mirror image in Her Majesty's Opposition. None of them, frankly, has your winsome public-schoolboy charm, nor for that matter the incentive that you have."

Slocock mulled it over. "If I'm to do this, if I'm to stick my neck out for you, I'll really have to know why. Is it a journalist? Someone snooping around, threatening to blow the lid?"

"We've already had several of those," Lambourne replied with a dismissive air, "and they've been dealt with. It's amazing how little one has to pay to spike a story these days. I blame the internet. All those nosey-parker bloggers, tapping away for next to nothing, queering the market. The smallest of bribes, and crusading instincts go out of the window, along with scruples. No, if you must know, Giles, it's simply the consortium. The three of us have got a lot at stake here, no pun intended. We haven't been able to PFI the new project, thanks to Mr Wax and his ethics. Principled *and* stubborn—it's a bad combination. So my colleagues are getting restless and wanting to know when there'll be returns and how soon they'll start coming in. That coupled with the fact that in other areas we've been... well, rather too successful, if you see what I mean."

Slocock did indeed see.

"The storm is rising faster than our projections predicted," Lambourne said. "If we don't bring the deadline forward, it may break, and if it does"—he splayed out his hands and shrugged his shoulders—"we all get drenched."

"Not much choice then," Slocock said. "I have to win Wax over."

"Not much choice at all, I'm afraid." Lambourne patted Slocock's hand. "But I'm more than confident that you're up to the challenge, my lad. In addition, I'll be able to provide you with leverage to help."

"Leverage?"

"Make sure you're home tomorrow morning. Something will arrive that will give you what you need should negotiation fail."

As Slocock was pondering on this, the *maître d'* shimmied up to the table.

"All iz well, gentlemen? Ze food iz to your lahkeeng? Zere are no, 'ow you zay, issues?"

"All is marvellous, thank you," said Lambourne.

Slocock's fork paused on its journey to his mouth. On it was impaled a lump of steak so rare it looked raw.

"Yes," he said, smiling, as the meat dripped at his lips. "Yes, I think everything's absolutely bloody marvellous."

CHAPTER FOUR

REDLAW WAS IN the canteen, having his first coffee of the night, when Khalid walked in. Redlaw stood, scraping back his chair. He and the sergeant had unfinished business.

Khalid didn't take too kindly to being seized by the shoulder and being made to turn round.

"Take your hand off me," he said, adding, "Sir," with as much of a curled lip as he dared.

"Where'd you run off to last night?" Redlaw demanded. "I said I wanted words."

"And I wanted to avoid precisely this sort of thing," Khalid replied.

"A dressing down from a superior officer?"

"No, a scene."

"I'll give you a scene." Redlaw was conscious of the dozens of eyes on them, the colleagues and ancillary staff watching. "You came barging in, all guns blazing. You reignited a situation I'd managed to defuse. You lost me an informant."

"I think you'll find you did that last one yourself, captain."

"But what really matters is you were just letting that riot happen."

"Forgive me, sir, but I value the lives of the people under me, and going into that SRA would have been suicide."

"I went in. I'm still here."

"Then you're clearly a better man than I am." Quite a few of the SHADE employees in the canteen smirked at this remark. A couple even laughed out loud—cronies of Khalid's, Muslim brothers. Khalid was emboldened. "Permission to speak freely?"

"Go on then."

"What you did was admirable, undeniably. But it didn't save those truck drivers, did it? You know as well as I do that they were dead long before you got there— long before any of us got there. So what would have been gained by us trying to rescue a pair of corpses, except possibly more corpses?"

"It would have shown we mean business. SHADE has a reputation to uphold."

"You mean *you* have a reputation to uphold, as a full-on hard nut."

That was when Redlaw decided to deck Khalid. Not for being impudent; for being right.

Khalid got up off the floor, rubbing his chin. He rose to his full height, which outdid Redlaw's by a good three inches.

"Captain or not," he rumbled, "no one sucker-punches me and gets away with it."

"Then let's go, sergeant. You and me."

"Everybody here's a witness. You hit first."

"Don't worry, I won't have you up on an insubordination charge. Let's sort this out."

Khalid dived into Redlaw, pushing him back so that he collided with the serving counter. Crockery went flying. Redlaw was winded but still managed to retaliate, ramming his elbow down onto the crown of Khalid's head. The sergeant reared up with a roar. Redlaw blocked his first two punches, but the third got through, a roundhouse to the ribs that left him gasping. Khalid drew back his fist to repeat it, but Redlaw seized him by the ears and yanked his head down, bringing a leg up at the same time. Knee and face made crunching contact. Khalid groaned and staggered back, putting a hand to his mouth. It came away bloody, with a fragment of tooth cupped in the palm.

Khalid cursed in Arabic, then lunged for Redlaw once more.

Redlaw braced for impact.

"*Stop!*"

The shout resounded across the canteen, bringing instant silence and stillness. Even Khalid was halted in his tracks.

Commodore Macarthur strode between tables, her face bunched tight and radiating cold fury.

"What the hell is going on here?" she barked. "Two grown men brawling like school kids in the playground?"

"He started it," said Khalid.

Redlaw shrugged. "It's true. I did."

"I don't bloody care," said Macarthur. "In headquarters? In full view of staff and officers? What's got into both of you?"

Redlaw was about to speak, but Macarthur cut him off with a chop of her hand.

"John. My office. Now."

She said this in the tone of voice she had perfected as a major in the Royal Highland Fusiliers, a sharp, commanding bark that must have been the terror of the lower ranks. Redlaw didn't even try to protest. He about-turned and made for the canteen exit.

"Yeah, you slope off, Redlaw," said Khalid. "And take your midlife crisis with you."

"That's enough from you, Ibrahim," said Macarthur. "Go and clean yourself up. The rest of you? Finish whatever you're doing. Sun's setting. Time for work. Go be the watchmen on the walls, the guardians at the gate."

"MARM, I CAN explain..."

"Not interested." Slamming the door, Macarthur brushed past him and went to her desk.

"But—"

"You do not get into fights with fellow officers, John," she said. "You do not. End of story. Whatever the provocation. Especially not you, a captain. I'm aware there's long been bad blood between you and Khalid, but still. Give me one good reason why I shouldn't suspend you without pay for a month. Actually, one good reason why I shouldn't just have done with it and sack you."

"Because I'm the best shady you have?"

"Are you, John?"

"You know I am."

Macarthur held his gaze for several seconds, then sighed relentingly. "Well, maybe so. But you're also, not to put too fine a point on it, knocking on a bit. If this were an ordinary police force you'd have been put out to pasture years ago. At best, you'd be reduced to pushing paper at a desk and getting fat on Danish pastries. That still might happen. We're desperately short-handed in the admin department and I'm seriously considering taking officers off the streets to whittle down the backlog of casework. You'd be a prime candidate for that."

"Please, God, no."

"It isn't up to God, alas. Would that it were. It's up to me. And right now I'm looking at a plainclothes field operative of mature years who's done his bit tackling Sunless and keeping the peace and who, on recent showing, looks like he could do with considerably less stress in his life."

"On recent showing? One minor infraction in the canteen?"

"John, I could at this point turn to my computer here," Macarthur said, indicating the terminal beside her, the sole occupant of a desktop that was otherwise bare of paraphernalia and ornament, "and pull up your HR file and scroll through a list of—let's call them infractions, then—dating back several months. I could do that, but I don't need to. I have them memorised." She tapped her head, with its shock of choppily cropped blonde hair. "All up here. Because I've been going through that file over and over lately, and wondering just what's got into you, why you've become so damn erratic."

"Erratic?"

"Don't make out like you've no idea what I'm talking about. It won't wash. Especially not while you keep fingering your ribs like that and wincing."

"Bruised not broken, I think."

"Glad to hear it." She steepled her fingers. "Once upon a time there was a man who worked for me called John Redlaw who could be relied on to act with complete probity and do whatever he needed to to ensure 'Lesses stay where they belong and humans don't get molested. I don't see that John Redlaw standing before me right now."

"Who do you see?" He was feigning indifference, but not very well.

"I see, for starters, a man who's been cited seven times for failing to follow up on reports of Sunless attacks."

"People lie about getting bitten, make up stories. Waste our time."

"Nonetheless we have a duty of care. Every single claim must be investigated fully and with due diligence."

"Even when it's just attention seekers taking the mick? Or wonky-headed Goths messing around with fake fangs and suction pumps? Or nutters who just bite people for the sake of biting?"

"Even then. You have to prove it conclusively, with hard evidence to back your findings up. Not take one look and judge."

"One look's usually all it takes."

"I know that, you know that, but we still have to go through the process."

"Go through the motions, you mean."

"Whatever." Macarthur's Scottish burr, faint after years in the south, still rolled the odd "r," especially when she was in an irritable mood. "Whatever" became "whateverrr," and Redlaw's surname was almost growled: *Rrredlaw*. "The point is, we have to be seen to be doing our job. Otherwise people get anxious, more anxious than they already are. We're the thin blue line between ordinary folk and a phenomenon they don't understand but fear greatly. We're a shield, and we need to seem impeccably sturdy. They depend on us."

"So I should pretend it matters when some old biddy's cat goes missing and she thinks Tibbles has been snatched by a vampire? Okay, I get you. Message received. I'll try harder in future."

Macarthur chose to ignore the drollery. "As long as you pretend convincingly, that's fine. Then there's the matter of the charges of assault that have been brought against you by civilians on no fewer than five occasions. Including a new one just today."

"Don't tell me. The Stokers from last night." Redlaw rolled his eyes heavenward. "They had it coming."

"You put two of them in hospital, John."

"They should count themselves lucky that's all I did."

"One of them will never walk again unaided."

"I'm fed up with ruddy Stokers. Giving their gang a fancy name and making out as if they're some kind of grass-roots activist movement—it doesn't legitimise what they do. Unless you have a government mandate to deal with the Sunless, you're just criminals, meaning I have not just the authority but an obligation to stop you."

"Nicely put. I'm sure you told them that, too."

"They didn't strike me as the type to listen to sermons."

"According to their testimony, they'd unearthed a rogue 'Less. Doubtless, after you'd finished with them, you dusted it yourself."

"I didn't, as a matter of fact."

Macarthur tweaked one eyebrow high. "Why ever not?"

"In all the confusion, he disappeared," Redlaw said.

"Not like you to let one slip through your fingers."

"You said it yourself—I'm knocking on a bit. When I was younger, four thugs wouldn't have taken me nearly so long to polish off."

The Commodore looked sceptical, but decided not to pursue that particular angle any further. "Broadly speaking, John, I'm on your side, you must know that. Stokers and the like need suppressing. The odd rap on the nose with a rolled-up newspaper does them good. Which is why I'm prepared to keep giving you my full backing when it comes to these charges. We'll argue self-defence, and as long as we hold firm, any lawsuit will be dropped before it gets to court. However— and it's a big however—you can't rely on my support indefinitely. I can't keep putting myself out for you, not without compromising my own position."

"I understand, marm."

"Do you, John? Really?"

"Really. May I go now? There's work to be done. Watchmen on the walls and all that."

"No, you may not go. I'm not done with you."

Redlaw stifled a sigh of impatience.

"The way you've been acting lately..." Macarthur was trying to sound sympathetic, conciliatory. "Is it Róisín? Is that what's eating you?"

"Leary? That was a year and a half ago, marm. I think I should be over it by now."

"You were close, you two."

"She was a hell of a shady," Redlaw said stiffly. "A hell of a partner. I don't know if I'd call us close, exactly, but we worked damn well together."

"I'm not suggesting you and she were romantically involved," said Macarthur. It seemed as preposterous to her as it was to him. "Nothing like that. But for a loner like you to stick with a partner at all, let alone the same person for, what was it, four years?"

"A hair over five."

"Exactly. When, prior to that, you could barely put up with anyone for longer than a week."

"We shared similar views. A similar approach to the job. Leary talked a bit too much, but never about her private life. That sat well with me."

"I'm sure it did. And I'm sure you miss her still. I think..." Macarthur hesitated. "I think we all do. But ever since what happened to her, you've not been yourself. You've been unpredictable, reckless—a ship without a rudder. It's like you don't care any more, or care too much, I can't make up my mind which. God knows, this is demanding work. The hours we keep, the things we have to face on a regular basis... It's not as though the salary's much compensation, either. You could stack shelves at a supermarket and probably earn more. And personal relationships? Forget it. You sacrifice those the moment you sign on the dotted line."

"When you put it in those terms, marm, I want to go and kill myself."

"Join the queue. What I'm getting at is, we need one another in this line of work, even if we don't realise we do. We tether one another. Róisín was your tether, and you may well have been hers. If you could find someone else to fulfil that role, I think you'd benefit from it. That's all I'm saying."

"I should go out and find a new partner? Good plan. How about Sergeant Khalid? He and I definitely bonded in the canteen just now."

"John, if you're going to be a snitty wee prick about this…"

Redlaw felt a little ashamed. The Commodore was only trying to help.

His apology was this: "Marm, I'd like to take a look into last night's bloodlust riot, if that's okay with you."

Macarthur frowned. "Why? What about it? Bunch of Sunless got carried away. It's happened before, loads of times. It's in their nature. When blood's involved, they can't help themselves."

"But it's been happening a bit too often lately."

"You reckon?"

"Don't you?"

"I don't have the statistics to hand. There are more Sunless than there used to be, I do know that. Maybe it's the SRAs. Overcrowding. Too many residents, not enough space. Pressure cooker environment. I don't honestly feel it's worth your time and trouble."

"And I beg to differ. I had to post mortem neutralise two men last night in Hackney. Two men whose last few minutes of life must have been spent in utter, abject terror. Two men with families. That isn't right. There has to be a root cause to the riots, something more than simple thirst."

"Thirst isn't simple when you're talking about vampires."

"You know what I mean."

"I know what you mean. I just don't get why you're making such a big thing out of it all. A riot's a riot. Sunless lose control. That's just the way it is."

"If I can prove it's something else, though, that there's some other factor involved, some underlying rationale…"

"What are your suspicions based on?"

"Nothing. Yet," said Redlaw. "Instinct. A feeling."

"Oh, dear Lord, please don't say a hunch."

That would have been the very next word out of his mouth. "I patrol the streets every night. Have done for a decade and a half. It'd be fair to say that I've developed a... sensitivity for how 'Lesses think and behave. What I witnessed at Hackney, the savagery, the intensity—it wasn't normal."

"Normal?" said Macarthur. "Normal got parcelled up and posted off the day the first Sunless turned up on these shores."

"Will you let me do this, marm? Will you sanction it? At least let me have a try. What did you call me earlier? A ship without a rudder. Well, maybe this is a way of me getting my rudder back."

"I don't respond well to any kind of blackmail, John, especially not emotional."

"And I would be a fool to attempt it on you." The ghost of a smile touched the corners of Redlaw's perpetual scowl. "Let me rephrase, then. What have I got to lose? Or you, for that matter?"

"Only my sanity," Macarthur said, clutching her temples in mock despair. "All right. All right. Have a sniff around, see what you can turn up. If it'll make you happy."

"It won't."

"I can believe that. Just don't go moaning to me when you find you've wasted your time, because I'll only tell you I told you so. I'm guessing you have some kind of subtle strategy in mind? Some tactful, well-thought-out approach you can take to this that won't upset anyone or cause any ripples?"

"I thought I'd go back to Hackney, give the hornets' nest a kick, see what comes buzzing out."

"Yes," said Macarthur, lips pursed, nodding. "I was afraid it would be something like that."

CHAPTER FIVE

REDLAW DROVE EAST from SHADE HQ. It was an overcast night. A thin sleety rain began to fall, misting the windscreen.

London was quiet.

His route from Paddington to Hackney wound through St John's Wood, Primrose Hill and Islington. Each of these upmarket neighbourhoods boasted its quota of gated enclaves, where wealthy homeowners had erected defensive measures around clusters of houses and hired ex-servicemen to patrol outside. In many instances the perimeter fence supported a circuit of plastic tubing through which water was pumped in a continuous cycle. Redlaw had to smile. The old superstition about Sunless being unable to cross running water was just that. After all, they could travel overseas, couldn't they?

Many of the fences also carried notices declaring "YOU ARE NOT INVITED IN." Another superstition, another waste of effort.

Metal crucifixes, stars of David, star-and-crescents, yin-yang circles and even the odd sacred swastika were a further adornment. But again, not an effective countermeasure, not unless there was a significant proportion of believers among those within the enclave. A religious symbol did not, by itself, repel a vampire. Faith was required—unwavering faith—to give it potency.

Redlaw felt the edges of his crucifix digging into his breastbone, and shifted it to a more comfortable position.

The security guards, though, were the greatest absurdity. *Amateurs*. He watched them striding up and down with their black jumpsuits and their air of big-bellied self-importance, and he knew they wouldn't last ten seconds if any Sunless ever did get it into their heads to launch an assault on one of their enclaves. No question, these were competent, even well-intentioned individuals, experienced in combat, scared of little. But vampires were a whole different order of opponent, like nothing they'd ever confronted. It took more than nerve and martial prowess to handle them. It took more, even, than a stake-firing crossbow, the only offensive weapon this kind of unlicensed protector could legally carry. It took authority and righteousness. Whatever your strengths and aptitudes, without those two qualities you were to a Sunless as the antelope is to the cheetah: ambulatory dinner.

A number of the security guards waved at the patrol car as it drove by—*hail, brother in arms*. Redlaw did not acknowledge or return the gesture.

At the Hackney SRA, he parked and got out into the seeping rain. He turned up his coat collar, both warding off the weather and adding to the neck protection already afforded by his steel-reinforced shirt collar.

At the entrance he nodded to the two SHADE officers on sentry duty. The younger of the pair demanded to see credentials. The older tutted at the younger's ignorance and unlocked the gate.

"Not sure why you'd be wanting to go in, Captain," he said.

"Me neither," said Redlaw, and went in.

GIVE THE HORNETS' *nest a kick, see what comes buzzing out.*

He'd said that partly to wind up Macarthur, partly to entertain her. It was what she expected to hear; it jibed with Redlaw's public persona.

In truth, he was going to tackle matters with a little more finesse.

But not much.

The Residential Area was calm tonight. The rain helped—one type of running water that did have an effect on Sunless, in as much as they didn't relish getting wet and so preferred to stay indoors. The streets were more or less deserted, just the occasional resident to be seen scurrying through the drizzle from shelter to shelter.

Not that Redlaw didn't think he was being watched. Of course he was being watched. Vampires always watched.

He followed the route he had taken when chasing the squat little informant, Grigori. Soon he was nearing the outcrop of modern flats which, a sign informed him, were called Livingstone Heights, christened in tribute either to the great Victorian missionary explorer or, possibly, to one of London's more notorious civic leaders from recent history. Somebody had amended the name so that it now read Unlivingstone Heights, proof that the Sunless weren't without a sense of humour.

The decrepit recreation ground was where Redlaw took his stand and waited.

They came for him eventually, creeping out from cover, as he had known they would. He let them encircle him, keeping his empty hands low, non-threatening. Red eyes blinked in the rain. Breaths huffed wheezily around him, little gusts of vapour that spoke of a reflex the creatures no longer truly needed but somehow hadn't managed to dispense with—a piece of core code that survived the system reboot of vampirism.

"Her," Redlaw said to the dozen or so Sunless that had softly assembled around him. "I want to see her."

"Who?" somebody grunted.

"You know who I mean. Bring her out here or take me to her, I don't mind which."

"Or we maybe kill you, heh? How about that instead? Kill you to drink."

"Yes, yes. Heard it a million times before. Not impressed. I just want to talk to her. I'll even let you take my weapons if that'll convince you."

"Night Brigader give up his weapons?" Incredulous.

"All of them, to show I'm sincere."

There was debate among the vampires. One of them was delegated to go indoors with a message. Several minutes later he returned.

"She says okay. You come. No weapons."

Redlaw removed his weapons-laden vest and passed it over to the Sunless. They handled it like a ticking bomb. When it came to his Cindermaker, he took the precaution of sliding out the clip and ejecting the round in the chamber beforehand. Even so, the Sunless treated the gun like something red hot.

"Your cross?" one of them said.

"It stays," Redlaw replied. "Or do you really want to hold it?"

They all, in unison, shook their heads.

"Thought not. Now, take me to your leader. Oh, and whichever of you's keeping an eye on my stuff, look after it. I'll be wanting it back in the same condition. You'll be sorry if it isn't."

THEY LED HIM up the cloacal staircase, eleven flights to the top. The vampires trod blithely—many of them barefoot—through the globs of faecal matter that had piled up on the steps. Redlaw placed his feet with care and fought to keep from gagging.

He was ushered into a flat with low ceilings and poky little rooms. Its redeeming architectural feature was a covered balcony overlooking the darkened SRA to the bright parts of the city beyond. The London where Redlaw lived was, through the gauzy rain, a thing of dazzle and distance, as shimmeringly unattainable as Atlantis.

The female Sunless stood on the balcony, silhouetted against the glow of the skyline. Redlaw was prodded to join her. The access door, whose window panel was lined with several thicknesses of newspaper, closed behind him. A key clicked.

He was aware that he was at close quarters with a vampire, in a limited space, and he'd been deprived of an exit route. There were no other balconies within leaping distance. In fact, his only way off the balcony was a sheer drop of some hundred feet straight to the ground.

Well done, Redlaw. Another fine mess you've got yourself into, you tactical genius, you.

The woman turned.

She was—and Redlaw could not hide his surprise—striking. Pale-skinned, yes, but she lacked the greasy pallor common to the Sunless, and her eyes were not scarlet, just dark. Dark like a starless night. There was, too, none of the familiar slouchy cadaverousness about her. She held herself straight. She had presence. Her hair was thick, glossy and black as ink. Her features were fine, not feral. Even her clothing—jeans, tailored jacket, a blouse, knee boots—was a cut above the shabby vampire average. Not brand new, to be sure, but in good condition and showing signs of having been laundered not so long ago.

She smiled at his confusion.

"You're asking yourself, 'What is this?'" she said. "'I do not recognise this. What am I looking at?' Oh, John Redlaw. Captain in the Night Brigade, valiant vanquisher of the undead, who believes he has seen everything there is to see—how discomfiting it must be for you to learn that there is more than you thought you knew."

"A name," Redlaw said, clawing back some of his composure. "I'll take a name, for starters."

"My name, old bean? What use would that be to you? I'm nothing more than vampire filth, am I not?"

"You seem to have a very low opinion of me."

"How shocking, when you people have such a high opinion of my kind."

"You prey on us. You kill us for our blood. You can see how we might have formed the view that you're not very nice," said Redlaw.

She grinned, and her fangs were the sharpest and most even that Redlaw could recall ever laying eyes on. Not a tangled snaggle of teeth but a neat array, like spears in a rack or knives in a drawer.

This wasn't Sunless. This was something else, a whole other order of the species, a different class.

"I am," she said, "Illyria Strakosha. And the answer to the question your eyes are asking, and your stumbling tongue is not, is that I am a vampire but not merely that. I share many of the traits and characteristics of my vampire cousins, but I am of a special bloodline, as it were. There are few of us. Very few."

"Shtriga." It had swum up from the depths of memory. "But shtrigas are—"

"A myth? And vampires aren't?"

"I take your point."

"And before you say it, no, we do not feed on the blood of infants. That *is* a myth. A scurrilous slander that was put about by certain vampires to foster resentment against us. Hatred of the more powerful is common in all walks of life."

"And non-life."

"Indeed. So, having satisfied your curiosity, I would now ask you to satisfy mine. Why are you here? Why do you wish to see me?"

"For the sparkling repartee, of course," Redlaw said evenly. "When we met last night, something clicked between us. Didn't you feel it too?"

Next thing Redlaw knew, he was bent painfully backwards over the concrete parapet, Illyria's fists bunching the material of his coat. He was accustomed to how quickly vampires could move, but this hadn't been just fast. It had been *lightning*.

Eleven storeys' worth of freefall yawned beneath him, and Illyria was both pushing him over and supporting him. The edge of the parapet bit into his lower spine. He was almost upended. If she let go, there would be nothing he could do except plummet.

"Mockery," she said. "Not a wise course of action, I think you'll find, Redlaw. I have a very low tolerance for disrespect."

Redlaw, in response, tugged his crucifix free from inside his shirt, at the same time latching firmly onto her wrist with his other hand.

"How's your tolerance for *this*?"

He expected her to recoil, and in recoiling pull him back onto the balcony. Instead, Illyria just looked at the crucifix and laughed, merrily, scornfully.

"A small piece of wood on a chain?"

"It represents the Holy Cross on which our Redeemer suffered and died," Redlaw said. "It is a constant reminder of the grace of God, through which even the most sinful may be saved. It is hope in the shadows, a beacon in the dark. It is the promise of resurrection and the life eternal."

"Right you are, Redlaw."

"It is *not* just a small piece of wood."

"If you insist."

With an abrupt, effortless motion Illyria drew him up so that he was standing on the balcony once more. The blood rushed from his head and he teetered. Shock set in, belatedly. The balcony seemed unsteady beneath his feet. He waited for the shaking to pass.

"I do not share all the frailties of a vampire," Illyria told him. "I am superior in almost every way. And now that we have established this, I will ask you politely, for the last time, what is it you want? What brings you to the ghetto on such a dismal night?"

"Because there was a riot in this ghetto," said Redlaw, "and I want to know what caused it."

"You know what caused it," Illyria said. "Vampires went mad for blood. Their primal urges came out. They could not control themselves."

"Did you witness the events yourself?"

"I did not. I choose not to stand in line to have my sustenance handed out to me. I send others to fetch my share."

"Handy. You run a little gang in this building here, then?"

"I have... followers. Loyal associates. Livingstone Heights is exclusively ours."

"Your own turf. A ghetto within a ghetto."

"Should you be saying 'ghetto' so much?"

"You used it first," Redlaw said. "I reckoned that gave me the green light."

"You would be censured for it, if one of your colleagues or a member of the public heard."

"Report me to Commodore Macarthur. See if she gives a damn." Actually, in light of her current attitude towards him, she probably would. It might even be the final straw for his career. Not that Redlaw cared.

Illyria appraised him with haughty curiosity and, he thought, a hint of wry amusement.

"You feel there was more to the riot?" she said.

"I feel there have been too many incidents like it in recent weeks," Redlaw said. "This year so far, to April, at least two major breaches of the peace have occurred in each of the main inner-city SRAs, and countless minor ones. Last year, guess how many there were? Five. In the entire country. Almost all of the outbreaks of violence have been centred around the blood deliveries. That means something, although I'm not sure what."

"Maybe it means vampires are not content to drink cattle blood."

"That did cross my mind. It's supposed to be an acceptable substitute for your preferred diet. Is it?"

"It will do," Illyria said after a pause for thought. "It certainly slakes the thirst and keeps the agonies at bay."

"The agonies of having nothing to drink?"

"It's a need, Redlaw. You must understand this. It isn't just about filling our bellies. We suffer a compulsion. We *must* drink. If we do not... To go without blood for any length of time is to crawl through Hell with a thousand devils pricking you with their goads."

"Good practice for the real thing."

"Am I destined for Hell?" She seemed tickled by the idea. "Perhaps so. If one believes in such things."

Redlaw decided he wouldn't be drawn into *that* argument. Not with a Sunless, or even a shtriga.

"Cattle blood isn't good enough, that's what you're saying. It doesn't quite hit the spot."

"It sends the pain away, but not entirely, not in the way human blood does. A gnawing ache remains even after one has had one's fill. We accept the cow blood. Tolerate it. It's given to us, on a plate as it were, sparing us the effort of having to hunt. We take it because it's on offer. I cannot claim, however, that anyone truly relishes it."

"Heroin addict forced onto methadone."

"I have no experience of drugs, but I imagine that is a fair comparison."

"So when a shipment comes in, 'Lesses fall on it, consume it, then get peeved because it isn't human? That seems a little, well, feeble. They know it's from cattle. So what are they expecting? That one day, magically, it won't be?"

"I agree. It isn't in itself a reason to go berserk. But perhaps there are other considerations. Dwelling in one of these places, for example." Illyria waved, straight-armed, to indicate the SRA. "Confined in one area. No freedom. A city full of potential prey, and no liberty to go out and stalk and slay. Everything instinct demands is forbidden. It's a recipe for insanity, eh what?"

"So we'll let you all out." Redlaw made an expansive gesture. "Why not? That'd be a great idea. Off you go. Have fun. Run rampant. Fill your boots."

"Sarcasm, Redlaw," Illyria said, "is as offensive to me as mockery. Watch your tongue, or I shall rip it clean out of your mouth."

"I was aiming for irony."

"Irony is simply sarcasm in formal dress, and no less deserving of contempt and punishment."

Illyria Strakosha was, Redlaw thought, a very touchy individual. This being his first encounter with a shtriga, he wondered if all of them were so sensitive.

"I still have this feeling that it's the blood that's key to this," he said. "The correlation seems too clear cut. Delivery, then riot."

"And I'm inclined to agree with you," said Illyria.

"In which case, would you help me?"

Those eyes—pitilessly, unfathomably dark—bored into his. "Help you? Why ever would I wish to help the Night Brigade? You people are our sworn enemy."

"That's putting it strongly. We have a responsibility to safeguard our kind from your kind. That doesn't make us your enemy."

"It hardly makes you our friend."

"I'm not asking you to swap sides, Ms Strakosha. Nor am I after some form of alliance. You need to realise that the riots are causing widespread unease. Last night's especially, with those two men dying. Having Sunless among us is a source of tension in itself. Having restless, angry Sunless among us is bound to make matters worse—for you."

"You're appealing to my own interests."

"Absolutely I am. If I can get to the bottom of what's going on, it could save you 'Lesses a whole heap of trouble. Because, mark my words, trouble is what's coming your way if the situation continues to worsen. There's going to be a backlash, a crackdown of some sort. You know this as surely as I do." He was laying it on thick, exaggerating for effect, although nothing he said seemed unlikely. "People aren't going to let vampires think they can kick up a fuss any time they feel like it. They won't stand for it. You might find SHADE officers being sent in here to bash down doors and pump residents full of ash wood, simply to make a point. I really don't think you'd want that, would you? Not least because, with me in charge, this is the first address I'd direct my officers to."

"So it's threats, is it?"

"Your own interests, like I said. That's all."

Illyria nodded, giving the matter some thought.

"Perhaps," she said at last, "I could make a few enquiries. Grigori, for instance, would be somewhere to start. He was present at the riot."

"Grigori would've been my first suggestion," said Redlaw.

"If I come up with anything..."

"I'll drop by in the next couple of days. Do your best. I'd regard it as a personal favour."

"Oh, such an attractive proposition—to have the mighty John Redlaw indebted to me."

Redlaw half smiled. "Sarcasm?"

"I was aiming for irony," Illyria replied.

"Lucky for you I'm not as judgemental as you are." He turned towards the balcony door. "Tell your underlings to let me leave now, please."

"He's coming through," she called out, and the door unlocked and swung inward. "Until we meet again, old bean. This has been... entertaining."

"Not for me," Redlaw said, with a grimace.

ILLYRIA WAS NO longer on the balcony as he walked away from the building buttoning his weapons vest back on.

It puzzled him that he had looked up to check whether she was.

Annoyed him, too.

CHAPTER SIX

"I WAS RATHER hoping we could settle this like gentlemen," said Slocock to Wax. "You know, come to an arrangement over subsidised G and T's in the Strangers Bar. Thrash out a deal without one or other of us resorting to bodyline bowling."

"It's midday," Wax said. "I never drink before evening. I have standards."

"Then we'll just have to do it sober in this ratty little office of yours. Funny, I thought Cabinet ministers got grander cubbyholes to work in than the rest of us."

"The senior ones do. Sunless Affairs is very much a junior post."

"Ah well. Decent view, though. Way better than mine."

The Thames stretched outside the narrow windows, with Lambeth Palace and the London Eye dominating the opposite bank. A rubbish barge was chuntering by along the turbulent brown water, taking its cargo to some recycling centre, or to a dumping ground in the North Sea—Slocock didn't much care which.

"So, I've asked you nicely, Maurice," he said.

"And I've told you that Nathaniel Lambourne can go hang," came the reply. "I turned him down in person. I'm hardly going to shift my position when his errand monkey comes calling, now am I?"

Errand monkey. Slocock swallowed the insult, making one last effort to remain civil. "It could be the shrewdest move of your entire political career, you realise that, don't you? The kind of decision that makes a media darling out of someone who's—well, no offence, a dull and not especially loved MP. The kind that puts a chap in line for the highest of high office."

A glint came and went in Wax's eyes, like a torch flash in the dark. This was not a rare sight in Westminster. Some hid the ambition better than others, but everyone had it.

"Be that as it may, I simply can't go along with what Lambourne is proposing. It's a step too far. I can't offer official government approval."

"Why not? It promises to resolve the Sunless situation more conclusively than anyone's managed so far."

"But the ramifications... the possible repercussions..."

"What are you scared of? A few hand-wringing liberals? A bleating editorial in the *Guardian*? Trust me, the general public will be overwhelmingly on your side. It could even swing the election in Labour's favour, which, let's face it, would be nothing short of a miracle."

Wax fixed Slocock with the only kind of smile he knew how to give: wan and fleeting. "Surely you want your lot at the wheel next time round."

Slocock blew out his cheeks noncommittally. "Frankly

it doesn't bother me. I find MP-ing pretty boring, as a matter of fact. I thought it would be fun helping run the country, the thrill of power and all that, but mostly what it involves is endless committee meetings, late-night sittings that go on ad nauseam, and hours spent in my surgery listening to constituents whinge on. Opposition, government, what difference does it make? I'd still have to do the same sort of shit either way. I might not even stand for re-election come October. I've other irons in the fire. Plenty more fish to fry."

"Pick your cliché," said Wax dryly. "The fact is, Slocock, I couldn't sell Lambourne's master plan to the PM even if I wanted to. He just wouldn't wear it. He's a man of high moral fibre and a statesman well aware of his standing on the international stage."

"The Prime Minister can be made to see sense. Anyone can." Slocock's expression tightened. "It just takes the right application of pressure."

"Oh, and is that how you're intending to make *me* see sense?" Wax sat back in his chair, folding his arms. "You can try."

"It needn't have come to this, Maurice. Let's be clear about that. You've brought this on yourself."

"What's it going to be? Bribery? I know Lambourne's pockets are deep. I'd be curious to see how deep—not that I *can* be bought, at any price."

"No, you can't. I'm not even going to waste my time waving money about."

"Blackmail, then. Yes?"

"Afraid so."

"You have nothing on me. No one does."

Slocock had to admit, Wax had a hell of a poker face. The man could bluff for England.

The trouble was, everybody had some sort of secret they didn't want the world to know. There wasn't a person alive you couldn't get dirt on if you looked hard enough and dug deep enough. Nathaniel Lambourne had the resources and the wherewithal to winkle out the ugly truths and bring them squirming into the light. He'd prepared a dossier on Wax months ago. It was part of an arsenal of precision-targeted blackmail weapons aimed at all of the nation's great and good, which he stockpiled in case of need. The contents of the Wax file had been delivered to Slocock's door that very morning by courier in a card envelope. Slocock now produced the envelope and fished out a four-gigabyte memory stick from within.

"It seems," he said, "that Maurice Wax, Member of Parliament for Washington and Sunderland West, has a very seamy side to his life."

Wax's naturally grey complexion greyed just a fraction further.

"I've watched the footage myself." Slocock winced. "Fair put me off my breakfast, I can tell you."

"There's nothing," Wax said. "Nothing on there."

"Really? Then you wouldn't mind me running off a copy and sending it to the *Daily Mail*."

"You're lying. This is a barefaced bluff."

"How do you know I'm lying?

"Because…"

"Because there aren't video cameras at Mistress Sterne's Parlour of Correction just round the corner from Tooting Broadway? Well, none that you know of. But Mistress Sterne, a.k.a. Nadine Blevins, is not a stupid woman. She takes covert film of all her clients, especially the high-profile ones. Insurance policy;

you're not going to get prosecuted if you have images of girls tying up and whipping high court judges and top-ranking cops safely stored on a hard drive in a lockup somewhere. It's how she's managed to survive several busts for pandering and keeping a house of ill repute. And you, Maurice, are a regular visitor to her rather bijou terraced property, so there are plenty of shots of you here in all sorts of compromising positions." He waggled the memory stick. "Gimp masks and ball gags and butt plugs—oh my."

Now Wax's face had taken on a ghastly sheen of desperation.

"What would the lovely Anthea say?" Slocock went on. "And young Philip, and little Sandra."

"Shauna," Wax said numbly.

"Shauna. How do you think they would react seeing your saggy white behind on *Newsnight*? Bit of a shock, I'd have thought. Hubby, daddy, seemed such an upright man, but all along, this fetish, this perversion he was harbouring. Your 'vampire' session is a particular delight. I can see the media having a field day with that. Young ladies dressed up in thigh boots and batwing capes, fake plastic fangs, even faker Transylvania accents... Not to mention the riding crops. The riding crops! Surname like yours, the headlines write themselves. What on earth possessed you, Maurice?"

Wax buried his face in his hands. Then, with a sharp intake of breath, he looked up over his fingertips at Slocock.

"You use prostitutes on a regular basis," he said. "You take cocaine. You understand—a man has needs."

"Oh, I'm not criticising. Definitely not. That would be hypocritical. The difference between us is that I don't pretend to be anything other than what I am. You do. You make a big thing out of being a family man, a faithful husband, the perfect father. And I'm sure you are. But with that comes certain expectations, most of which involve staying away from places where they handcuff you to steel frames and twist leather thongs tightly around your privates. It's a question of degrees of honesty. I make no bones about my bad habits, and that's why I get away with it. If you'd tried the same approach, maybe we wouldn't be having this conversation now. Mind you, with your proclivities you probably wouldn't be an MP in the first place, but that's another story."

"It's not fair," Wax lamented. "It's just not fair."

"No, it's not, Maurice, old chap. But it is politics, and that's the donkey we're all riding. So, to recap. This is how it's going to go. You think Lambourne has come up with an ingenious method for handling the Sunless, putting them out of harm's way. You'll recommend to the Prime Minister that Lambourne is given full government backing to pursue his project and bring it to fruition. In a couple of days' time, you'll announce the scheme to the world at a press conference, with its architect standing right beside you. You'll spin it so that it looks like an act of extreme benevolence, which shouldn't be difficult, since it does. It is. And that, my friend, will ensure that this memory stick does not stray from my safekeeping. It's not much to ask, is it, in exchange for your life and career staying on track? You might even, if you do this right, emerge as a national hero."

Wax sighed, heavily, bleakly.

"I'll take that as a 'yes,'" said Slocock.

Popping the memory stick back into the envelope, he exited the Cabinet minister's office.

Job done. Lambourne would be happy.

In fact, the memory stick was blank. The information about what Wax got up to at Mistress Sterne's Parlour of Correction had been contained on a two-page printout enclosed in the envelope, the text drawn from private testimony provided by Mistress Sterne herself. She did not video her clients, unless they requested it specifically so that they might have a keepsake of the occasion, but she was prepared to furnish details of their preferences and peccadilloes to anyone who wanted to know, as long as the price was right (six figures would usually cover it).

The stick had been a prop, a conjuror's wand, nothing more. The rest was embellishment and misdirection.

Wax had been successfully blagged, and Slocock had every reason to feel pleased with himself.

CHAPTER SEVEN

REDLAW ROSE EARLY—three in the afternoon. He opened the curtains and raised the blackout blinds, screwing up his eyes against the slanting spring sunshine. With age, his vision seemed to be getting more sensitive to bright light. Or maybe it was the job, the owl hours, perpetual estrangement from the sun.

He took the Tube to HQ and spent an hour at his desk, researching. It was drudge work—chasing up facts, filling in background detail, checking, cross-referencing. He'd not done the like since his time as a policeman, an eternity ago. For a shady, results were more or less immediate. You didn't have to painstakingly build a case against a Sunless. You didn't have to satisfy the criteria for a warrant. There wasn't much, where vampires were concerned, that couldn't be resolved on the spot with a stake or a Fraxinus round.

His efforts proved fruitful. By the end of the hour he had established a framework of knowledge which, if flimsy, nevertheless supported his suspicions. Armed with this, he took a patrol car from the pool and drove out to Park Royal where, in a huge warehouse on an industrial estate, could be found BovPlas Logistics' London distribution depot.

The site supervisor was a man named Nigel Hutchings. He was politely obstructive at first, but a bit of arm-twisting by Redlaw soon had him being politely compliant instead.

"This," Hutchings said, giving Redlaw a tour of the premises, "is where we load the trucks with their consignments of CG."

"CG?"

"Short for crimson gold. It's our euphemism. We're not squeamish about the blood itself, so much as its end use. Calling it CG helps. That way it sounds like an inorganic chemical or some such."

Forklifts fetched pallets of blood pouches from room-sized refrigerators and slid them into the backs of waiting trucks. The place was frenetic and loud: workers shouting, diesel engines idling, vehicles moving about with intricate mechanical choreography.

"You've caught us at our most manic." Hutchings kept tugging at one corner of a bushy moustache. Redlaw noted the nervous tic. Here was someone who did not thrive on stress. "During this and the next hour, until the trucks head out, we're like chefs at a restaurant, rushing about trying to get the dishes ready on time."

"Not that much of a stretch as metaphors go," Redlaw observed.

"I suppose not."

"And where does the blood—excuse me, the CG—come from?"

"Cows."

Obtuse little beggar. "I'm aware of that. What I mean is, where's it stored prior to coming here?"

"The hub facility up near Watford. The CG is shipped there from slaughterhouses all over the country, pouched up and parcelled back out to depots in thirty-seven locations. We, of course, are the largest of those." Said with pride. "London's where the 'Lesses want to be, isn't it? Some emigrate to the northern cities, some even to the countryside, but London's like a magnet to them, a Mecca. Why is that, I wonder?"

"Do I look like an expert?"

The BovPlas supervisor gave an impertinent frown. "If not you, then who?"

"I round Sunless up and corral them and make sure they stay corralled," Redlaw said. "Doesn't mean I have any special insight into their psychology. But if I had to guess, I'd say cities are like planets. The larger they are, the greater their pull. Why does anybody come to London? Because there's so much of it. It's inescapable. And the numbers of Sunless in the capital keep going up because so many are there already. They cluster, like with like. It reassures them. That answer your question?"

"Adequately."

"So here's one in return. Were you, Mr Hutchings, aware that of the bloodlust riots that have occurred since the New Year, not one has taken place in an SRA that hasn't had its supplies from BovPlas? Not a single one."

Hutchings was taken aback, but only momentarily. "Well, that's not what you'd call surprising, is it, Captain Redlaw? Name me an SRA that *isn't* supplied by BovPlas."

"I can name you several. The one in the Gorbals, Glasgow, for instance. The one in Cardiff's Billy Banks. BovPlas's network of distribution covers most of England, does it not?"

"All apart from the West Country and the remoter parts of Northumbria and the Lake District. Small independent firms have the contracts there, catering to tiny communities of Sunless, some of them no more than five or six strong. It isn't economical for us to supply on that sort of scale."

"And there are no records of riots in those regions or, indeed, anywhere outside England. In other words, anywhere not served by BovPlas. You have to admit, that's something of a coincidence, isn't it? At the very least."

"On the contrary. We furnish every SRA in this land, one or two excepted, with product. What about the ones covered by our distribution network where there've been no riots? What about those, eh? You're misusing the data, if I may say so, Captain Redlaw. If there's some sort of link between our CG and these disturbances, as you seem to be implying, surely it would be universal? The fact is, BovPlas works hard to help keep Sunless pacified. The CG is there to disincentivise them from aggressive and potentially lethal behaviour. It's not logical for us to give them something that would aggravate them. I'd say, in fact, that that would be the very definition of counterproductive. Bad for business."

Hutchings was pulling on his moustache quite agitatedly now, like a milkmaid pumping an udder.

"Two of my drivers have died," he went on. "I sent them out there. I signed their order manifests, and therefore their death warrants. I have that on my conscience. And you have the nerve to come here and suggest that I was in some way responsible?"

"Not you. BovPlas. The blood."

"Ridiculous! What's worse, this whole affair has got my workforce all riled up and militant. I've had drivers phoning in sick. I've had 'em demanding pay rises—danger money—and threatening to go on strike if they don't get them. Insurance premiums are through the roof. I'm trying my damnedest to keep things on an even keel, but it's not easy. And now I've got the Night Brigade accusing me of—"

Just then one of the forklifts collided head-on with a loading dock at speed. Its burden of blood pouches was knocked off onto the floor, slithering in all directions. Many of them popped on impact, and a smooth slick of blood started spreading around the forklift's tyres.

"For the love of—!" Hutchings exclaimed. "Look at that. Just look. This is what I'm having to contend with, Captain Redlaw. Everyone's got the jitters. Now we're going to have to shut operations down for who knows how long while the biohazard team get in there and mop up. Oh joy. I need to oversee this, so you'll just have to make your own way out. Sorry if I haven't been helpful. No, I take that back. I *have* been helpful. Your accusations against BovPlas are completely unfounded. Bordering on slanderous."

He bustled away, gesticulating angrily at the forklift operator with one hand and yanking frantically at his moustache with the other.

Lucky, Hutchings, thought Redlaw. *Saved by the spill.*

As he headed out to his car, Redlaw couldn't help feeling that the BovPlas supervisor had been straight with him.

Corporate stooge though he was, Hutchings had seemed justifiably indignant. His outrage over Redlaw's line of questioning had been genuine. His counterarguments had been plausible.

Perhaps Redlaw was barking up the wrong tree.

On his way back into central London, he stopped off at St Erasmus's in Ladbroke Grove. It wasn't his usual place of worship, by any means. That honour went to the unimposing, modestly appointed Anglican church two streets away from his flat in Ealing, where he attended evensong most Sundays. St Erasmus's was a much larger and more grandiose affair, complete with a neo-Gothic spire that towered above the Westway flyover and a belfry whose bells were so loud their peal easily held its own against the thunder of daytime traffic.

The parish priest, Father Graham Dixon, had done a stint as visiting pastor at SHADE HQ, ministering to the spiritual needs of officers alongside a Catholic bishop, a rabbi, an imam, a lama and representatives of other religions, including a Wiccan druidess and a Class XII Scientology auditor. In that time Father Dixon and Redlaw had developed a friendship which was pretty much confined to meetings for auricular confession, but was no less cordial for that.

"Bless me, Father, for I have sinned," said Redlaw as he knelt at the communion rail, facing the sanctuary.

"No, you haven't, John," Father Dixon replied from the other side of the rail. "Don't talk rot. If *you've* sinned, then it's truly a sign of the End Times and I should be looking out the window for my first glimpse of the Four Horsemen. What's troubling you? Care to share?"

For a time Redlaw said nothing, his gaze on the reredos behind the altar. It was a triptych, depicting Christ's journey through suffering from Earth to Heaven, from Gethsemane via Calvary to the Ascension. Candlelight flickered on the carved, plainly coloured reliefs, lending them a strange liquid animation.

"Is it the job?" Father Dixon prompted. "What am I saying? Of course it's the job. What else could it be? Captain John Redlaw has nothing else in his life."

"And does Father Graham Dixon have anything else in his life beyond the Church?"

"*Touché*. Well, I have my allotment, actually. Those vegetables mean the world to me. But when you get down to it, yes, basically I'm a trad, boring-old-fart vicar who serves his congregation and visits the sick and elderly and tries to get by on an astonishingly meagre stipend. Nothing exciting about me. Not like the two-fisted, all-staking, all-dusting shady Redlaw. Surely he feels fulfilled in his work. Saving us from the Sunless scourge? Now that's a glamorous existence. Men want to be him, women want to be with him..."

"Stop," Redlaw said. "Please. Not in the mood."

Father Dixon let the genial smile ease from his somewhat pudgy features. A frown appeared in its place. "That bad, eh? Come on, fill us in. Me and the Man Upstairs. We're listening."

"I know *you* are, Father. But..."

"Oh. Ah." Father Dixon nodded. "I see. Is *He*? Is God paying attention?" He leaned forwards, dropping his voice but not the concern in his expression. "How long have you been feeling this way, John? Is it a recent thing or has it been brewing a while now?"

"How long since I last saw you?"

"I don't know. Months."

"Months, then. Maybe longer."

"You seemed okay last time, as I recall. Bit dour, bit down in the mouth, but that's default setting for you. You didn't appear to be having any problems. No existential crises I was aware of. Routine confession followed by a chat and a cuppa in the vestry."

"I just..."

"Go on. Honestly, He is here. Even if it doesn't feel that way, He is."

The church yawned around the two men, chilly and cavernous and full of whispering echoes.

"I'm not sure," Redlaw began.

"About?"

"Anything, anymore. There was a time when I had no doubts. None. Everything was straightforward. Cut and dried. God wanted me to work for Him. That was the alpha and omega of my life. In my early twenties I seriously considered taking holy orders."

"I know. You had a narrow escape there."

"Became a copper instead. More practical. A better way of helping people. Tangible results."

"Are you implying I've wasted my life?" said Father Dixon with a chuckle.

"No. I simply don't have the knack for guiding others, the way you do. I lack empathy. I think with my head, sometimes with my hands, seldom with my heart. Served me well enough on the force. Model plod, I was, if not outstanding. A reasonable arrest record, a few solid prosecutions, no black marks, not one public complaint lodged against me. Then, after I'd been pounding the beat a few years, the Sunless began appearing. The population explosion in Eastern Europe. The diaspora.

The mysterious deaths and then the first confirmed sightings. They came out of the murk of legend, into the light of reality. In no time, SHADE had been set up and I was one of the first to sign on the dotted line, one of the initial pioneers. I joined because I knew this was what I was meant to do. Sunless were self-evidently evil, unholy, an aberration, an abomination in the sight of God. People of faith were needed to combat them, people who also had some professional experience of the grimier side of life. I fit the bill perfectly."

"No argument here."

"The Lord had shaped me for this, I understood. He'd been nudging me in this direction all along. There wasn't a moment of blinding-light epiphany, just the cool, calm realisation that my destiny had arrived. I was a machine. I worked tirelessly from dusk 'til dawn. We unearthed 'Less nests all over the city. We captured when we could, dusted when we couldn't. I never hesitated, never questioned. I was righteous beyond righteousness."

Father Dixon knew all of this already, but it didn't even occur to him to interrupt and say so. Redlaw needed to vent. Let the man vent.

"I fought the good fight with all my might," Redlaw said. "I worked with teams, or with partners, but I never gelled with anyone, and that never really mattered to me. I was happiest and best on my own. Then Sergeant Leary came along."

"Róisín. Ah, yes. We all loved Róisín, John. She was— to use my choristers' favourite adjective—awesome."

"Love wasn't it, Father. I don't think I even know what love means."

"Love is what God feels for you, John, constantly.

When you're least certain of it, that's when it's at its strongest."

"Perhaps. What I had with Leary, it was pure compatibility. We knew what each other was thinking. Out in the field, we barely had to speak. We were the right hand and left hand of the same body. She had my back, I had hers. We could be up against hordes of 'Lesses, just the two of us, isolated, alone, in deadly danger, and I never for one second was worried because Leary was with me. Between us, together, I knew we'd be fine."

"And then she died."

"And then she died."

"And you weren't there."

"I wasn't there. Laid low with a case of shingles, of all things. Never had a night off sick before then. Leary was by herself, chasing up a lead—a sighting of a rogue 'Less up in Walthamstow. Turned out the intel was bad; and it wasn't a single vampire but a whole nest of them, occupying the crypt of a deconsecrated church, of all places. She didn't stand a prayer. Or at least, she would have stood a prayer if I'd been with her, or *someone* had been with her. But Leary was as headstrong in her way as I am. I was the only other shady, apart from Commodore Macarthur, she really respected. Certainly the only one she'd work with in the field. So she went it alone that night and the 'Lesses got the jump on her and..."

Redlaw's throat felt tight. He had to force the words out.

"According to the scene-of-incident report, Leary used up two full clips of ammo on them, plus all her stakes. There must have been just too many, though. Dr

Wing, in her autopsy, counted at least thirty separate bite marks on the body, from different sets of fangs. Child-sized fangs, what's more. I reckon that'd be why Leary got caught out. They were child vampires. Compassion got the better of her. That was her one weakness: compassion."

Father Dixon cocked his head. "Compassion is a weakness?"

"For a SHADE officer? Oh, yes. The younger vampires, the kids, you see, they really troubled Leary. She always hesitated over dusting them. She'd say they weren't to blame for their condition. To which I'd say that most Sunless weren't, and she shouldn't let what they looked like when they were turned colour her judgement over what they had become since. It's hard, though, I appreciate that. I've perhaps been known to think twice before dusting a kid. I've even..." He paused, then carried on. "These particular children, though, they showed her no mercy, once they'd overpowered her. They feasted fast and hard. There wasn't a drop of blood left in her. Should be grateful for that, I suppose. At least she wasn't turned and I didn't have to hunt her down and dust her."

"Would you have done that?"

"I'd have made it my mission. I wouldn't have stopped, I wouldn't have slept, until I'd put her out of her misery. As it was, I took it upon myself to carry out the beheading. Dr Wing kept the body on ice in the morgue for me until I was well enough to go in. Out of courtesy. Leary obviously wasn't coming back, but a post mortem neutralisation had to happen anyway. Standard procedure. Macarthur said she wanted to do it, but I insisted. I couldn't see why anyone else should have the right. I was Leary's partner. We had a bit of a set-to over that, Macarthur and I, but I won in the end. The Commodore backed down, once she realised *I* wasn't going to. I think I may even have threatened resignation if I didn't get my way."

"You still feel guilty over Leary's death." Father Dixon pitched the remark carefully as both statement and query. He already had a clear notion of the answer.

"Of course. If I'd been with her, it never would have happened."

"It was bad timing, rotten luck, but you must see, John, that it had nothing to do with you. Regret's a reasonable thing to feel, under the circumstances. But don't mistake it for guilt. You were seriously ill. What, you should have risen from your sickbed and gone in to work that night? You could barely move."

"But why was I ill?"

"Something to do with germs? I'm a vicar, not a doctor."

"It's almost as if... as if..."

"...God arranged the whole thing?"

Redlaw nodded numbly.

Father Dixon *pshaw*ed. "Don't take this the wrong way, my friend, but I've never heard such complete and utter bobbins in all my life. God hit you with a rash and a fever, then had a bunch of vampires murder Róisín? Why? To prove what point? To make you miserable? To plunge you into despair?"

"He moves—you may have heard this, Father—in mysterious ways."

"Too right, He does. But He's not vindictive, He's not a psycho, He's not some divine Mafia don. The God I worship isn't, at any rate."

"He's omnipotent. He could have prevented Leary's death."

"Maybe. But that obviously wasn't in His plan."

"But torturing me is?"

"Oh, John!" Father Dixon's exasperated cry resounded to the rafters. "How egotistical are you? God's got it in for you specially, that's what you're telling me? He's decided John Redlaw needs taking down a peg or two? One of His staunchest admirers, His biggest fans, deserves a good smiting? It doesn't make sense."

"He did it to Job, didn't he?"

"Yes, and He's allowed any number of martyrs to be put to death, horribly, on His behalf. Not to mention you-know-who, His own son, what's the guy's name again? It's on the tip of my tongue. Jesus... Jesus somebody. I'll get it in a moment. That one who had the fun day being crucified. Him." He jerked a thumb towards the reredos. "John, God isn't trying to hurt you. Don't be childish."

"What is He trying to do, then? What does He want from me?"

"That's for you to work out for yourself."

"Come off it, that's a total copout."

Father Dixon could only shrug. "Way it works, I'm afraid. No easy answers. No multiple-choice tick-the-box. Just the long, arduous process of sifting through the contradictions and the inconsistencies and the sometimes outright absurdities to find some kind of truth. Takes most people a lifetime."

"You've managed it, though," said Redlaw.

"Oh, no. Don't be under that illusion. I grapple with my faith on a daily basis. Sometimes I get so depressed about it all—the suffering in the world, the countless prayers that go unanswered, God's apparent indifference to the human condition—that I feel like jacking it all in. I want to tear off the dog collar and go and live like a hermit in a croft in the Hebrides. But you know what keeps me going? What reminds me that there probably is a supreme deity and He's watching out for us? You'll like this."

"I will?"

"Sunless."

"What?"

"The fact that there are Sunless."

Redlaw was flummoxed. "'Lesses prove the existence of God? You're going to have to explain that one, Father."

"Think about it," said Father Dixon. "Vampires. Supernatural beings. They're immortal—as long as they steer clear of you chaps. They have abilities that some might call superhuman, godlike even. They skulk in the dark, forbidden the light. They're compelled to leech off the living, to drink blood, kind of an anti-Eucharist. They're dead but they mimic life. What are they, looked at like that, but a parody of God? His warped reflection. The negative to His positive. We infer the shape of Him by the shadows the Sunless create. They provide the outline, leaving a blank for us to fill in. He made them, John, just as He made the Devil, in order to show us Himself. Unholy and blasphemous as they are, vampires are the clearest evidence we have that God is real and wants us to know it. Do you see that? Often I'm asked by a parishioner why doesn't God ever just give us a sign, something concrete and undeniable, so that we can be sure, one hundred per cent, that He's there. I reply: He already has. Go to an SRA and look. There's your sign."

Father Dixon slapped both hands on the communion rail with all the satisfaction of a barrister who has just conclusively proved his case and exonerated his client.

"Now, any more silly questions, Captain Redlaw? Or can we all go back to our appointed tasks as defenders of faith and vessels of the divine will?"

"I suspect," Redlaw said evenly, "that we can."

"Then I absolve thee from all thy sins, in the Name of the Father, and of the Son, and of the Holy Spirit. Amen. Now go forth, be fruitful, and make the streets safe for people with a pulse."

The consolation of absolution was, like the interior of St Erasmus's, cold. But, like St Erasmus's, it was also solid and uplifting.

Redlaw drove.

Two PHONE CALLS zigzagged simultaneously through the network.

One was from Nigel Hutchings to Nathaniel Lambourne, on a private mobile number that very few employees in the Dependable Chemicals family of firms had access to.

The other was from Father Dixon to his old boss, Commodore Macarthur, on the direct line to the latter's office at SHADE HQ.

Both calls pertained to recent conversations with Redlaw.

Hutchings's was plaintive and anxious. It sought reassurance. It got it.

Father Dixon's was probing and solicitous. It did not breach the seal of the confessional. It merely conveyed a general apprehension about Redlaw's mental wellbeing.

Hutchings complained to Lambourne.

Father Dixon compared notes with Macarthur.

Lambourne, when he had convinced the site supervisor that interest from a SHADE officer was nothing to lose sleep over, sat in quiet contemplation for several minutes. He looked unruffled, but a muscle at the base of his jaw kept writhing under the skin.

Macarthur, when she had told Father Dixon his concerns were duly noted, thanked him for voicing them, and set down the receiver, also sat thinking. The creases at the corners of her eyes deepened, as though she were pained by a memory, or a presentiment, or both. They smoothed again as she reminded herself that Redlaw was a SHADE officer of the highest calibre. His first and only allegiance was to the Night Brigade. That, surely, would save him.

Then her phone rang again.

CHAPTER EIGHT

OVER THE COURSE of the night, there was a spate of bloodlust riots all across England.

Birmingham saw the worst of it. Sunless ran amok in all six of the SRAs in that city. BovPlas trucks were attacked, their drivers besieged in their cabs. Fatalities hit double figures.

In Bristol, the trouble didn't stay confined to the Residential Area in Eastville. Blood-drenched vampires spilled over the fence, onto the streets. The city's full complement of SHADE officers was deployed to herd them back where they belonged. Sunless who refused to co-operate were summarily dusted.

Leeds saw a breakout, too. There, however, a posse of civilians joined the Night Brigade in re-containing the vampires. The help wasn't asked for, or officially endorsed, but the beleaguered SHADE officers weren't ungrateful.

The Sussex coastal town of Hastings also saw citizens taking up arms against the Sunless. No actual riot occurred in that once genteel, now run-down seaside resort, but the place did boast a sizeable contingent of Stokers, who commanded general sympathy and support among the populace. The town's pier, which had been condemned as an unsafe structure due to storm damage and closed to the public, had been put to use as the local SRA. The Stokers set fire to it with petrol bombs, and half of Hastings turned out during the small hours to watch it burn and the vampires along with it. All along the promenade and on the balconies of the Regency seafront buildings, fascinated, gleeful faces were lit up by flames, and cheers went up as the century-old pier crumbled section by section and collapsed into the sea. Fire crews arrived suspiciously late—too late to do anything about the blaze except ensure that none of the bystanders were hurt.

In Oxford, on the notorious Blackbird Leys estate, a similar sort of pre-emptive action was taken against neighbourhood Sunless, although it met with less success. A gang of youths followed the BovPlas delivery truck into the SRA and set about the waiting residents with improvised weapons. It soon dawned on the kids that they ought to have done their homework properly. Their stakes were lengths of sharpened dowel and chair-back spindle, but none was made of ash wood. What began as a concerted effort to give the vamps what-for, ended as a rout. The carnage was appalling. Teenagers, even a few twelve-year-olds, ran screaming from the enraged vampires. None of the young invaders made it back to the gate and safety. Many sobbed and cried for their mothers as fangs tore chunks out of their flesh and mouths sucked greedily at the blood that welled from the wounds.

At SRAs in Coventry, in Milton Keynes, in Bradford, in Stevenage, in Middlesbrough, in Stoke-on-Trent, the story was much the same. It seemed as though virtually every vampire in the land was in the grip of blood madness, helpless to do anything but obey their savage thirst.

REDLAW STOOD IN front of an electrical goods shop window, watching the soundless televisions within. All were tuned to the same twenty-four-hour news channel. Reporters in various locations spoke to the camera, wide-eyed, hunched anxiously as if expecting to be attacked from behind at any moment. Captions scrolled along the bottom of the screens, tickertaping the latest statistics—the tally of the dead, the number of SRAs affected—and soundbites from politicians. Maurice Wax: "No cause for alarm. Stay in your homes. Take reasonable precautions." Giles Slocock: "Blame lies with government's lamentable failure to grasp Sunless nettle." These were interspersed with texted-in contributions from viewers, which ranged from "gr8er understanding is called 4" to "stake em all."

So far, London itself had been surprisingly incident-free. Redlaw had been monitoring the verbal traffic on the SHADE band on his patrol car's shortwave. There'd been a few minor flare-ups here and there in London SRAs out of his jurisdiction, and none at all on his patch, the north-east quadrant of the capital. He was feeling oddly useless, like the reserve player on a team looking on from the touchline, willing but unable to take part in the game.

He was almost relieved when Macarthur called.

"Marm. At a loose end. What can I do?"

"Get me to a desert island," said Macarthur. "Anywhere without phones. Mine's been ringing off the hook all night. And don't even get me started on the emails. I think my inbox just exploded. Everyone wants a piece of me and there's not enough to go round."

"London's been keeping its nose relatively clean, though. Commodore Choudhury up in the Midlands, him I could understand having a hard time tonight, but you?"

"That's just it. Everybody's badgering me to do something, but if it's not happening in London, how am I supposed to help? Wax has been the biggest pain in the behind. He's all but told me he'll have to sack me if I can't keep a lid on this. 'We'll be looking to collect a major scalp, and I shan't be afraid to wield the tomahawk.' His exact words. He even hinted he and the PM have some kind of contingency plan they're considering, which, if they are, it's news to me."

"The army?"

"Could be. Hope not. Anyway, my problem, not yours. No need to be burdening you with it. I don't deserve the commodoreship if my shoulders aren't broad enough to bear the weight."

"I don't mind, marm."

"Yes, but still. How's the hornets' nest kicking coming along?"

"It's ongoing. Nothing to report yet, but at least I haven't been stung."

"I still think you're wasting your time."

"I still think not."

"But you're at a loose end right now?"

He eyed the televisions. "Nothing I can't tear myself away from."

"Then I have a little job for you. The Isle of Dogs. Reports of possible Sunless activity there. Could be a rogue nest."

Redlaw stifled a groan. "And when it turns out to be a wild goose chase...?"

"If it does," Macarthur said, "you file a comprehensive statement to that effect. *After* you've investigated thoroughly. Didn't we discuss this? I'm not having you skimp on the meat-and-potatoes stuff, John."

"There are bigger things going on."

"Not at this precise moment."

"Send a sergeant. Send Khalid."

"Actually, I thought about him, but he's off tonight."

"Send him anyway."

"You're close to being insolent, Captain Redlaw."

Even over the phone Macarthur's anger was palpable. Redlaw could easily picture the thundercloud in her face, the lightning in her eyes. Her military background was coming to the fore again. Chain of command was important, and everyone needed to know their place on it.

"You have been given a direct order," she said. "You damn well obey. Otherwise, you can come back to HQ and everyone can watch as I take your badge and Cindermaker off you and strip you of your rank and kick you out on your ear. Don't think that's an empty threat, either. I'm reaching the end of my rope with you. You'd be advised to remember who you are and what you get paid to do."

Macarthur continued in the same vein for another couple of minutes. At the end, Redlaw felt as though he'd been flayed alive, and the prospect of unearthing a Sunless nest seemed positively pleasant by comparison.

Which, he could only assume, had been the Commodore's intention all along.

NEW MET OLD on the Isle of Dogs, and it was an awkward encounter. Sky-raping towers of commerce glittered to the north. Docklands conversions twinkled smugly along the riverbank. In between lay decayed wharves, disued printworks, and tangles of back-to-back tenements which had been young in Dickens's day and not much jollier then. The areas City money had touched were pristine and clean, but this effect did not extend to the inner reaches of the Isle, which remained historically grubby and undesired and looked all the more so when bathed in the cold radiance given off by the surrounding developments. So near, yet so far. There could not be a starker illustration of the ineffectiveness of trickle-down economics than this.

Sat-nav led Redlaw to the address Macarthur had given him, an abandoned unit on a trading estate overshadowed by the elevated track of the Docklands Light Railway. He checked the building's perimeter first. No sign of a break-in, but vampires were sneaky that way. They knew better than to leave visible evidence of forced entry. Also, premises like this often had skylights, easily accessible to Sunless if not to humans.

Indeed, that was how suspicion had fallen on this place, according to Macarthur. Someone on a train had glimpsed a figure lurking on the unit's roof. It had been dark and the train had been going fast, so the witness couldn't be certain that the figure was a Sunless, but the balance of probabilities suggested it was. Why else would anybody be up there at night? Burglary?

An opportunist burglar would be more likely to take a ground-level approach, and a professional burglar wouldn't bother with the unit at all.

There was a large rolling door for vehicle access, a smaller personnel door beside it. Both were padlocked securely. Round the back there was a flight of fire escape steps leading up to an emergency door, hinged to open outwards. Redlaw found a length of rebar among the weeds and detritus at the rear of the building and used it as a crowbar to pry the door open. He tried to work as softly as possible, but the odd splintery *crack* and *creak* was unavoidable. If there were vampires inside, their sharp ears might well pick this up. Alerting them was a risk he would have to take. Couldn't be helped.

Into the building he went, Cindermaker drawn, night vision goggles in place. He passed through a series of back rooms, trying doors, peering into stripped-bare office spaces and empty supply cupboards. Nothing. No trace of Sunless. None of their spoor. No faeces. No animal remains—bones or shrivelled corpses—that spoke of the undead trying to lead a clandestine existence, denying themselves humans as food and subsisting on dogs, cats and whatever other small mammals they could find.

Nonetheless a gut instinct was telling Redlaw the unit was not uninhabited. *Something* was here. And why not? The Isle of Dogs was known for being a place of refuge for Sunless freshly arrived off the boat. Situated at a bend in the Thames, nestling inside a looping curve of river that in a million years' time would be an oxbow lake, it was the first point on the inland journey when the city began to look like a city rather than an industrial sprawl. Sunless, whether stowed away on a freighter or smuggled in below decks on some trafficker's yacht, were apt to wade ashore here and hole up in the nearest available dark crevice. A unit like this suited them down to the ground.

Stairs led down into the unit's main section. Redlaw's goggles revealed an expanse of rough concrete floor with a rectangular trench at the centre. A car exhaust repair firm used to rent the premises; the trench was an inspection pit. It was also, in Redlaw's experience, just the kind of dank burrow vampires liked to huddle in when resting.

He approached it cautiously, stepping toe to heel to deaden his footfalls. At the lip of the pit he swung his Cindermaker down, quartering every corner with the barrel. The pit was empty apart from a few congealed puddles of motor oil.

He stepped back and scanned around in every direction. All he saw was bare corrugated steel walls. Shadows were few and far between. There was a dearth of places to hide.

All the evidence pointed to there being no Sunless here.

Yet still Redlaw was sure there were.

Too late, he thought to look upwards.

A shape plunged from the ceiling joists. It would have struck Redlaw squarely if he hadn't managed to twist aside in the nick of time. It caught him a glancing blow instead, but that was still enough to send him sprawling. He hit the floor beside the inspection pit, knocking the wind from his lungs and the Cindermaker from his grasp. The gun tumbled into the pit, discharging as it landed. The percussion of the gunshot was instantly followed by a stutter of pings and pops as the bullet ricocheted around inside the pit.

Redlaw dived in headlong after his weapon, scrambling across the pit's greasy floor to where it lay.

Behind, there was a thud as his attacker jumped in after him. He snatched up the Cindermaker and whirled around. A vampire was lunging at him, point blank range. No hesitation. He fired.

It was a perfect heart shot, bang on target. The Fraxinus round was already working its magic even as the force of the shot propelled the Sunless through the air to the far end of the pit. Flakes of flash-charred flesh spiralled out from the entry hole as the creature flew, and its chest disintegrated completely when it collided with the side of the pit. Within a few seconds the whole of its body had crumbled to a pile of grey-black powder. It never even had a chance to scream.

Other vampires dropped to the floor from the joists where they had been lying in wait. Redlaw counted five, six, seven of the creatures. He flung back the flaps of his overcoat, exposing his weapons-festooned vest.

"All right, then," he said. "Ashes to ashes, dust to dust."

They came at him as one, in a snarling mob. He eliminated two of them with his Cindermaker before they reached him, and winged a third. Then he was cornered, his back against the pit wall, the vampires closing in fast. An allium sativum bomb repulsed them long enough for him to clamber out. The pit was six feet deep, so it was a struggle, and no sooner had he hauled himself up on the unit floor than the vampires joined him there, nimbly leaping their own height or more from a standing start. Still flat on his belly, Redlaw shot the nearest of them in the ankle. Then he was up on his feet and running.

He glimpsed figures descending all around him from the ceiling. Damn it, how many of the things were there? One landed directly in his path and he emptied a round into its face. The vampire's entire head vanished in a detonation like a bag of flour bursting, and the rest of it followed suit as its headless body crumpled to the floor. Redlaw ran straight through the cloud of swirling dust, to find himself confronted on the other side by three more Sunless. He shot the first, at which point the slide on his Cindermaker snapped back.

No time to reload. Holstering the gun, he unclipped an *aqua sancta* grenade, pulled the pin and lobbed it at the two vampires. It burst, and they screeched and recoiled, their skin blistering and smoking as though splashed with acid.

Two Sunless appeared, one on either side of Redlaw, phosphorescent green blurs in the goggle lenses. They charged, fangs bared, talons outstretched.

Redlaw tugged a pair of stakes from their sheaths on his vest and hurled them right and left. Both vampires were impaled simultaneously. They went down with wails of distress, their chests imploding around the wooden implements and becoming powdery cavities.

Redlaw armed himself with a fresh pair of stakes.

"The old-school method," he said, hefting them in his hands. "Can't knock it."

Vampires converged on him from all sides. Redlaw stabbed out as they came within range. Occasionally he missed. More often he didn't. He kept turning his head to compensate for the limitation the goggles put on his peripheral vision. He could feel ash coating his hands and face. It clogged his throat, too, almost choking him. The taste was bitter—bonfires and barbecues gone wrong—but he was used to it.

Finally a Sunless got past his guard. He had known this was going to happen sooner or later. There were just too many of them.

The creature pounced, slashing his right shoulder with its talons. The entire arm went numb, the stake falling from useless fingers. Then pain hit, like a charging rhino.

Redlaw, reeling, managed to dust the vampire with his other hand. Blood gushed down his arm, a hot wet sleeve. The remaining vampires, inflamed by the smell of it, cried out in a kind of ecstasy and redoubled their assault. Redlaw staked them one after another with his good arm. He was in bad shape, though, and he knew it. The pain from his shoulder filled his entire torso, constricting his breathing and making him dizzy. All at once the simple act of staying upright seemed a Herculean feat. He fought on, only because that was all he could do. If he stopped, he was dead. It was that simple. The single stake lashed out, but accuracy and control with it became increasingly hard to achieve. It was just a short piece of wood, but seemed to weigh a ton.

Redlaw sagged to one knee, still maintaining his defence. His right hand was slick with blood. A vampire lurched at him and he punctured its ribcage, but lost his grip on the stake. The creature staggered away, losing cohesion, its face becoming all cracks and craters like a parched riverbed. Redlaw tried to pull another stake from his vest, but somehow he couldn't do it. His fingers would not work. It was as though they'd been replaced with a bunch of bananas. Detaching an *aqua sancta* grenade was no less an impossible task. He was weaponless. The pain from his shoulder pounded like a gong. He was a sitting duck. The next Sunless that came at him would be the end of him. He bent his head, waiting for the leap, the snarl, the killing blow. So be it. He was ready. Let it happen.

There was only stillness and silence. Redlaw lifted his head. The goggles showed him images of the unit's interior through a haze of dispersing ash particles, like streaks of green ground mist. No figures loomed. Nothing crouched up among the ceiling joists.

"God..." Redlaw breathed.

He never took the Lord's name in vain. This was simply an imprecation to the Almighty, gasped out in relief and gratitude.

It was also the last word on his lips as a tide of emptiness rushed up inside him and he keeled over, unconscious.

CHAPTER NINE

SLOCOCK'S OPPONENT CIRCLED round the sparring ring, light on his toes and wary. The man had been introduced to him as Abiade or Adebayo, something Nigerian and unpronounceable like that, and he looked tough—tough enough to give Slocock a run for his money, at any rate. Which was how Slocock liked it. Too many of the victories in his life were easy ones. Now and then he relished a challenge. The possibility of defeat, however remote, added an edge to things.

"Don't hold back," he told the man. "That's not what I'm paying you for. Try and do some serious damage."

Adebayo—Slocock was pretty certain that was the name—just nodded. No smile. Businesslike.

Good. That meant he was taking the fight seriously. It also meant he didn't think this white Englishman, who conceded ten years and six inches of height to him, was going to be a pushover. Slocock didn't mind being underestimated—it enabled him to spring surprises—

but he had no problem with being respected either.

From the ringside Khun Sarawong said, "Fighters, when you are ready... *chok*!"

At the command, Slocock triple-stepped towards Adebayo and landed the first blow, a straight punch to the chin. He followed it up with an elbow thrust, taking power from the shoulder. Adebayo responded with a curving knee strike, which Slocock blocked. The Nigerian then attempted a clinch, but Slocock danced backwards out of reach.

Two decent hits, but Adebayo shrugged them off. He had come with a reputation. Slocock was pleased to see that he lived up to it.

It was midmorning and Slocock had booked out the ring room at the Soho Dojo for his exclusive use. A crowd of onlookers would have been an annoyance, and the last thing he wanted was some idiot with a camera phone uploading footage of the bout onto YouTube. *Kickboxing MP In Action.* But, more pertinently, they were fighting without pads, gloves, gum shields, head guards, any kind of protection, nor a referee, all of which was illegal.

Adebayo launched a blistering attack, opening with a roundhouse kick to the midsection—which Slocock parried with his shin—then moving in close for some fist and elbow work. Slocock bore the brunt with his forearms, impressed by the power and rapidity with which the hits came. Cobra punch, elbow uppercut, spinning backfist, corkscrew punch—Adebayo was running through the whole repertoire, keeping Slocock on his mettle. Eventually Slocock made a misjudgement and a right cross got through. Though it stunned him, he managed to retaliate with a jumping knee strike which connected with Adebayo's solar plexus and repelled him enough to allow Slocock to recover.

He aimed a quick glance at Khun Sarawong. His instructor's face said it all: *I thought I taught you better than that.* Khun Sarawong was seldom anything but disappointed with a pupil's prowess. His approval was hard to gain, and all the more desirable for that.

Slocock sprang across the ring and brought an axe heel kick slamming down on Adebayo's shoulder. Next he went for an angle kick to the ribs, but his opponent deflected it with a sideways foot thrust and answered with an angle kick of his own to the other flank. Slocock got his shin up in time, but a reverse horizontal elbow strike from Adebayo caught him unawares, smack on the temple.

Stars? Slocock saw supernovas.

Adebayo drove home the advantage with a succession of elbow chops and shin kicks, pressing Slocock back towards the ropes. The Nigerian was being paid on a sliding scale: a set fee for taking part in the bout, double that for victory and treble for victory by knockout. He had every incentive, then, for going at Slocock as viciously and relentlessly as he could. No question he was a formidable foe, and it vaguely entered the Member for Chesham and Amersham's thoughts that there was a chance he might lose here.

That galvanised him. Giles Slocock never lost. The instant his back touched the ropes he thrust Adebayo away with a *thip* kick—a sharp shunt with the toes—then set about him with a barrage of diagonal kicks and knee strikes, reversing the journey so that now it was Adebayo being propelled backwards across the ring. Each kick required rotational movement of the entire body, but Slocock snapped back to basic stance every time, never allowing himself to be off-balance a millisecond longer than necessary. He was sweating now, and his breathing was getting heavy, but as fit as he was, he could have carried on the assault for several minutes.

With Adebayo hemmed in at one corner of the ring, Slocock went for a clinch. Both hands locked onto the Nigerian's head while both forearms pressed onto his collarbone. Adebayo tried to get out of the hold by hammering Slocock with his knees, but Slocock kept him close, weakening the force of the counterattacks.

There was a saying in *muay thai*: "Kick loses to punch, punch loses to knee, knee loses to elbow, elbow loses to kick." It was the fundamental mantra of the Eight-limbed Science, something that every practitioner was meant to ponder and appreciate. It implied that there was no single all-prevailing form of attack, there was only a perpetual cycle of blow and block, strike and parry.

Khun Sarawong had tried to drum this into Slocock, but Slocock remained unconvinced of its truth. Maybe it had something to do with him being, as Khun Sarawong often called him, a *nak muay farang*—a foreign boxer—but Slocock had found that once you were the dominant half in a clinch, you had the contest pretty much sewn up. Your opponent could try to "swim" his arm up inside your arms, as Adebayo was doing now, in order to turn the clinch about and establish himself as dominant. But as long as you stopped him from doing it—and it wasn't all that difficult—then his body was yours to do with as you wished. His fate was literally in your hands.

For Slocock, that meant bringing Adebayo's head down and his own knee upwards repeatedly. The first dozen times, Adebayo resisted. Slocock had to wrench his head down with some force. After that, though, it got easier. Adebayo's strength ebbed with each strike. His struggles faded. Slocock's knee continued to ram into his face.

In a normal bout, the referee would have called "*yaek!*" by now and broken up the clinch. But of course there was no referee. Soon blood was flowing, and it wasn't long before the Nigerian had gone completely limp and Slocock was supporting him as much as battering him.

When Slocock at last let Adebayo go, the Nigerian slumped to the mat in a heap. He wasn't conscious anymore, and he didn't have much of a face left. What he had was a bulbous mass of contusions and broken flesh that looked like some sort of poorly cooked pudding.

Slocock stepped back, panting, flushed with success. He turned and looked to Khun Sarawong. He resented his need for affirmation from the instructor, but was unable to keep from seeking it.

Khun Sarawong merely put his palms together and gave a curt bow. "Not bad," he said. "For a *nak muay farang.*"

It wasn't much, but given the source, it was high praise indeed. Slocock retired to the showers happy. In the toilets, he helped himself to a quick toot of the old Bolivian marching powder from a golden snuffbox, a family heirloom that had seen his great-grandfather through the First World War and his grandfather through the Second. *Muay thai* and a prodigious cocaine habit might seem incompatible bedfellows, but in fact the cardiovascular training helped counteract the drug's harmful effects, while the coke mitigated the post-exertion aches and pains and boosted his depleted energy reserves. It was almost as if the two things were made for each other, a perfect marriage of opposites.

He then spent some time studying himself in a wall mirror. His physique was superb for a man in his mid-thirties. Hell, it was superb full stop. Not an ounce of flab to be seen. The muscles seemed to glide across one another with every movement he made, smooth as cloud shadows on a hillside. The face wasn't bad, either. A little long, perhaps, a little too pointed at the chin, and the nose was slightly larger than the ideal, but all in all a symmetrical, well-put together face. Slocock looked at it and, as usual, did not fail to like what he saw. Political pundits frequently commented on his appearance, his "public schoolboy good looks," his "athletic build." In any number of blogs and online surveys he was rated the handsomest man in Westminster, although that wasn't saying much, given the troll-like quality of the competition. One website, politiciansidliketofuck.com, placed him in the top three most shaggable elected officials in the world. A rival site, politiciansidliketofuckoff.com, ranked him similarly highly, but that was far less of an accolade.

A bead of blood bulged suddenly from his reflection's left nostril. Slocock sniffed it back up, but the blood would not be restrained, swelling from the nostril and then dribbling down his upper lip. He stemmed the flow with a twist of toilet paper. Had Adebayo punched him in the nose? Possibly. More likely, though, it was the coke.

The coke, which even now was forming a hard nucleus in his brain, defining his thoughts, sharpening his convictions until they were certainties. Oh, glorious coke, which took a man who was already considerable and made even more of him. Slocock felt his personality expanding until he was no longer merely full of himself, he could barely be contained, like a universe in a bottle.

His mobile trilled. He dug it out of his gym bag and flipped it open.

"Yes?"

"Slocock? Wax."

"Maurice! Maurice, old mate. How you doing, Maurice, Morrie, the Maurice-meister? What up? ¿Qué pasa?"

"Slocock, are you all right?"

"Don't I sound all right? I'm all right. I'm fine. Never better. What can I do for you? To what do I owe the thingummy of this call? How can I help my fellow duellist across the dispatch box, my other half, my oppo?" During his few weeks at Sandhurst, before getting booted out for conduct unbecoming, Slocock had managed to pick up a few pieces of military slang, which he liked to drop into the dialogue now and then to suggest the army career he'd not actually had.

"Ah," said Wax. "I see. You've had a little... pharmaceutical assistance, haven't you?"

"No idea what you're talking about. Just been working out, that's all. I'm charged with endorphins. Riding a natural high." He inhaled hard through his unplugged nostril and hissed the air noisily out through pursed lips. "Pure and undefiled, that's me. My body is a temple."

"Yes, well... Listen, Slocock. I've got some news for you."

"Oh yes?"

"Yes. I've managed to bring the PM on board."

"Really? No shitting?"

"He wasn't having any of it at first, but I talked him round. What swung it was something you said, about all of this looking like an act of benevolence."

"Well, it is. I mean, let's be honest, it's for our own security, and that's paramount, but the Sunless gain something too. Everybody wins."

"And Lambourne can have these things up and running how soon?"

"The first's already been completed," said Slocock. "Far as I know, it's ready for use."

"Completed? But I was led to believe the project was only at the blueprint stage."

"What you were led to believe, Waxy old pal, and what's actually the case, are two very different kettles of fish. Nathaniel escalated the project to priority status once it became clear how restless the Sunless are getting in their SRAs. One facility's been built, there's a further two well on their way to being finished, and the land's been surveyed and the materials purchased for at least a dozen more. All the sites are on property Nathaniel owns, so he hasn't even had to apply for planning permission. The work falls within the category of legitimate change of use."

"From factories to... to whatever these places are going to be called."

"That's right."

"What *are* they going to be called?"

"Nathaniel's publicists are working on that right now. We'll let you know. The main thing is, you did it, Mo. Well done. Bent the PM's ear and wormed some sense into him. I knew you had it in you."

"And I'm safe now? You promise that memory stick isn't going anywhere?"

"Nowhere except somewhere safe that only I know about."

"I don't suppose... I don't suppose I could have it, could I?"

"What, to watch? For your own personal viewing pleasure? *Maurice Wax's Greatest Hits?*"

"No. Not for that. Not at all. Just so that it doesn't fall into the wrong hands. To make sure."

"Oh, Mo. Mo, my foe. Mo the Joe who likes a low blow from a 'ho. That's not going to happen. No way. The stick stays with me. Something to keep you honest. A stick to beat you with, as it were. Which of course, you being you, I think you'd quite enjoy."

Wax's voice turned icy. "You're an utter turd, Slocock. You know that?"

"Know it, don't care," Slocock replied blithely.

"One day you're going to get your comeuppance."

"Perhaps. But not, Wax, from you. Never from you."

"You know what my grandfather would have called you? A *putznasher yutz.*"

"I do love those Yiddish insults. They're so expressive, so onomatopoeic. Did your grandpa yell that over this shoulder as he fled from the Nazis? I bet that told them."

"Fuck you, Slocock."

"And a very good day to you too, Wax," Slocock said, and slapped his phone shut.

He re-examined himself in the mirror. The screw of toilet paper was soaked red, but when he tugged it out there was no renewed flow of blood. Triumph was blazing in his reflection's eyes, but it was nothing next to the triumph Slocock felt inside. He'd done it.

He'd moulded the malleable Wax, and Wax in turn had brought the Prime Minister into the fold. All was going swimmingly.

If only Wax knew the full potential of Lambourne's scheme.

Maurice Wax, whose grandparents had escaped Germany a few weeks before Kristallnacht and who liked to brag how they had instilled a strong sense of fairness and justice in him as a young boy, along with a loathing for intolerance and oppression...

Oh, *there* was irony. Irony galore.

CHAPTER TEN

IT WAS BOTH dream and memory. A memory within a dream.

The day Leary gave him the crucifix he now wore.

Until then, Redlaw had made do with a small silver cross on a slender chain.

Leary had told him that wasn't good enough. Too modest. Too restrained.

"What you need," she'd said, "is something nice and ostentatious and Catholic. Like mine." She waggled the crucifix she wore, with its carved Christ. The whole thing was the size of the palm of Redlaw's hand. "Not that piddly little whatnot no bigger than an ant."

Accordingly, one evening she presented him with a velvet-covered box. Inside lay the wooden crucifix, strung on a strong-looking steel chain that looked like the kind used in making handcuffs—same diameter, same density of links.

"Think of it as an anniversary gift. Celebrating five

years, to the day, since we first partnered up."

"No figure on it like there is on yours," Redlaw remarked, holding the crucifix up for inspection.

"In deference to your Protestant sensibilities. Didn't want to go too far. There's only so much showiness you C of E types can take before your heads explode. We left-footers, by contrast, we love a bit of holy bling. Now, are you going to put it on or what?"

He did as bidden.

"Feels heavy," he said.

"So it should. Can't have you mincing around not accepting the full weight of your faith. Christianity's not simple. It uplifts, but it's also a millstone round our necks. All the stuff we're supposed to do and not supposed to do. All the sins we try not to commit but commit anyway."

"Speak for yourself."

"I forgot, it's a monk I'm talking to," said Leary. "Ever thought of getting yourself a tonsure, Redlaw? It'd suit you, *and* no one would realise you have a bald spot."

"I don't have a bald spot."

"Trust me, you do. But it's our secret. Ours and your barber's."

"Shut up, Leary."

She just laughed. She never took him seriously, even when he was at his most serious. "So you're not going to thank me, then?"

"For what? Informing me I'm going thin on top?"

"That and the cross."

"I haven't decided if I'm keeping it or not."

"That's okay. I know you will. See, the thing is, as with everything where God is concerned, it might not be what you want, but it might just be what you need."

"Thank you for that insightful little aphorism, sergeant. Now, are we going to stand here all night jabbering, or are we going to get out there and wrangle Sunless?"

"Lead on, boss. To the SHADEmobile! I'm driving, mind."

A week later Redlaw contracted shingles. Two days after that, Leary was dead.

The crucifix stayed on. He hadn't removed it since.

Surfacing from sleep, he groped for it now, in his hospital bed. His right arm wouldn't budge, so he used his left. His fingers closed around the familiar contours, that axis of pity and sorrow.

"Redlaw."

He opened his eyes. Commodore Macarthur was seated at his bedside. They two, and a host of purring machines, were the only occupants of the small private ward. Venetian blinds ruled the daylight like lines on a sheet of foolscap.

"Marm," he croaked.

"There you are," Macarthur said. "You poor thing. Came a real cropper this time, didn't you? And it's all my fault. I should never have sent you to check out that nest. Not alone, at any rate."

"There were dozens of them. You weren't to know."

"Still, I should have made you take backup, instead of sending it along afterwards. If we weren't so stretched right now..."

"I'd never have accepted backup."

"I'd have insisted. How are you feeling?"

Redlaw glanced at his shoulder, which was tightly and thickly bandaged, his arm in an immobiliser sling. "Sore," he said.

"What have the docs said?"

"That I'm lucky those officers arrived when they did and that one of them knew how to tie a tourniquet, else the blood loss might have done for me. And that I've lost a significant chunk of my deltoid muscle and some of the triceps, but the surgeons did a good repair job and I should still have the use of my arm. They tell me it'll require weeks of physio, but I reckon if I get back to work as soon as possible, and stay active, then things'll fix themselves."

"Oh, no," said Macarthur, with an emphatic shake of the head. "Not going to happen. Not on my watch. You're staying put and you're following doctors' orders, Redlaw. Those are *my* orders."

"Forgive me, marm, but with all that's going on, we are, as you said, stretched. We need all the resources we can muster. We need feet on the street."

"We need your backside in bed. I can't have you going out there with a half-crippled arm. However much I could do with you, I'm going to have to cope without. Until you're in tip-top condition again, you won't be an asset, you'll be a liability—mostly to yourself."

"Marm—"

"Redlaw." She thumped the mattress, and a shockwave of pain shivered across his chest from his shoulder, although he tried not to let this show. "Listen to me, you pigheaded... *man*. You almost died and I'm beating myself up into wee little pieces over that. I'll not be responsible for you risking your neck again, at least not until I'm certain you're back to full fitness. Look on this as providence. You've a chance now to lie back, take things easy for a while, rest, have some space, get some perspective. Don't squander it, make the most of it. Think about what you want from life, and from SHADE, and from yourself. Take a good hard look at yourself and try and figure out what you're about and what you're after."

"Are you telling me to think about taking the gold carriage clock?"

"Retirement? No. Not unless it's something you're already thinking about. Is it?"

"No."

"Then just give yourself a break. Call it a sabbatical, if you like."

"The last time I was stuck in bed, someone I thought highly of died. I can't let something like that happen again. But also, there's this to consider." Redlaw felt it was best to get it out in the open now, while events were still fresh in his mind. "In that industrial unit, those 'Lesses were lying in wait for me."

Macarthur did a double take. "What?"

"I'm almost sure of it. I was as stealthy as I could be getting inside, and I suppose there's a chance they heard me and got themselves into ambush positions. But that isn't how Sunless normally operate. They're not that organised. More likely, if they'd got wind of me coming, they would have tried to make a run for it, or else headed straight for me and attacked at the first opportunity, like termites defending their mound. The way it went down, it was as if they were expecting me."

"That's preposterous, Redlaw."

"Maybe so, but that's how it felt," Redlaw said. "There was something off about the whole thing. So I'm asking you, who else knew about the nest? Who, apart from you, knew I was going there?"

"The possibility it existed was on the wires. Common knowledge. The eyewitness statement was logged earlier in the evening. Anyone with access to the SHADE database could have pulled it up."

"In other words, just about anyone at HQ."

"And as for knowing I was sending you there, I mentioned to several people I was doing that."

"In advance?"

"Yes. Redlaw, you're not really thinking what I think you're thinking? That someone inside SHADE set you up? Somehow tipped off the vampires that you were coming?"

"I'm *trying* not to think that."

"For heaven's sake, I've never heard anything so insane in all my life!" Macarthur exclaimed. "What could this person hope to gain?"

"My death. Or, failing that, something like this." He indicated his injury.

"But why?"

"Revenge is the only motive I can come up with."

"In which case, who? Who at SHADE would be after revenge on you? Granted, you've rubbed a few people up the wrong way, but..."

"Did Sergeant Khalid know about the nest?"

"Did Sergeant—? I'm not even going to entertain this idea."

"Did he? You said you'd thought about sending him instead of me."

"Redlaw." Macarthur stood, fists clenched by her sides. "If you didn't happen to be in hospital already, I'd put you there myself for talk like that. As it is, I'm going to blame whatever medication it is they've got you on. That and post-traumatic stress. Do you realise how irrational you sound? A SHADE officer knowingly, deliberately endangering another?"

"Maybe I'll ask Khalid myself."

"You will not. You will not be going anywhere near Sergeant Khalid, and that's because you will not be going anywhere near HQ. Not 'til you're fully recovered. And it won't be the medical professionals who'll decide when that is, it'll be me. Do you understand? Let me put it a little more bluntly, in case I'm not getting through that thick skull of yours. You are hereby suspended. You are no longer on active duty. I will reinstate you when I, and only I, believe you are ready for reinstatement. Until then, you may consider yourself on indefinite leave. Have I made myself clear?"

"Crystal, marm," said Redlaw.

"Good."

Macarthur stomped out, and Redlaw settled back against the pillows.

To be honest, that had gone better than he'd thought it would. At least she hadn't sacked him. And he now knew that his suspicions about events on the Isle of Dogs weren't pure paranoia; they carried a grain of possibility.

The fact was, there'd been grief between Redlaw and Ibrahim Khalid for years. Interreligious tensions were not uncommon in SHADE, and officers tended to group according to faith, Christian with Christian, Muslim with Muslim, and so on, which exacerbated matters. With Redlaw and Khalid, however, it was a clash of personalities rather than creeds. The sergeant's attitude towards the job was a blend of cynicism and bludgeoning overkill that Redlaw found unprofessional and unpalatable.

Added to that, Khalid had *really* not got on with Róisín Leary. Redlaw had never quite fathomed why, although he reckoned it had a lot to do with Leary's being a woman, and a forthright, forceful one at that. Khalid did not seem to mind being answerable to Commodore Macarthur, but that was probably because he had no choice in the matter and was, at any rate, in no position to criticise her, at least not openly. For Leary, a fellow sergeant, Khalid had shown little but contempt, and she in turn, who usually had a good word for everyone, could find none for him. Many was the time, indeed, when she had muttered darkly that if Khalid kept pushing and needling her the way he did—going on about how Sunless control and enforcement was not an appropriate occupation for a female and how much he disliked trouser-clad, unwomanly women—one day he'd wind up on the wrong end of a stake.

"Ignore him," Redlaw would counsel. "It's just a cultural thing. It's not personal."

But it had felt pretty personal to Leary, and that had made it personal to Redlaw. He couldn't bring himself to be open-minded and even-handed towards Khalid, especially now that Leary was gone. He was defensive of her memory in a way that he hadn't had to be defensive of her while she was alive, when she'd been perfectly capable of standing up for herself and hadn't needed or welcomed protection from anyone else. He was jealous of everything she'd been to him and resentful of any person who had ever misjudged or maligned her. Khalid seemed to sense that, and so a vicious circle had developed, a mutual grudge that now and then spilled over into outright hostility.

The question was, just how low would Khalid stoop?

* * *

HOURS CAME AND went. Nurses came and went. Redlaw dozed and, in between dozes, brooded.

TV news provided some distraction. There was widespread coverage of the aftermath of last night's rioting, accompanied by dire predictions of what tonight might hold. Politicians pontificated meaninglessly. Maurice Wax was a hyper-cautious wimp and his Conservative nemesis, that Slocock person, a loudmouthed opportunistic grandstander. Neither was offering anything like a practical answer to the problem at hand, doubtless because neither had one. Both seemed to be in a holding pattern, recycling the same old bromides and jibes. Wax did, however, hint at some kind of alternative strategy, making public what he'd already vouchsafed in private to Macarthur. All would be revealed at a press conference tomorrow.

Night fell, and Redlaw was seized by the urge to get up, get dressed, get out into the city. He made it as far as the foot of the bed before dizziness overwhelmed him. It felt as though a hole had opened up inside him and he was tumbling into it. He had to sit for several minutes on the edge of the bed until his vision cleared and the quasi-vertigo passed.

The powerful painkillers he was taking were the cause. The doctors had warned they might have side effects—nausea, disorientation, and the like.

Simple solution, then. Stop taking the painkillers.

When an orderly came to give him his next dosage, Redlaw pouched the pills in a corner of his mouth, pretended to swallow, then spat them out after the man had left and secreted them inside his pillowcase.

Over the next few hours his resolve was tested to the limit as the pain from his shoulder mounted, crescendoed, crested into waves of sheer agony. He gritted his teeth and bore it. The pills in the pillowcase were a terrible temptation—gulp them down and in no time blessed relief would come—but he resisted. Commodore Macarthur had benched him, but that wasn't going to stop him. He was John Redlaw and there was work to be done. London needed him. The small matter of a suspension was neither here nor there.

The television was not allowed to be on after 10pm—hospital rules—but emergency vehicle sirens in the streets told him all he needed to know. They wailed their song of chaos and alarm until well past midnight.

By then, Redlaw was getting ready to leave. Now was the ideal time, when there was almost no one around to stop him or get in his way. He girded himself to clamber out of bed. Starting—levering his upper half upright—was bad. The slightest jolt added fuel to the blaze in his shoulder. Swinging his legs out from under the covers was worse. And as for standing and detaching the sling... He managed it, but it almost made him faint. He swayed on the spot, clutching the bed frame for support, hospital gown flapping around his bare thighs. He'd never known anything like this—the feeling of being utterly enfeebled, paralysed by pain, his entire body jangling and malfunctioning. The agony was not isolated; it seemed to permeate every nerve he had, even down to the tips of his toes.

Minutes elapsed, and at last he regained sufficient self-control to walk towards the closet where his clothes hung. His coat and shirt were torn and bloodstain-browned, but they would do until he could get home and replace them. His Cindermaker and weapons vest were gone, removed by his fellow shadies when he was bundled into the ambulance, but he had a remedy for that, again at home. Losing the accoutrements of SHADE was something he wasn't unprepared for. It had looked to be on the cards for a while.

He was reaching for his underpants and trousers when a doctor unexpectedly entered the room, without knocking. Redlaw froze. There was no way he could pretend to be doing anything other than what he was clearly doing. If the doctor started giving him grief, he would just have to brazen it out.

In addition to the long white coat and stethoscope the doctor had on a surgical mask, looped around her ears. The mask seemed incongruous to Redlaw, to say the least. He noted her long dark hair and her black, black eyes, and all at once he was diving across the room—shoulder be damned—in search of something, anything, to defend himself with.

But there was no piece of ash wood to be found anywhere. And he knew his crucifix would be no use.

For the woman masquerading as a doctor was the shtriga from the Hackney SRA, Illyria Strakosha, and she was coming across the room towards him with purposeful, menacing strides.

CHAPTER ELEVEN

REDLAW SNATCHED UP a metal drip stand from the corner and swung it at Illyria one-handed. She caught the end of it and wrenched it out of his grasp in one swift, supple movement.

Instantly Redlaw lunged for her, hoping to barge her aside and make for the door. It was a desperate ploy but, unarmed and outclassed, it was all he had. The one thing she might not be expecting was a direct frontal assault.

Next he knew, Illyria's hand was around his throat. Her grip, implacably tight, forced him to his knees. His head began to swim, heartbeat roaring in his ears.

"Don't be foolish, Redlaw," she hissed, bearing down on him. "You'll gain nothing by fighting me except pain."

"Rude... not to... try," he gasped out.

"Listen well." The black eyes glittered like polished onyx. "I have you in my power. I can snap your neck easily. One twist of my wrist, that's all it will take, and no more John Redlaw. However, that is not what I came here for. I'm going to let go of you now, but only on condition that you don't attack me again. I cannot guarantee that my patience with you will be endless. Do you agree to those terms?"

Redlaw saw no alternative. He gave a nod.

The hand relaxed its throttling grasp.

"So now," said Illyria, setting the drip stand back down on its castors, "we're going to talk, you and I. Peacefully. You may remain on your knees if you like. Then again, you may prefer to take that chair over there."

Redlaw chose the chair, crossing his legs tightly to preserve his modesty, of which the gown left him in short supply.

"You're out of your SRA," he said. "That's in direct contravention of the Sunless Settlement Act."

"So impale me."

"I would if I could."

"I know, old bean. That's what makes you so spiffingly entertaining—your relentless dedication to your job. To the point of masochism."

"I... entertain you?" Redlaw snorted. "Well, that's a first. I've *frightened* plenty of 'Lesses in my time, but never entertained one."

"But I am like no vampire you have ever encountered."

"That's for sure. You can pass as human, for one thing."

"Indeed." She lowered the surgical mask. "The fangs are the only real giveaway. Were it not for the need to speak, I could go without any disguise whatsoever. Since I was looking for you in hospitals, this mask seemed— let's say, serendipitous."

"Hospitals, plural?"

"This is the third I tried. They're dashed unforthcoming at Night Brigade headquarters about their officers' whereabouts. All the person on the switchboard would confirm was that Captain Redlaw had been injured in the line of duty and hospitalised."

"You rang SHADE HQ?" Redlaw almost laughed. "Some nerve."

"Why not? It seemed the most straightforward method of locating you. I *can* use a phone, you know. We vampires are not the animals you think we are."

"I don't think you're animals," said Redlaw. "Frankly, I've never been able to make up my mind what you are. The best I can come up with is 'people but not quite'."

"Meaning less than people?"

"In some ways more."

"Interesting," said Illyria. "At any rate, you said when we last met that you would be coming back to find out what, if anything, I had discovered about the blood deliveries. You have not done so, and with the situation deteriorating as it is, I felt it best to seek you out instead."

"Deteriorating? How bad are things actually getting?"

"Aren't you aware? It is you lot who are stirring up the most trouble."

"My lot? SHADE?"

"Humans in general. SHADE officers are carrying out what they are calling 'pre-emptive strikes'—charging into SRAs, inflicting casualties and then pulling out again as quickly as possible. It's either punishment or deterrence, nobody's sure which, perhaps not even they themselves. Civilians, meanwhile, are taking matters into their own hands—not just Stokers, although they're at the core of it. There are bands of them going about like paramilitaries. They cut through the SRA fences, plant fire bombs or else simply use stakes, whatever gets results. Naturally, vampires aren't taking any of it lying down."

"How do you know all this?"

"Beyond what I have seen for myself in Hackney?" She shrugged. "Half an hour pretending to drink tea in a café where there's a television on. It isn't difficult."

"Nor, it seems, is leaving your Residential Area."

"I come and go as I please. The boundary is hardly impenetrable, and looking as I do, no one has grounds to be suspicious."

"Why stay in an SRA at all?"

"I have my reasons. Besides, would I be welcome among so-called normal people, if they knew what I was?"

"I suppose not," Redlaw admitted. "So, what have you managed to learn about the causes of the rioting? Is the problem just that it's cattle blood, or—"

At that moment, the night-shift ward sister popped her head round the door. She was a jovial West Indian, so fat her body seemed to be composed entirely of spheres.

"I thought I heard voices in here." She wagged a stubby forefinger. "Mr Redlaw, you can't be sitting up having guests at this hour. How you going to heal, if you don't get your proper rest?"

Redlaw noted a sudden rigidity in Illyria's body, as when a cat spies a mouse. He did the only thing he could, which was gesture at her and say, "Dr Strakosha isn't a guest. She's giving me an examination. Aren't you, Dr Strakosha?"

Illyria hesitated. Then she turned and smiled at the nurse, without parting her lips.

The ward sister should have been mollified but wasn't. Her gaze flicked to the surgical mask round Illyria's neck, then to Illyria's knee boots, then back to Illyria's face.

"You a specialist?"

Illyria nodded, again making sure her lips stayed firmly together.

"Never heard of no specialist making patient calls at one in the morning."

"It's a private consultation," Redlaw said. "She's a... a personal friend of mine."

The ward sister made little effort to hide her scepticism. "Personal friend, huh?" she said and sucked her teeth slurpily. "Yeah, and I'm Naomi Campbell."

"It's true, I assure you." Redlaw wasn't, he knew, the world's greatest liar. He'd had almost no practice. "She's seeing me as a favour."

"Tell you what," the ward sister said, "I'm going to my station and I'm sitting down at the computer and I'm checking to see if there's a Dr Strakosha registered anywhere. And when I find there isn't, which I will, I'm coming back here with security and I'm having you, lady, kicked out of this building on your skinny behind. Favour! Is that what they're calling it these days? And you, Mr Redlaw. A SHADE officer. A man of faith. You ought to be ashamed of yourself."

She was gone before Redlaw could remonstrate any further.

"Well, that's torn it," he said to Illyria. "You'll have to leave."

"Why?"

"She thinks you're a prostitute, that's why." It would have been funny if it wasn't so offensive.

"No, I meant why, when all I have to do is go after her and kill her?"

"Over my dead body," Redlaw snarled.

"If that's how it has to be..."

"It is. Why do you think I came up with that cock-and-bull 'consultation' story just now? To save that woman's life. If I'd done anything but cover for you, you'd have pounced on her and ripped her heart out. And if you try it now, I will do everything I can to stop you."

She eyed him loftily, and at the same time probingly. "Why do you care about her? You don't know her. She's no one."

"She's a human being. It's my responsibility to protect her from your kind."

"And not us from your kind?"

"That too."

"You aren't doing a very good job, on present evidence."

"I'm stuck in this wretched hospital, aren't I?" he said. "I want to be out there helping sort things out, believe me, but it's not easy. I was trying to get myself dressed when you turned up and I wasn't managing even that."

"You need someone's help, don't you?"

"Why, you offering?" Redlaw asked facetiously.

"Yes, I am."

It took him a moment to accept that she was sincere. "And what on earth would you want to do that for?"

"I'm not entirely sure, except that I have a feeling that together we may achieve more than either of us could alone. You will clearly have difficulty fending for yourself, with your arm the way it is. You need my aid, eh what."

"And what would you be getting out of it in return?"

"If it's at all possible to find a way of ending the hostilities between humans and Sunless before they escalate completely out of control, I must do so, and that would be markedly easier in the company of someone such as you. You can go places I can't. You have contacts and resources that I don't. It's not something that I particularly desire, forming an alliance with a SHADE officer—John Redlaw, no less—but circumstances make it necessary."

"It'd be no great source of joy for me either, I hope you realise."

"That's fine. As long as we both understand that it would be a marriage of convenience and nothing more. I speak strictly metaphorically, of course."

"Of course," said Redlaw. "A temporary coalition. A deal with the Devil, even."

"For both of us. But we should hurry. It wouldn't be good to run into security men—not good for *them*, that is."

"I take your point. Pass me those trousers, and if you don't mind, turn your back."

"Won't you have trouble getting them on with just one arm?"

"I'll manage."

"How about undoing those ties at the back of your nightdress?"

She thought she was being cute and sly, but as far as Redlaw was concerned she was simply being annoying.

"Turn. Your. Back."

"Oh, very well."

*   *   *

SEVERAL EXCRUCIATING MINUTES later, Redlaw was dressed and hobbling down the fire staircase to the ground floor, accompanied by Illyria.

The central lobby heaved with people. One after another, ambulances decanted casualties and raced off to fetch more. A&E medics were busy performing triage, establishing the hierarchy of the injured. Mainly there were Sunless-inflicted wounds—claw marks, bites, abrasions—and burns resulting from incompetent use of homemade fire bombs by amateur arsonists. Groans and low, urgent conversations filled the air.

Redlaw and Illyria skirted the edge of the room, heading for the door. A man, seeing the white coat and mistaking Illyria for a real doctor, reached out and grabbed her arm.

"Please," he demanded. His other hand clamped a bloodied cloth to the side of his head. "How much longer have I got to wait before I get seen?"

Illyria's face contorted. Redlaw couldn't tell whether she was affronted to have been latched on to like this by a human or her thirst had been aroused by the sight of the blood soaking the cloth. Either way, he needed to intervene, in case she was unable to control herself.

"It should be your turn any moment," he said, unpicking the man's fingers. "Just be patient."

"I could have dealt with him," Illyria muttered as Redlaw led her away.

"That's exactly what I was afraid of," he replied.

They had almost made it to the exit when somebody called out, "Captain!"

A uniformed SHADE officer numbered among the

wounded. Redlaw recognised the face—a recent recruit who worked London's north-east quadrant too—although the name eluded him. He was finding it increasingly hard to keep abreast of who was who among the junior ranks. All those twentysomethings had begun to look alike to him—the same smooth features, the same brightness about the eyes, the same hopeful air.

"Captain, sir, it's you," the young man said. His hand rested gingerly in his lap, wrist puffy, either sprained or broken. "You're okay. I heard you were at death's door."

Redlaw decided to ignore him. He pushed Illyria on towards the door.

"Captain?" said the shady, perplexed. "Captain, what's up? Why are you—?"

Then Redlaw and Illyria were outside, in the chilly spring night air, and Redlaw could hear the junior officer saying to the person next to him, "See that? One of the top men in my quadrant. Just waltzed out without a word. He's got a reputation for being standoffish, but honestly! That's plain rude."

"You hurt the poor chap's feelings," said Illyria.

"I'll get over it and so will he," said Redlaw. "It's a pain that he spotted me. My boss is going to find out sooner than I'd hoped that I've done a bunk, and when she learns I was in the company of some unidentified female, she's going to get very inquisitive indeed."

"Does it matter to her if you're no longer in hospital?"

"Very much so," said Redlaw, "seeing as I'm not actually formally on the SHADE payroll right now."

"What the deuce do you mean?"

"I mean I'm on suspension and I'm supposed to be lying in that bed upstairs re-evaluating my life and career."

"In other words, this is making you a fugitive," said Illyria.

"After a fashion."

She looked at him askance. "But you're John Redlaw, the quintessence of a Night Brigade man. What's happened to you? How can things have gone so awry?"

"I don't know. They just have. Taxi!"

A black cab had pulled up at the hospital entrance to let out an intern who'd been summoned from home to cope with the rush. Redlaw hailed it, and was then faced with the unpleasant task of hunching over and climbing in. Illyria offered him a hand, but he waved it away and managed by himself, with arthritic delicacy and stiffness.

"Where to, guv?" the cabbie asked.

"Ealing," said Redlaw, and gave the address of his flat.

"Why there?" said Illyria as she settled in beside him in the back.

"I need to arm myself. I'm not doing anything 'til I've got some weaponry on me."

"Don't like being around me without a stake handy?"

"That has some bearing on it."

LONDON WAS NOT London that night, not London as Redlaw understood it. It had become a city of insomniacs; an eerie, transformed place where the horizon was lit up by the glow of a dozen major fires, and whole areas were cordoned off by police and SHADE officers, and lights shone in most windows, and there wasn't a single street where people weren't gathered on the pavement in huddles or someone wasn't running somewhere or away from something. Sirens were an almost constant refrain, whooping and dopplering, the sounds playing hide and seek among the buildings. Helicopters—police and media—jackhammered overhead.

"Been ruddy pandemonium, it has," the cabbie said over his shoulder. "From sundown on. Yesterday night wasn't much to laugh about, but this..." He clucked his tongue. "The wife told me not to go out. Said she had a feeling it would get messy. Woman's intuition. Turns out she was right. But I said to her, 'What am I going to do, luv? Stay at home and not earn a penny? Cabs still ran during the Blitz,' I said, 'and this ain't the Blitz. Not quite. Not yet.' Oh, will you look at that. More bleedin' looters."

Some youths had smashed a mobile phone shop window and were scurrying off with armfuls of goods. An alarm bell shrilled in vain.

"I'd give them a smack round the earhole, the lot of 'em, if I had the chance," the cabbie said. "Little tossers, pardon my language, missus. Not as bad as vampires but near as. Vamps, now, they're just trouble and have been from the start. Why couldn't they have stayed put? That's what I want to know. In their own countries, I mean. Up 'til twenty years ago we didn't even know they existed! They were just, you know, Dracula, Christopher Lee, virgins in floaty dresses and that. Now they're flippin' *everywhere*. What was so wrong with lurking in secret in East Europe or wherever? That not good enough for them? Better prospects overseas? Thought they'd have an easier time of it in soft-touch Britain? Hah!"

"Perhaps they had to leave," said Illyria, "to escape persecution."

"Yeah, but only because there'd got to be too many of them and the people in those countries were fed up and were doing something about it."

"Is it wrong to flee from violence and seek asylum elsewhere?"

"Asylum? Don't make me laugh. That's for genuine refugees, victims of ethnic cleansing and torture and what have you. Not for bloodsucking monsters. That accent of yours, that's French, innit? I'm surprised to hear you sticking up for vamps. Your government had exactly the right idea. Round them up and put them on a train back where they came from, and keep doing that 'til they finally get the message. Don't see Paris going all to hell like this, do you? No, you do not."

Illyria was going to argue further, but Redlaw stilled her with a shake of his head. *Not worth it*, his look said. *Let him prattle on*.

Eventually, circuitously, the taxi got them to Ealing.

"That'll be forty-five," the driver said. "Bit steep, I know, but I had to go all round the houses, didn't I, and then there's night rates, and a bit extra for the added risk..."

Redlaw paid up grudgingly, then said, "How would you feel if I told you you'd just had a Sunless in the back of your cab?"

The cabbie studied him for a moment, then barked a laugh. "Nice one. I like your sense of humour. Sunless in a cab. As if. Besides," he added, tapping his rearview mirror, "you both showed up in this. Vamps don't do reflections, do they?"

He drove away, still chuckling to himself.

"I thought everyone knew the thing about mirrors was untrue," said Illyria.

"Myths die hard," said Redlaw. He stuck his key in the lock. "And now, '*mademoiselle*,' let's get inside."

"French!" said Illyria with disdain, and followed Redlaw in.

THE FIRST THING Redlaw did was gulp down four ibuprofen tablets from the bathroom cabinet. Next, he went to the bedroom and delved into the wardrobe where his emergency spare set of weapons was stashed. The Cindermaker was one he claimed he'd lost while pursuing a Sunless along the Regent's Canal. The gun had dropped into the water, allegedly, during a hand-to-hand tussle on the towpath. Redlaw had been concerned that replacing it would be a headache, but the armourer at HQ had authorised the issuing of a new one with barely a murmur. "Normally I'd be obliged to report this upstairs and there'd be a ton of paperwork," the armourer had said, "but as it's you, Captain Redlaw, I think we can just nod this one through." Redlaw had felt almost guilty, as though he were abusing the trust of others, but now, as he loaded the Cindermaker, he knew the deception had been a necessary one, and forgivable.

"Better?" Illyria said as he entered the living room with the gun strapped prominently to his waist. "Feel safer?"

"Much."

"I really have no intention of harming you, you know."

"I'd rather I had some say in the matter, instead of just having to take your word for it."

"Are you this mistrustful of everyone?"

"Only 'Lesses," said Redlaw. "But you're in my flat, so that must tell you something."

"I should feel honoured? Oh, then I am." Illyria cast an eye around the room—white walls, basic furniture, no carpet nor even a rug, nothing fancy anywhere. "Such a charmingly uncluttered and... *simple* living space. Tell me, do you have an aversion to décor of any kind?"

"There's that." Redlaw pointed to a plain oak cross that hung above the fireplace. "Only décor I need. Maybe you'd prefer it if I bashed some holes in the plasterwork, tore up a couple of floorboards, smeared excrement everywhere. Then you'd feel more at home."

"So material comforts aren't important to either of us," Illyria said. "It seems we have that in common, we just show it in different ways. Having said that, the state of the accommodation in the SRAs was never that palatial to begin with."

"No reason to make it worse, though."

"Redlaw, must we bicker all bally night long? I get it—you have no great affection for me, it aggrieves you to be in my company. The point's made. Let's set that aside and get down to brass tacks."

"All right." Redlaw took a seat. The ibuprofen had begun to dull the edge of the pain. From being unbearably sickening, it was now bearably sickening. "The BovPlas blood—it's contaminated in some way. Is that what you've found?"

"As far as I can discern, it is just cattle blood, but if it was contaminated, it would be hard to tell by taste alone."

"Why?"

"Blood from cows has a strong, coarse flavour, unlike human blood, which is more delicate and subtle. If I cast my mind back to my wine-drinking days, it's the difference between some cheap, rough table wine and, say, a Château Margaux or some other top-notch Bordeaux. You drink the one because it's there and the other because you want to, and if you had a choice in the matter, you would never touch the table wine and you'd take the Margaux every time. There really is nothing to compare with the stuff that runs through human veins. Anything else comes a poor second."

"So you're saying if it were human blood and it had been tampered with in some way, you'd know."

"Almost certainly. It doesn't take much to upset the balance of flavours in human blood. Vampires are sensitive to that. Alcohol, sugar, milk—they all have an effect on its acidity and sweetness. Garlic is the worst. This, I think, is the real reason the French have been so successful in expelling vampires from their borders. Their diet."

"You're kidding."

"A little. But garlic undoubtedly sours blood, and of course, in its purest form it is repugnant to vampires—so yes, maybe we're less willing to sup from French veins than we are from those of other nationalities."

Redlaw gave a low whistle. "I've learned something new today."

"I'm just surprised that you seem to have no problem discussing a subject that most of your kind find deeply disagreeable."

"I've been in the Sunless-handling business a while now. I'm pretty much immune to the nastier aspects. The taste of cattle blood, then, could be masking something else, some added ingredient?"

"It's perfectly possible. Something which sparks aggression in those who drink it."

"Does it make *you* aggressive?"

"Not that I've noticed. But then I am not your average vampire."

"So you keep saying."

"I do not need to drink blood in any great quantity. I'm able to survive on far less than other vampires. I'm more... fuel-efficient. So if BovPlas blood has any ill effects, I wouldn't be in the best position to judge. Besides, having asked Grigori—"

"Your little round minion."

"—Grigori about what happens when the blood arrives, it seems that it isn't so much the blood itself that triggers a riot as the eagerness to get to the blood. If the pouches aren't distributed quickly enough, or someone shoves someone else aside or snatches a pouch out of another's hands, then frenzy can result. Vampires are a touchy, undisciplined breed. They can be stirred to anger by the slightest of provocations."

"And that coupled with blood that is somehow more potent or intoxicating than usual," said Redlaw, "would lead to every delivery becoming a potential flashpoint. Additives combined with mob psychology. Someone's manipulating the Sunless, deliberately messing with them in order to cause mayhem."

"It seems that way. But who? And why?"

"Those are both valid questions, but before we begin trying to answer them we need proof, something that'll confirm that this isn't all pie-in-the-sky conjecture."

"We need a pouch of BovPlas blood."

"We do. And I know where we can get one. It's only a couple of miles from here, in fact."

CHAPTER TWELVE

THEY TRAVELLED FROM Redlaw's flat to Park Royal on foot. Redlaw now had a spare overcoat on, his second best, and Illyria had ditched the doctor-wear. A scarf, looped around her mouth and chin, fulfilled the same function as the surgical mask.

The atmosphere in the city was still febrile. The whiff of burning hung everywhere, and distant columns of smoke, rising like immense trees, shed an ochre haze across the moon. Detours were unavoidable. Wherever crowds had gathered, Redlaw switched to an alternative route, in case a disturbance was brewing. He led Illyria in a dogleg over Hanger Lane and across the broad sweep of Western Avenue via a footbridge. Soon they were closing in on the BovPlas depot.

Once there, Redlaw ascertained that his plan—march into the depot, requisition a blood pouch on some official-sounding pretext, march out again—was not going to work. There was a substantial SHADE presence on the premises. SHADE, it appeared, was providing an escort for every truck that went out to make a delivery; one patrol car per truck, four uniformed officers in each car.

"I'm not running the gauntlet of dozens of shadies all demanding to know what I've come for," Redlaw said.

"You're a captain, aren't you?" Illyria said. "Can't you just tell them to mind their own business?"

Redlaw squinted through the spiked railings of the depot's perimeter fence. "I see at least two captains swanning about. Not so easy to play the 'superior officer' trump card with them. Plus, there's no telling if Commodore Macarthur's spread the word that I'm suspended yet. If any of them knows, then I'm not going to get anywhere."

"Do we have a back-up plan?"

"Send you in to slaughter everyone, Illyria."

"By Jove, tell me you're not serious."

"Of course I'm not serious! What do you take me for? The back-up plan is we waylay one of the trucks as it leaves."

"What about the SHADE car with it?"

"The day I can't browbeat a bunch of uniforms..."

Minutes later, Redlaw was flagging down a patrol car and the truck behind it, some two hundred metres from the depot gates. He showed his badge and his vest, so that the shadies could see at a glance that he was one of them but plainclothes.

The sergeant driving the car braked and wound down his window.

"I take it you know who I am," Redlaw said.

The sergeant nodded. "Is there a problem, Captain Redlaw?"

"None as such. So BovPlas are still making deliveries, in spite of everything?"

"Trying to. That's why we're along for the ride. Accompany the truck to its designated SRA, recce the situation, make a judgement call. If all's quiet, go in. If not, abort the dropoff. It's orders from the top. The policy is, better that some 'Lesses get their feed than none do. Going hungry might just make them worse behaved."

Redlaw let that pass without comment. "I'd like to give the truck a once-over, if that's all right with you."

"Might I ask what for?"

"You might, sergeant, but I'm under no obligation to explain myself to you—any of you. I have my reasons, and I outrank you. Fair enough?"

The sergeant did not like being put in his place but was sufficiently seasoned to take it on the chin. "Can you at least tell us who *she* is?" he said, gesturing out of the window at Illyria. "Scarf-face over there."

The other three in the car thought this a hoot. "Scarf-face!" *Guffaw, guffaw.*

"A colleague," said Redlaw. "Got any further inane remarks, sergeant? How much more of my time are you going to waste?"

"None, sir," the man said, both sharply and sullenly.

"Good."

Redlaw turned and made his way to the truck. Sometimes it worked to his advantage that he was renowned as a tough-nut with limited social skills. He didn't have to worry about winning people round when he could simply steamroller over them.

He knocked on the truck cab door and invited the two drivers to get out.

"SHADE business," he said. "Open up the back, will you?"

Both men looked towards the patrol car for endorsement. The sergeant, who was standing out beside the car now, gave them the nod.

One of them pressed a lever on the dashboard and the rear doors opened automatically, releasing tendrils of chilly vapour. Redlaw stepped up into the truck's fridge body. Blood pouches in their hundreds were stacked around him on pallets, looking somewhat like house bricks. He made a show of inspecting them, running a hand over their plastic skins, peering between and behind the stacks.

"What're you looking for?" one of the drivers asked.

"Nothing. This is just routine, a precaution—things being as they are and all."

"Don't hassle him," the other driver said to the first. "Whatever the shadies need to do is fine by me. You think I'd have even come in to work tonight if we hadn't been promised they'd be helping?"

Redlaw squatted down at the far end of the fridge body with his back to the drivers. His overcoat billowed out around him in such a way that he was able to slide out a pouch, left-handed, unseen, and tuck it into one of the coat's inner pockets.

Nice one, Redlaw. If all else fails, there's always that career in shoplifting to fall back on.

He stood up, wincing with discomfort. He was trying to avoid using his right arm, but almost anything he did seemed to involve that shoulder somehow or other.

"Right," he said. "Everything seems to be in order. I'll just get out of here and you can be on your way."

As the rear doors swung shut, Redlaw saw Illyria striding swiftly towards him.

"Redlaw," she murmured. "Snag. The sergeant is contacting SHADE HQ. I just heard him. He told the others he's decided to check up on you, because you're outside your usual stamping ground and he finds that strange."

"Damn." Redlaw threw a glance towards the patrol car. The sergeant was leaning in through his door, speaking into the radio handset. He cast a look in Redlaw's direction, making eye contact and almost instantly breaking it. That clinched it; that, and the fact that the other three officers all then looked at Redlaw.

He'd been rumbled. The game was up. HQ had broken the news that John Redlaw was not at this moment officially a SHADE officer. He was, in essence, a civilian pretending to be a shady. A civilian, what's more, who was interfering with a blood delivery for no readily apparent reason.

The sergeant straightened up. The other three officers, in unison, opened their doors and climbed out of the car. One tugged down the ends of his jacket in businesslike fashion. Another angled his head from side to side as though working out kinks in his neck.

"Redlaw," said the sergeant. No *Captain*, note. Just the surname. "Seems you're not only outside your jurisdiction, you're operating without authorisation. 'Relieved of duty pending assessment.' That's from the Commodore herself, as is this: 'Detain and transport to headquarters.' Which, I reckon, applies to your girlfriend as well. Please come quietly, if you would. Let's not make a fuss, eh?"

The sergeant's face said Redlaw had made him look a fool and he was not best pleased about that. It also said he was rather hoping Redlaw would *not* come quietly.

Redlaw was in a quandary. The logical course of action would be to go to HQ with these men, meek as a lamb. There he could face Macarthur, endure the inevitable verbal laceration, then present her with his findings and secure her consent to have the BovPlas blood analysed.

On the other hand, he didn't have any findings as such. What if the blood turned out to be untainted and innocuous? He would be twice as deep in the mire then. Moreover, he doubted Illyria would let herself be taken into SHADE custody.

Before he could reach a decision, he felt himself being seized by the arm and propelled towards the cab of the truck. Illyria shoved him roughly up into the driving seat, then thrust him along into the passenger seat and slid in behind the wheel. One of the drivers yelled an objection—"Oi! Gerroff out of it! That's my truck!"—and clambered up after them. Illyria grabbed him by the front of his BovPlas coveralls and flung him smartly outwards. He hurtled through the air, landing almost at the kerb on the far side of the road. Something cracked as he hit the tarmac, and he let out a shriek.

The key was in the ignition. Illyria cranked the engine, then slammed the door. She threw the truck into first, stamped on the accelerator, and aimed for the patrol car and the four men standing, slack-jawed, near it.

"No!" Redlaw cried.

"Don't get your bloomers in an uproar, old fellow," Illyria said, yanking the wheel to the right. The four officers scattered as the truck roared past. Its front bumper caught the nearside wing of the car a glancing blow, knocking out a tail light and denting a door. Illyria shifted up into second and poured on the speed. The truck responded as well as any fully laden twelve-ton refrigerated goods vehicle, with armour plating, could—which is to say with loud but sluggish enthusiasm.

Redlaw checked in the wing mirror. The second BovPlas driver had rushed to his colleague's aid. The shadies, meanwhile, were piling back into the patrol car, ready to take off in hot pursuit.

"Why on earth," he asked Illyria, "did you do that?"

Illyria pulled down her scarf. "To stop you from doing something very counterproductive. You'd rather we had gone to SHADE HQ? Do you honestly think I would let any of those men lay even a finger on me?"

"I'm sure we could have worked out some sort of compromise with them."

"I'm just as sure we couldn't have. You're the one who doesn't wish me to hurt people. This way, everyone gets a chance of coming out of this with their hide intact."

Redlaw had to admit she had a point. "But we only came for one pouch of blood. Now we've a thousand of the damn things."

"Then we have been a thousand times more successful than we hoped."

Redlaw consulted the wing mirror again and saw the patrol car coming up at the rear, fast. The sergeant was hunched at the controls, looking resolute.

"We're going to have to shake them off somehow," he said.

"We certainly can't outrun them in this galumphing great rattletrap," said Illyria. "It's your city. Where should we go? Where, Redlaw?"

"I'm thinking."

"Then think harder."

Illyria made a screeching left turn at a junction, the

truck heeling over onto its shock absorbers. They were now heading towards the Hanger Lane Gyratory.

"Big roundabout coming up," she said, spying a road sign. "Suggest an exit."

"Okay. The North Circular." It was a big road with plenty of turnoffs but no sharp bends or corners. It would give them some breathing space, him some time to formulate a plan.

Illyria gunned the truck up the ramp to the Gyratory, passing through the lights at the top as they turned amber. They were red by the time the patrol car reached them but the sergeant didn't stop. A night bus, just pulling out in front of them, honked angrily.

Illyria took the first exit onto the North Circular, northbound. Multiple neon-lit lanes stretched ahead, almost devoid of other traffic. It was 3.30am, and tonight even fewer people than normal were out and about in their cars. Illyria used the splitter switch on the gearstick to shift the truck from fourth low into fourth high, and the needle on the speedo edged towards sixty.

The patrol car was right on their tail now, and the sergeant pulled out into the adjacent lane. The officer in the passenger seat had his window open. Illyria glimpsed a Cindermaker in his hand.

"It won't do any good them shooting at us," she said. "We're armoured. Everything's bulletproof, even the windows."

"Not the tyres," said Redlaw. "That's what he's going to aim for. I would if I were him."

Sure enough the man loosed off a round at one of the truck's rear tyres.

Illyria growled something in Albanian—"*Ta qifsha nanen!*"—which was unmistakably uncomplimentary.

The bullet had missed, but the patrol car was now parallel with the truck and the officer was lining up his second shot with great care.

"Are you buckled in, Redlaw?"

"No."

"Then do so. Now."

Redlaw grabbed his seatbelt and fastened it. The next instant Illyria, bracing herself on the steering wheel, hit the brakes. The truck squealed and juddered and slewed. The patrol car barrelled on, the officer squeezed the trigger and a spark flashed as once again he expended a Fraxinus round on the innocent roadway.

Illyria did some complicated gear-shifting and got the truck going again. Now the truck was chasing the car, although the sergeant performed a nifty deceleration and drew back so that the car was, as before, hovering alongside the truck's rear wheels. Illyria's response was to veer out of lane, forcing the sergeant to swerve accordingly.

"Easy," Redlaw said. "You could kill them."

"And they're not trying to kill us? I know what I'm doing. Believe it or not, I used to drive a truck for a living."

"You did?"

"At the docks in Marseilles."

"Before or after...?"

"After. Night shifts only, loading and unloading cargo ships. I have done many varied things during my decades as a shtriga. You'd be surprised."

"I probably would. Shall we just focus on what we're doing right now, though? Like not steering into the back of a lorry full of flammable liquid."

Illyria overtook the petrol tanker lumbering along

in front of them. The patrol car continued to follow doggedly, although the sergeant was being somewhat more circumspect now. The near-miss Illyria had engineered a few moments earlier had given him a definite case of the willies.

The truck was soon hitting sixty again and got flashed by a speed camera.

"Forty pound fixed penalty for BovPlas," Redlaw commented. "I think they can afford it."

"I'd be going even faster if I could," Illyria said, "but it's as if the truck doesn't want to."

"Fitted with a limiter. It can't."

"Then we're never going to be able to lose those men. Unless..."

"Unless...?"

Illyria floored the accelerator, hoping to squeeze just that last little bit of extra juice out of the engine. At the same time she scanned the dashboard until her eye alighted on a small lever. With a grim smile she depressed it and nudged the truck out in front of the patrol car.

The truck's rear doors began to open. A warning light winked on the dash, indicating this action was not advisable while the vehicle was in motion.

Illyria then began swerving from side to side, and Redlaw gripped the door armrest to steady himself. Objects began to *clunk* and thump in the fridge body behind them—the pallets of blood pouches shunting around. Illyria kept twisting the wheel hard left, hard right, until eventually one of the pallets was bumped to the threshold of the doors and tipped out.

Redlaw saw it in the wing mirror: a spectacular explosion of dark red liquid as dozens of pouches struck the road at speed, along with the plywood pallet. The sergeant swerved to avoid ploughing headlong into the obstacle; one flank of the patrol car was spattered with cow blood, but that was all.

Illyria continued to snake the truck along the road. Another pallet tumbled out, and another, splashing gallons upon gallons of blood across all three eastbound lanes. The patrol car skidded but carried on, its wipers frantically scrubbing its windscreen.

When, however, a fourth pallet landed almost slap bang on its bonnet, the sergeant concluded that the game wasn't worth the candle. Personal safety was more important than mission success. He slowed almost to a halt, and the patrol car receded rapidly in the truck's wing mirrors. Illyria laughed.

"Take that, *budol douch*," she said with satisfaction and hit the lever to shut the doors.

"Pull off at the exit ramp coming up," Redlaw said. "There's a retail park, load of superstores and malls. We can lose ourselves amongst them."

Organ chords crashed in his coat pocket. He opened the phone and winced when he saw the display:

GAIL MACARTHUR
calling
Accept   Reject

"I'd better take this," he said, sighing as he selected *Accept*. "Marm?"

"John." She sounded calm, and that was not a good sign. It was the lull ahead of the hurricane. "I think I gave you pretty explicit instructions, did I not? I doubt I could have made myself much clearer. You're inactive.

You're not even supposed to be out of your hospital bed."

"Marm, I can explain..."

"And now I'm hearing reports that you're tooling around London on some sort of crime spree. You've assaulted BovPlas employees and hijacked one of their vehicles. You've also put the lives of four SHADE officers in jeopardy. I keep thinking there must be another John Redlaw out there, a lookalike who's passing himself off as you. You don't have an identical twin who's just escaped from a mental institution by any chance?"

"No."

"Pity. I felt I should ask, because that would at least make sense. Otherwise I'm left with no alternative but to assume that you've gone *stark staring mad*." Here it came, the howling Gail. "In the name of all that's holy, John, what is going on inside your head? What the hell am I meant to make of all this? Never mind that you've stolen property and inflicted criminal damage and trampled over about half a dozen different SHADE regulations—what are you hoping to achieve? And who is this woman with you? What's her story? Does she have some sort of hold over you? Blackmail? Is that it?"

"Nothing so straightforward," Redlaw said.

"She's strong, by all accounts. Way more than she should be. Is there something you need to tell me, John?"

Plenty, thought Redlaw. *But I doubt you'll give me a fair hearing. Not now.*

"Commodore," he said, "will you just trust me here? I'm on the cusp of something big, I think. Something relevant to the troubles we're experiencing. I just need a little more time to get my facts straight and sort out what's what. If you can see your way to—"

"*TRUST YOU?*" Macarthur boomed, so loud that Redlaw had to hold the phone away from his ear. "You lost my trust the moment you set foot outside that hospital. You are so far beyond me trusting you now, I might as well have never met you. Forget about suspension, John. Forget about the sabbatical and the time to reflect. I handed you that little fig leaf so that you could take the hint and do the decent thing. I was expecting you to come back to me in a couple of days and tell me you'd decided to hang up your weapons vest for good. That would have saved us both a great deal of heartbreak and indignity. As it is, we're going to have to do this hard way. No more beating about the bush."

Her voice took on an icy formality.

"John Redlaw, I am hereby stripping you of all rank and entitlement pertaining to your role as an officer in the Sunless Housing And Disclosure Executive. Effective immediately, you are no longer permitted to function in any capacity in, for or on behalf of SHADE, and any attempt to do so shall constitute a breach of the law, punishable by incarceration."

It wasn't unexpected. It had, in fact, been more or a less a foregone conclusion from the moment Redlaw threw in his lot with Illyria. It came as a shock, nonetheless, to hear Macarthur actually utter the words—to listen to the convoluted phrasing which, boiled down to its essence, amounted to *You're fired*.

"I'm not glad I've had to do this," she concluded. "It's a sad day for us all. But you left me no choice, John."

"I understand, marm."

"I hope you do. And all I can advise now, as a friend, is turn yourself in. Abandon this path you're on, this lunatic crusade or whatever it is. It won't do you any good. Come in to HQ and we'll see if we can't smooth things over and make it easy on you. I'm sure I can convince BovPlas not to press charges. Maybe, given your long and exemplary service up to this point, we can even salvage your pension, which, needless to say, as matters stand, is forfeit. Otherwise..."

"Go on."

"Well, otherwise, John," Macarthur said, and sorrow vied with severity in her tone, "there'll be nothing for it but to regard you as an enemy of SHADE, hostile to the Executive and all its aims."

"No better than a rogue Sunless."

"If you like."

"Off-reservation and liable for dusting."

"I wouldn't put it quite so melodramatically."

"But to be arrested on sight, captured by force if necessary."

"You'd have no one to blame but yourself. One last time, John. Give it up. Come in."

Redlaw was silent a while.

"John?"

"It's going to have to be a 'no,' marm," he said finally. "What I'm uncovering here, if it is what I think it is, is major-league. But I need my freedom if I'm to have any hope of excavating all the way to the truth."

"At the expense of your whole future?"

"My future set against the future of countless humans and Sunless, maybe even the future of this country."

"Care to elaborate?"

"If I'm wrong, I'm wrong," said Redlaw. "But if I'm right, then somebody is trying to caused a rift between us and 'Lesses, for some self-serving purpose. Could be Stokers, could be another party we know nothing about yet. But if I don't nail this soon, there's going to be curfews, martial law, reprisal attacks, civil strife and Heaven knows what else."

"John?"

"Yes?"

"You're a fool," Macarthur said, and hung up.

Illyria negotiated a series of mini roundabouts, passing between the hulking, temple-like edifices of outlet, DIY and department stores. At last she brought the truck to rest in a car park wedged between a railway embankment and the rear of a supermarket. She killed the engine and looked across at Redlaw.

"That was not a good phone call."

"Not especially." He tried to smile, but it just looked forlorn. "On the minus side, I've sacrificed almost everything I hold dear and made myself a wanted man. On the plus side... Well, there is no plus side as far as I can see."

"At least things can't get much worse."

"There is that." Redlaw got out of the truck for a breath of fresh air. "Oh, and my shoulder's still hurting like hell. I forgot to mention that. Not helped by all your driving shenanigans."

"There's gratitude for you." Illyria also exited the cab, leaping down with a lithe, feline grace. "You wanted me to get us away from those Night Brigaders without causing any injury or loss of life, I managed it, and now you complain because it made the journey a bit rough? Are you always so damn hard to please?"

"Are you always so damn prickly?" Redlaw snapped back.

"Prickly? *I'm* prickly?"

Their voices rose, echoing across the empty parking spaces and the conga lines of chained-up shopping trolleys.

"Yes, prickly," said Redlaw. "Sensitive to criticism. Quick to take offence. And snooty, too. What were you, some kind of Albanian aristocrat before you were turned? Or were you a commoner but you think you're special now because a shtriga isn't your average vampire, as you never tire of telling me? One way or the other, you've got several world-class tickets on yourself, Miss Strakosha."

"Oh, and you haven't, Mr Redlaw?" Illyria retorted. "The way you barged into Livingstone Heights that first night, into my home, without so much as a by-your-leave..."

"I was entirely within my rights, as stipulated in the Sunless Settlement Act. I had due cause to enter the building, being in pursuit of a Sunless who was germane to an enquiry that was ongo—"

"Bureaucratic balderdash. My home!"

"Technically, the borough's, not yours. You have no property rights. You're not even a tenant. If you're anything, you're a squatter. But we'll overlook that little nicety, shall we?"

"I live there."

"Live? Again, technically..."

Illyria let out an infuriated growl, baring her fangs. "Are you trying to provoke me to violence? You've hit rock bottom and this is some kind of coward's suicide bid?"

"You couldn't take me. Not even on your best day."

"Don't tempt me. Gun or no, I could still—"

She broke off and raised her head, sniffing the breeze.

"What?" said Redlaw. "Finish the thought. Gun or no, you could still...?"

"Redlaw," she said softly. "You know I told you things can't get much worse?"

"Yes."

"I may have been mistaken, old bean."

At the brow of the railway embankment a stooped figure appeared, silhouetted against the orange-brown sky. More figures joined the first, loping into view, heads up, questing.

Illyria glanced at the truck. There were streaks of wet cattle blood on the bodywork. Not much of it, not even a pint in total, but enough. Enough to give off an alluring aroma to those that could detect it.

The vampires atop the embankment gave moans of appreciation, and hunger, then set off down the slope, bounding through the dense growth of brambles and nettles like hounds on the trail of a hare.

There were perhaps a score of them in all, and nothing stood between them and the BovPlas truck.

Nothing except Illyria and Redlaw.

CHAPTER THIRTEEN

REDLAW'S HAND IMMEDIATELY, instinctively, went to his Cindermaker, and a sudden burst of agony left him bent double, almost whimpering. His shoulder felt as though it was tearing itself open.

Trembling with the pain, he groped for the gun with his left hand and fumblingly unholstered it. The Cindermaker felt ungainly and off-balance as he lifted it. What had been a trusty servant on his dominant side was an unruly mutineer on his non-dominant. Then there was the matter of drawing back the slide, which his right arm refused to make easy for him. Even aiming was tricky. Sighting along the barrel with his left eye just seemed wrong.

Never mind, Redlaw. You'll just have to do your best.

The vampires flowed across the car park, fanning out into a ragged line. Their focus was on the truck, their prize, but they were all too aware of the presence of Redlaw and Illyria.

"Neasden," Redlaw muttered to Illyria. "That's where this lot are from, I'll bet. The Neasden SRA's not far from here. They've broken out."

"Or been driven out by humans laying siege."

"Still, not where they should be."

"It isn't wrong to run away from somewhere if you're not safe there."

"Dusting them's the only answer, though."

"No!" Illyria said, with vehemence. "Not necessarily. Maybe I can resolve this without you resorting to blasting away with that weapon of yours—which, by the by, you look like you can barely hold. I'm a vampire too. I can talk to them."

Redlaw weighed it up. He wasn't, he had to accept, anywhere near his fighting peak. He wasn't, for that matter, a SHADE officer any more, and so was under no professional imperative to destroy these or any other vampires. The only good reason to start shooting at them was self-preservation, and Illyria was holding out the possibility that that might not be an issue here.

"All right," he said. "Let's give it a bash. Your way first, and if that fails, then mine."

Illyria gave him a look of approval that was just discernibly condescending. Then she turned and addressed the approaching Sunless, who were now only a few metres off.

"Listen to me, my friends. It may not look like it but we mean you no harm. You want what's in this truck? Then have it. Feel free. In return, all I and the human wish is to be allowed to go on our way, unmolested. Do we have a deal?"

The vampires halted, exchanging glances. They were nonplussed, unconvinced. Redlaw himself wouldn't have made as generous an opening bid as Illyria was making, especially considering that the blood might well be dangerous. But it was her show. For now.

"Who are you?" one of the vampires demanded, a girl who must have been barely in her twenties when she'd been turned. She was dreadlocked and nose-ringed and spoke with a London accent—a local victim from the early days, most likely, before the UK government girded its loins and started implementing measures like the Settlement Act and SHADE.

"I am Illyria Strakosha and I am one of you."

"No, you're not," the girl shot back. "You don't look right. You don't *smell* right. I'm not sure what you are, but I don't like your face and I really don't like you being with him." She jabbed a finger in Redlaw's direction. Her talons gleamed with black nail varnish. "Fucking shady there. You and him, all cosy together, and him waving his ruddy great cannon at us. You're 'one of us,' why ain't you ripped the bastard's lungs out?"

The others grunted and growled in accord.

Illyria gazed at them, placid, imperious. "Redlaw and I have set aside our differences for the time being, in pursuit of a common goal."

Probably shouldn't have told them who I am, Redlaw thought. Mention of his name brought agitated hisses from the tongues of several of the vampires, and the crimson malevolence in their eyes darkened.

"So you're Redlaw," the girl said, looking him over from head to toe. "Shorter than I expected. I always imagined you was a giant, the way everyone goes on about you. But you're just an old man. Bit wobbly on your pins, too, looks like." She put her hand on her hip. "Can't say I'm impressed."

"Your opinion is of no consequence, child," said Illyria. "Let me repeat. We don't want trouble. The truck is yours. It has most of its load left—more cattle blood than the twenty of you can possibly drink in one go. Gorge on it. Enjoy it. But leave us be."

One of the vampires muttered something about a trap, and others agreed.

"Yeah," said the girl. "Talk about too good to be true. We've just left our Residential Area, where we're supposedly protected, and where all night long shadies have been garlicking and holy watering us all to buggery and Stokers have been lobbing Molotov fucking cocktails at us over the fence, and now here's another shady and some hoity-toity cow offering us a BovPlas truck to do with as we please, no strings attached, and we're meant to just go 'Oh, okay, that's nice, thank you very much'? Yeah, right. Pull the other one."

Redlaw could see that Illyria was making every effort to keep her cool and finding it next to impossible. The Sunless girl had no idea what she was dealing with, just what sort of beast this was whose tail she was tweaking.

"Why should I deceive you? Why betray my own kind? I'm presenting you with a generous free gift. You can do me the courtesy of accepting it."

"Free," said the girl, "but it buys you and the shady your lives."

"My life," said Illyria hotly, "is not yours to take, you ignorant little slut."

Redlaw knew then that this was not going to end well.

"Slut, am I?" the girl replied. "Least I'm not a dry-titted old hag who hangs out with Sunless Public Enemy Number One. What d'you get out of it, being with him? A cheap thrill? Tips on how to knock us off? Because obviously we're lesser beings, not good enough to mix with the likes of—"

She didn't say anything further. She couldn't. Where she had had a throat there was suddenly a cavity, tatter-edged, running crosswise over the front of her neck, narrow but deep. Had she been human, blood would have fountained out, drenching the ground. As it was, the wound merely oozed drips of the glutinous fluid that suffused a vampire's body.

The girl lifted a disbelieving hand; touched the gouge; frowned at the sticky dark stuff that came away on her fingertips.

Then, with a single swiping blow, Illyria finished what she'd started, taking the girl's head clean off. Decapitated, the body crumpled to the tarmac, turning to ashes as it fell.

There was a moment of shock. No one moved. Then another of the vampires, grey-haired and bearded like a grandfather, sprang at Illyria with a vengeful yowl. He was fast, but she was faster—infinitely faster. He looked almost astonished to discover that she had evaded his leap and punched a hole clear through his ribcage. His baffled face was the last part of him to disintegrate.

The other vampires crowded in on Illyria, attacking because she was the adversary and Sunless looked after their own. When put on the defensive, invariably they went on the offensive. It was in their nature.

They paid for it. Illyria flickered among them like a mirage, here one moment, there the next. Redlaw could scarcely follow her movements. She was eel-quick, and impossibly agile. The supermarket car park was an Olympic arena in which she performed like some inhuman gymnast, making the vampires look like flatfooted circus clowns by comparison. For all their lunging and clawing and artful leaping, they never laid a finger on her. She darted among them and around them, avoiding their every attack, and her hands slashed and punched and sliced, delivering terminal blows every time. In less than a minute the twenty vampires were whittled down to just a few. The rest had become long, low heaps of ashes which the wind swiftly set about dispersing.

At last the Sunless, seeing sense, halted their assault. The remaining few backed away from Illyria in a huddle, heads bent, looking cowed and sheepish.

"So," she said, squaring her shoulders, "what's it to be? Further opposition? Or have you learned your lesson?"

One of them sank to his knees, and the others followed suit.

"Better," said Illyria.

"Please," a Sunless man piped up in broken English. "We are your. We belonging to you. Master. We call you master."

"You submit?"

"We submit. We all."

"Then you survive." Illyria walked among them, touching each bowed head in turn, like a priest bestowing a blessing. The vampires writhed in fawning delight. "I have defeated you and made you mine. You are bound hereafter to render me service. Should I need you, I will find a way to summon you. In the meantime, leave this place. Return home. Go!"

The vampires scrambled to their feet and scuttled off up and over the embankment. One of them paused at the top to throw a glance Illyria's way—a last, adoring look—before disappearing from sight.

"Impressive," said Redlaw, trying not to mean it. "If I could, I'd clap."

"They are like dogs in many ways." Illyria brushed ash from her hands and sleeves. "They simply need to be shown who's boss. Once that's established, you have their loyalty forever."

"That how you run your gang at Hackney, is it?"

"Some fear me, some love me. It's all the same."

"You could rule the entire SRA if you wanted to. Queen of all you survey."

"Too much like hard work. I have what I have, and it's enough. Now, your shoulder."

"What about it?"

"I distinctly heard stitches ripping as you reached for your gun," said Illyria. "Would you like me to take a look?"

"No."

"I have some experience in the treatment of wounds."

"And in the making of them."

"I was a nurse with the resistance in the Second World War, during Mussolini's occupation. 'Before,' before you ask."

"Still no." Redlaw clumsily re-holstered his Cindermaker. "I know we've got a pact going, you and I, but I'm not letting a Sunless, a shtriga, whatever, anywhere near a big hole in my arm."

"It has begun bleeding again."

"Even more reason not to."

"I *am* able to control myself around blood."

"If you say so, but I'm not willing to put that to the test just yet." He checked his watch. "Getting on for four. Sunrise is due in about an hour and half. I think it's time you thought about finding somewhere to bed down for the day, unless of course you're impervious to sunlight along with everything else. Frankly, I doubt it."

"Frankly, you'd be right." Illyria nodded at the BovPlas truck. "And we just leave that here?"

"Can't very well go joyriding around in it any more. SHADE will be looking out for it, as will the cops. Supermarket staff will report finding it when they come in to work and BovPlas will come and retrieve it. Meanwhile, I've got my pouch of the blood here"—he patted his overcoat—"and I'll get going on having it looked at once I've crashed for a couple of hours."

"Where do you intend to 'crash'?"

"Where do you think? Home."

"But your flat—will it be safe?"

"What do you mean? Of course it'll be..."

And then it hit him. He had just never had to think this way before. He had never been the outsider, the outcast, the outlaw. He'd always been within the establishment, confident of his place there and content with it. Now, at a stroke, all that had changed. He had left the beach and swum into the cold, murky waters of an unknown ocean, and there might not be any chance of getting back to shore.

"Won't SHADE have it under observation?" Illyria said. "Surely it'll be the first place they think of to look. You can't go back there."

Glumly, deflatedly, Redlaw acknowledged this. "Well, that's certainly a drawback."

"You need to get rid of your phone as well. It's a GPRS model, yes? They might try to trace you."

Reluctantly, Redlaw took out his phone and let it drop onto the ground. Illyria, without pausing to ask his permission, stamped it to smithereens.

"There. Now, do you trust me?"

"No."

"Can you at least try to?"

"Maybe."

"Because I'm good at this—going to ground. Like the fox, I know how to find new burrows. Many times I've been cut off from my home, prevented from reaching it by lack of time or by circumstances. I'm still here because I have learned a trick or two. Will you let me do this for you—for us?"

Redlaw was too drained, and in too much pain, to come up with a better proposal. "Just make it somewhere not too grotty, will you? I know about you 'Lesses and your standards of creature comfort."

"Have a little faith, old bean."

That, thought Redlaw as he traipsed after Illyria out of the car park, *is about all I do have now. A little faith*.

So little, it was virtually nonexistent.

CHAPTER FOURTEEN

"GILES?"

Lambourne.

"Nathaniel, do you have any idea what time it is?" Slocock said blearily into the receiver.

"Big day. Can't have you lolling around in bed. The news this morning is good—which is to say bad. Widespread violence throughout the night. Sunless on the rampage. Humans on the rampage. All the ammunition Wax and the PM need for their press conference. Nobody'll even turn a hair at what they're announcing, not after a night like that. It won't be a hard sell. Like tossing a lifebelt to the drowning."

Slocock succumbed to a jaw-cracking yawn. "That's lovely, Nathaniel, but couldn't you have waited to share this with me 'til a reasonable hour? Like, say, anything past five o'-fucking-clock."

"Sleep is overrated, Giles. I get by on three hours a night, four at most. Sleep is the enemy of success."

"But it is the friend of the hard-working MP who's been up late at an emergency session of Parliament, debating the Sunless crisis."

"Is that what they're calling it officially? A crisis?"

"The Leader of the Opposition is. Wax insists it's not nearly that, though even he's hardening his language."

"Softening everyone up," said Lambourne. "Good, good. I'm looking forward to standing shoulder to shoulder with him and the PM later today before the ravening hordes of the Fourth Estate. I had a delightful chat on the phone with him yesterday afternoon, where he was all but crawling up my arse. My, how he's altered his stance. I think he thinks I'm the light at the end of a singularly dark tunnel."

"And not the oncoming train?" Slocock murmured.

"Eh? Didn't catch that."

"Must be a bad line. I just said Wax takes some beating, doesn't he?"

"Oh, very good." Lambourne laughed—a brutal sound, a hammer pounding in nails. "He is a bit of loser, isn't he? I'd feel sorry for the fellow, if I knew what feeling sorry felt like."

After Lambourne had hung up, Slocock tried to get back to sleep but couldn't. Eventually he went downstairs, brewed coffee, and practised at his punching bag for half an hour. It wasn't hard to picture Lambourne's face superimposed on the bag and imagine his cries as knee, elbow, fist and foot made contact. Slocock hated the man, and yet their destinies were so tightly bound together, he had no choice but to take whatever the CEO of Dependable Chemicals dished out.

The relationship reminded Slocock of his schooldays. His father, a middlingly successful solicitor, had only been able to afford to send him to one of the minor public schools, Starkely College, a third-division place which modelled itself on the upper echelon establishments but lacked the budget to compete when it came to teaching staff and facilities—a kind of Happy Shopper Eton. At that time the tradition of personal fagging was still upheld there, meaning that for his first two years Slocock was effectively the unpaid scullery maid to one of the senior boys.

The boy was Harry Parker-Hollingbury, a sixth former who could most fairly be described as an utter cunt. If Parker-Hollingbury's study bedroom was not immaculately tidied, if there was a scrap of mud left clinging to the cleats of his rugby boots, if a cup of tea was not waiting for him at his bedside punctually at 6.30am every day, Slocock suffered for it. Sometimes Parker-Hollingbury would let him off with just a cuff round the ear. Sometimes it was a closed-fist punch. Mostly, though, the penalty was exacted after lights out, when Slocock would have to sneak out of the junior boys' dormitory, go to Parker-Hollingbury's room and wank him off on his bed. Once or twice Parker-Hollingbury made him lick him, but manual masturbation usually sufficed.

"Slow cock," Parker-Hollingbury would say. "No rush. Slowww cock. That's it. Slowwwww."

Of course Slocock despised every second of this, but there was nothing to be done. He couldn't complain to the housemaster, as schoolboy *omertà* forbade it. He couldn't baulk or fight back, because Parker-Hollingbury, who played second row in the 1st XV, was built like a conspicuously large brick shithouse and Slocock was, during his early teens, a scrawny little streak of piss. He couldn't even prevail on his father to send him to a different school, since Slocock senior was himself a product of the independent system and seemed to regard an all-male boarding school as some sort of educational nirvana; he wouldn't hear a word said against Starkely College and would never have credited his son's tales of inter-pupil sadism and sexual abuse.

Slocock had no choice but to suck it up, as it were. Which he did for two long years, all the while fantasising about elaborate revenges on Parker-Hollingbury that he never actually got round to enacting.

Since then he had vowed he would be no one's bitch ever again. That was why he hadn't lasted long at Sandhurst—no good at taking orders, especially not from drill sergeants born on council estates and educated in the state sector—although his habit of turning up for parade drunk and disorderly hadn't helped. That was why a career in banking hadn't worked out too well either. His bosses had a tendency to be, well, bossy, telling him to do stuff all the time and bollocking him when he failed to jump to it.

Politics seemed to be the ideal vocation for a young man who wanted to be on top, dishing out, not underneath, receiving. There was no question that Slocock's ascent up the rungs of the Conservative Party ladder, from well-connected wannabe to fully fledged MP, had seen him having to take a certain amount of shit from higher-ups along the way. His two years as a research assistant to one of the more reactionary old-guard Tory backbenchers had been no picnic, as the man was cantankerous and gaffe-prone and apt to blame others for his own shortcomings.

For the most part, however, Slocock had felt quite at home in the corridors of power and had found that the more he let his own inner bully out, the faster he rose through the ranks. There was a strange dichotomy in effect at Westminster: those who wished to rule also liked to be ruled. So important was status to them that it almost didn't matter how much they had, as long as each knew exactly where he or she stood. All you needed to gain an edge on someone was to be a slightly bigger bastard than him. For Slocock this presented no problem at all.

Throughout his adult life, until he met Lambourne, Slocock had kowtowed to nobody in any meaningful sense, with the exception of Khun Sarawong. The little Thai, who came up to Slocock's breastbone and couldn't have weighed more than eight stone soaking wet, was the only person he allowed to get away with chastising him, criticising him or treating him with open contempt. A *muay thai* pupil never spoke back to his instructor; that was a tradition Slocock could respect, and Khun Sarawong had valuable knowledge to impart. Thanks to his strict, rigorous coaching, Giles Slocock had become physically unafraid. The Harry Parker-Hollingburys of this world could never intimidate him again. No matter how big or brawny they came, he knew he could kick their arses seven ways to Sunday.

Nathaniel Lambourne was a Parker-Hollingbury of sorts, but his hold over Slocock was subtler and more insidious.

They had first got to know each other at a party fundraiser which Slocock helped organise. Right-wing worthies with plenty in the bank were invited to a slap-up dinner aboard a pleasure cruiser on the Thames and then, after the coffee and *petits fours* had been cleared away and while the port was still being passed, subjected to a PowerPoint presentation on the future of the Conservatives. It laid particular emphasis on the party's bias towards big business, its lax attitude towards the income tax dealings of citizens with non-domiciled status, and its promise to deregulate working hours and employee pension provision. Then the guests were expected to write the party large cheques, which to a man and woman they did, regarding this—correctly—as a downpayment to be offset against substantially increased profit margins in the years ahead, once Labour was ousted and the Tories took the nation's reins again.

Later that night, Lambourne was out at the cruiser's stern, leaning on the taffrail, puffing on a robust Stradivarius Churchill and enjoying the breeze and the solitude. Slocock bumped into him there, having just emerged from an alcove somewhere amidships where he had been helping himself to a little booster from his gold snuffbox. *Bumped into him* was almost literally how it happened, since the river was full and turbid that night and the cruiser had just cut across the wake of a freighter inbound for Chatham docks, so was yawing somewhat. This was well downstream of the Thames Barrier, approaching the estuary, on a broadening sweep of water all aglitter with moonlight.

"Oops," Slocock said. "Boat's rolling a bit. Not got my sea legs."

Lambourne dismissed it with a wave of his cigar. "Accidents happen. It would take a lot to spoil my mood right now."

"Been a good evening, hasn't it? We really appreciate your donation, Mr Lambourne, all the more so when it's given with such good grace."

"Oh, that's not why I'm smiling," said Lambourne. "Couple of hundred thou—I sneeze that kind of sum into my handkerchief. No, I'm smiling because I've just inked a deal to supply almost every SRA in the land with cow's blood. The PM gave it the go-ahead this morning. I've taken what is basically a waste product in the cattle slaughtering process and turned it into a marketable commodity. If that isn't spinning straw into gold, I don't know what is."

"Congratulations, Rumplestiltskin." Slocock didn't intend it to come out quite so sarcastic-sounding, but unfortunately it did. The coke often impaired his ability to gauge the tone of his remarks. He was conscious that he might have just upset a very generous benefactor. Cheques, until cashed, could always be taken back and torn up, couldn't they? *Fuck*.

In the event, Lambourne seemed amused rather than annoyed. "Well, now that you've found out my true fairy name, I can't hold you to your promise to give me your first-born, can I?"

Slocock laughed, perhaps too loudly, brittle with relief. "I don't have or ever have any intention of having a first-born. Kids only slow you down. How can you hope to achieve anything with a couple of rug rats clinging to your ankles? It's like trying to run a race with a ball and chain attached to both feet."

"A man after my own heart. It's Slocock, isn't it?"

"Giles." He wasn't fond of his surname. It, too, was a bit of a ball and chain.

"Heard good things about you, Giles. Your star's on the rise. Research assistant for now, but a likely candidate for nomination soon. A young man who's going places. You remind me of myself at your age. Of course, at your age I was a millionaire a dozen times over. I'd just sold my business selling on people's cars for them at a commission. But that excepted, a close match. Forever looking ahead, sharp elbows, unwilling to rest, keen for power, for influence, for *more*."

"If you ask me, you're still that same man," said Slocock. "Just, you know, older."

Not exactly phrased with tact, for a compliment, but again Lambourne seemed not to mind. "Age is the one foe none of us can defeat."

"The vamps can."

"Well, yes, them of course—they're the exceptions to the rule. But tell me, would you really buy immortality at the price of becoming a hideous, hunched, ratlike creature, living off blood, despised by all? Is that a reasonable exchange? What use is eternity if you can no longer enjoy the finer things in life? This cigar, for instance, or that stuff you still have clinging to your right nostril."

Slocock quickly rubbed his nose clean.

"Nothing on earth would tempt me to become a vampire," Lambourne went on. "I know there are some who've voluntarily got bitten. They want to live forever. But is it truly living? I'd prefer death myself over that kind of ghastly semi-existence. I like the sun, too. Couldn't do without that. Useless owning a Caribbean island if you can't bask in the sunshine. And then there's always that lot to consider."

He gestured to a small speedboat that was passing to starboard. Its searchlight and markings identified it as a SHADE patrol vessel. It was scouring the lower reaches of the Thames for suspicious craft, with board-and-search orders that no captain, pilot or boat owner could legally refuse to comply with.

"Those chaps can bring it all to an abrupt end," Lambourne said, "which rather defeats the object, doesn't it?"

"Frankly, they creep the hell out of me," Slocock said.

"Shadies?"

"Sunless."

"I know; I was being obtuse. Funny how vampirism used to be so glamorous, once upon a time. You know, in the books and movies."

"An attractive lifestyle choice."

"Then the real thing came shambling into our lives, and now, not so attractive."

"Not that you mind, when you're going to be making a buck out of them."

"Many, many bucks, I expect. God bless PFI. But what I'm getting at is, it's the sheer unpleasantness of the vamps that makes anything possible where they're concerned. The powers that shadies have, to take one example. Far in excess of any powers that have been granted to custodians of the peace in the past. Men and women permitted to openly carry guns on our streets and use them at their own discretion—no government could have pushed through a draconian piece of legislation like that were vampires not so subhuman, so damn repugnant. It makes me wonder what else our lawmakers might be prepared to do, just how far they'd be willing to go."

"Or, perhaps more to the point, how far the Great British public will be willing to let them go."

"Indeed. Indeed. Frightened, anxious, desperate for some kind of assurance that everything's going to be all right, people will swallow any new policy, however extreme, if they think it'll make them feel just that tiny bit safer in their beds at night."

"The *Daily Mail* reader mentality."

"There's a reason why that rag is as popular as it is," said Lambourne. "It mines a seam of middle-class paranoia, the dread of the comfortably-off that their prosperous existence could be upended at any moment, all their meagre privilege and material advantage snatched away. It exploits a flaw in the psyche of a particular stratum of society, very profitably. If one day I could perhaps tap into that same fear-fuelled market, I too could benefit."

"Cut me in for a slice of that action," Slocock said.

It had been a facetious comment, offhand, not intended to be taken seriously. He had no way of realising that it was to change the course of his life.

"Maybe I will," Lambourne said, eyeing the younger man speculatively, as though he were a racehorse he was about to lay a bet on or a share option he was about to buy. "Play your cards right... maybe I will."

A half-dozen phone calls followed in the next few months, Lambourne ringing "just for a friendly chitchat," wanting to keep abreast of how Slocock was getting along career-wise. Then came an invitation to dine at the great man's Surrey mansion in the company of industrialists, knighted financiers, multimillionaire entrepreneurs and a host of skinny, frosted, too-young wives. Then the two of them played a couple of rounds of golf together, Slocock losing on both occasions; even if he hadn't been the lesser golfer, winning might have been ill-advised. Then came days out at Goodwood and Henley as a guest of Lambourne, in the best-placed private box at each event. Slowly, by degrees, Slocock found himself been drawn ever closer into the plutocrat's orbit, and although it was an agreeable process—who could resist the extraordinary luxuries that were on offer?—there were times when he felt like a virgin being seduced by a wealthy suitor, and this rankled with him.

A year after the cruiser dinner, Slocock won the nomination for the Chesham and Amersham seat, replacing the incumbent MP who had keeled over from a fatal heart attack while mowing the lawn one afternoon. (That, at any rate, was the official story. The man in fact died doing something not dissimilar from lawn mowing, but much more strenuous, with his nineteen-year-old mistress at a spa hotel in Gerrards Cross.) Slocock was touted as a fresh start, the photogenic face of young Conservatism, a bellwether of the way forward. The *nouveau riche* and the blue-rinsers all loved him, while the traditionalists grudgingly admitted that he looked the part and would serve the party's purposes well. Lambourne himself put the idea about that Slocock, whom he had taken to referring to as his *protégé*, was right for the job. The rest was plain sailing.

Subsequent scandals rocked the boat somewhat—revelations about Slocock's partiality to class-A substances and class-A prostitutes. He weathered them, however, and the journalistic vitriol was noticeably more diluted than it might normally have been. Lambourne swore blind that he had nothing to do with that, but Slocock didn't entirely believe him. A quiet word in a newspaper proprietor's ear was all it would have required. Equally, mightn't his own Teflon charisma have been enough to deflect the tabloids' ire? He liked to think so.

It wasn't until he was chosen to be Shadow Spokesman for Sunless Affairs that Slocock realised he had, in almost imperceptible ways, been manipulated. Lambourne had been steering him into this position all along. By then, of course, it was too late to do anything about it. Slocock was too far in. He was Lambourne's bitch, as he had been Parker-Hollingbury's. This time, though, carrot and not stick was the tool of mastery.

"You live beyond your means, Giles," Lambourne told Slocock once during an awkward lunch at his Pall Mall club where Slocock was guardedly expressing his resentment that the CEO of Dependable Chemicals seemed to regard him as his proxy in Parliament and nothing more. "You're in debt up to your ears, thanks to your various predilections, and you may not be aware of it but I have been helping to keep your creditors at bay."

"You have?"

"Why do you think your bank's been extending your overdraft limit time and time again? Out of the goodness of its heart? And the interest rate on your Visa card loan repayments is awfully generous, isn't it?"

Slocock could think of nothing to say as he digested this information.

"I'm happy to continue bailing you out for the time being," Lambourne continued, "but the day will come when that's no longer desirable or possible. Being on the board of Dep Chem will save you. You'll be able to stand on your own two feet financially then."

"While still being under your thumb."

"Take it or leave it. Either way, you aren't there yet, and until you are, you do as I ask, you keep your objections to yourself, you *behave*. Any problem with that?"

Plenty, Slocock thought, but "None" is what he said.

10AM, AND IT was time for the weekly visit from his dealer. Ronaldo Peake made house calls and offered the kind of personalised, user-friendly service that suited his time-poor but cash-rich client base. "I'm the Ocado of the drugs world," he liked to say.

He and Slocock did a couple of lines in the living room, as was customary after the money had been handed over, to celebrate the completion of the transaction. It irked Slocock that it was *his* charlie they were snorting, but that was how Peake operated. His terms. No concessions. Nothing for free.

"Jesus, was last night a mess or what?" Peake said. "London's a disaster zone this morning, like fucking Rwanda or something. What're you lot going to do about it, eh? Can't let things carry on like this."

"Wait and see," said Slocock, using a moistened fingertip to mop up a few stray grains of powder from the tabletop and rub them onto his gums. "It's all in hand."

"You need to get your skates on. My suppliers are getting well antsy. In the early days it was great. When the vampires came along, suddenly it was a damn sight easier shifting stuff into this country. Funds for customs and the coastguard got siphoned off to run SHADE instead."

"Priorities."

"Exactly. But now the bloodsuckers are kicking up a fuss, my guys overseas are flapping. They reckon England's in trouble, serious shit like, and that's going to screw the import and buying side of things no end."

"Hence your prices have gone up."

"Yeah, sorry about that, man, but, you know, market forces. Market fucking forces. Makes you think, though. We're all, like, dependent on one another, aren't we? You, me. Me, them. We're all, like, feeding off each other in a way. Our relationships are parasitic. Vampiric. Yeah?"

"I hear what you're saying," Slocock said.

"We're all leeches. Maybe that's why everyone hates the vamps so much. They're us. They're just us, man, people, with all the politeness and the smooth talk and the bullshit stripped away. They're us as we are, not as we think we are or would like to be. They're the fucking truth—the mirror we don't wanna look in."

Peake helped himself to another line of the coke he'd just sold Slocock, using a rolled-up twenty from the wad Slocock had just paid him with.

"Fuck yeah," he said, inhaling hard. "No wonder so many people'd be happy to see them gone from the face of the earth. It's like waking up one morning, you thought you were a man, you realise you're actually a cockroach. So, like, let's stamp out the reminder. Let's smash that fucking mirror. That's what it's all about, underneath everything—the firebombing, Stokers, all that. Exterminating the roach us."

THE LOGIC OF Peake's cocaine philosophising had started to fade, along with the buzz, as a ministerial limousine ferried Slocock along the M4 into London.

Traffic was abysmal. From Heston Services onwards the Lexus was stuck in a slow-crawling cavalcade of vehicles, moving in lockstep with the riffraff in their white vans, people carriers and National Express coaches. Slocock's driver tutted and huffed and, etiquette be damned, joined in the occasional bouts of horn-tooting to express his frustration. Once the motorway became a flyover past Osterley, then at least there was the distraction of something to see while inching along, something exceptional and startling: the patches of the city where fires still smouldered and smoke still twisted upward in filmy strands.

Peake had been right. *Fucking Rwanda or something.*

From Hammersmith to Westminster—five miles as the crow flies—was another tortuous hour and a half's driving, diversion after diversion threading the car through the dreary Sloane dormitories of Fulham and even across the river and back. Slocock arrived at Parliament with barely twenty minutes to spare before the all-important press conference began.

The Central Lobby, where the Houses of Commons and Lords intersected, teemed with TV reporters doing live pieces to camera, setting the scene for the main event. Slocock was waylaid by a rather tasty bit of totty from Sky News, who asked him if there was anything he could tell the viewers about the content of the Prime Minister's upcoming statement.

He feigned ignorance. "Not a clue. Shadow Cabinet—we tend to be kept in the dark by the other side. Your guess is as good as mine."

"But you must have some inkling what he's going to say, Mr Slocock," the reporter insisted. "Anything you'd care to share with us?"

"There's plenty I'd like to share with *you*, love," Slocock said, with a caddish leer. "None of it suitable for broadcast."

Her smile said coy amusement. Her eyes said *I'd slap you if I didn't think it would cost me my job.*

Soon, it was time. Slocock settled down with a coffee at a table in the Pugin Room, where a TV had been set up, tuned to BBC News 24. He and an assortment of ministers, permanent private secretaries, personal assistants, aides and spin doctors watched as, onscreen, the PM entered the Grand Committee Room to a lightning storm of flashbulbs. Maurice Wax followed, and behind him strode the cocksure, leonine figure of Nathaniel Lambourne.

"Isn't that your sugar daddy, Giles?" some Labour wag quipped.

Slocock flicked him a V.

"Boyfriend, I heard," someone else said, a wonky-chinned Lib Dem from the Midlands. "They meet in Soho for long candlelit dinners *à deux*."

There was widespread chuckling over that, which Slocock silenced by saying, "The next smartarse remark from any of you, I will seriously fuck that person up. You want to be eating meals through a straw for the next six weeks? Then make a joke. Go on. I dare you."

Nobody believed he would actually make good on this threat. At the same time, he was volatile enough that nobody was going to take the risk.

"Now shut up, all of you, and let's see this."

"LADIES, GENTLEMEN," SAID the Prime Minister, seated between Wax and Lambourne behind a long oakwood table. "I come before you today at a critical juncture in British history, when our nation faces a grave dilemma. We're all too aware of the regrettable events of the past forty-eight hours or so. There's no need for me to rehearse them here. Nor is it for me to apportion blame. Responsibility lies on both sides and neither. There's no right or wrong, as I see it. There's one viewpoint and another, one culture clashing with another culture.

"For nearly two decades now, we in Britain have attempted to handle the increasing influx of Sunless as best we can. We have allowed them to reside among us. We have, for their wellbeing and ours, assigned them clearly demarcated portions of our cities and towns. We have provided them, out of the kindness of our hearts, with refuge and sustenance, expecting nothing in return but that they remain put and do not trouble us. We have, I believe, been exemplary in devoting time and resources to them. Other countries have not been so charitable. Our generosity, in terms of both material goods and spirit, has been second to none.

"I regret to say that the time for such boundless tolerance seems to be past. For the sake of the Sunless community, and of the people of this great nation, a change of approach is called for. The state of mutual antagonism that presently exists cannot be allowed to worsen any further. We must perforce take drastic steps. We must act in a manner which may seem to some unforgiving, even harsh, but which I assure you is not only necessary, but advantageous to all.

"I'll hand over now to the Secretary of State, Maurice Wax, who can give you further details. Maurice."

Wax asked for the lights to be dimmed. He moved to stand beside a digital projection screen, on which a map of the British Isles loomed into life, measled with red dots of various sizes.

"These dots," said Wax, "represent the locations of SRAs. The larger the dot, the greater the Sunless population. As you can see, the highest concentration of Sunless is down here in the south-east. It's where most make landfall from the continent. They tend not to move north and west, but stay more or less where they arrive.

"They are scattered nonetheless. This results in logistical and administrative challenges. It makes it hard to keep track of their numbers and meet their needs accordingly. Hence, we believe, the root cause of these so-called bloodlust riots. Maintaining consistent supply when demand is so diverse and disparate has led to issues of resentment and deprivation.

"Our solution... is this."

The image on the screen changed. Now there was an aerial shot of a geodesic dome, a flattened hemisphere made up of hexagonal sections. The metal framework was black, the inset panels made of some gleaming, dark grey material. It nestled in the lee of a hillside, with outcrops of coniferous forest all around. A sense of scale was hard to get from the picture, but the impression given was that the dome was enormous, football stadium size or even larger.

"It looks not unlike a theme park or a holiday park," Wax said, "or perhaps a giant greenhouse. Within, however, lies this."

From exterior to interior. A kind of open-topped labyrinth now occupied the screen, with the dome forming a darkly opaque, overarching firmament above. The labyrinth was composed of clusters of roofless, single-storey dwellings arranged in a grid pattern. Filling the spaces between were plazas, streets and squares, all radiating from a hub lying directly beneath the apex of the dome. It all had an air of beehive tidiness, a kind of pristine, microcosmic perfection.

"We are calling it Solarville. To be precise, what you're looking at is Solarville One. The first of a proposed fifteen such ventures."

The chatter from the assembled journalists had started

as a hum when the shot of the dome came up. Now it was a rumble, rising to a clamour.

"Please," said Wax, "we will answer questions—and I'm sure you have many—once we're done with the announcement. Until then, if you could quieten down..."

The noise abated.

"A man better able than I to explain the workings of Solarville is sitting over there." All eyes turned to Lambourne. "I'm sure you all recognise Nathaniel Lambourne of Dependable Chemicals. He is, I suppose you could say, the father of the whole project. It is his brainchild. Nathaniel? Over to you."

Lambourne beamed beatifically.

"Solarville is the ultimate SRA," he said. "It's the next generation, version two-point-oh. Purpose-built, a safe haven, self-contained, secure, ideal. A good three thousand Sunless will fit comfortably within its environs, each at liberty to roam its streets, occupy one of the berths on offer, enjoy independence and a good quality of living, free from interference and intervention from outside. The dome affords shelter from the elements, hence the lack of a need for roofs within. We feel this arrangement suits the Sunless temperament and social disposition to a T."

He held up a finger, as if in objection.

"'But isn't this a form of confinement?' is what you're thinking. 'A glorified prison?' Well, you couldn't be more wrong. I concede that admission into and out of Solarville will be closely monitored. There is only a single entrance."

A three-dimensional schematic of the dome rotated to show one access point at the base: large double gates that formed two halves of a hexagon.

"This will be SHADE-guarded. However—and it is a significant however—in return the Sunless will be granted something that has hitherto been denied them. Something we humans regard as essential, even life-giving, but which to them is fatal. Something... wonderful."

The sun filled the screen, shimmeringly bright.

"The dome's individual panes are made of glass. Darkened, light-inhibiting glass. It's designed to screen out the worst of the sun's radiance while allowing some light to penetrate still. Put simply, Solarville is an environment in which Sunless may walk outdoors during the day without fear of being burned to a crisp. We are offering them that which we take for granted and which has been anathema to them throughout all generations 'til today. It's what's known in the business sector as a trade-off—or, if you prefer, a damn good deal."

SLOCOCK DRAINED HIS coffee. A hush had fallen in the Pugin Room, everyone intent on the TV, absorbed, mesmerised.

Alea iacta est, as his Classics teacher used to say, every time the class handed their test answers in. *The die is cast.* No going back now.

THE QUESTIONS FROM the press pack came thick and fast.

"Mr Lambourne? Mr Lambourne! How do you know it'll be completely safe for the Sunless under that dome? Have you run tests?"

"Thank you for asking that," said Lambourne. "We've not actually tested whether the glass will provide perfect immunity from the effects of the sun. There are two reasons for this. First off, were we to do so and the experiment failed, it would be tantamount to committing murder. Second, as in all things Sunless we are dealing with the supernatural—facts which cannot be ascertained or verified by empirical methods. However, what we have done is calculate the rate at which sunlight burns Sunless, based on extensive study of all the available video recordings of Sunless perishing in that manner, which amounts to nearly two and a half hours of footage. It was grim viewing, but all in a good cause.

"We then," Lambourne continued, "devised a formula relating speed of cremation, if I may use that word, to level of solar exposure. The pace of the burning process depends on several factors including the time of day, the time of year, thickness of cloud cover and density of atmospheric pollution. Assembling all the data, we were able to extrapolate what an acceptable level of daily exposure would be. We have computer-modelled extensively, and we are confident that we have judged the occlusion rating of the glass—some ninety-six per cent—with absolute accuracy. A Sunless may stand under our dome all day long, in cloudless conditions, with no more ill effect than you or I spending a summer's day outdoors."

"Can you be certain of that?"

"I'm personally investing a small fortune in this, as are the other two members of my consortium. We are all experienced businesspersons and none of us, I can assure you, is the sort to part with money rashly."

"Mr Wax, how do you know that this is something the Sunless themselves want?"

"You'd have to ask them yourself," said Wax. A sheen of perspiration glistened on his upper lip. "I can't see, however, that they could reasonably object. As Mr Lambourne said, Solarville is a better SRA, a marked improvement on their present living conditions. If you arrive at the airport to find you've been given a complimentary upgrade from economy to business class, do you say no?"

"Will they have any choice in the matter? Will this be a compulsory relocation?"

"There are times when the public good must come first, over and above individual freedoms—times when... when..."

He faltered. He seemed lost for words. The Prime Minister leapt to his rescue.

"What Maurice is saying is that the Sunless already understand the terms on which they are permitted to stay in this country, the conditions we expect them to abide by. It is implicit in clause two of the Settlement Act, which, if I can remind you, reads 'Sunless are entitled to a status commensurate with but not equivalent to full British citizenship, allowing for their unique attributes and distinctive differences, in so far as they remain subject to the laws of the land at all times and submit to sequestration in whatsoever fixed locations as the government shall decree.' I had a hand in drafting the document, of course, back when I was Home Secretary, so I'm more than familiar with the wording. Now, if I as Prime Minister, with the support of my Cabinet, decide that Solarville should be one of the aforementioned 'fixed locations,' then there's really nothing to argue about. The Sunless can be sent there whether they like it or not— although I have no doubt that it'll be the former."

"Sunless didn't actually sign the Settlement Act, sir."

"Is that a question, young lady?"

"Did any Sunless sign the Settlement Act? Did they actively consent to its stipulations?"

"Well, that is now a question, although it sounds mostly like a rhetorical one. Don't tell me—*childrenofthenight. com*, yes?"

It was a good guess. The woman he was talking to nodded. She had artificially dark hair and Nefertiti eye makeup and was dressed in multiple layers of black and purple clothing, with plenty of crushed velvet, taffeta and corsetry on show.

"The official website of the People for Ethical Sunless Treatment," said the Prime Minister.

"It's People for Ethical Treatment of the Sunless, actually. PETS."

"Of course. Silly mistake. My acronym would spell PEST, wouldn't it?"

Several journalists laughed.

"Well, miz," the Prime Minister went on, "you tell me how exactly would you go about obtaining their consent and making sure it was unanimous, or even a majority opinion? If there were some sort of Sunless spokesperson, someone elected to represent them, a community leader, that would give us someone to deal with directly. But there isn't, is there?"

"Count Dracula?" somebody near the back of the room offered.

"I said elected, not hereditary peer."

Now everybody laughed, apart from the PETS woman.

"As it is," the Prime Minster went on, "the Sunless are this amorphous, undemocratic mass, and we're left with the unsatisfactory but unavoidable compromise of a legal contract that had to be imposed from above rather than bilaterally agreed upon. There was no other way. I know you and everyone in your pressure group believe the Sunless have a voice that deserves to be listened to, and I'm broadly sympathetic to the notion, but where is it, this voice? If it existed, surely we'd have heard from it by now."

"Have you really tried? Aren't you hearing it now, with the riots?"

"You've had your turn. Next question, please. Someone else?"

"So you'll be shipping Sunless off to the Solarvilles as soon as they're built, is that it?" said a television reporter.

"What makes you think they're not built already?"

"Well, that was a computer-generated simulation, wasn't it? Work hasn't begun yet."

"Mr Lambourne? Perhaps you can enlighten the gentleman from Sky News?"

"Of course, Prime Minister," said Lambourne. "That's no simulation you're looking at. That is the actual thing, the working prototype, situated on Dep-Chem-owned land in Hertfordshire, near Hitchin. Those hills in the background are the eastern tip of the Chilterns. The venue is ready to receive its first residents right away. As soon as tonight, even."

"And tonight," said the Prime Minister, "is indeed when we'll commence the task of moving Sunless out of certain SRAs and into Solarville One, in the hope of defusing present tensions. SHADE will be overseeing the operation, with the assistance of the army. It'll be a mammoth, complex undertaking, but I think you'll agree that the end-result will make the effort more than worthwhile."

THE CONFERENCE WAS wound up soon after. On the way out each journalist was handed an electronic press kit containing images and easy-to-assimilate information about the Solarville project. Shortly after that, Lambourne summoned Slocock via text message for a debrief.

"Reckon it went well?" he said as they took a turn together through Victoria Tower Gardens. Traffic grumbled on one side of the small park, the Thames tumbled along on the other.

"Apart from Wax muffing it, yes."

"Yes, he did seem to lose the plot all of a sudden, didn't he? Weak man. Panicked by tough decisions. Not like you and me. I wouldn't be surprised if he quits the job soon, maybe even before October. Wax is definitely on the wane." Lambourne chuckled; Slocock didn't. "Too corny?"

"Ever thought of writing headlines for the *Sun*?"

"That bad? Anyway, at least we don't have need of him any more, not now that the proverbial ball is rolling. In fact, I'd go so far as to say that there are no further obstacles facing us. We're free and clear. The PM's agreed, in principle, to buy Solarville One and take out an option on the others. He'll have to okay it with the Chancellor first, but that's purely a formality."

"Really? He likes the idea that much?"

"Doesn't *like* it, as such, but recognises that it's his least unpalatable option and best hope. I get the impression he senses it could be an election winner, too.

It's the sort of forthright, robust policy decision that might just halt his decline in the polls, perhaps even reverse it."

The pathway they were following had led them to a small Gothic monument near the river bank, the Buxton Memorial Fountain. They stopped beside it while the bells of Parliament tolled twelve o'clock. It was the most pleasant day of the year yet, and the buds on the trees were pushing out their leaves like a choir breaking into song.

"Well, we can't have that, can we?" said Slocock. "Labour getting in yet again. You'll have wasted all that donation money, for one thing."

"I told you at the time, a hundred K isn't a big deal for me."

"Two hundred, actually."

"Even so. I dropped ten times that much on a Bugatti Veyron last week, and you know what? I'm probably never even going to drive it. I just had to have one—because I can."

"You're honestly saying you don't care whether there's a Conservative victory?"

"I'm above caring," said Lambourne. "You don't seem to appreciate, Giles, that for a man in my position, political partisanship is an irrelevance. Left, right, red, blue, it's all the same to me. What counts is whether I have them in my pocket or not. As I do with our dear leader. We're best buddies now. I've reinvigorated him with Solarville, given him a new lease of life. Brought him back from the dead, even. We're firmly on track, he and I."

"But I thought we were working towards putting the Tories back in charge."

"A wise man hedges his bets. When circumstances change, one needs to be sure that one can change with them. The unveiling of the Solarville project was originally scheduled for after the election, but that became, as we know, unfeasible. Long-term was telescoped to short-term. We couldn't hold off. Net result: Solarville is now a Labour initiative. I don't see what the problem is. It doesn't materially affect you."

"No, it doesn't, but... but you had me pressurise Wax into it."

"Pressure, not pressurise. To pressurise is to perform a specific physical procedure relating to the atmosphere of an enclosed system. Did they not teach you anything at that school of yours? And yes, I enlisted your aid in twisting his arm. I used an asset I had. What of it?"

"That's all I am to you?" said Slocock. "An asset?"

"And what am I to you, Giles?" Lambourne replied. "A meal ticket. Let's not pretend we have anything more between us beyond what each of us can get out of the other. Certainly let's not pretend we're yoked together by a shared ideology," he scoffed. "That would be absurd."

"I felt we... we had a sort of... understanding?" Slocock was aware how pathetic he sounded, like a girl asking a boy if he loved her.

Lambourne leaned close. "Let me explain to you something about power, my boy. You think power is being in government? That's not power. That's a glorified parish council. Power—true power—is being able to move people around like the pieces on a chessboard, without an opponent to thwart you with counterattacks. Power is getting your own way, all the time, and being answerable to no one. Power is the position I'm in, a position you will never be in. I'm sorry to state it so baldly, but I feel it has to be said and now is as good a time as any. Gaining absolute, unfettered control of others is the only thing that motivates me. My wealth is simply the means to that end, as well as a happy by-product of it. You and your aspirations and those of all the political class are of as much consequence to me as the mewling and squabbling of pre-schoolers."

Secretly, in that dark corner of the soul where people stow the things they don't want to admit to themselves, Slocock had known all along how little he meant to Lambourne. He had kidded himself that they were fellow-travellers, in order to maintain some self-respect, but deep down he'd understood almost from the beginning that they were—and only ever would be—motorist and hitchhiker.

Having his nose rubbed in this truth was not a pleasant experience. The urge to break some portion of Lambourne's anatomy was strong, but happily Slocock had more sense than to give it free rein. He could physically injure Lambourne, but Lambourne, in return, could *destroy* him.

He settled for a bit of carefully calibrated snittiness instead.

"So then," he said. "You've got everything you want. Bully for you. You've sold your Solarvilles, complete with built-in failsafe in case things go tits up."

"Yes," said Lambourne curtly, "and I'll thank you not to speak of that again."

"Does the PM even know? Does he realise what he's signed up for?"

"He does, as a matter of fact. He's been fully apprised of what a Solarville is capable of. But it's not a matter of public knowledge and, save for a crisis, will never have to be. And that, Giles, is the last I'll hear from you on the matter. We do not mention the failsafe, at all, to anyone, even each other. I'm not sure why I ever told you about it in the first place. It was, perhaps, a lapse of judgement. I saw no harm at the time in letting you in on the game. Don't make me regret that decision. It would really not go well for you if you did."

Slocock nodded, a stiff show of contrition. "It shall not pass my lips again."

"It had better not. Same goes for Subject V. You are implicit in that, don't forget."

Slocock could not suppress a small shudder as he recalled the first and only time he had clapped eyes on Subject V. The memory was etched in his brain, repugnant at every level imaginable.

"That you know of Subject V and have taken no steps to report it makes you an accessory," Lambourne said. "Don't even think of ever using his existence as leverage against me. Try to topple me, and you'll be the one going down. And on that note..."

Lambourne took out his iPhone and summoned his chauffeur with a tap of an icon. By the time he reached the park gates, his Bentley Continental would be there waiting for him, door open.

"A useful chat, Giles. I hope you'll come away from it with a slightly clearer grasp of the state of our relationship."

"Oh, I have, Nathaniel, don't you worry."

After Lambourne had gone, Slocock loitered a little longer in the shadow of the Memorial Fountain. The monument had been erected in 1865 by an MP, Charles Buxton, to celebrate the abolition of the slave trade. The drinking fountain which sheltered within the ornate gothic structure bore an inscription saluting William Wilberforce and other emancipators, including Buxton's own father.

Slocock found sympathising with the downtrodden difficult at the best of times. But this was not the best of times, and as he bent to take a drink at one of the fountain's four marble basins, he felt that he understood the thirst of the shackled and indentured to be free.

CHAPTER FIFTEEN

REDLAW AWOKE WITH a start. His Cindermaker rested in his left hand, his index finger curled loosely around the trigger. His right shoulder was still a nexus of pain, but hurt markedly less than earlier.

He was sitting propped up against a bare brick wall. He smelled dust, dankness and the stale-sweet aroma of beer. He blinked into a cavernous gloom, fuzzily piecing together where he was. He had slept hard—the deep dreamless slumber of the lost and dispossessed.

He was in the cellar of a pub. An old pub—old, out of business and closed down. A sliver of light fell from between the flaps of the steel trapdoor overhead like a guillotine blade, dust motes turning to gold as they drifted through it. Midday, by the angle of the light. Damn it. He'd been out far longer than planned.

He creaked upright. Illyria. Where was she? He looked over to a corner of the cellar, the one furthest from the trapdoor, where empty wine racks and a few sticks of furniture from upstairs had been piled up tightly and carefully. Together they formed a kind of lean-to tepee, and inside it, balled like a foetus, she lay.

Redlaw was struck by how vulnerable she seemed, in sleep. There was no hint here of the lithe, lethal creature he had witnessed just a few hours ago, tearing a dozen Sunless apart with virtually no effort. This, now, was a slender, frail-looking thing, huddled behind a makeshift bulwark in fear of even the slightest touch of sunlight.

He had no choice but to leave her there. It surprised him that this even bothered him; Illyria Strakosha could unarguably fend for herself. It felt like an abandonment nonetheless.

He climbed the steep cobwebby staircase up to the bar and retraced the route he and Illyria had taken through the building, after they had broken in last night. He found the back door whose boarded-up window Illyria had punched through. He stepped out, shading his eyes, into a backyard where locals had fly-tipped all the rubbish they couldn't be bothered to carry down to the proper waste dump. He picked his way through to the back gate and out to the street.

The pub—The Cross In Hand; he recalled Illyria pointing out the sign to him and making some crack—stood on a corner. He was a while getting his bearings. One tract of north London suburbia looked much like another. NW2, the street signs said. Borough of Barnet. He followed his nose until he reached Cricklewood Broadway. The blood pouch in his coat pocket sloshed gloopily with every step, as if to remind him what he had to do.

He would attend to it. First things first, though. He was famished. A Starbucks lured him in, and he wolfed down two croissants and a massive cappuccino. That wasn't enough, and he went in search of a greasy-spoon café serving all-day breakfasts, ordered a full English and polished it off in record time. Using his right hand to carve up rashers of bacon was a small torture but, again, he was aware that his shoulder was nowhere near as bad as it had been.

In the café's toilet he removed his coat, rolled up his sleeve, peeled back the dressing and inspected the wound in the mirror. It was puckered, puffy, flaring-red, very ugly. He noticed that, while most of the stitches were surgical sutures tied in neat square knots, two weren't. Another type of thread had been used for them—it looked like ordinary sewing cotton—and the knots were tidy in their fashion but still cruder than the rest.

He had no recollection of Illyria mending the stitches he had torn. She must have done it while he slept. Dear God, how insensible did you have to be for someone to put two fresh stitches in you and not be woken by it? He was both alarmed and oddly touched, picturing her ministering to him in the dark. Any other Sunless would have taken advantage, ripped a hole in his neck and drunk from his jugular as though slurping water from a spigot. Illyria, instead, had deftly, delicately fixed him up, knowing he would never have given his consent had he been conscious.

You let your guard down, Redlaw.

No, wrong tense.

You've let your guard down.

HE CAUGHT THE Tube at Kilburn Park. Redlaw loved the Underground. You could go down a rabbit hole almost anywhere in London and emerge from another rabbit hole almost anywhere else. It was magic—he'd known that since a child. Dirty, noisy, smelly, overcrowded and unreliable, but magic all the same.

He felt safe and anonymous among the milling throngs of passengers. Shadies as a rule didn't travel by Tube, certainly not during daylight hours, so it was unlikely he would bump into someone he knew. The Metropolitan Police might be on the lookout for him, he supposed, London Transport Police too, but the odds on running into a representative of either force were slim. As for CCTV, as long as he kept his head down, half buried in the upturned lapels of his overcoat, he should be all right. Calm and unobtrusive, that was the way to play it.

He rode the rumbling rails southward, then westward.

A short time later, he came up at Ladbroke Grove. Outside the station a newsvendor had just finished installing a recently arrived headline sheet behind the grille in his stand. Redlaw glimpsed the words "PM's BOLD SUNLESS RELOCATION SCHEME." The newsvendor began cutting the twine on a bale of *Evening Standard*s, hot off the press. Redlaw snatched up the top copy and hurried to a nearby bench.

Most of the front page was taken up by a picture of Solarville One, squatting on the landscape like a big fat black blood-blister. Inside there was an array of images of its interior, and the accompanying text reproduced the Prime Minister's statement verbatim along with facts and figures about the dome and houses and, in a boxout, a profile of Nathaniel Lambourne. The *Standard*'s editorial was broadly in favour of the Solarville project. "It severs the Gordian Knot of a seemingly intractable problem," was its conclusion. "Some may carp, but the right-thinking majority will surely heave a sigh of relief."

Redlaw read and reread. Nothing in the article changed anything. The Sunless were swapping one form of internment for another, that was all. He could see a kind of sense to it.

All the same, he was uneasy. The involvement of Nathaniel Lambourne in the Solarville project set his antennae twitching. BovPlas was a subsidiary holding of Lambourne's Dependable Chemicals. That seemed more than coincidence.

Redlaw was conscious of events moving fast, the stage scenery shifting around him. That made it all the more urgent that he get on with the matter at hand.

The spire of St Erasmus's rose clear above the rooftops, visible from some distance, like an immense finger pointing the way. Redlaw binned the newspaper and started walking.

"JOHN REDLAW IN full daylight. Wonders will never cease. Aren't you afraid you'll burst into flames?"

From Redlaw's expression, Father Dixon gathered that jokes were unwelcome—not even a little light teasing. Well, tough.

"Come in, come in," he said, and in no time he was plonking a mug of steaming tea in front of his guest. The mug bore the inscription *Vicars Do It On Their Knees*. It was a gift from a parishioner, one of many cat-loving spinsters in Father Dixon's flock who'd developed a complicated, daughter-like crush on their pastor. "Don't suppose you'd care for a dash of cognac in that?"

Redlaw fixed him with a stony look. "I couldn't think of anything more revolting."

"Only asking. You look like you could do with some, that's all. Me, I rarely take tea without, when I'm at home." As if to prove the point, Father Dixon charged his own mug with a generous dash of Courvoisier. "Makes everything slip down more easily."

The vicarage kitchen was modest and unmodernised, all fixtures dating back to the 1970s, the golden age of Formica. The vicarage was also modest, a little redbrick cube crouching across the road from the church on the edge of a housing estate. The original official residence of the priest of the parish of St Erasmus was a huge, beautiful Victorian manse, but that had been sold off to property developers decades ago and converted into luxury apartments. There was a fine, uninterrupted view of it from the kitchen window, which Father Dixon could enjoy every time he did the washing-up at his tiny sink.

"I feel I'm going to need it," he added. "What's on your mind?"

"I have a favour to ask," said Redlaw.

"It's the Pope grants favours. We in the C of E just go in for a bit of light mutual back-scratching." Still only po-faced blankness from Redlaw. "Oh, come on, John. This is interdenominational comedy gold. I could go on stage with this kind of material."

"Don't give up the day job."

"Tough crowd," Father Dixon muttered. "What sort of favour, then?"

Redlaw wasn't sure how much to reveal. "You've seen the news, I take it."

"'My husband's no love rat,' claims footballer's wife.

Poor lass. The phone footage of him and that nightclub stripper are pretty conclusive evidence. Or are you referring to the Prime Minister's Solarville statement? I'm going to chance my arm and say it's that one."

"And the riots that have prompted it. I'm halfway convinced this isn't just some random sequence of events. Something bigger and more far-reaching is going on, and I aim to find out what. That's where the favour comes in."

"I'll help if I can. I've no idea how, though. I'm just a humble pulpit jockey."

"The thing is, it so happens I can't go into HQ right now."

"Why ever not?"

"Long, complicated story. Let's just say I'm persona non grata at SHADE."

"Persona non...? You mean fired?" Father Dixon was genuinely flabbergasted. "What have you done? It must have been pretty severe. You're John Redlaw, for you-know-who's sake. Poster boy for the Night Brigade. Wait. Did you criticise Macarthur's hair? That would do it."

"I'm not prepared to go into it," Redlaw said patiently. "All I want is for you to go to HQ and take something down to the forensics lab for me. Ask Dr Wing if she'll analyse it ASAP."

"'Something' being...?"

Redlaw placed the blood pouch on the table.

Father Dixon peered at it, frowning particularly over the BovPlas sticker. "What should I tell the delectable Delilah Wing to look for? Assuming I do this for you."

"Anything anomalous. Anything that doesn't belong."

"Meaning it mightn't be pure cattle blood in there as

advertised on the label. But why...? Oh. *Oh*. And that's what... That could be the reason for..."

All at once he was regarding the pouch with suspicion and a touch of wariness.

"I could be wrong. It could be nothing," Redlaw said. "Dr Wing will be able to establish that one way or the other."

"And what excuse should I give for being at HQ in the first place?"

"You pop in now and then, don't you, for old times' sake? No excuse necessary."

"You realise you're asking a priest to lie," said Father Dixon sternly.

"I'm asking a friend to go out on a limb for me, in the name of the greater good."

"But it's still a sin. We reverends are held to a higher standard of morality than your average punter. I could go to Hell for this."

"Look, if you're not up for it, for whatever reason, that's fine. I'll figure out some other way of—"

"John, I'm messing with you." Father Dixon chortled. "Of course I'll do it. It'll be a laugh. Besides, I've nothing else on this afternoon. Nothing that can't be postponed, at least. The sick and dying of St Erasmus's parish will still be sick and dying tomorrow—apart from the ones that don't last 'til tomorrow, but they'll just have to lump it. God'll welcome them to His bosom regardless of whether they had a chat with their vicar immediately beforehand. He's decent that way. Doesn't demand deathbed confessions, not like the other lot's God."

"I appreciate this, Father. Really I do."

"In this context, John, it's Graham, not Father. And if it's okay with you, I'm going to help myself to another nip of cognac, without the tea this time. The old nerves could definitely do with some steadying."

FATHER DIXON LEFT for SHADE HQ an hour later. He had stowed the blood pouch in the battered leather holdall in which he normally carried his stole, chasuble and sacrament when visiting parishioners. He gave Redlaw a cockeyed salute as he set off down the front path—man on a mission. Redlaw last's sight of him was him straightening his cardigan and adjusting his clerical collar as he stepped through the gate onto the road.

Half an hour to walk from Ladbroke Grove to Paddington. He'd get there around four. Dr Wing was an early bird by SHADE standards. She would probably have just arrived.

Beneath the superciliousness, Father Dixon was a decent man. But was he capable of being discreet and wily?

Redlaw had to hope so.

CHAPTER SIXTEEN

SHADE HEADQUARTERS OCCUPIED a former set of council offices a stone's throw from Paddington station. Only its sheer size—extending the length of a city block, nine storeys tall—hinted at importance. Otherwise it was outwardly unimpressive, a nondescript specimen of municipal architecture, all prestressed concrete and unopenable windows.

The place was busier than Father Dixon had anticipated. The SHADE working 'day' didn't usually start until shortly before sunset, but this afternoon, with nightfall not due for another three hours yet, the building thrummed with activity. Out in the street, patrol cars had already begun to surface from the sub-basement garage. In the lobby, shadies by the dozen were clocking in, yawning as they swiped their ID cards through the barrier sensor.

Father Dixon signed in at the front desk. The duty officer asked him if he had an appointment.

"No, this is just a social call," he replied.

"Who to?"

"The Commodore." It was the only answer Father Dixon could think of. He didn't want to say Dr Wing in case it aroused suspicion. Dropping by to see Macarthur was a plausible pretext—he'd done it before.

"You're in luck, Father. She's in. Let me just call up and tell her you're here." The duty officer picked up the phone.

"Oh, that won't be necessary," Father Dixon said hurriedly.

"I think it will. We've got a nightmare of a night ahead of us. In case you haven't noticed, every shady in town's been drafted in to help with the 'Less relocation. The Commodore is rushed off her feet organising it all. You can't just wander up to her office and walk in willy-nilly. She won't like it."

He dialled an extension number. Father Dixon waited on tenterhooks.

"All right, well, she must be away from her desk." The duty officer put down the receiver and gestured to a row of chairs. "You sit over there and I'll try her again for you in a minute."

"How about I just go up anyway?"

"How do you expect to find her? Rabbit warren up there. She could be anywhere."

"I'll stand outside her office like a supplicant 'til she returns. She's bound to sooner or later."

The duty officer eyed him sceptically. "Hmmm. Anyone else, I couldn't allow it, but I don't suppose there'd be any trouble with you..."

"Bless you," said Father Dixon, affixing a visitor's permit to the lapel of his cardigan.

HE TOOK THE lift down instead of up, and after wandering lost in the basement for several minutes, eventually found his way to the forensics lab. He was feeling flushed and exhilarated as he rapped at the door. Cloak-and-dagger stuff wasn't his forte—not much call for subterfuge in the daily life of your average vicar— but here he was, bluffing and bamboozling with the best of them. God evidently approved of what he was up to, otherwise He wouldn't have given him such an easy ride so far.

Delilah Wing, one quarter Chinese, three quarters Caucasian, dumpy-cute, blinked up at him in surprise through her bottle-bottom spectacles. She was wearing scrubs, a plastic apron and a pair of latex gloves smeared with traces of blood.

"Oh. I wasn't expecting anyone."

"Father Dixon. Remember me? Used to work here. May I come in?"

"Um, sure, okay."

"I won't shake hands, if you don't mind."

Dr Wing closed the door as she had opened it, with her elbow, then peeled off the gloves and tossed them in a hazmat bin.

The lab was sparsely furnished and equipped. Not a high proportion of the SHADE budget went on forensics. In fact, Dr Wing's specialty was almost bottom of the list of priorities here. Her responsibilities consisted largely of autopsying officers who had been killed in the line of duty and analysing Sunless spoor at the sites of rogue nests to determine if the number of occupants tallied with the number of Sunless dusted. Signs of her lack of full employment were all around, from the countless magazines scattered over the work surfaces to the *World Of Warcraft* game that ran almost nonstop on her computer. When she worked, she worked diligently, but opportunities to do so were infrequent.

As it happened, right now her services were in demand. She had a dead shady on a slab in the next room and four more in drawers in the morgue, all awaiting cause-of-death pronouncements and post mortem neutralisation certificates. She gave this as the reason why she couldn't carry out a job for Father Dixon, however small he assured her it was.

"And that's not counting the sixteen other bodies currently lying in police morgues," she said. "It was carnage out there last night. I've been pulling an all-dayer as it is to clear the backlog. I can't possibly fit anything extra in."

"Please," said Father Dixon. "It's not for me. It's for Captain Redlaw."

"Redlaw?" Dr Wing's hazel eyes widened, filling the lenses of her specs. "Redlaw's flipped his wig. That's the rumour that's going round. Cracked under the strain. He nearly killed some of our boys in a car chase, so I heard. All officers are under a blanket order to bring him in if they see him."

"He's got his back against the wall, that's certainly true. But I've known him long enough to believe that he'll always do what's right, no matter the cost, no matter the consequences. He does God's work. And what I have here in my bag could help settle things in a case he's involved in. It could even help settle doubts about his sanity. I need you to examine it, find out what you can. Preferably straight away."

"Like I said, no can do, Father."

"I'm begging you, on Redlaw's behalf. It shouldn't take too long, and those dead fellows next door aren't going anywhere, are they? At least, I hope not."

A smile flickered across Dr Wing's face. She was at home with gallows humour. You needed it in this line of work.

"The one on the slab, a Sunless took off most of his head," she said. "Frankly if he gets up and walks it'd be a ruddy miracle."

"On a par with Lazarus, I'm sure. And while I may be one of Jesus's sunbeams, I'm not actually Him, so I think we're safe on the resurrection front. Come on, Dr Wing. Just a few minutes of your time. If Captain Redlaw's track record still has any currency here..."

Dr Wing sucked on the end of one stem of her specs. "He has been SHADE's star performer 'til now. Perhaps..."

"Perhaps you will?"

She put the glasses back on. "I should have my head examined for this. What do you want me to do?"

ONCE SHE GOT started testing the blood, Dr Wing quickly became absorbed in the work. She ran a sample through a centrifuge to separate cells from serum, then studied both parts under a microscope. She added reagents to other samples and jotted down each result. She took cultures, introduced inoculants into them and placed the phials in an incubator to warm. She filtered some of the blood, set the filter papers in a gel-filled apparatus and ran in a charge through the gel to activate the separation process.

An hour went by; two. Father Dixon occupied himself by flicking through the magazines that festooned the lab. They ranged from *Nature* to *Hello!* and all points between. It was hard to find a periodical these days that didn't mention the Sunless in one context or other, so here was a recent *National Geographic* photo spread on the effects of the diaspora as it began to make inroads into the east coast of America, while here was a piece in *Empire* previewing a hard-hitting Hollywood blockbuster in which a team of A-list actors battled hordes of Sunless in a near-future post-apocalyptic world overrun by the creatures.

Finally, seated at her computer terminal, Dr Wing uttered a soft "Ah."

Father Dixon looked up. "Good 'ah'?"

"Well, it's an 'ah.' No idea if it's good or not." She took off her spectacles and began massaging her forehead. "I've checked for pretty much every organic and inorganic toxin I can think of. I've done basic metabolic panel, immunoblotting, protein electrophoresis, cell count, even blood gas analysis. Everything sits well within the normal reference range for cattle blood. The only peculiarity I've found is... Well, I'm no farmer. Maybe it's just what they do to livestock these days to increase milk yields or improve the taste of beef or something."

"What do you mean, what they do?"

"Inject them with hormones."

"You're saying this blood comes from cows that have been mucked about with?" said Father Dixon.

"No." Dr Wing's fingers moved to her cheekbones. "I'm saying there's an abnormally high concentration of one particular hormone in this particular sample. Statistically that doesn't mean anything. It's like looking at a cabbage patch and inferring from that that the entire planet's landmass is full of cabbages. I'd need to test blood from the whole herd, and several other herds, to be sure this isn't just a freak one-off."

"But you think it might be significant."

"Only because the hormone is at a higher level than naturally occurs. I checked with the literature online. So there's a good chance it has been artificially introduced into the animal. Again, though, I'd be wary of reading too much into this. The agricultural industry will do anything to enhance its product and up profit margins, and cattle farming's the worst culprit. Only drink organic milk, Father. There's enough oestrogen in the ordinary stuff to make you grow ovaries."

"I'll take that under advisement. I don't think my flock are ready to start calling me Mother."

"What is curious," said Dr Wing, "is that the hormone is vasopressin."

"Which does what?"

"Increase aggression. It also boosts sex drive and territoriality. Which isn't of much pertinence when it comes to cows. Experiments have been done on prairie voles and golden hamsters. Again, I looked this up online. Arginine vasopressin, to give it its full name, is a neuropeptide secreted in mammals by the hypothalamus, principally after mating. Once it's released into the bloodstream the male voles and hamsters turn vicious, seeing off other males who come sniffing round, sometimes killing them. Basically the vasopressin, while its effects last, transforms cute cuddly rodents into little furry berserkers. You cross one of them at your peril."

"Does this happen in humans as well? After... mating?"

"The men I've known tend to roll over and start snoring, not lamp the first virile rival they come across."

"I must say I've not had much experience in that field myself."

"There's no Mrs Father Dixon?"

"Are you auditioning?"

Dr Wing tried not to smile. "No disrespect, Father, but you're not my type. Not by about twenty years."

"Damn, I knew I should have started chatting you up twenty years ago."

"You didn't know me then, and besides, I was eleven, so that's a bit creepy."

"You're right, it is." Father Dixon grimaced. "Pretend I never said anything. The reason I enquired about humans is: how would this vasopressin affect Sunless?"

"That's anybody's guess. Their physiology's still something of a mystery. Difficult to perform necrotomy on one of them because, well, how much can you deduce from a pile of ashes? And using live specimens to find out what makes them tick, that's a huge ethical no-go area. It's not as if they volunteer themselves to be examined. I'm sure somewhere some covert black ops agency has a bunch of them chained up in an underground facility, probably in the middle of a desert, and is cutting them up while keeping them alive, all in the name of science and the military-industrial complex. But whatever they've learned, they're not sharing with the wider world."

"But drinking blood loaded with the hormone could conceivably drive vampires wild, like the hamsters?"

"It's not beyond the realms of possibility. Vampire metabolism must mimic that of humans to some extent. They still have the same underlying architecture as us—the same physiological chassis, just ramped up and customised in ways we don't and can't understand. Added to that, they have an extremely limited diet, so if they've been receiving nothing but vasopressin-enriched blood for months on end, then the hormone will have been accumulating steadily in their systems. They won't have had time to flush the excess out as waste product when more keeps coming in daily. I'm surprised I haven't noticed this before, all the 'Less poop I have to sift through. But then hormone concentration is one of the few things I haven't been checking for. This is what Redlaw's been looking into?"

"It is. The blood and the riots."

"Oh, this could be big, then." Dr Wing fetched herself a can of Red Bull and popped the ringpull. She didn't offer one to Father Dixon, not that he would have accepted. "I've been on the go twenty-eight hours straight. Caffeine and glucose are all that's keeping me sentient." She polished off half the can at a single gulp, then belched discreetly into her fist. "So what we have to ask ourselves is, is it accident or design? Did the vasopressin get into the blood before it was extracted and put in pouches or after? Who's to blame, farmers or Big Pharma?"

"That isn't up to you or me to establish, fortunately for us," said Father Dixon. "What I'd like is if you could type up your findings, please. Doesn't have to be much, just a page or so. Then I'll have something to bring back to Redlaw. He can decide where things need taking next."

"I can do that," said Dr Wing. "I warn you, it'll be science only, no conjecture, no insinuations. Hard facts."

"The harder, the better. And Dr Wing?"

"Yes?"

"Maybe you'd best not mention this to anyone else. Should it, you know, turn out to be nothing. Or indeed something."

"Don't worry. Mum's the word, Father. Unless Redlaw manages to uncover a whole huge sinister conspiracy and becomes superhero of the year, in which case I want everyone to know the part I played. I want my share of the credit, dammit."

Father Dixon laughed. "I'll see that you get it. Thank you, Dr Wing."

FATHER DIXON LEFT the forensics lab with two sheets of A4 printout that stated plainly and disinterestedly everything Dr Wing had discovered about the vasopressin in the blood. He rode the lift up to the lobby suffused with confidence and a sense of grace. He was surer than ever that Redlaw had not, as Dr Wing put it, "flipped his wig." Redlaw was a troubled soul these days, but at the core of him there was something unshakeable and unbreakable. It wasn't faith, though faith formed a part of it. It was rock-solid righteousness, which God had put there in His infinite wisdom, knowing there needed to be people on earth with that quality... even if those people often stood alone and rejected and were out of step with the rest of humanity.

To be the owner of an unerring moral compass was not a gift, not in this topsy-turvy world where crooks and charlatans rose to the top and the good sank without a trace. No, it was most definitely a curse.

But at least in John Redlaw, God had found a sturdy

vessel, one that could withstand the worst that life had to offer.

As the lift doors opened, Father Dixon made a mental note to remember the 'sturdy vessel' metaphor. There was the germ of a Sunday sermon in there.

The very first person he spotted after stepping out into the lobby was Commodore Macarthur.

He felt a sudden clenching in his belly, like a snake tightening its coils.

Macarthur was deep in discussion with a half-dozen men, two of them uniformed shadies and the rest mid-ranking military personnel. Through the windows Father Dixon saw a row of canvas-topped troop transport lorries parked in the street outside, armed soldiers standing guard beside them. He'd been downstairs just a couple of hours, and in the interim everything had turned olive-drab and martial.

The only thing he could do was try to make it across the lobby and out the front door without attracting attention. Macarthur had her back to him, and she and the men with her were all poring intently over a map. If he moved swiftly and stealthily, chances were she wouldn't look up. He'd have to be desperately unlucky if she did.

"God?" he murmured under his breath. "Come on, big chap, don't fail me now."

He was almost at the door—three paces from it, if that—when somebody called to him.

"Father?"

It was the duty officer.

In his head, Father Dixon said a word vicars aren't supposed to use. Or even know.

"Yes?" he said, turning, smiling.

"You were a while."

"I know. Well, that's how it is. The Commodore—busy, just as you warned me. I had a long wait."

The duty officer didn't seem completely convinced by this. "Funny, because she came down not long after you went up and she's been here ever since."

"Did I say we actually met up? I didn't, did I? We missed each other, you see. Yes. Such a shame. I'll catch up with her another time, when she's not snowed under."

"She's just over there, though. Now's your chance. You can at least say hello."

"No, really, she's doing something important with some important-looking people. Ex-military herself. She looks quite at home with them. So I shan't bother her. I'll just—"

"Father Dixon? Graham?" Commodore Macarthur was looking his way. "Thought I heard a familiar voice."

Father Dixon's pulse pounded in his ears. *Keep a grip*, he told himself. *You can do this. Be innocent. Act like there's nothing untoward going on. There isn't. There really isn't.*

"To what do we owe the honour?" said Macarthur.

"Been waiting for you upstairs, he has," said the duty officer. "Two hours."

Couldn't this busybody jobsworth keep his mouth shut, Father Dixon wondered.

"Have you? What for?"

"No reason. Just happened to be in the area and passing," Father Dixon said. "Bad timing, though, obviously, I can see. Mustn't disturb you. You carry on with your meeting."

"If you were waiting for two hours..."

"Honestly, it doesn't matter. I had my Bible with me. I didn't let the time go to waste. Lost myself in a Good Book, as it were."

"Commodore?" said one of the military men, tapping his wristwatch. "If we could perhaps get back to finalising the deployment ratios of our men..."

"Yes. Yes, of course." Macarthur nodded to Father Dixon. "Sorry we couldn't coincide, Graham. I suspect I'd have been very interested in what you had to say to me."

"Yes, well, I'll be sure to come by again soon. Goodbye, Gail."

"Goodbye."

Father Dixon stepped lively to the door and out into the cool, early evening air.

Yes!

He cast a glance up to the sky and winked.

"You and me," he whispered, "what a team," and began the journey back to Ladbroke Grove.

As HE LEFT, a thought struck Commodore Macarthur and she interrupted her strategy meeting again, this time in order to go off to a quiet corner of the lobby and make a quick phone call.

"Khalid here."

"Ibrahim, what are you doing right now?"

"Routine vehicle patrol to check SRA perimeters, then heading off to help the soldier boys."

"Cancel that. I've got something else for you. Who's in the car with you?"

"Qureshi and Heffernan."

"Good. Heffernan's a bruiser. You might well need that. Do you remember Father Dixon? Used to be a pastor here?"

"Sort of. I know his face."

"He's just left, and he was behaving... 'squirrelly' springs to mind. Not like himself at all. Said he'd come to see me but wouldn't say why."

"So?"

"'So, *marm*?'" she corrected.

"So, marm?"

"He's a friend of Redlaw's. They still keep in touch."

"And?"

"And I wouldn't be at all surprised if it was Redlaw he came to see me about."

"Meaning? Aaah, I get it."

"Exactly. This is where he lives." She gave Father Dixon's home address. "Go round there. I'd lay good money that's where our errant Captain is."

"And then?"

"You know what to do. Arrest and detain."

"And if he resists?"

"Try reasonable force first," said Macarthur. "Escalate only if that fails. I want him here where I can keep an eye on him, and I want him in one piece."

"I'll do my best," said Sergeant Khalid, but his tone said, *No promises*.

CHAPTER
SEVENTEEN

As DUSK GATHERED and night fell, the streets grew increasingly deserted. It had been business as usual during the day, London dusting itself down, picking up the pieces and carrying on. There'd been inconveniences, like the traffic holdups, but there'd also been a determination in the capital—as everywhere else in the UK—not to let the events of the night before overshadow the day. People had gritted their teeth and forged on, as though battling through a massive collective post-binge hangover.

Besides, you could afford to be courageous during daylight hours. So long as the sun was up, even when screened by a layer of cloud, there was nothing to worry about. The Sunless were paralysed, unable to venture outside, stuck in whatever dark, cataracted hovel they called home. While a glimmer of solar radiance remained in the sky, you were safe.

But the sun had now moved on, curtsying over the

horizon. The terminator between night and day had passed across Britain.

And tonight was when the relocations began.

SHOPS CLOSED EARLY around Father Dixon as he walked through Bayswater and Notting Hill. twenty-four-hour convenience stores put up apology notices and brought down the steel grilles. Commuters dived into Tube stations or crammed themselves onto buses. Cinemas, pubs and restaurants shut their doors. At the enclaves of the wealthy—and W11 had a fair few of them—the spotlights went on and the ex-servicemen commenced sentry duty. Front doors slammed, latches were locked, bolts shot, blinds drawn.

By the time Father Dixon reached the vicarage, he was one of the last few pedestrians abroad. Motor traffic was still dense, but foot traffic was negligible. He strode briskly up the garden path and could not deny that he was glad once he was indoors, within walls.

He found Redlaw conked out in an armchair in the lounge, feet up on a pouffe. The man had plainly been through the mill and was exhausted. Father Dixon let him sleep a little longer while he helped himself to a pale ale and some leftover chow mein from the fridge. Then he went round the house turning on lights and drawing curtains to ward off the dark. Redlaw came to with a sudden sharp intake of breath.

"What's the news?" was the first thing he said. "What did Wing find out?"

"See for yourself." Father Dixon triumphantly presented Redlaw with the two sheets of printout.

Redlaw began reading:

Lab results—Delilah Wing, PhD

<u>Abstract</u>
Presence of unexpectedly high concentration of arginine vasopressin (AVP) in sample of bovine haemoglobin taken from BovPlas pouch, batch # BP5/7601H/PR.

<u>Materials and Methods</u>
Sample was subjected to a battery of standard tests, but for the purposes of this text only the results of endocrinology testing are relevant. AVP was found in the blood at a level of 25 pg/ml (picogrammes per millilitre), 500% higher than the median level commonly found in...

"You were right," Father Dixon said. "Something very dodgy going on with the blood. Been tampered with."

Redlaw, still studying Dr Wing's conclusions, set his mouth in a grim line of satisfaction. "It fits. It's cynical in the extreme, but it fits. Nathaniel Lambourne's been manipulating the 'Lesses, and Parliament. He's manufactured a crisis, and the Prime Minister has played right into his hands, giving his Solarvilles the go-ahead. All this is—all this has ever been—is a business proposition. The 'Lesses get out of hand, people get scared, but oh, look, Lambourne has the tailor-made solution. How handy." He gave a disgusted grunt. "Never mind that people have died and vampires have been put to the torch. No, that doesn't matter one bit. Long as Lambourne and his consortium make a killing on this."

"What do you intend to do?"

"Put a stop to it, of course. Expose the whole miserable fraud for what it is."

"But how do you—"

The doorbell chimed, startlingly loud.

"You expecting someone?" Redlaw asked.

"No," came the reply. "But folk call on me at all hours. It'll be some parishioner in a tizzy about something or other. It always is. That or Jehovah's Witnesses. I tell them I'm at the rational end of the Christian spectrum but they keep coming back."

"Ignore it."

"I can't."

"Pretend you're not here."

"Every light in the house is on. The place is screaming 'The vicar is in.' What are you fretting about, anyway? No one knows you're here."

"I don't know," said Redlaw. "I'm just not happy."

"When are you?" The doorbell went again, sounding somehow more urgent this time. "Whoever it is really wants me," Father Dixon said. "And if they've made the effort to come over on a night when everyone is battening down the hatches, they must have a good reason. I have to go and let them in."

"All right," Redlaw conceded. He drew his Cindermaker and flicked off the safety.

"The gun, John? Seriously?"

"Seriously."

"Well, keep it out of sight. If you must."

Father Dixon set off down the hallway. He didn't have a spy hole in the front door. Spy holes were for the mistrustful, and that wasn't him. He did, though, have a security chain. He wasn't a complete idiot. He twisted the catch and cracked the door open.

A size-thirteen boot kicked from the other side, hard, snapping the security chain and ramming the door into Father Dixon's face with stunning force. He was thrown back against the wall, and fell sideways. He grabbed the coatrack for support, but it toppled with him, and he hit the floor tangled up in an anorak and a mackintosh. He heard feet thudding down the hallway. Next thing he knew, hands were grabbing him, freeing him from the coats, hauling him unceremoniously into a sitting position. He stared up into the face of a uniformed SHADE officer.

"Just sit there, reverend," the man said. One side of his face was badly scarred. "Be a good boy and don't move a muscle. This'll all be over in no time."

SERGEANT KHALID BURST through the lounge doorway to find Redlaw standing in the centre of the room, his Cindermaker levelled. He skidded to a halt. The second shady, Qureshi, pulled up behind him. Redlaw covered both of them with the gun, which trembled slightly in his grasp.

"Now then, Redlaw," said Khalid. "There's no need for that. Put that thing away. No one here wants any gunplay. We've come to take you in. Just let us."

"Why would I let you? So you can dump me in a holding cell and hand me over to the cops?"

"That's the general idea, yes."

"I can't allow that to happen."

"You can't afford for it not to happen. What are you trying to prove, anyway? You've been haring all over the city like a lunatic. Give it up. Just admit that you've snapped. Whatever's been eating you these past few months has finally got the better of you. I'm sure with counselling and medication you'll soon be right as rain."

Redlaw laughed, roughly. "I've not gone crazy, Sergeant. You're the one who's crazy, thinking you can just bash down my friend's door and come stampeding in. If Father Dixon's not all right..."

The gun-wielding arm drooped. With effort, a grimace of pain, Redlaw raised it again.

"You'll what?" said Khalid. "You can barely keep that gun up. And you aren't going to shoot me or anyone, because that's not who you are, Redlaw."

"Try me. This injury's your fault, anyway. Don't think I don't know it was you who set me up on the Isle of Dogs. You somehow warned those 'Lesses I was coming."

"I have no idea what you're talking about."

"Of course you'd say that, wouldn't you? But I know."

"Honestly, Redlaw, this isn't just crazy any more. It's beyond crazy. I don't like you, yes, but not so much I'd arrange to have you killed. I'm not that... that *petty*."

"Well, maybe you aren't." Redlaw firmed his grip on the Cindermaker. "But maybe *I* am."

Khalid took a step towards him, arms out to the side, presenting his own chest as a target. "Go ahead, then. Do it."

"Don't tempt me."

"You're not that sort of man."

"You keep telling me I'm crazy. Crazy people do all sorts of things they wouldn't normally."

"Even so, you don't kill. You won't. Especially not a SHADE officer."

"All right. Perhaps not." Redlaw angled the gun so

that it was pointing at Khalid's thigh. "But how about shoot to wound?"

"Too great a risk with Fraxinus-round calibre. You could easily hit my femoral artery. I could bleed out. You want my death on your conscience? I think not. Sura 5:32, 'If anyone slays a person, it will be as if he slays the whole people.'"

"Forgive me for not being swayed by a quotation from a scripture that has no value to me."

"Do not belittle the holy Qu'ran, Redlaw," Khalid rumbled. "Do not dare mock my faith."

"Out of my way. You too, Qureshi. I'm leaving. You'll regret trying to stop me."

Redlaw sidestepped around the two officers, making for the doorway. His Cindermaker remained poised between him and them, but the cost of keeping it there was too great. The gun dipped, and Khalid smashed it sideways with a whipcrack backhand swipe. Redlaw's hand hit the door jamb and he involuntarily discharged a round into the floor. In the ear-ringing aftermath of the gunshot Khalid drove the heel of one palm into Redlaw's collarbone. Redlaw howled like a whipped dog as his shoulder impacted with the wall, and Khalid twisted his wrist, forcing him to drop the Cindermaker. He attempted to follow this up by putting Redlaw into a wrist lock, but Redlaw jerked his hand back, driving a left-handed uppercut at Khalid's jaw. Off-balance, he cuffed Khalid on the ear instead.

Khalid sneered and drew back a fist. "The Commodore said 'in one piece.' But I might risk disappointing her."

The blow never landed, as Redlaw took advantage of Khalid's little moment of preening to ram his knee up between the Sergeant's legs. Khalid's cheeks and eyeballs bulged and he sagged to the floor, letting out a sound like a steam whistle. Redlaw snatched up his Cindermaker and staggered out into the hallway.

Qureshi knelt by Khalid. "Sir, are you all right?"

"Get him!" Khalid said, red-faced, spewing spittle. "Blow the damn *kafir* away if you have to!"

Qureshi took a few steps into the hallway, where he found Redlaw confronting the third SHADE officer, Heffernan. Father Dixon was slumped at Heffernan's feet, looking dazed and ashen. Blood trickled from a cut to his forehead.

"Move," Redlaw said. "That's an order."

Heffernan was a former doorman who had found God during an unusually violent bar brawl, when a vision of the Virgin Mary appeared before him and prevented him from walloping a troublemaker who was brandishing a broken bottle at him. He now bore the facial scars from that encounter, along with an unyielding sense of mission. Very little intimidated him.

"I don't take orders from ex-shadies," he said. "You're not getting past me."

"I'll shoot."

"He won't," said Qureshi.

Redlaw didn't glance round. "You've hurt Father Dixon. Right now I'm in the mood to put a bullet in all three of you."

"I'm okay, John," Father Dixon said wanly. "It's nothing, just a bump on the noggin. Don't be shooting anyone on my account."

"This is unacceptable," said Redlaw to Heffernan and Qureshi. "You're SHADE, not thugs."

"Put the gun down," said Heffernan. "You're not leaving this place unless it's with us."

"I beg to differ."

Redlaw squeezed the trigger, and a hole appeared in the front door just inches from Heffernan's head. Heffernan recoiled, clutching his cheek, which had caught the splinters. Redlaw charged him, driving his left shoulder into Heffernan's meaty midriff, clubbing the shady's skull with the butt of his Cindermaker. Heffernan yowled and groped blindly, angrily, for his attacker. Redlaw twisted under the man's flailing paw, and grabbed the door handle. He was just seconds from making good his escape.

He heard a bellow behind him. Khalid came furiously out of the lounge, his Cindermaker out and pointed straight at Redlaw. In his maddened, streaming eyes there was clear, murderous intent. A bullet in his gun had Redlaw's name on it.

"No!"

This from Father Dixon, who lurched to his feet.

Khalid fired.

Father Dixon, throwing himself in front of Redlaw, took the round in his upper abdomen. He was hurled back against his friend, and both men struck the door.

"No!"

This from Redlaw, who clutched Father Dixon. All at once, any thought of getting away had left him. He took Father Dixon's weight, lowering him gently down onto the doormat. The vicar's body was going into spasm. Blood spilled down his shirtfront from a teacup-sized cavity in his ribs.

The three SHADE officers were too aghast to move. All stared at the wounded man, none more wide-eyed or gape-mouthed than Sergeant Khalid.

Father Dixon turned his head to Redlaw. He tried to speak.

"You've... you've got to..."

"Save it," said Redlaw. "We're getting you an ambulance. Ambulance!" he shouted at the shadies. "Somebody bloody call one!"

Qureshi delved into his pocket for his phone.

"It's... I hope to God I've been right all this time," said Father Dixon. "Otherwise... it'd really not be funny."

"Let's not have any of that. You're going to be okay. I don't think it's too bad."

But the wound was making a sucking sound, and Father Dixon's breath was rattling wetly at the back of his throat.

"God's work, John," he choked out, spitting blood. "Never forget... you're doing..."

He shuddered. His head lolled. He went limp.

St Erasmus's parish no longer had its pastor.

CHAPTER EIGHTEEN

THE AMBULANCE ARRIVED, futilely. As paramedics rushed up the vicarage's front path, Redlaw was frogmarched the other way at gunpoint. Heffernan, jowl quilled with splinters, shoved him into the back seat of a patrol car and slid in beside him. Sergeant Khalid tossed Redlaw's Cindermaker and weapons vest onto the passenger seat and took the wheel. Qureshi had been assigned to stay behind to handle the paramedics and, when they came, the police.

"Shouldn't have resisted," Khalid said as he pulled out into the road. His groin was still tender. "It was your fault. You brought this on yourself."

Redlaw said nothing, just stared fixedly at his knees.

"If you'd only come quietly, none of it would have happened. Things wouldn't have got so out of hand."

Redlaw continued to stare. If he was listening, if he could even hear Khalid, he gave no sign.

"If it wasn't for you, he'd still be alive."

Khalid checked in the rearview mirror. Redlaw had raised his head. Their eyes met, and the sheer venom that radiated from Redlaw's glowering gaze made something inside Khalid shrivel, like wax in flame. He focused his attention back on the road, knowing that he was hated by the man in the back seat as he had never been hated by anyone.

"*Allahu akbar*," he consoled himself under his breath. Everything was God's will. Even accidental deaths.

THE HOLDING CELLS were on the third floor of SHADE HQ. Khalid and Heffernan took Redlaw straight up there from the sub-basement garage. Both were handling him brusquely, as though he were still a potential threat and flight risk, but the fight had gone out of him. Father Dixon's death had left him hollow and raw.

He went meekly, numbly into the cell. The officer in charge of incarceration, Noakes, closed the door on him and shot home the locking bar.

"It's a crying shame," Noakes said with a wistful shake of the head. "I mean, Stokers, vampire wannabes, druggies who think they've been bitten, the odd Sunless, yes, I'll happily bang them up for the night... But *Redlaw*?"

"An object lesson to us all," said Khalid. "Look after these." He handed Noakes Redlaw's gun and vest, then turned to Heffernan. "You should go and have your face seen to."

Heffernan fingered the splinters gingerly. "It's not so bad. Not compared to this." He traced the bottle scar that ran in a jagged line down the right side of his face. "I'm just as pretty as I ever was."

"Still, don't want it to go septic, do you?"

"True."

Heffernan trotted off to the minor injuries unit on the second floor. Khalid headed in the opposite direction, up to the Commodore's office on the eighth. Concerned though he was for Heffernan's welfare, he had sent him downstairs mainly so that he could bring Macarthur news of Redlaw's capture on his own. That way the credit would not have to be shared, and he could come clean about the shooting of the vicar. If he gave Macarthur his side of the story first, before she heard about it from anyone else, she would be more understanding and, he hoped, more lenient.

There was, after all, a captaincy going begging in the north-east quadrant. Khalid felt he was long overdue for promotion, and bringing in Redlaw ought to have clinched it for him. Father Dixon notwithstanding, the position might still be his, assuming he played his cards right.

Macarthur was on the phone when Khalid knocked and entered. She looked harassed and irritable. "I have nothing to tell you right now," she said to whoever was on the other end of the line. "Events are in motion. Perhaps by the end of the night, when the first phase of the transfer operation is complete, then I'll be in a position to make a statement. Until then, stop bothering me. Goodbye."

Clunk went the receiver. She looked up at Khalid. "Bloody journos. Bet you anything you like there'll be another one ringing in a moment or so. Press time's looming and everybody wants a comment. Anyway, I'm guessing by the glint in your eye that you did it. Mission accomplished."

"He's down in the cells," Khalid said with a nod.

"That's a relief. Well done. Were there any problems?"

"There was... collateral damage, I'm sorry to say."

"He's hurt?"

"Not Redlaw. The priest, Dixon."

"Oh, no. How badly?"

Khalid did not reply, and that told her how badly.

"What happened?"

He explained: Redlaw resisting arrest, attempting to flee, causing grievous bodily harm to both Khalid and Heffernan, not to mention discharging his firearm twice with intent to wound, possibly to kill.

"When I fired, it was meant as a warning shot, to bring him to heel, but I did feel that my life was in danger, so it was more or less self-defence. Father Dixon just got in the way. He moved unpredictably. A split second earlier, a split second later, all would have been fine. The situation was fluid, chaotic. I deeply regret the loss of life. I can hardly express how saddened I am. I know Father Dixon and you were on friendly terms. I'm sorry, marm, truly I am."

It galled Khalid to have to abase himself before this... this *woman*. In a fair and just world, a world that lived according to the tenets of the One True Faith, the likes of Macarthur would not hold positions of public responsibility. She would cover herself appropriately, as Khalid's wife Zaina did, and remain out of sight, in keeping with the Prophet's decrees. She would not cut her hair so short, either. She would not unsex herself like that and deny the feminine attributes God had given her—such as they were, for Gail Macarthur was not one of life's great beauties.

"I feel Redlaw must bear some of the burden of blame," he went on, biting back his resentment. "If not most of it. Had he not been there, hiding behind the priest's skirts..."

The phone rang shrilly. Macarthur picked up the receiver and dunked it straight back down in its cradle.

"Well," she said after a lengthy, ruminative silence. "What's done is done. I'll expect a full report, of course, corroborated by whoever was there with you. As for Redlaw, I'm minded to leave him to stew in his own juices for a while. On the other hand, any excuse to get away from this damn phone..."

A SHARP RAP on the door was followed by Noakes calling out, "Occupant of cell two, stand facing the opposite wall, hands on head, fingers linked."

Redlaw did as instructed. The camera embedded in a corner of the ceiling was watching him, relaying an image to a small screen inset next to the door.

In came Commodore Macarthur.

"Do you need me in there with you, marm?" Noakes enquired.

"No," she replied. "I'm perfectly safe with this man, I'm sure of it."

"Very well. I'll be right outside."

The door clanged shut.

"Turn round, John."

Redlaw turned.

Macarthur slapped him across the cheek, hard enough to leave a crimson imprint of her hand.

"That's for getting Graham Dixon involved in your nonsense," she said.

She slapped him again, harder.

"That's for getting him killed."

And a third time, snapping Redlaw's head sideways.

"And that's for the crap you've pulled on me this past couple of days."

Redlaw touched his smarting cheek.

"You know you deserved those," Macarthur said. "That's why you're not even thinking of hitting me back."

She was right. It hadn't once crossed Redlaw's mind to retaliate.

"You stupid, stupid bastard," she went on. "Look at you. Look where you've ended up. Standing there without your weaponry, you know what you look like? Like a useless, pointless old man. Not a SHADE officer, just a washed-up has-been. Someone who had it all and threw it all away."

Redlaw winced.

"Now, sit down."

Redlaw lowered himself onto the cell's thinly padded cot. Macarthur remained standing.

"So here it is. A one-time-only deal. I've got a million demands on my attention this evening. The army's going into seven separate SRAs, accompanied by every shady I can muster, and they're rounding up a total of one thousand Sunless, putting them on trucks and driving them out to Solarville One. I can spare you five minutes of my time, but that's all you're going to get. This is your one and only chance to explain yourself before the cops come and drag you off to Paddington Green nick on charges of taking a vehicle without the owner's consent, reckless endangerment, affray, and anything else I can think of. You'd better have a reason for what you've been up to and it had better be phenomenally good."

"Will it change anything, however good it is?" said Redlaw. "Will it get me my job back?"

"Almost certainly not."

"Then why should I bother?"

"Because I think you need to tell me. You need to get it all off your chest."

"Confession's good for the soul?"

"Clock's ticking, so you'd best get on with it, if you're going to."

"Actually, marm," said Redlaw, "I was hoping I would see you and you'd give me this chance. We might still be able to salvage something out of this mess without anyone else getting killed. Here." He fished inside his coat and produced the printout, which was folded into quarters. "Should take significantly less than five minutes, unless you're a slow reader."

Macarthur unfolded the two sheets of paper and studied them.

"I don't know what to make of this," she said. "What am I looking at here?"

"Evidence of a plot to mislead Parliament and the British people, and secure construction contracts worth, I'm guessing, close on a billion quid."

"Or, an abnormality in the contents of a single blood pouch. I mean, I'm no biochemist, but if this vasopressin stuff is a naturally occurring substance, one dead cow having a lot of it in its bloodstream—surely all that signifies is that one cow had something wrong with it, some kind of hormone imbalance."

"But don't you see? It's not just one cow. It's all of them. Or all of the blood, rather. BovPlas has been shipping adulterated product into the SRAs for months, turning the 'Lesses gradually more and more violent until a tipping point was reached. The blood deliveries become a focus for their aggression. It's the moment when they're all together, jostling, eager. Tempers fray. Squabbles break out. Sometimes it peters out into nothing, other times it develops into a full-blown riot. That's the intent behind it all—organising chaos, then exploiting that for gain."

"There could be other causes for the riots. Maurice Wax said something on TV about inefficient distribution."

"Maurice Wax couldn't find his own backside with both hands and a map. He was probably just parroting something the Prime Minister told him to say, or Lambourne."

"And it's Lambourne who's engineered this whole thing, just to make a bit of money?"

"A lot of money, for him and his consortium."

"That's awfully coldblooded, isn't it?"

Redlaw shrugged. "There's capitalism for you."

"It's also nothing short of impossible to prove." Macarthur tapped the printout. "This is flimsy wee stuff. Not nearly enough to secure a prosecution, or even an arrest."

"Maybe not, but it's a start."

"What I'm really having trouble accepting is that a high-profile public figure like Lambourne could think he could get away with this—if it's true. It's so overt. So brazen."

"That's precisely it. That's why it's credible. It *is* brazen. Almost contemptuous. The act of a man who truly considers himself above the law. A lesser mortal would have taken the subtle approach. Lambourne's gone all-out, pulling off a con so big, nobody would ever think to suspect him. I don't know him personally, but from what I've read about him he's a high-functioning sociopath, an egotist and narcissist of the first order. Anything less than a bold, audacious strike like this would be beneath him."

Macarthur perused the printout one more time. "If you're right—"

"I am."

"If you are, I still don't see what we can do. It's too late. The Solarville project is already up and running."

"You could halt the transportation, for starters."

"I could not. How? The army's calling the shots. It's out of my hands. I'm aiding and abetting, but not administrating."

"All right, but we could still expose Lambourne."

"On what grounds? This?" She tapped Dr Wing's work. "I told you—not enough."

"Then we requisition more blood pouches. Test more samples. Raid the BovPlas hub facility at Watford, even. My guess is that's where the vasopressin gets added, in bulk, before the pouches go out to the distribution depots."

"I don't have the authority to do any of that, and I doubt we could obtain a search warrant anyway."

"Talk to the Chief Inspector of Constabulary, see if he agrees."

"It's all so simple to you, John, isn't it? So cut and dried. But the world's not black and white the way you see it. You're asking me to try to prompt an investigation into the affairs of a billionaire businessman who's working hand in hand with the government. How can I? I'm just a glorified game warden. All shadies are, when you get down to it. The Sunless are a natural hazard, like tigers in the jungle or sharks in the sea, and we're paid to keep people and them apart. That's it. That's all we're here for."

"I never thought you'd be so defeatist."

"Pragmatic," she corrected. "Like it or not, our elected representatives want to put Sunless in Solarvilles, so that's where they're going. It's not necessarily a bad thing, either. They'll be better protected from humans and vice versa. If you were in your right mind—if you still had a sense of proportion, which I think you've lost—you'd think so too. Whatever the method that's got them there, the net result is a positive one."

"The ends justify the means, eh?"

"Sometimes. What's still bothering me is this woman you were running around with last night. Who is she? My guess would be an activist from one of the pro-Sunless pressure groups."

"Oh, I've fallen under someone's spell, is that what you're thinking? I've become a convert to a cause."

"She's quite striking-looking, judging by the couple of fuzzy CCTV images I've seen. Am I on the right track? Is she some PETS-type do-gooder?"

"Does it matter?"

"It might account for your sudden obsession with BovPlas and bringing down Lambourne. Here's my theory. She found you when you were vulnerable, this woman, shortly after Róisín's death, and she's been working her wiles on you ever since, wearing down your resistance. You've been keeping quiet about it. Now it's finally all out in the open. This is your new creed, Sunless rights. Yes?"

Redlaw smiled bleakly. "You couldn't be more wrong."

"Then tell me, John," Macarthur said with the patient insistence of a parent wanting to know who kicked the football through the greenhouse. "Explain to me what she is to you. I'd like to gain some insight into how my most trusted and dedicated officer could turn against his own and—"

She was interrupted by Noakes thrusting open the door. "Marm?"

"What?"

"Bit of a commotion downstairs. Thought you ought to know."

"Commotion?"

"Just got a call from the front desk. Seems there's been some sort of break-in."

"Here? Who by?"

"Don't know. Details are sketchy. Far as I can gather, it's just one person."

"Well, where are they?"

"That's it. No one knows. Braithwaite, duty officer, says she came through the main door, took down three uniforms who happened to be in the lobby, then hit the lifts. Not sure where she is now."

"Took them down? They're dead?"

"Battered, unconscious, but otherwise not injured. That's all I've been able to gather. This was a couple of minutes ago."

"Then we need to go into lockdown," said Macarthur. "Close all exits, shut down the lifts, task all able bodies in the building to look for the intruder. Why do I even have to say this? It should happen automatically."

"I'll see to it," said Noakes, and hurried off to his station at the end of the corridor to pick up the phone.

Macarthur spun round. "It's her, isn't it, John? Your friend. Must be."

"I have no idea."

"Be honest. She's come for you."

"If she has, it's nothing to do with me. I didn't ask her to. I don't know how she even knows where I am."

"And she waltzed straight in through the front door and got the drop on three shadies—three armed, combat-trained individuals. Never mind who she is. *What* is she?"

From outside the cell there came a sudden gruff shout, the sounds of a struggle, a muffled cry, the thump of a body falling to the floor. The echoes faded along the corridor. Then silence.

"Noakes?" said Macarthur. "Noakes, you still out there? Noakes?"

No reply.

Macarthur took a step towards the doorway.

"Marm," said Redlaw, "I advise you not to move. The safest place for you, now, is right here beside me."

"Safest...?"

"She's not killing anyone. At least"—he raised his voice a little—"she'd better not be. But I'd hate to see you accidentally get hurt."

"For God's sake, Redlaw, what are you mixed up in? What have you got yourself into?"

"You make it sound like he had no choice in the matter."

Both Redlaw and Macarthur looked to the doorway.

There stood Illyria, insouciantly dangling Redlaw's Cindermaker from one hand and his weapons vest from the other.

"What-ho, old bean. We haven't got all night. Time we were gone."

CHAPTER NINETEEN

REDLAW HESITATED.

"Come on," Illyria urged. "I'm officially busting you out of here."

"My God," said Macarthur, staring. Illyria's scarf had fallen down from her face. "Those teeth..."

Illyria didn't bother trying to cover them up. She seemed to enjoy the effect they were having on Macarthur. "Impressive, aren't they?" she said.

"Real. Not filed. Fangs. You're..."

"...losing patience. Redlaw. Men are coming. I hear them. We go now, together, this moment, or I leave you to make it on your own."

Redlaw took a step towards her.

Macarthur regained some of her composure. "John," she said, "you realise, if you do this, there's no turning back. You'll be a wanted man for the rest of your life."

"Marm, there's already no turning back," Redlaw replied. "I think we both know that. I can't belong to this institution any more—especially not now one of its members has killed the only man I counted a friend. SHADE is blighted for me, tainted beyond redemption. At least if I'm free I still have the chance to do some good, even if it has to be from the wrong side of the law."

"But *she*"—Macarthur nodded at Illyria—"whoever, whatever she is, is no friend of yours."

"How can you be so sure?"

"She's just using you for what you can do for her. She'll ditch you once she's got what she wants."

"And maybe I'm using her for what she can do for me. Did you ever think that?"

"Redlaw," said Illyria. "Really, there's no time for this. We must go *now*."

"Just another moment. Listen, marm. You keep Dr Wing's report. I'll leave it to you and your conscience what to do with it. Go public with it if you want."

"Maybe," said Macarthur. "Or I keep a lid on it for the time being. Wait until the transportations are over and the dust has settled. Maybe Lambourne will say or do something then, something careless that'll make what we have on him more incriminating."

"If you like. But whatever you choose to do, I'm going to continue working on the case at my end. Lambourne's still firmly in my sights and I won't stop until I've got him. I'm sorry that it's had to end on this note, marm... Gail. But the only way I can continue to do my job is not to be in my job any more."

"*Redlaw...*" said Illyria.

"Yes, yes." To Macarthur: "For what it's worth, I'm sure Leary would have approved of what I'm doing."

"John, I like to believe Róisín's watching over me every day. And I hope to hell she's watching over you too. Go on, get out of here. Do what you feel you have to. Enjoy your liberty. I doubt it's going to last long."

"As long as it's long enough." Redlaw snatched his vest and gun off Illyria and set off down the corridor.

"And you," Macarthur said, poking an index finger at Illyria. "I don't pretend to understand what your game is, but mark my words, there'll be a reckoning between us. You'll get what's coming to you. No one beats up my officers and walks away scot-free."

"Noted," said Illyria. "I love what you've done with your hair, by the way," she added. "Not many women can pull off the toilet-brush look. And those blonde highlights—they almost completely cover up the grey."

"Bitch," Macarthur hissed.

"*Kurve*," Illyria retorted, in her own language. Then, slamming the door, she strode off after Redlaw.

NOAKES LAY IN a crumpled heap beside his station. Redlaw, as he went past, knelt to check for a pulse. Faint but steady.

"Non-lethal force," Illyria said. "You should be proud of me. I've been very restrained."

"Make sure you keep it that way. These are good people. Innocents."

"No shady is innocent in my book."

Redlaw thought of Khalid. Some shadies weren't, it was true.

"But I shall do my best," Illyria carried on. "Those men I mentioned. They're on the floor below, doing a sweep."

"You can hear...? What am I saying? Shtriga. Of course you can."

"They're making for the main staircase, the one I used. This will be the next floor they try. The lift..."

"Out of action. Macarthur's ordered a lockdown. This way—we'll take the fire stairs."

Redlaw led her to a door marked with a green emergency exit sign and pushed on the panic bar. As they descended the narrow stairwell he asked, "How did you find me? How did you even know I'd been arrested?"

She tapped her nose.

"You... smelled me?"

"I have your scent. I can detect you from far away."

"How far?"

"Miles. Like a bloodhound. When I woke up, I got wind of you—you were in distress. It was like a clarion call."

Redlaw couldn't help but shake his head in wonder. "All vampires have an acute sense of smell, we know that, but yours is..."

"Extraordinary?"

"I was going to say 'better,' but we'll go with extraordinary if you like."

One more flight, then Redlaw said, "So, what do I smell like? What's my scent?"

"When distressed? Like vinegar and urine."

"And when not distressed?"

She grinned. "Roses and incense. The odour of sanctity. Saintly incorruptibility."

"You're mocking me."

"Only somewhat."

They halted at the door to the lobby. Redlaw motioned Illyria to stay back and peered through the narrow slot of safety glass.

"Damn. Should have known this'd be too easy."

"What is it?"

"Main entrance is guarded."

"How many?"

"Six. No, seven. Guns drawn."

"Not a problem."

"It is for me. I'm not getting involved in a shootout."

"Then don't. I'll deal with them."

"Will you kill them?"

"If they're shooting at me, then it'll be hard not to. If my life is in peril, their lives are forfeit. It's only fair."

"Then I'm glad I checked beforehand," said Redlaw. "There's another way out. Come on."

They climbed to the second floor and passed through an open-plan section. On any other night there would have been a score of officers here in their cubicles, taking calls, gathering intelligence on reported rogue sightings. As it was, the place was deserted. On every terminal the standard screensaver, a SHADE logo, glided to and fro like a skater on a rink. Phones chirruped once, twice, and went to voicemail.

There was a back room—a coffee lounge with a couple of vending machines and a handful of not quite comfortable plastic chairs. French windows opened out onto a smokers' balcony situated on top of a one-storey extension. It overlooked a parking area shared with one of the neighbouring office buildings, the London branch of a Middle Eastern commercial bank. Vehicle access was obtained via a side-street.

"There's our escape route," Redlaw said, pointing to the large barred gate on the far side of the car park. "Think you can manage the jump down to ground level?"

"Never mind me. Think *you* can?"

Probably not, thought Redlaw. *Not with my knees.* But he straddled the safety railing anyway, giving the drop on the other side a wary glance. It was nigh on twenty feet.

BLAM!

The pane of one of the French windows disintegrated, shards of glass pouring down in an avalanche. Out through the empty frame stepped Heffernan, holding his Cindermaker in a double-handed grip.

"Now that I have your attention," he said, "that's far enough, the pair of you. Redlaw, get back up on the balcony. You, woman—don't know your name—keep your hands where I can see them and don't move."

"You didn't hear *him* coming?" Redlaw said irritably out of the side of his mouth as he clambered back over the railing.

"He moves quietly for such a big blighter," Illyria answered.

"Well, well, well. Making a break for the border, eh, Redlaw?" Heffernan's cheek was stippled with surgical strips. "Not any longer. Give up your gun. Again."

"May I?" said Illyria.

"Go ahead," said Redlaw. "Be my guest. Non-lethal still—but you don't have to go so easy on this one."

"Less muttering, more surrendering." Heffernan gestured with the Cindermaker. "I'm not mad keen on the idea of using this on people, so don't make me do something I don't—*Whuff!*"

Illyria punched him in the gut, driving the air from his lungs. She had crossed from Redlaw's side to Heffernan's, a distance of five metres, in a fraction of a second.

"*Nnghh!*"

She rammed an elbow down onto his trapezius, forcing him to his knees like a hammer pounding in a nail.

"*Uggkk!*"

She chopped him across the back of the neck, and Heffernan toppled headlong onto the balcony's all-weather tiles as though every muscle in his body had suddenly turned to rubber. He lay there, head twitching spasmodically, mouth working like a goldfish's.

Illyria nudged his Cindermaker away from his limp hand with her toe. "Although I doubt he'll be holding it again any time soon."

"What have you done to him?" said Redlaw. "I heard a bone snap."

"Second cervical vertebra. It's called the hangman's fracture."

"Is he paralysed?"

"Probably. But it's not as permanent as it once was. Modern medicine can perform miracles. What? What's that look for? You said not to go easy on him, and he *was* threatening us with a gun..."

Redlaw bent down beside Heffernan, who was making a guttural, terrified moaning sound. "We can't leave him here like this."

"I can. More shadies are coming. They've heard the gunshot. I'm not hanging around to let them take pot shots at me." So saying, she vaulted nimbly over the railing as though it was nothing more than a fence between two fields and vanished down the other side.

Redlaw was torn. Self-preservation wouldn't let him stay. His conscience wouldn't let him leave.

SHADE officers appeared at the entrance to the coffee lounge, taking cover behind the doorway, guns out.

"This man is badly hurt," Redlaw called out. "Make sure he's immobilised and taken to hospital immediately."

Then he straddled the railing once more and surveyed the landing zone. His best bet was the bonnet of a BMW 3-series cabriolet—some banker must be working late; no shady could afford such a car—stationed just below. He launched himself off the balcony, hitting the bonnet feet first with a resounding *boom*, and the BMW's alarm started to warble. He slithered out of the deep dent his impact had created and raced to catch up with Illyria, who was already halfway across the car park.

Shouts from the balcony were swiftly followed by volleys of bullets. Redlaw zigged and zagged between cars, hunching low. The windscreen of a Rover shattered to smithereens just beside his elbow. A new-model Mini Cooper lost a wing mirror as he sped past.

Illyria was at the gate. It was a solidly made thing, several hundredweight of steel, which rolled across the entranceway on a track and was operated by a keycard. She braced one foot against the outer pillar and hauled backward on the bars. The gate squealed, screeched and shuddered as gradually, inch by inch, she heaved it open. Her body trembled with the strain. Her lips drew back from her fangs in a grimace. Bullets, meanwhile, zinged and whined around her.

At last she had made a wide enough gap. "Through!" she exhorted Redlaw. "Get through!"

Redlaw squeezed through, and Illyria followed him. They sprinted down the side-street to the junction at the end. The right turn led back towards SHADE HQ, so Redlaw chose the left, then cut through a cobbled mews to a parallel road. Traffic was almost nonexistent and they had the pavement entirely to themselves. Their footfalls resounded between the buildings. They ran and kept running, past glaringly lit display windows, until Redlaw was so winded he could scarcely catch a breath. Only when they halted, taking refuge in a bus shelter so that he could recover, did he realise that he was holding hands with Illyria. For the last few hundred metres she had been dragging him along.

He stared at their linked hands, then at her face, then at their hands again.

Illyria got the hint and let go.

"We needed to go faster," she said. "Well, *you* did."

"Sorry I... was slowing... you down," Redlaw replied, panting. His shoulder was on fire again, thanks to Illyria tugging so hard on his arm.

"Don't assume we're girlfriend and boyfriend now, just because we've held hands. I won't tell any of the other children at school if you won't."

"Ha... ha."

"I think your Commodore Macarthur might be a tad jealous of me, though, if she knew."

Redlaw scowled in puzzlement.

"You heard how she was talking," said Illyria. "It was like I was stealing a husband from her."

"Husband?" He started to chuckle mirthlessly. It ended up as uncontrollable wheezing.

"What's so funny?"

"Macarthur's hardly the marrying kind," he gasped out.

"She prefers women?"

"I don't know. I don't know if she has a preference at all. The job is her wife, husband, whichever. As it is for most of us."

"Was, you mean. For you."

"Oh, yes," said Redlaw, remembering. He was exiled from SHADE, like Adam from Eden. Forever. "Damn. Yes. Was."

"She really didn't want to lose you. I could see it in her eyes."

"Nevertheless, she has. SHADE has. For better or worse, I'm freelance now. My own boss."

"And what's your first instruction to yourself, as your new boss?"

The bus shelter had a scroller billboard that cycled through three different posters, with a soft mechanical hum: one for toothpaste, one for face cream, then one for Vamp-B-Gone, a garlic-based repellent spray. This came in a canister small enough to fit in a pocket or handbag but was strong enough, if the strap-line was to be believed, to *Stop The Undead Dead In Their Tracks*.

"I don't know," Redlaw admitted. "I'm stymied. I need time to think."

"You know what I used to do in Albania, during the Communist regime, when I needed to think?"

"I'm all ears."

"Caught a bus. Sounds silly, I realise, but you must understand, under that jumped-up little tinsmith Xoxe and then later under Enver Hoxha, there wasn't much freedom. Postwar, the country was rebuilt with Soviet Russian money and everything seemed good for a while, but Hoxha cut us off from the rest of the world and naturally the infrastructure went to pot. The buses were terrible. You were never quite sure where you were going or if you would even get there. That was part of their attraction for me—the randomness, the uncertainty. The state rigidly controlled every aspect of daily life, but the buses were a law unto themselves. You could rely on them only to be unreliable.

"So I'd board one and ride along and wait to find out where it ended up, and in the meantime I'd feel as though, for once, nobody was spying on me and I could allow my guard to drop and my mind to wander. An illusion of independence, perhaps, but it helped. And if the bus broke down—and they often would—I'd step out, and chances were I'd be somewhere unfamiliar, a district of Tirana I'd never visited before, say, or on the shores of the Adriatic, or near one of the huge black lakes, Shkodër or Ohrid. And if a Sigurimi, a secret policeman, should come up and demand to know why I was there, looking out of place, I'd simply say, 'The buses,' and he would nod in understanding and say back, 'Ah yes, the buses.'

"It was on one of those trips that I..." She stopped, reflecting.

"Was turned? Became 'shtrigafied'?"

"Yes. But that's a story for another day. Unless...?"

He didn't take the bait. "So you reckon we should catch the next bus that comes along. That would be the answer."

"It beats just sitting here, and who knows where it might lead? At the very least, it'll give us some breathing space."

As luck would have it, a night bus was approaching. Redlaw would probably have let it go by, rejecting Illyria's suggestion out of sheer perversity. But then he spied a SHADE patrol car some way off up the road, prowling towards them from the opposite direction. That decided it for him. He stuck out a hand and hailed the bus. It pulled up with a loud hissing and huffing, as though grumbling at the delay, and the doors flattened open. Redlaw flashed his SHADE badge at the driver.

"For her and me."

The driver had no way of knowing how meaningless the badge was. She jerked a thumb at the empty bus.

"Make yourselves at home, luv. If you can find a seat." She chuckled.

The SHADE car drove up on the other side, and Redlaw ducked his head. He couldn't be sure, but he thought the car slowed somewhat. When he looked up again, however, it had carried on past and was going its merry way.

"Hold tight, please," the driver called out.

Redlaw and Illyria climbed up to the top deck as the bus lurch-lumbered off along the road.

CHAPTER TWENTY

For all that it had been hastily arranged, the transportation programme—dubbed Operation Moonlight Flit—ran pretty smoothly. Two and a half thousand infantrymen were deployed to marshal the Sunless onto coaches, which then drove convoys up the M1, leaving the motorway just past the junction with the M25 orbital and heading off into the wilds of Hertfordshire. On each coach were a dozen soldiers and half as many shadies, and two dozen Sunless, who sat bewildered and for the most part passive, having no clear idea what was going on. All they knew was that people armed with guns, grenades and religious totems had rounded them up and were taking them somewhere else, somewhere new. They accepted this with equanimity, mainly because there didn't appear to be an alternative.

Of course things didn't go off without the odd hitch. Vampires at the Hounslow SRA took fright and resisted being herded towards the coaches. There were scuffles, gunfire, and casualties on both sides, before calm was eventually restored. At Stoke Newington, an over-the-fence breakout had to be curtailed by SHADE officers. At Kilburn, a nervous young private in the Royal Anglian Regiment got an itchy trigger finger and accidentally shot a Sunless with a Fraxinus round. The dusting caused what had up to that moment been an orderly procedure to dissolve into pandemonium.

On the whole, however, Operation Moonlight Flit could be deemed a success. Vampires were offloaded at Solarville One and filed through the entrance in a long queue. Once inside, they fanned out and started exploring the bounds of their new, permanent home.

WHILE THE TRANSPORTATIONS were getting under way, a movement of another kind took shape.

Throughout the day the committee of the People for the Ethical Treatment of the Sunless had been busy sending out mass emails and texts, as well using social networking sites, putting together a protest rally which would march on Parliament. The Solarville project was clearly prejudicial to Sunless, the equivalent of sweeping them under the carpet, and PETS wanted to make its outrage seen and heard.

Various vaguely likeminded groups got wind of the PETS plan and decided to throw their weight behind it. Anarchists, anti-globalists, anti-capitalists and both equal opportunities and animal welfare activists all came to the conclusion that the plight of vampires was an issue for them too, and invited themselves along on the march. PETS had been expecting perhaps a couple of hundred souls to turn up at the assembly point in Green Park, and so they did, resplendent in their blackest outerwear and purplest undergarments. However, an additional thousand gatecrashers also turned up, all toting placards declaring their opposition to heavy-handed government and planet-plundering multinationals, although a few of them had the courtesy to coin slogans that had at least a tangential relevance to the matter at hand: *Sunless Are An Oppressed Minority*, *Today Vampires—Tomorrow Jews/Blacks/Gays/Roma*, *Who Are The Real Bloodsuckers?* and so on.

Unfortunately, the Stokers also got wind of the rally and mounted a counter rally, a show of support for the Prime Minister's decision to put more than just a fence between vamps and the human population. By spreading the word at pubs, clubs, transport cafés and building sites they managed to drum up a decent turnout of six hundred or so. That included a number of hangers-on who had no strong feelings either way about the Sunless situation but fancied the prospect of a bit of a scrap with some leftie, pro-vamp whingers. They gathered on the other side of the river at Jubilee Gardens, beneath the skeletal gaze of the London Eye.

The PETS protestors set off along the Mall to Trafalgar Square and southward from there down Whitehall. At the head of the procession, six of them carried a coffin, on the side of which was daubed the word SUNLESS RIGHTS in blood-drippy red paint.

At roughly the same time, the Stokers and their sympathisers started trooping down the South Bank and across Westminster Bridge in an unruly rabble. While the PETS ringleaders initiated call-and-response chants through megaphones, the Stokers bandied obscenities, sang football terrace songs and tossed empty lager cans into the gutter. The PETS people waved their placards and banners, the Stokers baseball bats and crowbars.

Both groups were converging on Parliament Square.

SHORTLY AFTER 10PM, Nathaniel Lambourne got a call on his iPhone from Giles Slocock.

He let the call go to voicemail. He did the same with a second call, a minute later. With the third, he picked up and barked, "What the hell is this? What do you want? I'm in a meeting here."

Which he was. In his study at home he was teleconferencing with the two other members of his Solarville consortium, in Boston, and in Tokyo. 10pm was the sweet-spot hour at which all three could communicate simultaneously without it being ridiculously early in the morning or ridiculously late at night for any of them.

"It won't be on the news yet," Slocock said. "I thought you should hear about it as soon as possible, from the horse's mouth."

"Hear about what?" snapped Lambourne. "Your speech sounds slurred. Have you been drinking, Giles?"

"No. Well, yes. A bit."

"I expect your nose isn't any too clean, either."

"So frigging what? Listen, just listen..."

Lambourne made an apologetic gesture to the two screens in front of him. "Gentlemen, bear with me a moment. This is something I have to deal with. Shouldn't take too long."

The man in Boston with the blond blow-dried hair skewed his mouth impatiently, and the man in Tokyo gave a curt bow that was in its way no less indicative of irritation. Both were plutocrats in the same league as Lambourne, both breathing the same rarefied financial air. Each had more money than he could spend in several lifetimes and each took very personally anything that inconvenienced him or did not go precisely according to plan. That they were willing to let Lambourne call a hiatus to the meeting at all was testimony to the fact that he was one of the few people they regarded as an equal. From a lesser being, anyone outside their circle of a hundred or so peers, it would have been an unpardonable insult.

Lambourne took his iPhone onto the verandah outside the study, away from the webcam. The night air was cool, with threads of mist weaving across the lawn. Something rustled beneath the rhododendron bushes just across from the swimming pool, most likely a hedgehog rooting through the undergrowth for beetles and grubs. A fox barked distantly and forlornly in the woods.

"Make this quick," he said to Slocock. "You'd better have a damn good—"

"Wax," said Slocock. "Wax is dead."

"Come again?"

"Maurice Wax. It's all over Parliament. No one's talking about anything else. He didn't turn up for tonight's session. Wasn't answering the phone. Someone was sent round to his flat in Pimlico, one of his staff, some graduate intern, to find out what had become of him. Knocked. No reply. Couldn't get in. The landlord had a master key..."

"Dead how? What happened? Wasn't a sex game gone wrong, was it? Orange in mouth, belt round neck? Bloody stupid way to go."

"Close. Hanged himself."

"No."

"Yes. Dressing-gown cord tied to a light fixture. Poor little intern, he's completely freaked out by it. I just bought him the latest in a succession of stiff drinks. The way he described it to me—your neck stretches, did you know that? Under the weight of your body. To about three times its normal length. Like a piece of chewing gum when you pull it out from your mouth. And the smell. Wax had shat his pants. And his eyeballs—"

"Yes, yes, it wasn't a pretty sight, I get the picture."

"There was a note, too," Slocock said. "Word processed, not a single typo. Typical Wax, neat and tidy to the end. It said—I can't quote it exactly—but something about how he couldn't be a party to the Solarville project any more. His conscience wouldn't take it. As a Jew, as the grandson of people who'd only just managed to avoid getting sent to the death camps, he felt that putting Sunless into a bell jar was unacceptable. He definitely used that term, bell jar. He said it was a step too far. I think there was also some stuff about the relatives of his who did die, Treblinka, Auschwitz, *et cetera*, how he never knew them but felt a debt of obligation to them, felt he'd failed their memory, their legacy... Fuck. He topped himself, Nathaniel. Over this stupid Sunless business."

"Why are you so upset? You can't pretend you liked the man. You couldn't stand him."

"No, I didn't like him. It's just... Fuck. I feel like... I feel like *I* did this to him. I'm the one who pushed him over the edge. Me."

"How? With the threat of blackmail?"

"It couldn't have helped, could it? Added to the pressure he was under."

"He gave his reasons for suicide quite clearly enough. He thought he was complicit in some kind of new Final Solution. That was what was preying on his mind, what drove him to hang himself, not the fear of being exposed as an S and M fetishist."

"But the blackmail forced him into persuading the Prime Minister to go with the Solarville option. He wouldn't have done that if I hadn't... if *you* hadn't made me make him."

"Oh, so it's my fault too, is it?"

"I think you need to be prepared to take some of the blame."

"I never believed I'd hear this sort of thing from you, Giles," Lambourne said, lowering his voice but upping the anger a notch. "I thought you were made of sterner stuff."

"A man is dead, Nathaniel. A man whose wife is on her way down from Newcastle right now to view his corpse. Whose two kids are going to wake up tomorrow fatherless."

"Don't be so fucking maudlin. My father died when I was eleven and I couldn't have been gladder. I didn't have to run around scared all the time of him belting me. Stumbling drunkenly at the top of the stairs and cracking his head open at the bottom was the biggest favour he ever did me and my mother."

Lambourne had lived with this version of events for so long that he had almost convinced himself it was the truth. His father had been drunk at the time of his death, yes, but hadn't stumbled down the stairs so much as been shoved, with all the strength that the arms of a bruised and terrified eleven-year-old boy could muster.

"I've hurt people before," Slocock said. "I've screwed people over. Plenty of times. But I've never been responsible for someone's death."

"Well, get over it. Shit happens. If you want to get ahead in the world, this is the sort of thing you have to be ready to accept."

"I'm not sure I can accept it."

"You're going to have to try. Otherwise you're of no further use to me."

"I don't know if I want to be of any use to you any more."

"That's up to you," said Lambourne. "No skin off my nose. You won't be impossible to replace. You're not the only MP I have on a leash. What you have to consider is what you stand to lose by bailing out. Me, I stand to lose nothing if you do, but you, with all your debts, your outgoings, you could have a very rocky road ahead. You're relying on that position with Dep Chem to secure your future. Throw it away, by all means. Just don't come running to me when your finances fall apart and the bailiffs start knocking at the door. It can happen far more quickly than you realise, you know."

He could hear, from the breathing on the other end of the line, how Slocock was turning it all over in his mind. He could hear how hard the younger man was thinking.

"Call me in an hour," he said, "when you've had time to reflect and calm down a little. Then we'll discuss this again. That's if you still want in. If you don't, don't bother calling at all, and have a nice life."

He cut the connection and returned indoors.

"All sorted," he said into the webcam.

"Nothing serious, I hope?" said Tokyo.

"Nothing at all serious, Yukinobu. An employee with

an item of information for me. There's been a minor mishap, it shouldn't inconvenience us in any way."

"What kind of mishap?" Boston asked.

"Wax, the Sunless Affairs chap in Parliament, is dead."

"A politician? No big deal, then."

"Couldn't have put it better myself, Howard. In a way it's actually a bonus. He had been quite obstructive, 'til I leaned on him. Now he's out of the way, that's a loose end tied up. One less bleeding-heart liberal in the world. One less dandelion in the bowling green in need of uprooting."

"I prefer to stamp on my dandelions," said the Bostonian, grinning whitely.

"Weed killer for me," said the Japanese with a surprisingly girlish titter.

All three men enjoyed a moment in which to dwell on their common ruthlessness and the impunity that their stratospheric wealth afforded them. It was like belonging to the most exclusive club in the world, whose only rule was that you could do exactly as you pleased.

"So anyway, back to business," said Lambourne. "We have a Solarville deal in place, or as near as makes no difference. The PM's raiding the public purse to bring all fifteen of them on-stream within in a space of three years. Baseline projection sees us netting between four and five hundred mill."

"Dollars? Sterling?" said the Bostonian.

"Sterling. Each."

"Cool."

"Then, when they're a proven success, we can start rolling out the system across mainland Europe. I've already had expressions of interest from Germany and

Italy, and what sounds like an overture of partnership from Russia, though you can never quite tell with those damn oligarchs. Usually when they're enquiring about a deal, they're trying to figure out a way of ripping you off and cutting you out."

"I thought the Russians didn't have a Sunless problem," said the Japanese.

"They're worried they might. There's been some overspill across the Caucasus and they'd like to be ready in case the trickle turns into a flood. It's the same in the States, isn't it, Howard?"

"Hell, yes. There's not more than about four hundred vampires on our soil, that we know about, and the federal government's squawking around like Chicken Little, thinking the sky's falling on our heads. That's Americans for you—and I speak as a proud patriot. We sure know how to stir ourselves up into a panic. Anything that looks like it's going to impinge on life, liberty and the pursuit of happiness gets us frothing at the chops and reaching for the muskets. I could talk the President into buying a hundred Solarvilles right now and nobody'd turn a hair."

"We'll hold fire on that for the time being," said Lambourne. "Wouldn't want to overextend ourselves. Too much too soon is never good when you're growing a new brand. Besides, you've got our Porphyrian initiative in the pipeline. It'll suit the North American market better than Solarville, so we should try to avoid an overlap there. Same goes for you, Yukinobu, and your Shinobi Eternal. Horses for courses, eh?"

The trick to a good consortium was for each member to have his own discrete administrative sphere which he ran autonomously but with oversight from the other members. Then all felt in control, hands on the reins, while being mutually beholden, bound together by scrutiny as well as a share of the proceeds. J. Howard Farthingale III was in charge of operations in the Americas, Yukinobu Uona's territory was the Far East, while Lambourne claimed the bit in the middle. They had divided the world three ways. It was their very own block of Neapolitan ice cream.

"In a spirit of candour," Lambourne went on, "I feel bound to mention that a tiny fly has alighted in the ointment."

Frowns from the other two of the triumvirate.

"Again, like Wax, it's nothing serious," he hurried on. "Measures have been put into effect to neutralise the problem."

"What is it?" said Farthingale.

"Someone has twigged to the vasopressin augmentation. A SHADE officer, man name of John Redlaw. He developed suspicions about BovPlas and in the end stole a sample of blood to have it analysed."

"Stole!"

"It's not as bad as it sounds. He knows enough to have figured out what we've been up to. Counter to that, he's in no position to use that knowledge effectively against us. Latest reports have him being taken into custody by his own people. SHADE will hold him overnight, and by tomorrow it'll be too late and he'll be an irrelevance."

"Why so?" asked Uona.

"Because we've already stopped adding the vasopressin. It's done its job, achieved everything it was intended to. We don't need it any longer. As of this evening, all blood leaving the Watford plant is as pure as when it was running through the cows' veins."

"But this Redlaw guy still knows what he knows," Farthingale pointed out. "Surely we need to do something to fix that."

"By all accounts, he's become a loose cannon," said Lambourne. "Used to be SHADE's blue-eyed boy, but then had some kind of breakdown, failure of nerve, rush of blood to the head, something like that. Should he try and make life awkward for us—go to the media or some such—it shouldn't be too difficult to portray him as a crackpot, a fantasist who's put two and two together and come up with five. Dep Chem's publicity department is skilled at smearing anyone who's come gunning for the company. They've had years of experience discrediting healthcare quacks, investigative reporters, eco-mentalists and the like."

"But if he's with SHADE, won't that give him credence if he starts accusing us?"

"He isn't any more. He's had his licence revoked or whatever it is they do to shadies—hang up their stakes? He's a high flyer who's fallen to earth with a bump, a loser in a game he can't win, and I really don't think he need detain us further."

"Still," said Uona, "it might be as well to dispose of *all* the evidence, Nathaniel, if you see my meaning. Just in case."

"You're referring to Subject V, I presume."

"I am indeed. Surely he's outlived his usefulness by now. Frankly I'm baffled why you've insisted on keeping him at all, so long after you finished with him."

"I'm with Yukinobu," said Farthingale. "What's the point of hanging on to Subject V? He's not doing anyone any good, just chained up there, mouldering away. Now's the time."

"Get rid of V?" mused Lambourne. It wasn't that the thought had never occurred to him. He just disliked anything going to waste or throwing an asset away before he was absolutely certain he didn't need it any more. "I could, I suppose."

"No 'could' about it," said Farthingale. "He's got to go."

"I agree," said Uona. "I believe Howard would call it 'covering our asses.'"

"Damn straight I would. That's two votes for, Nathaniel, and being as this is a democracy, or as close to one as the three of us would ever care to get, that makes it a done deal. You have to terminate Subject V, no ifs, ands or buts, soon as you can."

LAMBOURNE, POWERFUL RECHARGEABLE SureFire torch in hand, exited the house and crossed the grounds of his estate to the old observatory. He did not like anyone telling him what to do. Equally, he understood that his consortium partners' recommendations made sense. Logic dictated that Subject V was surplus to requirements. So it must be.

The torch's 2,300-lumen beam lit the mist coruscatingly, picking out the dewdrops spangling the grass and, just briefly, the flash of a rabbit's eyes as the animal took fright and helter-skeltered into the shrubbery.

The observatory perched on a hilltop like a huge snub-nosed bullet, silhouetted against the dark brilliance of the sky. The previous owner of the mansion but one, a shipping tycoon, was a keen amateur astronomer who had discovered not one but two very distant objects, a moon and an asteroid, both now named after him.

The subsequent owner was a prog rock god, a 'seventies icon, who'd also been into star-gazing. The observatory, in fact, had been a key reason for his purchasing the house. However, his interest in the wonders of the cosmos waned, along with his record sales and financial fortunes, and he was eventually forced to sell first the twenty-eight-inch refracting telescope, then the entire property, in order to meet a swingeing tax demand.

A desperate vendor is a biddable vendor, and Lambourne had purchased the mansion at a knockdown price from the maestro of the twenty-minute live keyboard solo. He hadn't initially been able to find a use for the shell of the observatory and so had let the building crumble until it was little more than a hollow folly, its cracked stonemasonry shrouded with ivy. Then, two years back, he had had it shored up and renovated to new specifications.

The door was secured by a lock keyed to Lambourne's biometric profile. Look, touch, speak, and he was in.

A pit had been excavated deep into the observatory's foundations, and a monitoring gallery ran round the rim. Above, the hemispherical shape of the roof had been kept, but the original had been replaced by one composed of hexagonal panes of glass, a dwarf replica of the dome over Solarville. The construction workers responsible for these alterations had been told they were making a special hothouse intended for large, exotic specimens of rainforest plant life.

On entering, Lambourne quickly fitted a charcoal-filter mask over his nose and mouth to screen out the noxious stench from below. Extractor fans ran twenty-four-seven to clear the air in here, but their work was cut out for them. He went to the parapet at the centre of the gallery, on which four machine guns were mounted equidistantly, all aimed downwards and loaded with belt-fed Fraxinus rounds. Their firing mechanisms were hooked up to a motion sensor field located a metre below the parapet's rim. If the field's infrared meniscus was broken, the guns would be tripped. Once operational, each swivelled automatically, traversing back and forth through a forty-five-degree arc. When shooting began there would, for the occupant of the pit, be simply no escaping the crisscrossing streams of ash-wood bullets.

Down in the pit, something stirred.

"Vlad," said Lambourne softly.

Heavy chains clanked.

"Vla-a-ad."

A hoarse, grunting moan and a questing snuffle. From the shadows of the pit, two great red eyes suddenly shone.

Lambourne pressed a switch to disable the motion sensor field. Then he fetched a blood pouch from a fridge and tossed it over the gallery parapet. Barely had it landed before the creature in the pit dived on it, tore open the plastic and guzzled the contents.

A word came up, thickly uttered, scarcely recognisable.

"More."

"More, Vlad? Oh well, don't see why not."

Lambourne threw down a second pouch and, for the hell of it, a third. The blood was pure, unadulterated. The time for dispensing the other kind of blood, blood with a generous lacing of vasopressin, was long past.

The thing called Vlad consumed each pouch in one go, with lip-smacking gusto. Then he sank back onto the floor of the pit, the links of the chains settling with low metallic thuds.

"Go?" Vlad asked, longingly, plaintively. "Vlad go now?"

"No," Lambourne replied. He was used to this importuning. "No going. Vlad stay."

"Vlad want... free. Want... out."

"Not now. Maybe soon."

"Maybe?"

"Maybe."

Vlad heaved a sigh that Lambourne would have said came from the soul, if the undead had souls—if, for that matter, he'd believed in such things. He gazed down a little longer at the massive, misshapen figure hunkered amid his own filth, studying the hairless orb of skull, the body covered with swollen veins like vines, the musculature that spoke of a terrific, apelike strength. He had created this through feeding and nurturing. He had taken the raw clay of a Sunless and moulded it into something even more monstrous.

Vlad, as Subject V, had been the test bed for the results of the hormone on the Sunless metabolism and physiology. Long after it had been proven that vasopressin markedly increased aggression and fostered addiction, however, Lambourne had continued to dose the creature with it on a daily basis, at increasing levels of potency. He had wanted to see if there were long-term, even permanent effects. With the same cold, clinical curiosity that drives a child to dismember a beetle, he had extended the experiment, taking it to extremes, unhesitatingly.

The outcome was grotesque but satisfying. Amplified body mass, accompanied by a reduction in higher cerebral cortical functions. The outer Vlad grew while the inner Vlad shrank. Vlad had become both more and less.

Lambourne cast a glance up to the glass dome capping the observatory. It was dark and semi-opaque; the moon glimmered weakly through, but the stars were completely occluded. This was a second experiment that had been conducted on Vlad, in parallel with the first, a practical proof of the computer-model estimates of the levels of sunlight a vampire could withstand.

So, all this was to come to an end. Vlad's purpose had been served. Tomorrow morning, Lambourne would carry out a swift euthanasia, leaving nothing to show for months of painstaking dedication and application but a pile of ashes.

He could trip the guns, although they were primarily there for defence and deterrence. Another means of disposing of Vlad was open to Lambourne, however, and this was the one he would use when the time came. It was altogether quieter and more elegant, and perhaps also more humane.

Humane?

Lambourne was surprised at himself. Was he getting sentimental in his old age? He knew that vivisectionists could grow fond of the macaques and rhesus monkeys in their laboratories, even as they inflicted all sorts of suffering and indignity on them. The little primates represented progress and discovery, as well as, of course, potential profit. Their pain benefited the people who performed their scientific inquisition on them. They were appealing little martyrs, fellow travellers on the journey towards enlightenment and revenue.

Perhaps, then, it was inevitable that he had developed a kind of mild affection for Vlad. He'd nicknamed the creature, hadn't he? "Subject V" hadn't been enough for him, so he'd come up, on a whim, with something more colloquial. Vlad himself now believed this to be his identity. Whatever he might have once been called, he had forgotten. "Vlad" was what he was. "Vlad" was as much as he needed to know about himself.

All was quiet down in the pit. The condemned Vlad had eaten a hearty meal and, full-bellied, fallen asleep. His breathing was slow and stertorous.

With dawn would come the hour of his execution. Perhaps he would still be asleep when it happened. Then he might not feel a thing.

CHAPTER
TWENTY-ONE

THE NIGHT BUS swaggered like some boozy overweight marchioness through the streets of west London, past icy Georgian townhouse façades and frowning Victorian terraces. It skirted the darkness of Hyde Park, circumnavigated Marble Arch, and trundled down Park Lane. Throughout its itinerary, it halted at scheduled stops, even though nobody was there to climb aboard.

As they travelled, Redlaw noticed Illyria becoming subdued beside him, her gaze introverting. Her skin seemed to have got paler, if that was possible, and he detected a slight tremor in her hands.

His own hand went stealthily to the handle of one of the stakes on his vest.

"Please don't," Illyria said. "You won't be needing it."

"You're thirsty, aren't you? When was the last time you fed?"

"I don't know. Not long ago. I caught a rat in that pub cellar."

"A rat. That's not much."

"I realise that. You'd be surprised how little a shtriga can survive on. I'm often surprised myself. Even so..."

"Can you control it?"

"The thirst? Am I going to start chomping on your neck, that's what you're asking?"

"I'm more concerned about the driver. I can look after myself."

Illyria rolled her eyes. "Redlaw, you don't seem to realise—or else you're being deliberately thick-skulled—but I am not what you think I am. It's not just that a shtriga is to a regular vampire as a wolf is to a hyena. I am more ethical, more human, than you give me credit for, or at least I'm trying to be. I'm somewhat offended that you haven't noticed. Maybe you have but you can't bring yourself to say so. Would it hurt you to show some appreciation sometime? You've not even thanked me for coming to your rescue. A woman could get the impression she's being taken for granted."

For a moment, Redlaw didn't answer. "It all happened so fast," he eventually said. "And I suppose I didn't feel that I *should* be escaping from HQ. I'd resigned myself to the idea that I deserved to be a prisoner. I even felt I was kidding myself I could ever get Lambourne.

"And then you came for me. You came, and it completely changed my perspective. Opened up a new, unexpected avenue. Yanked me out of the dead end of despair I was in."

"You're welcome."

"And you'll forgive me if I haven't realised you're on your best behaviour with me, only I've nothing to compare it to. You're the only shtriga I've met."

"Apology accepted. Have you always had such a

problem opening up to others?"

"I'm a solitary man."

"Just you and the Lord, fighting the good fight together."

"Something like that. He's the only one I know I can count on—and even Him I'm not sure about these days."

"Crisis of faith?"

Redlaw brushed his fingertips unconsciously over his crucifix. "A flat tyre on the road to redemption. God doesn't seem to be paying me the attention I think I deserve. You dedicate yourself to someone, you expect it to be reciprocated."

"Like an one-sided love affair. You give the other person your all and get nothing in return."

"Worse—abuse."

"Ah, *that* kind of relationship. Isn't the best advice to walk away?"

"Hard to walk away from an all-seeing deity. Where do you go?"

"Into the arms of His Adversary?" Illyria suggested, jokingly. "That's the usual place."

"I've entered into a pact with one of Satan's minions, haven't I? So I daresay I'm halfway there."

"Satan's minion? Me? I thought we were past all that twaddle."

"I'm not being serious."

"Oh. It's so hard to tell with you. I must admit, for a while after I was turned, I did fear I was damned, Hell-bound. My upbringing was stalwartly Orthodox, and although I'd rebelled against that, I hadn't shaken off the shackles fully. I let myself believe that becoming a shtriga meant I had forfeited my mortal soul. It took a long time for me to come to terms with what I was."

"You said you were attacked on one of your aimless Albanian bus rides?"

"I wouldn't say 'attacked,' exactly," said Illyria. "And don't think I don't see what you're doing."

"What am I doing?"

"Getting me to talk so as to distract myself from my thirst. Really, I can hold out."

"You don't think I'm just curious? Interested to know?"

She eyed him. "Well, you may be. Perhaps at some level you're not prepared to admit to."

"Go on, then. You weren't attacked, but..."

She looked out of the window at the passing city. The bus was at that moment rolling alongside the gardens of Buckingham Palace. The high brick wall was strung with barbed wire, supplemented with a palisade of outward-jutting ash stakes. Sourced, in accordance with royal wishes, from a sustainably managed forest.

"I met him in the seaside town of Vlorë," she said, "the man who created me. I'd done a lot in my life before then. I had a privileged, some would say sheltered upbringing in Korçë, capital of the south of the country: my father was a doctor, my mother a schoolteacher with some inherited wealth. All very prosperous and educated and God-fearing and respectable. I studied music at university. My ambition was to become a concert pianist. I even spent a year at Oxford before the war, and learned English."

"Old bean."

"Old bean. But for all that, I was still quite a naïve creature, for a woman in her early thirties. I'd never had a proper boyfriend, a really passionate affair. The odd fling, including one with the son of a British aristocrat while I was over here, but nothing serious. I was too busy being self-determining and free. The middle of the last century was when women truly began to come into their own, and I was making the most of it. Albania itself was enjoying a new-found independence after half a millennium of Ottoman rule. Liberation was in the air, like the smell of spring, a determination never to be oppressed again. We fought off Mussolini, then Nazi Germany. We even got Stalin off our backs eventually, although we immediately gave ourselves over to Communist China instead, and for years afterwards... But you don't want a history lesson."

"Where does Norman Wisdom fit in? That's what I'd like to know."

"That's really all you can think of when it comes to Albania?" Illyria huffed. "A small but proud nation? Our love for imbecilic little Mr Pitkin?"

"It's just one of those cultural head-scratchers, like the French and Jerry Lewis. Carry on."

"All right. In Vlorë, where I fetched up one evening more or less by accident, I met a man in a bar. I was in the mood for another of my brief liaisons, a night or two of uncomplicated fun. It was 1953. The year Hillary conquered Everest. The year of your Queen's coronation. Dear Lord, nearly half a century ago. He was... quite beautiful. Didn't smile much. Spoke without fully opening his mouth, a trick I have not fully learned to copy. But how smitten I was! Thunderstruck. He was a Tosk like me, a southerner. We shared the same dialect and the same cordial dislike of anyone from the north of the Shkumbin river, those backwoods, backwards Ghegs. He bought me a shot of *rakia*. One shot turned somehow into four. I became giddy—not just from the alcohol—and chose not to notice that he himself wasn't drinking. He had such penetrating dark eyes. We went outside to take the night air. It was warm. We promenaded along the shoreline, arm in arm, my head on his shoulder. The moon was full and high and its light on the water was an expanse of pure shimmering silver."

She sighed, almost a parody of wistfulness.

"It still haunts me, the memory of that night. It had such promise, the potential to be so magical. Folk music spilled out of a restaurant, a violin scratching on top, a *lahutë* plunking away beneath, and we paused to listen. Further from the centre of town we heard the gasps of a couple making love, echoing from an upstairs window, and we paused to listen to that too. And then just the shush of water on sand, the Adriatic rubbing against the coast like a contented cat. I thought we were going to make love on the beach, in a secluded cove somewhere. I thought that was the plan."

"You can spare me the grisly details," said Redlaw.

"Instead we went uphill, and in the quietness of a pine grove he suddenly thrust me against a tree and opened his mouth wide and I was ready for the kiss, and then I saw his teeth, his fangs, and they shone so whitely in the moonlight, and I tried to scream..."

"Again, you can spare me the details."

"It was over quickly, anyway. It hurt—it was unimaginable agony—but pain is so hard to remember, isn't it? Even if you try. What I recall most is him lowering my body to the ground as he drank from me. I recall the smell of pine needles and soil beneath me, mingling with the tang of the sea air and the tang of my blood as it poured out, as he sucked it up in huge, wet gulps. The sound of his lips smacking, his tongue working—it reminded me of my father's old wolfhound Ari slurping water from his bowl. And then, as my consciousness faded, his final, parting words to me. 'This is an honour,' he said. 'Only the most accomplished and deserving earn this. You have been blessed. You have been made special.' It was months before I grasped fully what he'd meant."

The bus rounded Bressenden Place, turning left onto Victoria Street, eastbound.

"Months...?" Redlaw prompted.

"Months in which I lived like a hunted thing up in the hills above Vlorë, in what's now the Llogara national park, preying on rabbits and deer. I found a cave and called it home and only ventured out of it to catch food. Instinctively I knew sunlight was to be shunned. My hearing, my vision, my sense of smell—everything had amplified to the extent that I felt I might go mad. It was like leaving a darkened soundproofed room and walking straight out onto a concert hall stage where the spotlights are dazzling and the orchestra is in full swing. I was stunned and dazed, reeling from the immenseness of it all. Gradually I pieced together what had been done to me, what I had become. It appalled me. What was this 'honour' that was supposed to have been bestowed on me? It was surely a curse. I was a vampire. I would never again walk in the daylight, never know a normal life. I did not dare return to my family. What if my parents spat on me and spurned me? What if they tried to have me killed? Worse, what if I tried to kill them? There were times when I was so miserable, I came close to ending it all. I would wait in the mouth of my cave for dawn, but always retreat into the shadows just before the sun rose."

"What stopped you?"

"Cowardice, I would have to say. But also the growing awareness that actually I hadn't been abased as I thought—I'd been improved. My understanding of vampires came from legend, the stories that persisted in Mediterranean folklore about shambling bestial bloodsuckers, inhuman monsters. Yet clearly I was not that, and neither had been the man who made me this way. He had been urbane, handsome, mesmerising. I was less a victim, more a recruit. That's why I can't claim to have been *attacked* by him. It was more as if I had been specially selected. What confirmed it for me was meeting an actual vampire up in the hills. Our paths crossed when we were both stalking the same stray sheep. I outran him easily; out-hunted him. He couldn't come near what I could do. I caught and slaughtered the sheep, and when he swooped on me hoping to poach my kill, I repelled him with ease."

"I suspect he didn't survive the encounter."

"No, he jolly well did not," said Illyria with some zest. "I knew then for sure that I was not simply a vampire. I was something rare and exceptional. I felt ready to rejoin humanity, but on my terms. I became a wanderer, a night traveller. I roamed not just around Albania but throughout Europe, doing whatever work I could find, mostly playing piano in restaurants and cocktail lounges, stealing sometimes when I had to, feeding only off animals, never people."

"Did you ever run into him again? Your creator?"

"Once. Back in Albania, at the port of Durrës. He was travelling one way, I the other. Ships in the night—almost literally."

"How did it go?"

"Well. Enough time had passed that any resentment I might have had was gone. I no longer felt I had been misled, betrayed. We chatted like old flames who've got over the acrimony of their breakup and are content as friends. I knew by then, from poring over library books, what a shtriga was, but he filled in gaps in my understanding. The shtriga bloodline goes back thousands of years, to the earliest times, the dim pre-dawn when civilisation was just emerging from the primitive darkness. It is the purest form of vampirism, the stem from which ordinary vampires are merely a corrupt offshoot, and the Balkan region, ancient Albania specifically, was its point of origin, where it first took root. A shtriga turns only those he or she believes to be truly worthy. That's why we are so dashed few. Ordinary vampires can proliferate like fleas, and will, given half a chance, but the shtriga finds perhaps one person in every century to pass the priceless gift on to. Usually it's a fellow Albanian—we like to keep it in the family, as it were."

"Have you?"

"Passed it on? No, not yet. There hasn't been anyone I felt fit the bill. There've been a few who have come close. There's one man I'd even say met all the criteria... but you wouldn't be interested, would you?"

"Certainly not!" Redlaw exclaimed. "What do you take me for?"

"You have to want it, you see. Even if you don't know you do. I did, that night in Vlorë. I was at least a half-willing victim. At some subconscious level I realised my maker was more than he appeared, that his elegance and eloquence masked some dangerous secret. That was part of the thrill for me, why I found him so alluring. I let him have me, with scant regard for the consequences."

"Don't even think of trying any of that stuff with me."

"I get it, Redlaw. No need to keep harping on. I only mentioned you as a possible candidate because it is a shtriga's responsibility, among other things, to look after vampires. And that's what you used to do, isn't it? That's what a shady's job is, in essence."

"You look after vampires?" Redlaw said. "I thought you enslave them. Bend them to your will. Make them your docile little houseboys."

"Same difference. I keep them in check. An age-old duty. We of the shtriga line are the stern elder siblings, the babysitters, the shepherds minding the flock. We see lesser vampires as *us*, with the willpower and self-discipline stripped out. Someone has to stop them running wild, and that someone is the shtriga. If not for the actions of my kind, this world would long ago have become a vampire planet, infested with them, overrun."

"It's starting to get that way now. You lot obviously haven't been keeping your eye on the ball."

Illyria nodded, gravely. "Possibly we have become too discriminating in our choices, too picky for our own good. There aren't enough of us to go around. In fact, you see, the vampire population explosion has been going on longer than you think. It dates back to the war. Europe in turmoil was the perfect Petri dish for vampires to flourish in. Death and mayhem all across the continent. Entire countries transformed into killing fields. That was the catalyst for a surge in vampire numbers. There was easy human prey everywhere, and their depredations could go unnoticed amid the mass slaughter. They were turning people left, right and centre. After the armistice, every shtriga did what he or she could to thin the herd, and for a while we had some success. But still there were just too many. By the late 'eighties they were spreading out from their usual habitats—the Balkans, the Baltic states, *Mitteleuropa*—faster than they could be curbed. I myself had joined the effort by then, but it was clear we were fighting a losing battle. We weren't as organised as we could have been—should have been. It was like trying to contain a house fire with not enough hoses and nobody saying where to direct them. Eventually it got beyond our power to control. That's when humans started taking matters into their own hands."

"We had no choice."

"But we've kept at it too. We haven't given up. At the Hackney SRA, I was doing what I could to maintain order. Livingstone Heights was intended to be a model for others in the SRA to follow. Hundreds of vampires are beyond my ability to keep in check, but a few dozen I can, and that at least is a few dozen who definitely wouldn't be troubling the human population outside. I hoped the rest might learn by emulation. That was no doubt optimistic of me."

"No doubt."

"But it was the best I could do. So I've been working within your system, secretly, anonymously, striving to achieve the same goal as SHADE. And now this blasted Nathaniel Lambourne comes along and makes a mockery of it all. I could... Well, I think you can imagine what I'd like to do to him."

"Join the queue," said Redlaw.

"We have a saying in Albania, about those we hate. 'Let's fart up their nose.' Lambourne deserves that and a whole lot worse."

The bus had passed Westminster Cathedral and New Scotland Yard and was approaching Parliament Square. Here it began to slow, and all at once braked sharply and came to a complete stop.

Redlaw, peering ahead through the upper deck's front windows, whistled in disbelief.

"What the hell's going on there?"

CHAPTER
TWENTY-TWO

WHAT WAS GOING on was the inevitable outcome of one group of agitators meeting another group of agitators, as ideologically and sociologically antithetical as it was possible to be. Opposites had come together, but if there was any attraction it was of the mutual-loathing kind.

The PETS protestors arrived in the square first. The "pallbearers" at the front laid their coffin down at the foot of the statue of Winston Churchill. The rest gathered on the lawn facing the Houses of Parliament and quickly set about voicing their opposition to Solarville, the Prime Minister and Nathaniel Lambourne. With almost no traffic in the vicinity, the sound of their chants carried far.

Police soon appeared. They had been given no advance notification of the march, making it an unlawful assembly. And on Parliament's very doorstep. Through megaphones, officers instructed the PETS people to disperse.

The response from the dark-clad, pale-skinned crowd was to raise the volume. Placards were waved more emphatically than ever.

"Free the vamps!" went the cry. "Free the vamps! Free the vamps!"

Riot squads were mobilised, but by the time they had suited up and reached the scene, it was too late. The Stokers had already put in an appearance and the situation had become explosive.

The Stokers and their assorted hangers-on swept down Bridge Street like some thuggish tsunami. They burst onto Parliament Square at a run, charging headlong into the throng of PETS protestors. With little hesitation, they put the weapons they had brought with them to use. They were outnumbered by a ratio of two to one, but the baseball bats and crowbars evened those odds somewhat. The solid mass of PETS people broke apart as the Stokers drove into them in a rough wedge formation. All at once men and women in black were scattering in every direction, while skinheads in trainers and sportswear bludgeoned and battered.

Recovering from the initial shock of the attack, the PETS protestors regrouped and retaliated. The lengths of two-by-four to which their placards were attached were pressed into service as cudgels and pikestaffs. The coffin was unlidded to reveal a stash of clubs, knives, coshes, a couple of World War II bayonets, even a regimental sabre. Opposition had been anticipated.

Suddenly the Stokers were rivalled blow for blow. Everywhere, vampire lover and vampire hater clashed and clashed again, snarling, spitting, swearing. Running battles were fought on the lawn and in the road and on the pavement beside the railings around Parliament. The police who were present got out of the way, wisely. Coming between two brawling, weapon-brandishing mobs was not in their job remit. Let the Territorial Support Group boys with the shields and the training do that.

Blood, inevitably, flowed. A girl dressed equally well for her wedding or her funeral fell to the ground screaming, one eyeball bulging wrongly from its socket. A man in a Manchester United away-strip shirt staggered off with his arm held out, staring at a lump of flesh so broken and mangled he could barely recognise it as his own hand. A cadaverous creature in top hat and tails crawled on all fours gathering up lost teeth, two of which were the crowns that turned his upper canines into fake fangs. A skinny wretch with sovereign rings and jail tattoos tried repeatedly to smooth a flap of torn skin back onto his scalp, his efforts having a kind of pathetic patience to them, as if he was having difficulty with a stray lock of hair.

The tide of combat surged to and fro, occasionally spilling over onto the streets around the square. For a time, neither side seemed to be winning. It was all just universal mayhem and mêlée, weapons rising and falling, fists flying, strife as far as the eye could see.

Gradually, though, it became apparent that the Stokers were gaining the upper hand. Their opponents simply weren't a match when it came to naked aggression. Many of the Stokers were ex-servicemen, experienced football hooligans or former jailbirds with convictions for assault and GBH. They came from a world where violence was commonplace, and had no qualms about inviting others to join them in it and demonstrating how it worked.

The worst of the fighting was over by the time the riot police turned up. That didn't prevent them piling out of their paddywagons and starting to dispense justice straight away with their batons. Consequently, just as things had begun quietening down, trouble flared again, as a new front was opened up.

It was at this point that the night bus carrying Redlaw and Illyria came to a halt in Broad Sanctuary just west of the square, midway between the Queen Elizabeth II Conference Centre and the tremendous Gothic bulk of the Collegiate Church of St Peter at Westminster, better known as Westminster Abbey.

REDLAW TOOK IN the situation at a glance. Three clearly distinguishable forces were at loggerheads with one another. It was like watching three tribes, armed only with the most basic of weapons, vying for supremacy on some primeval plain—an ancient conflict brought to stark, bloody life in the heart of modern London.

"Well, brilliant idea," he said to Illyria. "'Let's get on a bus, see where it takes us.' Right into a massive great punch-up is where."

"Stop whining, Redlaw. We're in here, they're out there. We can't possibly get caught up in it."

"Don't you believe it." Redlaw headed down the staircase to the lower deck.

"Where are you going?"

"To tell the driver to turn us around and go back the way we came."

The driver flatly refused the request. "Can't."

"Why not?"

"It isn't the route. I'm round the square then down Millbank. That's the route. Can't deviate from it."

"But there's people fighting. Use your eyes. Look at

the blood. Look at that man sitting in the gutter over there with his face gashed open. That woman limping."

"So? Nothing's actually happening on my vehicle, is it? So I'll wait here 'til it all simmers down, then drive on. You just go back to your seat, luv. Shouldn't be standing here talking to me anyway. It's against regulations."

"Oh for—!"

"Redlaw," said Illyria, who had followed him down. "If you're so deuced bothered about it, let's just get off. We'll carry on on foot."

"Can't let you out," said the driver. "That's also against regulations. We're not at a stop."

"Open the door," Illyria demanded.

"No." The driver folded her arms beneath her bosom, looking priggish and adamant. To her, working for Transport For London wasn't just employment, it was a vocation. She was proud to be part of a service that met its targets and delivered on its promises, come what may—or at least tried its best to. That was why she was out driving—keeping up her end of the contract between journey provider and passenger—when many of her colleagues had declined to turn up for work at the depot this evening.

"Don't be so obstinate, woman," Illyria told her. "I can break the door open if I like."

"That would be criminal damage, resulting in prosecution and a fine, if convicted."

"I can break you open too."

"Transport For London staff have a right to work without fear of physical or verbal intimidation. Says so on that notice up there. See? So lay one finger on me, missy, and you'll—"

"Dammit."

This from Redlaw, who had spotted something out of the rear window.

"What?" said Illyria, looking. "Ah, yes. Dammit."

A SHADE patrol car was approaching from behind. The glare of its headlights made the two occupants difficult to identify, but Redlaw thought he recognised at least one of the silhouetted figures.

Khalid.

"Let's move. Now!" He hammered on the bus's central door. "Open up. Come on."

"No way," said the driver. "Shout at me all you like, but until we're at a stop that door stays shut. It's a health and safety issue."

"Don't say I didn't warn you," Illyria said to her. Then to Redlaw: "Stand back."

Grasping two poles to brace herself, Illyria gave the door a hearty kick, buckling it. Another kick and its windows shattered. A third kick and both halves of the door splayed outwards at skewed angles.

"Hoy!" the driver yelled indignantly. "This is all being recorded on CCTV, you know. I'll see you in court."

A few more kicks and Illyria had created an aperture wide enough to slide out through sideways.

However, the patrol car put paid to that plan by pulling up directly adjacent to the bus. Khalid was in the driving seat, and his window was gliding down and his Cindermaker was coming up.

"Back!" Redlaw cried out as a Fraxinus round entered through the doorway and exited through a window on the other side.

Illyria was already in motion. Ducking low, she raced along the bus to the rear. Bullets punched holes in the bus's bodywork, chasing her up the aisle. Khalid knew what she was. Macarthur had pegged her as some form of vampire, meaning SHADE officers had *carte blanche* to dust her on sight.

Redlaw loosed off a couple of shots at the patrol car, forcing Khalid and his fellow officer—Qureshi—to take cover. He didn't much care whether he hit them or not. Then he darted up the aisle after Illyria.

"Down!" he yelled. She flattened herself on the floor and he took out the rear window with a single bullet. Nuggets of safety glass showered everywhere. Meanwhile the bus driver cowered in her seat, shrieking something about her bus, vandalism, she'd be suing SHADE for trauma, personal injury, you name it.

Redlaw scrambled through the hollowed window, tearing his coat sleeve on one of the shards that fringed the frame like the tatters of a spider web. Illyria leapt nimbly out and landed beside him. Khalid and Qureshi were both exiting the patrol car.

"This way." Redlaw headed round the pavement side of the bus. He pulled Illyria by the wrist to make sure she came with him. They were going in the direction of Parliament Square and the fighting.

"Into the thick of that?" Illyria said. "Why not away from?"

"We'll be an open target out on the road. They won't shoot at us in the midst of all those people. Plus, I've had an idea."

"About time too."

Within seconds, they were surrounded by bloodshed. Two jumpsuited riot police were taking it in turns to stamp on a Stoker's head. A Stoker was giving a PETS protestor a hearty drubbing with the aid of brass knuckledusters. A PETS couple with matching scarlet contact lenses were beating up a riot cop, using his own baton and helmet.

Redlaw and Illyria ran diagonally across the square, dodging left or right when any of the combatants lumbered into their path. Khalid and Qureshi were close behind. Redlaw buttoned up his coat one-handed as he went, hiding his weapons vest. His Cindermaker was holstered out of sight.

They neared two large clusters of Stokers and PETS protestors, who had taken a breather and were now squaring off, ready to resume hostilities. On either side everyone looked wild-eyed, hot-cheeked and raggedly mad.

"Shadies!" Redlaw announced, gesticulating behind him. "Look! Bloody shadies!"

All eyes turned towards Khalid and Qureshi, who stopped dead in their tracks. If they'd been cars there would have been a screeching of brakes.

One of the Stokers snarled, "Fuck me. Fangbangers."

A PETS woman of Amazonian proportions pointed an accusing finger. "It's the Sunless Hounding And Discrimination Executive. They lock them up. They murder them."

Almost as one, both groups of people let out a furious bellowing roar. They might not agree on much, but on this they were unanimous: they despised SHADE officers.

"No!" said Khalid, as the Stokers and PETS protestors began to move menacingly towards him and Qureshi. "No! It's a trick. He's one too. That man."

He meant Redlaw, but nobody believed him. It was just some old bloke in an overcoat with a ripped sleeve. If he was SHADE, where was his uniform?

"Stop," said Qureshi, aiming his gun at the approaching rioters. "I'll shoot. I really will."

As if out of nowhere a half-brick came sailing through the air, and struck him on the forehead. Qureshi staggered and sank to his knees.

"Car," said Khalid. "Back to the car." He grabbed his colleague by the arm, hoisted him to his feet, and was off, hauling a rubbery-legged Qureshi with him. The Stokers and PETS protestors gave chase.

The two shadies almost made it to safety. They were within yards of the car when they were overtaken. Redlaw looked on with no small satisfaction as their pursuers dragged them to the ground and doled out a good kicking.

"'Vengeance is mine,' saith the Lord," he growled.

"Well, vengeance is Redlaw's, at any rate," said Illyria. "I'm not so certain the Lord would approve. I think you went a tad Old Testament there."

"Khalid had it coming. Anyway, look. Those riot squadders are wading in to help. Law enforcement solidarity."

Sure enough, Support Group police had spotted the SHADE officers' plight and were going to their aid. Batons rose and fell as they worked their way through the milling crowd to Khalid and Qureshi at the centre. They plucked the two of them out like prizes from a piñata and escorted them off to the sidelines within a stockade of polycarbonate shields. Both men were bruised, bloodied and bedraggled, and Qureshi was quivering and weeping in abject terror.

"It's almost like you knew that would happen," said Illyria.

"I didn't, as a matter of fact," Redlaw replied. "I was

rather hoping they'd get beaten to within an inch of their lives—Khalid maybe an inch the other side."

"And here's you telling me to hurt people as little as possible. Double standards, eh what?"

"This was a special case." Redlaw sidestepped as a PETS man came howling past with a stocky Stoker hot on his heels. "Anyway, we should make ourselves scarce. This isn't the safest of places to be."

They hadn't gone more than a few paces before they were confronted by a wall of advancing riot police. These were reinforcements, part of a secondary call-up, newly arrived. They were moving into the square en masse, with a view to herding the rioters towards the north-west corner and 'kettling' them in Great George Street. Another, similar-sized contingent was marching north up Millbank to do the same. All wore full-face gas masks.

Redlaw paused, quickly weighing his options.

From behind the ranks of police came a series of hollow, fluting detonations, the sound of CS gas canisters being launched. Moments later, clouds of white vapour bloomed in the square, spreading swiftly.

"I'll barge a hole straight through," Illyria said, gesturing towards the riot squadders. "We'll be out the other side in a jiffy."

"No. There's an alternative."

"I don't see one."

"There." He indicated the Houses of Parliament.

"We walk up to the gate and ask them to let us in?"

"Can't hurt to try."

The gas was drifting towards them in a thickening haze. Redlaw bunched his coat cuff over his nose and mouth and hurried towards the building's main entrance.

By the time he got there his eyes were streaming and his nostrils were dripping something that felt like acid. He thrust his SHADE badge through the bars of the gate and waved it at the police officers stationed on the other side—the Met's Parliamentary security team, all of them armed with semiautomatic carbines.

"Let us in, for God's sake!"

"Sir," said one of the police officers, "please step back."

"We're just bystanders. Do we look like we came here to protest?"

"This is a restricted area. We're on a state of high alert. Without proper authorisation, no one gets in."

"But I'm SHADE."

The policeman looked anything but impressed. "Don't care if you're the Queen of ruddy Sheba, mate. Now back off." He hefted his gun ever so slightly. "I'm not carrying this thing for fun."

"So much for law enforcement solidarity," said Illyria to Redlaw. "We're back to 'barge a hole straight through,' then."

The riot squadders were closing in from both sides, the jaws of a human vice squeezing the Stokers and PETS protestors together. Out in the middle of the square, where the CS gas was thickest, people were crawling on their hands and knees, choking and retching.

"Perhaps..." Redlaw began, but then someone on the other side of the gate spoke his name.

"Captain Redlaw? That *is* Captain Redlaw, right?"

Redlaw blinked. His eyes stung so badly that everything was a tortured, swimming blur. He could just make out the face of the young man addressing him. It was a familiar one.

"Gentlemen," the young man said to the police security team, "don't you know who this is? Why are you making him stay out there where he could get his brains bashed in? Let him in. Now."

"Will you vouch for him, sir?"

"Of course I bloody will. That's Captain John Redlaw, living legend. Don't know what he's doing here, but he needs sanctuary. Open the gate."

With a show of surly deference the policeman went to the gatehouse and pressed a switch. In no time Redlaw and Illyria were within the precincts of Parliament, safely separated from the turmoil in the square.

The young man stuck out a hand and gave Redlaw one of the tightest, firmest handshakes he'd ever known. His grip was almost painful.

"Giles Slocock," he said. "MP for Chesham and Amersham and, as I'm sure you know, Shadow Spokesman for Sunless Affairs. Pleasure to finally meet you in person, Captain. Big fan of your work. Big, big fan."

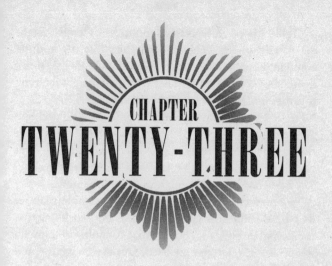

CHAPTER
TWENTY-THREE

SLOCOCK LED THEM across New Palace Yard and in through a surprisingly modest arched door, talking all the while.

"Something, isn't it? I've seen fights before but never anything on so epic a scale. Everybody else in the House has been watching from the upstairs windows but I wanted to get out and have a really good look. Kind of a ringside seat. Close enough to smell the adrenaline. Those security cops kept telling me to get back indoors but I wasn't having any of that. A classic piece of civil disorder going on right outside my workplace and I'm not going to check out the action for myself, first hand? I think not."

He swept them along corridors with chessboard-pattern flooring and portraits of eminent statesmen of yesteryear frowning down from the walls. The walls and ceilings bristled with ornate carvings, like a stonemason's fantasia, yet somehow the atmosphere remained coldly, echoingly austere.

"Talk about adversarial politics. Things might get rowdy in the debating chamber, but it's nothing compared with out there. That, out there, *that's* democracy in the raw. That's left and right coming together and thrashing out their differences."

He ushered them up a stone staircase, nodding deferentially to a pair of Lords who were peering out through a landing window, dressed in ordinary suits but carrying an unmistakable whiff of scarlet and ermine. They deigned to notice him and his companions.

"When sketch writers in the papers complain about us parliamentarians getting all 'yah boo sucks' across the despatch box, they forget that it could be so much worse. We're relatively civilised. Out there's what you'd get all the time if politicians weren't around to represent people's views. We keep the violence strictly verbal."

He steered them into an office, his, a tiny untidy room whose windows looked out onto a narrow, ill-lit courtyard. He shut the door.

"Make yourselves at home." He turned to Illyria. "I'm sorry, we haven't been introduced...?"

"Illyria Strakosha."

"Illyria. Lovely. The ancient name for Albania."

"Very good. There aren't many outside my country who know that."

"Benefits of a reasonably expensive education. *Twelfth Night*, that's set in Illyria, isn't it? That's where I remember it from. Our English teacher showed us Albania on a map, so we'd have some idea where the play's supposed to take place. Not that it helped much. It's all just fantasy land, is Shakespeare. Oh, and we did something in Classical Civilisation about the Illyrian Wars, which the Romans won, if I'm not mistaken."

"Your parents' money wasn't wasted."

Redlaw's nostrils no longer felt as if they were lined with paint stripper, and his vision was clearing. He took a long, hard look at Slocock as the politician vaunted his knowledge of Illyria's homeland, such as it was. Redlaw knew little about Giles Slocock beyond that he was famously dissolute and that he was proficient at some form of martial art. Macarthur hadn't a kind word to say about him, but that was only to be expected—she hadn't a kind word to say about most people, and politicians in particular grated with her. In his role as Shadow Spokesman for Sunless Affairs, Slocock had visited SHADE HQ a grand total of two times. On neither occasion had Redlaw been present, and he hadn't felt that he'd missed much.

In the flesh, Slocock cut a more impressive figure than he did on television. His floppy-fringed haircut was a little too youthful for a man on the cusp of thirty, but the body beneath the not-cheap suit and shirt was compact and well-muscled. His hands had incredibly callused knuckles and there was a thick ridge of horny tissue along the outer edge of each palm. Even as he lounged with one buttock on his desk, he held himself with a louche grace, the posture of a man with absolute physical self-confidence. Only the broken capillaries in the whites of his eyes—there were a few too many of them—hinted at bad habits.

"So how come the two of you wound up embroiled in that mess?" Slocock enquired. "Take a wrong turn somewhere?"

Redlaw threw an acerbic glance at Illyria, which she blanked.

"We trusted to providence," Illyria said. "Perhaps we shouldn't have."

"Providence," said Slocock. "Funny you should say that. Because actually it's more than a little fortuitous that we've met, Captain Redlaw. May I call you John?"

"Don't even try," Illyria advised. "I don't know what you have to do to be allowed to call him by his first name. Whatever it is, it's a test I haven't passed yet. Just stick with Redlaw."

"Redlaw it is, then. You see, Redlaw, you and me, we have something in common."

"We do?" said Redlaw.

"Not just a shared connection with the Night Brigade. Let me tell you what I know about your current situation. I know that you're not technically *Captain* Redlaw any more. I know that you're a fugitive. I know that you've lost your job."

"You're well informed."

"Shouldn't I be? Sunless Affairs is my brief. What goes on in SHADE, I have to keep on top of."

"Hmm. I suppose."

"I also know that the reason you're out on your ear is you've been trying to pin the blame for the bloodlust riots on Nathaniel Lambourne. Without success."

"So?"

"Well, he and I have a history." Slocock's face took on a sombre cast. He was no longer the genial, ebullient fellow of moments earlier. He was deadly earnest now. "A history that's come to a sticky end. You want to nail the bastard to the wall? Let me help."

SLOCOCK OUTLINED HOW he and Lambourne, having once been travellers on the same road, had come to a parting of the ways.

"Nathaniel helped me early in my career, there's no denying," he said. "Gave me a leg-up. I wouldn't go so far as to call him a mentor, but he was always there, introducing me to influential people, watching out for me, keeping potential enemies off my back. Everyone could do with a Nathaniel Lambourne in their corner if they want to get on in the world. I never thought there'd be any consequences. I thought I was using him. Turned out he was using me."

Slocock looked at his hands. He appeared to be struggling with deep, contradictory emotions.

"I know a thing or two about addiction," he said finally. "It's well documented that I'm a substance abuser. The trouble with drugs is you think you're in control. What you don't realise, until it's far too late and you're too far in, is the drugs are in control. You're their servant and there's nothing you can do about it. Same with Lambourne. He had his hooks into me, and I was helpless. You've heard about Maurice Wax, I imagine."

Redlaw shook his head.

"I'd have thought it was all over the mediasphere by now."

"I've been busy. What of him?"

"He's dead. Took his own life."

"Good God."

"Yes. And you know what drove him to it?"

"No."

"Go on, hazard a guess."

"Stress of work? Something to do with Solarville? Personal problems?"

"All of the above and none of the above," said Slocock. "Me. I'm the cause. Lambourne forced me to apply pressure on him. No, not forced. I was perfectly willing. He supplied me with information to use on Wax so that the whole Solarville enterprise could be kick-started into action. He handed me a loaded gun and I pulled the trigger. I barely thought twice about it. He gave me all that was needed to ruin a man's life, and it never even occurred to me to say 'no.' And then, after I'd done his dirty work for him, he treated me like I was something that had crawled out from under a rock. He felt contempt for me because I'd been so eager, so fucking puppy-dog thrilled, to do as he told me."

"And you're surprised by this why?" said Redlaw. "Men like Lambourne don't care about those beneath them. To them, everyone is the same—malleable, expendable."

"I know. I know. I was just too stupid—too naïve maybe—to realise it. I was his fire-and-forget missile and I'm worth nothing to him any more. I had a confrontation with him this evening about it. We argued on the phone. What he said, his whole attitude towards me, simply confirmed how little he thinks of me. Shit on the sole of his shoe would get more respect. His mistake, however, is he's underestimated me."

Slocock flexed his fists.

"You don't dump me like that and think you can get away with it," he said. "You're making a serious error of judgement if you do. I don't care how rich and powerful you are, fuck with Giles Slocock, prepare to suffer. I've never backed down from a challenge. The bigger you are, the harder you fall. Nathaniel Lambourne's gone from being my patron to being top of my shit list. I used to be proud to know him. Now I want to hang the arsehole out to dry."

"That's all very well," said Redlaw, "and all very commendable. I think we can all agree that taking down Lambourne would be a wonderful thing. But, practically speaking, what can we do? This is the problem. Lambourne's already got his way. He's won. I've done the best I could, and it was no good."

"Ah, but you see, I've got the dirt on him," said Slocock. "I know stuff that he doesn't believe I would dare use against him."

"You mean you'd be willing to testify against him at trial?"

"Better still. I can give you good, rock-solid evidence that's sure to put Lambourne in jail for a very long time."

"What sort of evidence?" Redlaw asked warily. "Because if it's a pouch of BovPlas blood, been there, done that. My boss—ex-boss—made it clear she doesn't feel it's a tack worth pursuing, and she's probably right."

"What if," said Slocock, "I could prove that Lambourne ran tests on a Sunless to see whether the additive he put in the blood would have the desired effect?"

"I'd say, if you knew at the time that he was doing anything like that, you should have told the relevant authorities. You're a Member of Parliament. You don't just make laws, you have to uphold them."

"Okay, so I'm compromised, I'm corrupt, I'm venal. Show me a man or woman in this building who isn't. Besides, is it actually illegal to experiment on vampires? There's nothing on the statute books that specifies either way. My point is, I believe this creature still exists. I know where it is. I can take you to it."

"And once I've seen it, what then?"

"That's for you to decide. Call in the shadies, maybe, or the police. If nothing else, Lambourne's keeping a

Sunless outside of an SRA. That's surely an offence under the Settlement Act, isn't it?"

"Very true."

"So, interested?"

"I might be."

"Need some time to think about it? I can step outside so you and your friend can confer." ·

"That's actually not a bad idea. Five minutes."

Slocock slapped the desktop with both hands and stood up. "Five minutes it is. I'll go powder my nose. But not," he added, "*that* kind of powder."

"WELL?" SAID REDLAW.

"Well?" said Illyria.

"You first."

"No, you."

"Fine. Know what I think? I think this is all very convenient. Rather too convenient."

"You don't trust the charismatic and accommodating Mr Slocock?"

"No further than I can throw him. With my bad arm."

"Agreed," said Illyria. "He's a politician. Enough said. On the other hand, though, he seems genuine in his hatred of Lambourne. He really does sound like he's had a change of heart there. Revenge is a great motivator. Never mind a woman scorned, hell hath no fury like a loyal henchman who's been abandoned by his master."

"He wants some payback, I can accept that. But why bring anyone else in on it? Why us?"

"He doesn't feel he can manage alone. He needs moral support. Accomplices. People with the same agenda as him. It's perfectly understandable. What you should ask yourself, Redlaw, is if you're going to get another opportunity like this. Slocock's offering you Lambourne on a plate. What is it they say about gift horses?"

"Don't go round the back end or you could get kicked in the teeth?"

NEVERTHELESS, AN HOUR later, Redlaw found himself in the back seat of a ministerial limousine as it ventured out of the gate, nosing tentatively into Parliament Square, Slocock at the wheel.

The unrest had been successfully quelled. The Stokers and PETS protestors had been corralled into Great George Street and crammed there in a tight, claustrophobic huddle with no room to fight, or barely even to breathe, until tempers died down. They had then been filtered onward into St James's Park where a fleet of paddywagons awaited to cart them off to various police stations. Debris littered the now empty square—placards, broken weapons, shreds of torn clothing. The lawn was churned up like a rugby pitch after a match. Puddles of blood glistened on the roads.

The limo purred south along the river bank, through Chelsea and down into Putney. No one spoke. Earlier, Slocock had phoned Lambourne, requesting an audience with the industrialist. He had given a very convincing impersonation of a man full of contrition, regretting the rashness of his decision to break off ties with Lambourne, desperate for one more chance.

"Please, Nathaniel," he had implored. "I shouldn't have said what I said. I was an idiot. I don't know what I was thinking. Let me drop by your place and we'll meet face to face and you'll see I mean it. Come on, what do you say? Kiss and make up? Seal it with a drink? Maybe a glass or two of that rather fine 'ninety-three Puligny-Montrachet you have in your cellar?"

Apparently, despite the lateness of the hour, Lambourne had said "yes." Then it was just a question of signing out a car and waiting for the trouble outside Parliament to end.

Redlaw understood that he was placing an inordinate amount of faith in the man in the driving seat, a man he scarcely knew. Slocock was as slick and glib as they came. He was not the sort of person you instinctively warmed to and yielded control to.

But.

If he was on the level...

If Lambourne did have a Sunless in his possession...

If the industrialist really was flouting the law so flagrantly...

Then Redlaw had a shot at clawing back some, if not all, of the ground he had lost. He was on course to redeem himself.

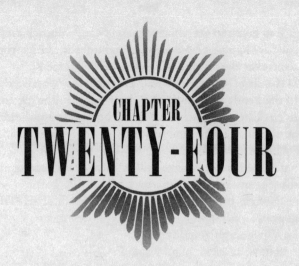

CHAPTER
TWENTY-FOUR

THEY CROSSED THE M25 and headed down into north Surrey, land of stockbrokers, A-list celebrities and a myriad of golf courses. Soon Slocock was turning off a trunk road onto a minor road and from there onto a narrow leafy lane. This, he informed his passengers, marked the start of Lambourne's property. It was a full five minutes before they reached the gate.

It was a high gate, spike-topped, solid. As the car pulled up in front of it, security lights flared into life, revealing surveillance cameras affixed to both pillars.

"Keep down," Slocock warned. Redlaw and Illyria were hunkering low in the back seat, out of sight of the cameras, while Slocock remained in plain view.

They waited. The cameras peered, beady-eyed. Finally the gate gave an enormous *clank* and rolled laboriously to one side. Slocock nudged the car through.

The drive snaked between folds of forested hill. The car's headlights formed a glowing tunnel in the dark.

"I'm going to get you as close as I can," Slocock said. "We'll stop just before we're in sight of the house. You remember the directions I gave you?"

"Go left," said Redlaw. "Through the woods. Up to the brow of the hill. Then bear right, following the ridge. When we reach the edge of the woods, we should be able to see the old observatory."

"If not, you'll have gone way off-course. There isn't much of a moon tonight. It'll be pitch black among all those trees. You all right with that?"

"Not a problem." Redlaw held up his SHADE goggles.

"What about you, Illyria?"

"I have excellent night vision."

A minute later the car coasted to a halt. "This is it," Slocock said. "Out you go. We rendezvous in an hour. Back at the gate, yes?"

"Don't be late," Redlaw said as he and Illyria slipped out.

"I won't. Best of luck."

"You too," said Illyria.

"Oh, all I'm doing is prostrating myself before the great man and begging his forgiveness. Don't need luck for that, just good acting skills. The ability to fake sincerity—any MP worth his salt has that."

The car glided off. Redlaw waited until its taillights were out of sight before putting on the goggles. He entered the familiar world of image intensification, phosphorescent green and slightly slippery. Illyria was already moving. He set off after her.

As they headed upslope through the woods, Illyria said, "Are you thinking we can retrieve this poor blighter and take him back with us?"

"I'm hoping so," Redlaw said. The trees were a kind of protection, deadening sound, but even so both of them kept their voices low.

"And if for some reason he won't come quietly...?"

"Then it's a good thing I've brought a shtriga with me, isn't it?"

"And once we have him, we persuade him to turn evidence against Lambourne."

"I can't see why he wouldn't want to, if Lambourne's been inflicting some kind of heinous torture on him."

"This could be the salvation of you, you know, Redlaw."

"I'll settle for it being the ruination of Nathaniel Lambourne. That's all I'm after now."

"By Jove, you really despise the fellow, don't you?"

"Not so much him," Redlaw said. "What he represents. Conscienceless greed. The anything-to-make-a-buck mentality. He doesn't care what he does, who he stamps on, how many lives he destroys, so long as it adds to his already obscene personal fortune."

"The rich man and the eye of the needle. The moneylenders in the temple."

"Meaning?"

"Just citing Biblical precedents, old bean."

"I don't need the Bible to tell me what's right and what's not. I've my own instincts to guide me."

"But it helps, surely, having scripture to back you up."

"It doesn't hurt."

At the summit of the hill Illyria had to pause for a few moments, steadying herself on the trunk of an oak.

"What's up?" Redlaw asked.

"Nothing. Dizzy spell. It'll pass."

"You're weak. You need blood badly. What if—?"

"No," she said curtly, interrupting. "Don't offer. You know perfectly well I won't do that."

"How do you know what I was going to say?"

"Because I know you. I won't take even a little bit. I refuse to."

"But we need you at full strength, just in case."

"And you too."

"I can survive losing a few drops."

"But there's a danger that once I start, I won't be able to stop myself. I'll drain you. Perhaps even turn you."

"I don't believe you'd be so careless."

"Never underestimate the thirst. I have enough strength for this," she insisted. "I'll be fine."

To prove it, she set a demanding pace for the next leg of the journey. Redlaw almost had to jog to keep up.

The forest ran out. They emerged from the trees to find themselves overlooking a shallow valley. Lambourne's mansion sat half a mile to the west, a sprawling H-shaped edifice surrounded by formal gardens, a tennis court, swimming pool, stable block, and countless other outbuildings. The roofs were all cupola, finial and spire. Light blazed from a hundred windows.

"Now there's a man who isn't bothered about his carbon footprint," Redlaw remarked.

"Or his electricity bill," said Illyria.

To the east, not far from where they stood, lay the observatory.

"Is the Sunless there?" Redlaw enquired. "What's your nose telling you?"

"Definitely I'm picking up traces of vampire scent. Male. It's... not usual. Extraordinarily musky. Plenty of waste product too. He's been imprisoned there a long time."

"What about noises? Hear anything?"

"About a thousand animals rustling around in the woods. Your heartbeat—rather rapid. Nothing from the observatory, though, except some kind of machinery whirring, I think an extractor fan."

"Let's go in closer."

Redlaw drew his Cindermaker, checked the clip—five rounds left—and padded towards the cylindrical building. Arriving at the entrance, he studied the door. Triple biometric security, as Slocock had warned. Retinal scan, voiceprint identification, thumbprint confirmation. But, according to Slocock, not fitted with an alarm. Lambourne didn't wish anyone apart from himself gaining access to the observatory, but neither was he anticipating that intruders might attempt to break in.

Not convinced that the source of this information was entirely dependable, Redlaw inspected the door frame carefully for wires, contacts, anything which suggested a circuit that could be broken. More or less satisfied that Slocock had got his facts straight, he turned to Illyria.

"You're up. This thing looks pretty sturdy. It's going to take some oomph to bust it open."

"Leave it to me."

"You'll need to be quiet, too."

"Brute force *and* stealth. You don't ask for much, do you?"

Illyria put her shoulder to the door, applied some pressure—and the latch gave and the door sprang open.

"Easy," she said.

"Too damn easy," said Redlaw.

The door swung inward. There was darkness beyond. Redlaw's goggles revealed an inner wall, and steps, curving up out of sight.

Illyria made to enter. Redlaw stayed her with a hand.

"This has all the hallmarks of a trap," he said.

"What's in there? Just a vampire. One that's been cooped up for months on end. I can't imagine he'll be much of a threat."

"He's been dosed to the gills with vasopressin."

"Still, only one of him and two of us."

"I really don't like this." Redlaw was remembering the Isle of Dogs, another trap. Someone had set him up there, he was sure. Khalid had denied involvement. But if not him, then who? "I vote we bail."

"When we've come this far?"

His shoulder was throbbing. Nothing felt right here. "Just not liking this gift horse very much at all."

"Oh, stop being such a nervous Nelly." Illyria strode decisively through the doorway and up the stairs.

Redlaw hesitated, although he knew he had no choice. He couldn't let her go in there alone.

"Stupid, impulsive..." he muttered under his breath.

"Heard that!" her words drifted down the stairs.

Redlaw crossed the threshold. Leading with his Cindermaker, he took the steps two at a time, but slowly. At the top, he looked around. He and Illyria were on a kind of ring-shaped viewing gallery. He noted the four machine guns perched like hungry vultures on the central parapet, angled downward and inward. He tried not to gag on the pervasive stench of vampire faeces.

"Well, he *was* here," Illyria observed.

Joining her at the parapet, Redlaw peered over.

The pit below was empty. Pats of black dung spattered the floor. A pair of heavy chains lay amongst them. One end of each chain was bolted to the floor, the other terminated in a manacle.

"Lambourne must have moved him," Redlaw said. "Or more likely got rid of him. Using these guns, no doubt. They're loaded with Fraxinus. See the black tips to the bullets in the belts?"

"Could he have known we were coming?"

"Not unless Slocock tipped him off, and he didn't. We've been with him the whole time since we told him we were taking him up on his offer."

"Then it's just coincidence. Rotten timing. Lambourne disposes of the last remaining piece of evidence shortly before we learn about it. Probably this very day."

"Which makes sense. Now Solarville's got the green light, he's tying up loose ends, making sure there's nothing left that'll connect him to the bloodlust riots." Redlaw grunted. "Damn frustrating."

"I'm sorry," said Illyria. "I know you had your hopes pinned on this."

"Not as sorry as I am. I've a good mind to go down to that house and confront Lambourne anyway. I might not be able to bring him to justice but I can certainly give him a hiding he'll never forget."

"And have him bring charges of assault and trespass against you? As if you're not in deep enough trouble already."

"Might as well be hanged for a sheep as a lamb."

"Maybe, but I think even you would draw the line at duffing someone up out of sheer spite."

"In that case, you don't know me very well at all."

Redlaw holstered his gun and tramped glumly down

the stairs. It was a relief to get back outside into the clean, cool, fresh-smelling night air. He inhaled lungfuls of it, glaring down at the mansion, which dazzled in the goggles like some emerald-encrusted treasure chest.

Something flitted at the periphery of his vision, to the right, and he spun. A pallid shape filled the entire scope of the goggles, massive, looming with horrifying swiftness. Redlaw felt himself being launched off his feet. He was in the air, hurtling. *Go limp!* He tried, but landed hard, rolling and rolling, fetching up face down in thick, night-damp grass. He thrust himself up onto all fours. He knew he hurt. He knew, too, that adrenaline was masking the worst of the pain, telling him he was well enough to do whatever was necessary, fight or flight. He tottered to his feet, reaching for his Cindermaker.

The shape came at him again, this time from the left. Fast. So fast.

The impact was like a thunderclap to the side of the head. Redlaw slammed to the ground. The goggles' green world stuttered, sparked, gave a shiver of static, then went black. Mechanism broken. Useless now. Redlaw ripped them off his head, scrambled to his knees, then up into a defensive crouch. As his eyes adapted to the darkness he squinted owlishly around for the shape, the thing, that was attacking him. All he could see were the dim silhouettes of trees, the bulk of the observatory.

Illyria. Where was Illyria?

"Illyria!"

The creature struck him once more, now from behind. He thought it must weigh at least four hundred pounds, and yet he hadn't heard it coming. He was propelled forwards like a ball whacked by a cricket bat, and hit the ground, furrowing headlong through the grass. He knew then how a small child must feel when being tossed about by an adult. This was no horseplay, though. This was the cold-hearted sadism of a cat toying with a mouse, doing all it could to make its victim feel tiny and terrified and helpless.

He was not helpless. At last he managed to draw his gun and cock it. He staggered upright, glimpsing the creature scooting off into the woods, vanishing among the trees like some immense, grotesque phantom. So that was the tactic, was it? Hit and run. Out from cover, then back in, in the space of a few seconds.

Illyria burst from the observatory. "You yelled?"

"There's something..." Redlaw panted. "The Sunless. The one Lambourne's been holding prisoner, experimenting on..."

"He didn't dust it?"

"The trees. Watch out!"

The vampire shot out from the woods again, rocketing across the grass. In three, four vast loping strides, feet barely seeming to touch the ground, he reached Illyria. His massive hands clamped around her neck. He hoisted her bodily into the air, Illyria writhing, her legs bucking.

This was Redlaw's first good look at the creature, and what he saw was loathsome even by Sunless standards. It wasn't just the unnatural hugeness, it was the over-muscled distension of the limbs, the face with its bear-like jutting jaw and huge slewed eyes, the lumpy, hairless scalp, the squat, thick legs. It was also the fact that this monstrosity had managed to catch Illyria off-guard and snatch her up so easily. That wasn't supposed to be possible. Redlaw's understanding was that no vampire could or should be able to overwhelm a shtriga.

Illyria resisted, twisting the vampire's wrists outward, trying to break them. Her attacker merely laughed and swung her from side to side like a pendulum, seemingly intent on detaching head from body by shaking. Redlaw lined up a shot with his Cindermaker. The vampire spotted him and flung Illyria at him just as he squeezed the trigger. Redlaw managed to jerk his hand aside in the nick of time, and their bodies collided, her full weight crashing into him. They fell together to the grass with brutal, bruising force.

Illyria was on her feet in an instant, tense, poised to renew the offensive. Redlaw remained sprawled on his back, seeing stars.

"You!" Illyria snarled at the vampire. "You can't beat me. I am shtriga. Your born superior. Your natural dominator. Your queen."

The vampire's retort was a mocking howl of laughter. "I am... Vlad," he said in a voice like rusty cogs grating together. "Vlad... no fear... shtriga. Shtriga is... shit to Vlad. Vlad is pounding shtriga bitch... into dirt. Then... Vlad is... let free."

"I order you to bow down," Illyria said. "Bow down and obey me, or be crushed."

"Vlad obey only... blood-giver man... Nathaniel. Nathaniel tell Vlad... do this thing... then no more chains... only freedom."

Redlaw realised he was no longer holding his Cindermaker. He'd dropped it, somewhere in the grass. He rolled over and began to hunt for it, feeling with his hands. Vlad might be super-sized, like three vampires combined, but no way was he impervious to a Fraxinus round. If it took more than one to do the business, if it took all five left in the clip, so be it.

"I will tear you apart," Illyria said.

"Vlad says... try."

She flew at him, hands clawed. Vlad sprang to meet her. They clashed in midair and came down brawling like tomcats. Blows rained in either direction. Vlad hammered Illyria with his fists. Illyria sank her fangs into Vlad's pectoral muscle and tore out a chunk. Vlad bellowed and slammed her head into the earth, spiking it down with one elbow. Illyria wedged her knees under his belly and propelled him off her.

Redlaw, meanwhile, continued to search on his hands and knees for his gun, in vain. Finally, admitting defeat, he pulled a stake from his vest. He stumbled towards the battling vampires.

Vlad was on top of Illyria again, bearing down on her with all his bulk, pinning her throat with one arm. His face loomed over hers, mouth agape to expose a bristling multiplicity of fangs, all cross-angled and overlapping like shark teeth.

"Vlad make... big smile. Bite off... pretty shtriga... face."

Illyria bared her own fangs, hissing defiance.

"Bite off... whole head... even," said Vlad, opening his maw wider still.

That was when Redlaw threw himself onto Vlad's back and plunged the stake in with all his might, next to the knotty ridge of spine.

With a roar Vlad reared, shrugging Redlaw off. He grabbed behind him for the stake. His fingertips couldn't quite reach the hilt.

He reeled round to face Redlaw, who was already drawing a second stake.

"Foolish... little man. Not nearly... deep enough. Hurt Vlad... but not kill."

"Then let's try again," Redlaw said, launching himself forwards.

Vlad parried the attack easily. He wrenched the stake out of Redlaw's grasp, and enveloped him in a rib-crunching bear-hug.

"Vlad now... use this... on you," he said, raising the stake, point downward. "Through eye... into brain. How about that? Human... impaled by... vampire."

Illyria jumped on Vlad from behind. Vlad plucked her off one-handed and tossed her aside as though she were nothing more than a bothersome insect.

"Vlad is... best," he crowed.

Redlaw wormed his hand between his chest and Vlad's.

"Vlad is... biggest."

Redlaw's fingers closed around an *aqua sancta* grenade.

"Vlad is... strongest."

Redlaw unclipped the grenade from his vest and thumbed out the pin.

"Vlad is..."

"Too damn talkative for his own good," said Redlaw, stuffing the grenade into Vlad's mouth.

It detonated.

Vlad shrieked.

He let go of Redlaw and recoiled, pawing at his face. Skin bubbled and sizzled. Thick grey foam vomited out over his lips, a frothing soup of consecrated water and melted tongue-flesh. Fangs came with it, unmoored from their gum beds. The whole of Vlad's lower jaw sagged as the tendons holding it in place deliquesced and snapped. Meat and bone within his head slitheringly parted company.

It was enough to incapacitate Vlad for several moments, to stagger him.

Not to stop him, though.

Vlad charged at Redlaw again. Redlaw threw himself to the side, managing to plant a stake in Vlad's thigh even as he dived out of his path. The vampire tugged the stake out with a throaty bellow of pain and rage. He hurled it at Redlaw, missing by a hair.

The flesh around the wound in Vlad's leg immediately started to blacken and atrophy. The flesh around the stake protruding from his back was doing the same. But not as rapidly as it would with an ordinary vampire. Redlaw wondered if Vlad would even succumb to ash wood poisoning at all, given his ramped-up physiology. Probably he could survive anything short of a heart-penetrating thrust. But none of the stakes Redlaw had on him would reach that deep, not into such a broad, dense body. Only a bullet could.

He was just thinking this when a dull glint in the grass caught his eye. His Cindermaker. He stooped for it, and at that very moment Vlad lunged and seized him by his injured arm, hauling him away from the gun. The pain was nauseating, crippling.

Vlad's mouth was a loosely hanging, blistered mess that was no longer capable of forming words. The murderous glare in his eyes, however, said plenty. With his other hand he grasped Redlaw's torso. He began to pull each way, slowly, deliberately. He was going to wrench Redlaw's arm out of its socket, like a butcher pulling the leg off a chicken.

Then Illyria barrelled into him at full pelt, with a cry of "*No!*" Redlaw was jettisoned from Vlad's clutches. Lying on his side he watched, dimly as though through a veil, the two vampires start to brawl again. They leapt, sprang, circled, feinted, struck, rebounded, slashed, grabbed, all at superhuman speed, almost too fast to follow.

Illyria, though she had ferocity and tenacity on her side, was dwarfed by her opponent. Vlad's reach far exceeded hers, and his blows carried considerably more heft. Inevitably this began to take its toll. Soon Vlad had her pinned to the ground once more and was dishing out piledriver punches one after another, almost as if trying to embed her in the turf like a tent peg.

Redlaw could barely move. He was semi-concussed, his shoulder immobilised by searing pain. Nonetheless he forced himself, teeth clenched, shuddering, nearly crying with the effort, to rise to a sitting position. He felt he was going to throw up or pass out, or both. His Cindermaker lay less than a yard away, but it might as well have been a mile. He extended a trembling left arm. He just couldn't seem to coordinate himself, to align hand with gun.

Illyria was making horrid grunting gasps. Vlad's blows continued to fall with metronomic regularity, each one connecting with a wet, meaty *smack*.

Redlaw's floundering hand finally fell on the Cindermaker. He lifted the gun—it felt like a hundredweight of metal—and curled a finger round the trigger.

Illyria wasn't moving now except in response to Vlad hitting her, her body twitching under the impacts.

Redlaw took aim. Tried to take aim. Took aim. Tried to. His target wavered in his vision. Vlad couldn't have been more than ten feet from him. Impossible to miss at that range. But he wouldn't seem to stay still. One moment he was solid, the next a juddering, smeary blur.

Fire anyway.

But what if the bullet hit Illyria?

If you don't shoot, she's done for.

Vlad swam into focus. Redlaw made every effort to fix his position in his mind's eye. Then he fired. And fired again. And again.

Had he got him? He couldn't tell. The barrel flashes had dazzled him, three gibbous blue afterimages floating across his vision. His ears were ringing from the percussion of the gunshots.

Time passed. Maybe quite a lot of it. Redlaw became aware that he was flat out on the grass. He was cold, chilled to the bone, his overcoat sodden. People were talking nearby. Two men. One was Slocock. The other...

"Shame about Vlad, but it was for the best. Despite what I promised, I couldn't have turned him loose, not really."

Lambourne?

"Still, at least he did what was required of him before he got dusted—subdued them both."

Lambourne. Redlaw stirred himself. *Get up. Go on, do it!*

"Hey, look, he's coming round."

That was Slocock.

"Can't have that, can we?"

A pair of legs presented themselves before Redlaw.

"Not yet."

An expensively shod foot lashed out.

Redlaw saw light, sun-incandescent, then blackness.

CHAPTER
TWENTY-FIVE

"WAKEY-WAKEY."

A slap on the cheek.

There was brightness and pain, so much of both that Redlaw immediately let himself slip back into the warm enveloping ink of oblivion.

Another, firmer slap.

"I said 'wakey-wakey.'"

Again, nothingness was preferable to consciousness. Consciousness meant sharp aches, jagged throbs of light that seemed to scorch his eyeballs.

"Come on, Redlaw. Can't have you dozing."

The voice—Slocock's—became insistent, as did the slapping. Finally, just to make it stop, Redlaw groaned and levered his eyelids apart.

"Enough," he said thickly. "All right. I'm here. Enough."

He was in a desk chair, hands fastened behind his back. Electrical flex cut into his wrists. The position was torment to his shoulder. Many other parts of him hurt too, though none quite as badly.

He was in the observatory, on the viewing gallery. With him were Slocock and Lambourne. Of Illyria he could see no sign.

The two men stood side by side. There was no animosity evident between them. Their body language spoke only of common purpose, unity. Their smiles matched, equally smug and superior.

"I should have known," Redlaw said, looking from one to the other, industrialist to politician, and back. "There was no great falling-out, was there? That was just a lie. A ruse."

"Well, Nathaniel and I did have something of a difference of opinion earlier today," said Slocock. "But we're over it. Once I agreed to bring him you, all was forgiven and forgotten. Think of yourself as a peace offering, Redlaw, a human olive branch. That's quite a beautiful thing to be, really."

"I knew you weren't to be trusted."

"Yet you trusted me anyway. Either I'm remarkably plausible or you're remarkably gullible. Probably it's a bit of both. Plus, you wanted to get hold of some kind of evidence against Nathaniel so badly. I could have told you I knew where to find photos of him strangling flower fairies with his bare hands, and you'd still have come along."

The flex wasn't only tying Redlaw's hands together, it was securing him to the chair back. Straining against his bonds did nothing but increase the pain.

"You, Mr Redlaw, have become a right royal pain in the arse," said Lambourne. "No, that's overstating it somewhat. A thorn in the side. You harass my site supervisor at the distribution depot, you hijack one of my trucks, you poke your nose into my affairs—you've been so persistent. A regular goddamn bloodhound. I've done all I can to get you off my back, pulled every relevant string I know of, and it's still not been enough. But at last, thanks to Giles—and Vlad, God rest his soul—I have you where I want you."

He sleeked back his silver hair.

"Sad that it's had to come to this, but let's be frank, you brought it on yourself. You didn't know when to leave well enough alone. You just kept doggedly at it, trying to knock down everything I've been building up this past couple of years. I don't take kindly to people who interfere with my deals. Don't take kindly to them at all."

"Let me go," Redlaw said. "You can't hold me like this. I'm a SHADE officer."

"What's the use of trying that, when we all know it's bollocks?" Slocock scoffed. "SHADE has disowned you. All you are to them is a runaway ex-employee who's had a brain fart and needs to be reined in. Which Nathaniel and I have done. You could regard this as us doing our civic duty, making a citizen's arrest. I can see the headlines: 'MP And Billionaire Nab Mad Vamp Cop.' That's got to swing a few extra thousand votes my way, come the election. Not that I need them."

"Except you aren't arresting me, are you?" said Redlaw. "It's gone too far for that. You're going to kill me."

"That hasn't been decided yet," said Lambourne. "There's still a chance for you, if you agree to play ball."

"You know I'll never do that."

"We're waiting for someone to arrive who might be able to convince you otherwise."

"Who?"

"You'll see. Won't be long."

Redlaw processed this piece of information. He had a suspicion he knew who Lambourne was talking about, and prayed to God he was wrong.

"Where's Illyria?" he asked.

"Ah, the luscious but somewhat intimidating Illyria," said Slocock. "Your raven-haired vampiress friend."

"We were watching from a safe distance while she was fighting Vlad," said Lambourne. "Quite the hellcat. There were moments when I wondered if she might not actually win. The odds were stacked against her, but she did well."

"Where. Is. She?"

"Not dusted, if that's what you're worried about," said Slocock.

"Not yet," added Lambourne.

"Unless you're keeping her buried under ten feet of concrete somewhere," Redlaw said, "neither of you is safe."

"Oh, I think we're fine." Lambourne nodded to Slocock. "Giles? Would you do the honours?"

"Of course, Nathaniel."

Slocock tipped back Redlaw's chair and dragged it, and him, over to the parapet.

"There. See?"

Down in the pit, Illyria lay prone, motionless. The manacles were fastened round her wrists. Her clothing was clotted with dust—the remains of Vlad.

"Those shackles held Vlad," Lambourne said. "They'll hold her. And should they not, there's always the guns. See those electronic eyes positioned about a metre down? Motion sensors. If anything bigger than a moth passes through that, the guns automatically open fire. A thousand Fraxinus rounds a minute from each. She won't be dusted—she'll be puréed."

"Do anything to her," Redlaw said, ferociously, "anything at all, and I will kill you with my bare hands."

"Woo-ooh!" said Slocock on a rising and falling note, in the manner of a gloating child. "Can it be you've got feelings for her? The great Redlaw's fallen for a vampire? Surely not."

Redlaw refused to dignify that with an answer. He realised, to his chagrin, that there might be a grain of truth in it.

"Mind you," the politician went on, "if I *was* going to do the dirty deed with a vamp, Illyria's the one I'd do it with. I mean, if necrophilia's your thing, might as well make sure it's with a looker."

"You aren't fit to lick her boots," Redlaw growled.

"Does she make *you* do that? Is that how it is? She does have that air about her, doesn't she, the whole alpha-female, ball-buster vibe."

"Now, now, Giles," Lambourne chided. "Stop being mean. The poor man's having a hard enough time as it is without you making it worse. Mr Redlaw, Giles and I need to pop out to meet our guest. We'll leave the two of you alone for a while. Not for long." He consulted his watch, a Patek Philippe with an alligator strap, worth the price of a medium-sized house. "Quarter of an hour at most. Enjoy your last few minutes together. And please don't try anything funny. We'll be right outside, and I have this"—he held up Redlaw's Cindermaker—"and no qualms about using it if the situation demands."

He descended the stairs, Slocock in tow. No sooner had the door clicked shut below than Redlaw canted his head over the parapet and hissed, "Illyria. Illyria! Wake up."

She stirred. Moaned softly.

"Illyria, please. You have to wake up."

She rolled her head round. Her face was a puffy mass of contusions, so severely bruised it resembled an aubergine in places. She opened one eye.

"Redlaw?" she croaked.

"Illyria, listen to me. Lambourne's got you chained up. You have to break free somehow. Shatter the manacles, yank the bolts out of the floor, whatever you can. But you have to do it right now, or we're both as good as dead."

"Can't," she said. "Can't move. Hurts too much."

"You have to. You have to move."

She tried her best to rise up, but it was like the tottering efforts of a newborn foal, feeble and pathetic. Even simply tugging on the chains from a lying position proved beyond her.

"It's hopeless," she said.

"No. No, it's not. It's not hopeless."

"You come down here and do something about it then."

"I can't. The guns. But there must be a cut-off switch for them somewhere. If I can just..."

Redlaw had another go at his bonds, but the flex was knotted tight and well, and the knots themselves were too high up his wrists for his fingers to reach. He jumped the chair up and down on the floor a few times, thinking he might be able to loosen a screw, perhaps even break the whole thing apart. No luck. The chair was teak and tubular steel, a sturdily constructed piece of office furniture.

"No," he said finally, defeated.

"What's... What's going to happen?"

"We're going to figure out a way out of this, that's what."

"No, Redlaw. Really. What's Lambourne going to do with us?"

"Nothing."

"No lies, Redlaw. The honest truth."

He wrestled with it, then said, "Me, I'm not sure. But you—I think he plans to use the machine guns to dust you."

A brief silence from Illyria, then: "Oh."

"He won't, though. Not while there's breath in my body. I won't let him."

"How very noble of you, Redlaw."

"I mean it."

"I know. And I appreciate it. We haven't known each other very long, have we?"

The sudden shift in her tone, from sardonic to sanguine, told him the direction Illyria was taking the conversation in. He didn't want to travel that route with her. Couldn't bear to.

"A couple of nights, is it?" she said.

"Bit more than that. Three days, two nights."

"But we can't count the two days, can we? Only the nights. So, not long. But we've done a lot together. Been through a lot."

"Yes."

"It's been fun, in a weird kind of way. You're a cantankerous, pompous old poop, but beneath it all you've a stout heart and even a sense of humour. I like you. I could have *really* liked you, had things been different, had we had more time."

"I doubt it. The longer someone spends with me, the less appealing I become. Only Leary could stand me, and she said that was only possible by ignoring me half the time."

"Deflect all you want, but I'm still going to say my piece," Illyria said. "You are a good man, John Redlaw. You may have stopped realising it, you may have lost your way somewhat, but you are. God chose wisely when he chose you to be one of his agents on earth."

"But you don't believe in—"

"Doesn't matter. Not the point. Now, as I'm not going to survive this, but you might, I want you to promise me one thing."

"What?" He should have said, *Name it.* Too late. *What?* would have to do.

"Promise me you'll continue to defy Lambourne and all the other bastards like him. Fart up all their noses."

"Of course I will. Of course."

"But specifically," Illyria said, "promise you'll defend vampires from his kind, and from anyone who means them harm. Vampires can't help being what they are. They're victims too, much as the people they prey on are victims. If I've learned anything being a shtriga, it's not to blame them for their behaviour. Curb them, control them, by all means. Cull where necessary. But have compassion for them as well. The great majority of vampires never asked to be bitten and turned. Always remember that."

Redlaw thought of the Sunless he had saved from those Stokers just three nights ago, before all this madness began, before everything went haywire—the not-long-turned Hungarian boy. Perhaps he had already started to become the person Illyria was asking him to be. He'd taken the first steps of his own accord, and there wasn't far to go to complete the transition.

"They're slaves of their appetites," she said. "They need a firm hand, and someone to defend them."

"You're asking me to be a shtriga."

"I am. A human one. If you can."

"I'm not sure I—"

"Just promise it," Illyria said. "You don't have to mean it. Cross your fingers or whatever. But I need to hear it from you."

"I don't make promises I can't keep."

"Then don't. Sorry I asked." Not bitter. Just disappointed.

Redlaw said nothing for a while. Then, with resolve: "All right. You've got it. I will."

"Thank you, Redlaw."

"John."

"Ah, now I get to be on 'John' terms with you. Finally."

"I tell you what, I'd much rather that than 'old bean.'"

"You don't like 'old bean'?"

"No."

She laughed, painfully. "It's not rather endearing in its archaic-ness?"

"No. Just annoying."

"Nice of you to tell me that," she said, "now it's too late to be of any use. John..."

"Yes?"

"It's been good knowing you."

Again Redlaw said nothing for a while, this time because he found it hard to speak.

"Come on," Illyria chided gently. "Don't be sad for me. I've had a very long life and I've managed to keep my looks. How many others can say that? I've travelled, seen and done so much. I was granted abilities most can only dream of, and I've revelled in them. I don't regret anything, except that you and I didn't meet under other circumstances, John, beneath kinder stars. And I'm not scared of what's coming, not in the slightest. I'm not saying that to be brave. It's true. There's nothing on the other side of death, and that's fine with me. That's how it should be."

"There is, though," said Redlaw.

"So you believe. I believe different. Let's hope I'm going to be pleasantly surprised. But if not, so what? I've made the most of the decades I've had. I haven't wasted them. I haven't allowed myself to become jaded. That, I think, is the best anyone can say about themselves, at the end of it."

The door clicked open. Footfalls on the stairs grew louder. Three sets.

Lambourne emerged first into the viewing gallery. Then Slocock.

Following them...

"You," said Redlaw.

Commodore Macarthur.

CHAPTER
TWENTY-SIX

SHE STUDIED REDLAW for a good length of time, lips pursed, eyes pitying.

Eventually she said, "John. Oh, God, John. Look at you. What it's come to? I gave you every chance, you know. Every chance in the world. I did my level best to steer you away from this vendetta of yours, get you back on course. But you just wouldn't listen. You wouldn't be told. You ploughed on, getting yourself deeper and deeper in 'til you were past the point of no return. I was helping you, I was trying to save you, but you were too obstinate, too blinkered, to see that."

"Helping?" In Redlaw's voice, contempt and despondency vied for control. He felt as though he had been gut-punched, and yet, deep down, he was somehow unsurprised. He should have known. Perhaps in some obscure way he *had* known, but had refused to acknowledge it. "How did you help, exactly? By hindering me at every turn? Sacking me? Having me arrested?"

"By trying to stop you pursuing Lambourne," Macarthur said. "By keeping you from making the biggest mistake of your life: getting on the wrong side of an enemy you haven't a hope of defeating. I didn't discourage you at the start, because I didn't think you'd get very far. But you were so persistent, so determined, after a while I felt I had to take drastic steps. I wanted to prevent precisely this—you ending up at his mercy, with everything you hold dear taken from you and your life in tatters. Whatever I've done I did for you, John, for your own good. Although, obviously, it wasn't enough."

"Drastic steps. Presumably that included sending me into that Sunless nest alone, knowing there were dozens of them there."

She nodded. "I had a pretty good idea how infested that business unit was. I'd visited it myself not long earlier, nosed around the outside and made plenty of noise. I rattled the cage so the vamps would be on the alert, expecting trouble, when you turned up."

"I could have been killed."

"No, not you, John," Macarthur replied calmly. "Not with your skills. And I sent backup, didn't I? Didn't reckon on you getting hurt, mind. All I was after was reminding you of what you were supposed to be doing. I wanted you to get your head back in the game, to remember what being a shady is all about. You'd lost sight of that."

"No, I think *you* have," Redlaw said. "How could you take Lambourne's side? Has he bribed you? Christ's sake, don't tell me he's bribed you. What's the going rate for a soul these days? What's the modern equivalent of thirty pieces of silver?"

"Such emotive language. Mr Lambourne—Nathaniel—he and I don't have that sort of relationship. Do we?"

"Not at all, Gail," said Lambourne. "Money doesn't enter into it. Which is refreshing, I might add. For once I have an influential collaborator who I don't have to dip into my pocket for." He patted Slocock's shoulder. "You could learn a thing or two from the Commodore, Giles."

The politician made a face.

"So then what *is* in it for you?" Redlaw asked Macarthur. "What are you getting out of cosying up to this scum?"

"Let's just say his vision for dealing with the Sunless dovetails with mine."

"Solarville."

"Indeed. The Residential Areas don't work, John, you know that as well as I do. It's a joke. The vampires come and go pretty damn well as they please. The government set up the SRAs as a sop to people's need to feel protected, a typical political quick-fix solution, bugger-all foresight or long-term planning involved. They're just not fit for purpose. Solarville on the other hand, that's the way forward. Once the vamps are in there, they're in there for good. We can keep tabs on them, do head-counts, censuses. They can be corralled, controlled. They can even, if they start to get awkward, be..."

"Be what?"

"He doesn't know," Macarthur said to Lambourne, a knowing eyebrow aloft. "About the failsafe. You haven't told him."

"No, but I'm going to give a practical demonstration

shortly. In about..." The Patek Philippe came out again. "I make it three minutes."

"She's down there, then?" said Macarthur, indicating the pit. "Redlaw's lassie?

"Take a look for yourself."

Macarthur did. Illyria hissed up at her from below, weakly but still with rancour.

"Shtriga," Macarthur said. "I thought shtrigas were a Sunless myth. I'd heard rumours they existed—a powerful, benevolent vampire elite—but it seemed like fantasy to me, wishful thinking. But here is one, in the unliving flesh." She looked round at Redlaw. "Is it true they have hypnotic powers? The ability to mesmerise others and make them do their bidding? Say they do, John. Say that's how she ensnared you. You've been under her influence all along."

She was giving him a get-out clause. Even now, at this late stage, she was still trying to help him, after a fashion.

"Everything I've done, I've done of my own free will," he said. "I haven't been dancing to anyone else's tune."

Macarthur caught his insinuation. "And I have? Don't make me laugh. You know me. I'm hardly the sort to kowtow. This is just me and Nathaniel working in tandem. He came to me for consultation, technical assistance, and I gave it him. I've not done anything on his behalf that contravenes SHADE regulations or my own code of ethics. I actually, genuinely believe Solarville is our best bet for the future, for humans and 'Lesses."

"And the riots? The deaths they've caused?"

"Undesirable, regrettable." Her eyes were hard. "But nothing worth having is gained without a price."

"Two minutes to go," said Lambourne.

"Is my death included in that price?" Redlaw said.

"You don't have to die today, John," Macarthur said. "It's very easy. Just renounce everything. Swear to me you'll leave Nathaniel be, you won't kick up any more fuss over Solarville, you'll quietly go on your way, act as if nothing ever happened. Then you get to live."

"And Illyria too?"

"Can't guarantee that. She is a rogue Sunless, after all."

"But I'm asking, hypothetically if nothing else: if I agreed to do as you say, would you let her go, unharmed?"

"John, no!" Illyria said from the pit. "Don't. Don't do this. Not for me."

"You're in no position to haggle, John," said Macarthur. "I'm holding out a lifeline here, but only to you."

"Both of us, or nothing."

"I really can't." She sounded sincere in her regret, and firm in her resolve. "When you get down to it, that's just a vampire there. An undead thing. She injured several of my men. Heffernan's in bad shape. It could be months before he walks again, if he ever does. I cannot see my way to leniency with her. It would be better for you, anyway, to be shot of her. She's a millstone round your neck, dragging you down."

Redlaw shook his head. "Then, no dice. I die here tonight." He nodded at the Cindermaker in Lambourne's hand. "Presumably by my own gun. Then my body buried somewhere on this estate where no one will ever find me. I'm curious. Who'll pull the trigger? Which one of you? You, Lambourne? Could you do that? Honestly? Put a bullet in my head? Execute a man in cold blood?"

"You have no idea what I'm capable of when it comes to protecting my interests," said Lambourne. "One minute."

"Oh, to hell with the countdown!" Redlaw barked. "What are you waiting for? If you're going to do this, for God's sake just do it. Get it over with. Send me to my Maker. I'm looking forward to meeting Him. I want to have words with Him about this crappy, corrupt world He made and all the liars and thieves He filled it with."

"The countdown," Lambourne said, unfazed, "is because what's about to happen is reliant on an event over which I have no control. Daybreak in this part of the world is due in a little over thirty seconds."

"Daybreak? So?"

"Look up, Redlaw. See the dome that's capped over us? See what it's made of?"

"Glass. Darkened glass."

"Quite. The exact same glass used at Solarville."

"Which shuts out almost all sunlight," Redlaw said. "That's the point, isn't it? It protects Sunless. You had that Vlad creature in here for ages. So what are you getting at? The sun can't harm Illyria when it comes up, as long as that glass does what it's supposed to."

"And it does," said Lambourne, and his smile was sudden and vicious as he added, "In its present state. But that isn't darkened glass up there, it's electrochromic 'smart glass.' Its opacity comes from a thin film of laminate within each pane which responds to an electric current. Introduce voltage into the laminate, and the randomly orientated particles it's made of start to line up nicely in the same direction and allow light to pass through. This control here..."

He moved over to a wall-mounted panel from which protruded a dial not unlike a large, revolving dimmer switch. It was encircled by markings that showed gradations of shading, from black to near-white.

"...lets me adjust the voltage level," he continued. "It's the ultimate deterrent at Solarville. Should the vamps try to start anything, we just threaten them with de-opaquing, if there is such a word. I was intending to deal with Vlad by this method, at this very moment, but it turned out he had other uses. One final use, I should say. However, I still have a guinea pig, don't I? And I have been rather looking forward to seeing for myself, with my own eyes, the effects of sun on a vampire."

He squinted, craning his neck.

"And there, I believe, it is. On schedule. The first glimmer of light over the hills. Rosy-fingered dawn bringing a blush to the firmament, banishing night. When the sun comes up, it'll come up fast. Let's clear the dome so we can get a better look at it."

He rotated the dial clockwise. A soft hum could be heard, and the panes of glass overhead lightened to reveal a smoky-grey sky.

"Giles, Gail, ringside seats for you." Lambourne motioned them to the parapet. He had become sinisterly gleeful, a master of ceremonies overseeing some ghastly ritual.

Redlaw realised Nathaniel Lambourne wasn't the sociopath he'd pegged him as. It was worse than that. He was, underneath all that moneyed sophistication, quite evil. And quite mad.

"Stop this," he begged. "Stop it. She's done nothing to you. It was me, not her. I'm the one you should punish. Turn that dial back. Do something to me, anything, whatever you like, but not her."

"Hush up, John," said Macarthur. "You're disgracing yourself. Pleading for mercy for a *vampire*?" She uttered the word with unusual contempt. "The man you used to be, the perfect SHADE officer, he'd spit on you if he saw you like this."

Slocock had his hands clasped together. He was gazing eagerly down into the pit. "Funny. It's only light. We can't even feel it—and it's going to incinerate her like a giant blowtorch."

"No!" Redlaw struggled and writhed, futilely. "You devils! You unspeakable monsters!"

Lambourne's smile sharpened into a grin, and he rotated the dial several notches further. The dome became almost entirely transparent. The sky was shot with silver streaks of brightness, some of them turning gold.

"Here it comes," he breathed. "Here comes the sun."

"John?" Illyria, from the pit, plaintively. "John, look at me. Please. Just look at me."

Redlaw leaned his head over the parapet as far as he could. Illyria's eyes were wide and sparkling.

He held her gaze.

Sunlight, lambently amber, spread into the observatory. It touched the rim of the parapet. It began to slide down the inside wall, erasing shadow as it went, like an eclipse in reverse. It was as though the darkness was a liquid, pouring from the pit, draining out.

Illyria lay still, resigned to her fate.

"Kill them," she said to Redlaw, barely a whisper.

Redlaw, no less helpless, nodded. Whether he could actually bring himself to do such a thing or not, he didn't know, but at that moment he meant it. He would kill them all.

The sunlight—so swift—reached the foot of the wall. It glided in a shimmering wave across the floor of the pit, picking out the black-red topography of Vlad's filth. Soon enough it touched Illyria's foot. Instinct overcame self-control and she shrank away. The light continued to advance. Illyria, shuffling backwards, ended up in a crouch, at the extremity of the chains' tether, nowhere left to go. Onward the light crept, remorseless. Lambourne, Slocock and Macarthur looked on, their faces solemn but their eyes greedy for the horror to commence.

Illyria found Redlaw's gaze again.

There was nothing left to say.

The light crawled over her feet, her legs. She started to buck and squirm.

Then to scream.

Then the charring began, the wisps of smoke rising, the crackle of burning, and Redlaw turned away, dropped his head to his chest, squeezed his eyes shut and tried not to listen, tried not to think, tried not to be present.

CHAPTER
TWENTY-SEVEN

A MINUTE PASSED, and it was over. Lambourne clasped his hands together in satisfaction, while on Macarthur's face there was an expression of grim rectitude. What needed to be done had been done.

As for Slocock, he felt queasy but pleased with himself. He had kept watching throughout, though several times he'd been sorely tempted to avert his gaze. He'd been brave, and so had chalked up another milestone in his life. He could now claim he had witnessed a person burn to death.

It wasn't quite the same as an actual immolation, of course, like seeing a witch put to the pyre in the dark ages or an Indian widow committing *suttee*. She'd been a vampire, and it had been unnaturally quick. Still, a horrific sight. The body blackly consuming itself. The clothes smouldering, flaring into flame, from the tremendous heat being released beneath them. The flailing and shuddering that gradually lessened until, by the time the sunlight had reached Illyria's waist, it had ceased altogether. The reduction of a solid physical form to a silhouette of ashes, in less than sixty seconds. Near-instantaneous cremation. Utter annihilation.

Slocock patted the snuffbox in his jacket pocket. God, he could do with a line or two right now. Three, even. He thought he might make himself scarce, nip outdoors for a moment. Lambourne disapproved of coke—of all intoxicants stronger than alcohol—so he would have to come up with a decent cover story. Maybe "I fancy a spot of fresh air" would do it. After all, the observatory did reek of shit, and now barbecued meat, cloyingly, chokingly. It wasn't easy, or pleasant, to breathe in here.

"Nathaniel, I—" was all Slocock managed to get out before Lambourne grasped him by the shoulder and said, "Giles. Another little job for you."

Slocock was about to ask what, but Lambourne pre-empted the question by planting Redlaw's Cindermaker in his hand.

"Here," he said. "You know what to do."

Slocock gaped in disbelief. "You can't mean... I can't..."

"Of course you can," Lambourne said cheerily, as though he were encouraging Slocock to help himself to seconds of dessert or cross a room to talk to a beautiful woman. "It's not difficult. Barrel to temple, pull trigger. What could be more straightforward? You were at Sandhurst."

"Not for long."

"Long enough to have learned about guns. And if you'd stayed the course, what else would they have taught you but how to kill a man? That's essentially what you went there for, to become a soldier, a trained killer. Think of this as making up for a part of your education you missed out on. Like going to crammer college."

"B-but..." Slocock stammered; actually *stammered*. "You want me to just... shoot him?"

Redlaw sat with his head hanging. He looked lost within himself, elsewhere. If he was registering any of the conversation, he gave no sign of it.

"Why not?" said Lambourne. "You beat people up for fun. I've heard you put an opponent in a coma once."

It was true. And the Nigerian from the other night had been left in a very bad way, needing urgent medical attention.

"How's this much worse than that?" Lambourne went on. "At least there's no chance of getting hurt yourself."

"But a man's life... I'm an MP." Odd how Slocock should fall back on that, his public office, his status, when it normally meant so little to him. "There's no possible way I can commit *murder*. You must have a goon who does this sort of stuff for you, Nathaniel, some professional bagman who makes all your problems go away. Call him in."

"I prefer to keep this one simple. The fewer people involved, the better. As for your career, your future prospects, let's just say you can quit Parliament tomorrow, come to work for Dep Chem the day after— *if* you do what I'm asking."

Lambourne gave the gun a shake, reaffirming Slocock's grip on it.

"Consider this a final test," he said. "Pass, and think of what awaits you. A seven-figure salary, and you'll barely have to do a lick of work. The odd board meeting, the occasional 'fact-finding' junket to somewhere nice and hot with sandy beaches and women in bikinis, flying first class everywhere, the best hotels... It's the life everyone dreams of, Giles, and it can be yours in, what, a minute from now?"

"I want no part of this," said Commodore Macarthur. "I'm not stopping you, but I've no wish to be here when it happens."

"Yes, of course, Gail," said Lambourne. "Go. Head down to the house. I'll be right behind."

She went, not before giving Redlaw one last lingering and distinctly sorrowful look.

"Well now, Giles," said Lambourne. "Over to you. What's it to be?"

"What about cleaning up afterwards?" Slocock asked, aware that he had more than halfway made up his mind.

"Not a problem. Toss the body into the pit. The guns will do the rest. There'll be hardly anything left of him by the time they're finished. Then, I think, perhaps tonight, a mysterious fire. The observatory goes up in smoke, taking the evidence with it. I'll have the debris bulldozed flat and a new observatory built in no time, and nobody'll be any the wiser."

Except me, Slocock thought. *I'll always know what I did here. And so will you.*

"Look at him." Lambourne pointed to Redlaw. "Beaten. Comprehensively crushed. A broken man. It'll be a mercy, Giles. A mercy."

As soon as Lambourne had left, Slocock whipped out his snuffbox and treated himself to those lines. Three felt good, instilling him with confidence, but a fourth was required before he could no longer hear his conscience prowling around, muttering its little messages of fear and discontent.

Not so much Dutch courage—Colombian courage.

He grabbed the Cindermaker and marched over to Redlaw. *Get it done, get it done.* Like tearing off a sticking plaster, one quick decisive action, minimal stress.

Except, Redlaw had raised his head. He was looking at Slocock with those deep-set, appraising eyes of his.

Slocock lifted the gun and jammed the tip of the barrel against Redlaw's forehead. The man didn't flinch, just kept on looking. Staring.

Slocock thumb-cocked the hammer.

Redlaw continued to stare.

"Stop it," Slocock said. "Stop looking at me. I'll do this, I really will. I can. I will."

"Go on, then," Redlaw said calmly. "Don't muck about. Pull the damn trigger."

"I'm going to. Only, close your eyes."

"No."

"I'm not having you watch me as I do it."

"Why not?"

"Because you're, you're judging me. I can tell."

"Judging? That's not my responsibility. Only one being can judge you, Giles Slocock. He's the one who'll weigh your soul in His scales when the time comes, and decide whether you've lived a virtuous life or not."

"That's bollocks. There is no God. There is no heaven or hell or any of that shit. Anyone with any sense knows that."

"Then what are you afraid of?" said Redlaw. "Shoot. Lambourne's presented you with a perfect murder.

There'll be no comebacks. You'll get away scot-free. You'll be richly rewarded, what's more. So where's the problem? Shoot. Go ahead and do it. Shoot, you gutless worm. Blow my damn brains out."

Slocock tightened his finger on the trigger, feeling it click softly. The tiniest further bit of squeezing, and the Cindermaker would leap in his hand, Redlaw's head would jerk back, a geyser of brain and skull fragments would exit at the rear, and that would be that.

Slocock's mind buzzed like a nest of wasps. He could do this. He *could* do this. No repercussions. A seven-figure salary. A life of idleness and sybaritic self-indulgence, in exchange for another man's life.

But...

He would know. Forever. It would always be with him, what he did here, if he did it. It would never leave him. He would never forgive himself.

But then could he ever forgive himself if he didn't kill Redlaw? If he failed Lambourne's "final test"?

"Come on," Redlaw urged. "Put me out of my misery."

The muzzle of the Cindermaker trembled ever so slightly.

"Come on."

Slocock screwed his face up, half turning his head away.

"Come *on*."

He shut his eyes.

No.

"No," he said.

The gun dropped.

"I knew it," said Redlaw. "I knew you couldn't. Coward."

Slocock lifted the gun again, lowered it again. He decocked it, then tossed it aside in disgust. Shame flooded through him. He had believed he was beyond morality, much as Lambourne was, but it seemed there was a line even he could not cross. It galled him to think he might, after all, be ordinary, as much in thrall to the taboos of society as the next man.

"Tell you what," Redlaw said, "how about I make it easier for you? Untie me and we'll fight, hand to hand. You're half my age and trained, but still, you won't find me a pushover. If you can't shoot me when I'm a trussed-up victim, maybe you can beat me to death when I'm presenting a threat to you. Then you'll be able to walk out of here with your head held high, higher than if you'd simply played firing squad with me. How about that?"

Slocock grabbed at the offer, almost absurdly grateful. "Yes. Yes, that might work. In the heat of combat..."

"Exactly. In the heat of combat, anything could happen."

Slocock knelt beside the chair. Within moments the electrical flex was undone and Redlaw was standing.

"Can I have a minute to get my circulation back?" he said. "Can't fight if I can't make a fist."

"Sure." Slocock began limbering up, rolling his shoulders, cracking his knuckles.

"You know, it all makes sense now," Redlaw said, massaging his wrists and hands. "I should have realised there was a connection between you and Macarthur. It was highly convenient, you being there to pull us out of Parliament Square. I thought so at the time, but chose to overlook it. But if the shadies who were chasing us had told Macarthur where we were, then she could have phoned Lambourne..."

"...and he could have phoned me to tell me to be on the lookout for you," said Slocock. "Which he did. Nicely pieced together."

"Too late to be of any use. I could kick myself."

"Leave that to me. I'll be happy to oblige." The cocaine was hot in Slocock's veins now, like magma, mingling with a surge of pre-fight adrenaline. He was supreme. He was unstoppable. Redlaw, this broken-down crock, was about to receive a beating like no other. Kill the old geezer with his bare hands? Yeah, Slocock could see himself managing that all right. "Ready now?"

"As I'll ever be."

"Said your prayers?"

"If He's even listening, He may not want to hear them."

"I'll try and make it quick."

"Less talk. Do your worst."

Slocock triple-stepped forwards, an angel of death, a lightning storm in the form of a man. His first furious flurry of punches all found their mark. Redlaw's defences were clumsy. He barely seemed to know how to mount an effective block. And he was slow—a tortoise, compared to Slocock. He reeled back under the onslaught with a baffled look that Slocock was familiar with, having seen it on countless opponents' faces in the past. *What is this? How can this be happening? What am I up against?*

Slocock kept the pressure up. The jabs, hooks and roundhouses landed thick and fast, driving Redlaw backwards until he butted into a wall. Redlaw was reduced to covering his head with both arms, the most basic method possible of warding off the attack. Slocock switched from head shots to body shots. His legs came into play, battering Redlaw's torso and hips. A spinning kick delivered the full stop to a long and complicated sentence of violence, scooping Redlaw's feet out from under him and leaving him flat on the floor.

Slocock danced back out of range as Redlaw first clambered to his knees, then got to his feet, clutching the wall for support.

Patches of Redlaw's face had the rough, reddened look of tenderised beef, and he was bleeding from nose and mouth. He wiped a hand across his lips, smearing the blood sideways. He spat a wad of pink sputum onto the floor.

"Yes," he said. "You're not bad, are you? Keep it up and you'll definitely be the death of me."

"You can always fight back, you know," Slocock said. "This doesn't have to be so one-sided."

"Oh, I mean to. I may not have your fancy moves but for two decades I've been dealing with creatures faster than you, and clawed to boot. I just wanted to establish the parameters here—how hard you can hit and all that."

"And how hard do I hit?"

"Very hard," said Redlaw, with feeling. "But then so do I."

He charged at Slocock, bull-like and with a surprising turn of speed. His punches had some serious weight to them, bludgeoning Slocock's midriff. His left fist was doing most of the work so Slocock concentrated on blocking on that side. When an opportunity opened up he dug in with an elbow strike to Redlaw's right trapezius, leaning back so as to give it full force. Redlaw grunted but didn't relent. A second elbow strike closer to the shoulder, though, brought a cry from him and he staggered away, right arm hanging limp.

Numbed? No. Slocock got the impression the arm was previously injured and still giving Redlaw grief. Therefore a vulnerable spot. Good.

That was where he focused on next, forcing Redlaw to turn out his left side and take most of the punishment there. At an angle, Redlaw's retaliatory options were limited, but he succeeded in sneaking a foot stamp past Slocock's guard, shearing his heel down the side of Slocock's ankle.

It was hobbling agony, as though part of the talus bone had been snapped off, and Slocock couldn't help but recoil. Redlaw threw himself at him, catching him in a clinch from behind. Using his own momentum he slammed Slocock's forehead against the edge of the parapet. He did it a second time for good measure, and then Slocock hacked backwards with an elbow, a flailing, undisciplined blow, but it did the trick, catching Redlaw full in the sternum and knocking the wind out of his sails.

"Oww, fucking oww," Slocock said, clamping palm-heel to forehead. Khun Sarawong would have told him not to show pain. He could almost hear the gnomic little instructor's voice: *Know pain but do not show pain.* Well, tough shit. Slocock felt like his skull had been cracked open, and it fucking well hurt.

He rounded on Redlaw, who was clutching his ribs, bent double.

"You old fuck," he snarled. "That was hardly fair."

"Have I ticked you off?" Redlaw wheezed.

"Yes, you have."

"Are you angry?"

"Yes, I am."

"What are you waiting for, then? Finish this."

Slocock beelined for Redlaw and almost immediately had him bound up in a clinch, a proper one, head to head like fighters should, with his hands locked round the back of Redlaw's neck. His right knee pistoned up and down, ramming into the other man's face. If he kept this going long enough, Redlaw would be done for.

A searing pain rose between Slocock's legs, as though a spike was being driven up into his groin. Redlaw had his balls in his hand and was squeezing as if to burst them. Slocock's head stretched back in a rictus of excruciation, mouth working soundlessly. Redlaw then cracked his brow down onto Slocock's upturned jaw, breaking the clinch.

Both men staggered away from each other, then clashed again, like magnets that could not be kept apart. Slocock was utterly content now with the prospect of killing Redlaw. The man deserved it. He had, in a perverse way, earned it. Slocock had no intention of ending the fight until Redlaw's lifeless body lay at his feet.

Together they lurched towards the parapet, colliding with it sideways. All at once, to his surprise, Slocock found himself being hoisted off the floor. Redlaw had lifted him up, using every ounce of strength he could muster, and panicky thoughts raced through Slocock's mind. This move wasn't in the *muay thai* rulebook, this wasn't something he had been trained for, this was an attack he had no defence against. He struggled, but Redlaw had him poised on the parapet, teetering over the pit, off-balance, legs scissoring wildly in the air. He lashed out but the blows had no power behind them, and anyway there was a maddened, implacable gleam in Redlaw's eyes that spoke of someone whom nothing would deter.

In a shocking, crushing instant Slocock realised he had lost. His life was in Redlaw's hands and not, as it should have been, the other way round.

"No," he said. "Please. I didn't... The gun..."

"I know," said Redlaw through bloodied, swollen lips. "When I was at your mercy, you couldn't go through with it. Sad to say, I don't have the same inhibition. Not any more."

He shoved. Let go.

Slocock plummeted.

The machine guns started firing before he even hit the floor, and they didn't stop firing until every Fraxinus round in their belts had been expended and the Conservative Member of Parliament for Chesham and Amersham, the Right Honourable Giles Slocock, was little more than a slurry of bone shards and pulped flesh.

CHAPTER
TWENTY-EIGHT

VICTORY. BUT IT couldn't have felt less like it.

With the cacophony of the machine guns still ringing in his ears, Redlaw stumbled over to pick up his Cindermaker. Next thing he knew, he was prone on the floor, the gun still inches from his hand. He groped for it, but it seemed just that bit too far away. The observatory was seesawing under him like a ship in heavy seas. Everything hurt, every part of him. He closed his eyes for a moment, hoping that when he opened them the pain would have gone away and the world would have stopped lurching nauseatingly up and down.

It was more than a moment. The sun was considerably higher, the sky brighter and bluer, when he next looked up. Somehow he summoned the wherewithal to stand. Somehow, Cindermaker in hand, he made it down the staircase to the exit.

He trudged downhill through dewy grass to the mansion. He crossed a shrubbery-fringed lawn. He crunched over a driveway covered in a drift of snow-white pea gravel. He dragged his feet up seven stone steps to a baronial front door.

Which stood ajar. Redlaw nudged it further open. He stepped inside, into a grand hall embraced by curving staircases, with a leaded skylight, Grecian statuary in alcoves, fresh lilies bursting crisply from crystal vases. There was a hush. Not quite silence. Unmistakably the place was occupied, there was someone other than him present. But nevertheless a waiting stillness, an ominous tranquillity.

Redlaw listened. Soft sounds reached him, coming from a doorway leading off from the hall. He approached warily, gun ready.

The door opened onto a drawing room. Twenty-foot ceiling. Moulded cornices. Murals on every wall, mimicking Georgian Arcadian landscapes. Lush drapery. A decorated piano.

And a body sprawled on the marble floor, twitching, uttering hiccupy little gasps.

Redlaw padded closer.

Nathaniel Lambourne lay on his back. He had one hand pressed to his neck, and his face bore a ghastly grey pallor. Beneath his head blood had pooled out in a circle like some obscene vermilion halo. His eyes rolled in their sockets, seeing everything and nothing, then all at once found Redlaw and fixed and focused on him. His gaze shone brightly, alive with horror.

"Oh, God," Lambourne said. "Oh, thank God. I need help. The bleeding... I can't stop it. I'm slowing it, holding it in, but... Ambulance. There's a phone over there. Use it. Call."

Redlaw didn't move. Lambourne's hand was slick with blood. It was oozing out between his fingers in slow, thick pulses. A wound to the carotid. Some kind of incision, a shallow one, but not so shallow that the blood could coagulate and form a seal.

A cut designed to cause a protracted, lingering death.

"Please," said Lambourne. "I can't get up. I don't dare. I've tried and I start to black out. Help me. I'll give you anything. Anything you want."

"Bring back Illyria Strakosha," Redlaw said. "Then I'll help you."

Lambourne's eyes darkened. Resignation set in. "That's how it's going to be, is it?"

"That's how it's going to be."

"Ha." Bitter. Mirthless. "So Giles bottled out, did he? Let you live."

"I'd hardly say let. I goaded him into untying me. Then we settled it like equals, only I was more equal than him. Who did this to you?"

"Who do you think? Funny thing is, I didn't see it coming. In every way, didn't see it coming. I turned my back for a second, and..."

He coughed, and the blood seeped out a little more freely. He did his best to keep the pressure on his neck, stem the flow, but he was fighting a losing battle. He knew it too. It was in his eyes: he had only minutes left.

"It was the letter opener. From the escritoire. Sharp as anything, that is. I nicked myself on it more than once, back in the days when people sent letters. She— she sneaked up on me from behind..."

"Macarthur," said Redlaw.

"Yes. Of course."

"But why?"

"I don't know. I don't sodding know. How should I? We were associates, that's what I thought. She was useful when it came to the designs for Solarville. A valuable resource. Then to turn round and stab me..." He sighed as if exasperated. *The sheer effrontery of it!*

"It happens. I'm getting used to betrayal. No one's worth trusting."

"But she's got everything she could have wanted, that's what I don't understand. She was all for Solarville from the start. Supported the idea the whole way. She even has the code."

"Code? What code?"

Lambourne was failing, fading out. Redlaw brusquely shook him.

"Macarthur, Lambourne. What code has she got? What for?"

The eyes drifted, then refocused.

"She absolutely detests them." The industrialist's voice was a papery rustle, like accounts books being flicked through. "Vampires. With a vengeance. You must know she does."

It was news to Redlaw, and his face showed it.

"No?" said Lambourne. "God, you should hear her sometimes. Maybe it's just with me, in confidence, but the way she speaks about them. The spite. The venom. Words like 'vermin.' 'Scum,' 'worms,' 'leeches.' Worse. It's just as well she's in administration at SHADE, stuck behind a desk. Otherwise she'd be out there exterminating every vamp she sees."

"Where is she now? Is she still here?"

"Gone," said Lambourne. "I heard her car."

"Gone where?"

"How should I know? Do I look like I'd care? Bitch has killed me. She can go to Hell as far as I'm concerned."

His face clouded.

"Redlaw?"

"Yes?"

"You believe, don't you?"

"In God?"

"Yes."

Lambourne seemed to be seeking some sort of benediction. Reassurance in his final moments. Extreme unction.

"You'll get what's coming to you," Redlaw said.

"I don't..." Lambourne's grip on his neck loosened. The blood frothed forth. "You know what this feels like? It feels like... Like falling."

His hand sank to the floor, limp.

"Falling."

His jaw slackened and his eyes glazed. His whole body went rigid, and up out of his throat came the gurgle of his last breath, the archetypal death rattle, sounding much like a dispirited groan.

Redlaw stayed with the industrialist's corpse for a while. In death, Lambourne had ceased to resemble himself. His face had lost its distinguishing features and become just a face, could be almost anyone's. The human body was merely a vehicle. The soul—and even a rapacious billionaire had one—was what gave it animation and character.

And right now, if there was any justice, Nathaniel Lambourne's soul was burning.

SHE ABSOLUTELY DETESTS *them*.

The remark went round and round in Redlaw's head as he pondered his next move.

Why had Macarthur killed Lambourne? What had possessed her to snatch up the letter opener and slit his neck? It was almost beyond comprehension. Lambourne didn't appear to have provoked her in any way. It had come seemingly out of the blue. What did she stand to gain from murdering him? Nothing. In fact, she had plenty to lose.

The sound of a car pulling up outside broke in on his deliberations. Through a window Redlaw saw a woman get out of a small Skoda, carrying newspapers under one arm, and walk round the back of the car to fetch groceries from the boot. Her age, dress and general demeanour all said 'housekeeper.' As she mounted the front steps, a frown of confusion creased her forehead. The open door.

Redlaw quickly undid the catch on the window and eased up the casement. He slipped over the sill into the flowerbed outside, even as the housekeeper entered the mansion and called out, loudly but tentatively, "Mr Lambourne? Sir?"

His initial thought was to take the housekeeper's car, but he remembered seeing her pocket the key. Instead, he stole over to the stable block, which had been converted into an open-fronted garage. Where horses had once snorted and whinnied, now a row of costly cars stood, some contemporary, some vintage, all with their front ends facing out and their bodywork gleamingly polished.

Sets of keys hung, handily, on a hook-board just inside. Even more handily, each was attached to a fob with a manufacturer's logo on it. The Lamborghini? The Ferrari? The Bugatti? Redlaw was spoiled for choice.

But not spoiled for time, as a scream emanated from the house, piercingly shrill. Once the housekeeper got over her shock, she'd be straight on to the police. They'd be here in quarter of an hour, maybe sooner.

He plumped for a Mercedes, a C-class saloon; he had no experience with snazzy Italian sports models and would probably crash one if he attempted to drive it. He unlocked the Merc, swiftly familiarised himself with the controls, switched on the ignition, and then was sailing off up the driveway. He felt a momentary pang of regret about the housekeeper. Ought he to have intercepted her before she went into the drawing room? Warned her what she would discover there? The poor woman was probably half out of her wits, finding her employer dead on the floor in a pool of blood.

But wouldn't it have alarmed her more to come across a stranger in the house? One who, moreover, looked as pitifully ragged and battered as the rearview mirror was telling Redlaw he did?

No, he'd done the right thing.

Now all he had to do was figure out where he was going.

Macarthur was his quarry. Catching up with her, catching her, was his priority. What had got into her? What was motivating her? He'd never thought of Gail Macarthur as the type to flip out and do something insane. She'd always seemed so sturdily reliable.

Then again, she had been busily undermining him throughout his investigation into the bloodlust riots, hadn't she? And, for all her protestations, the trap she'd set for him on the Isle of Dogs could have proved lethal.

Macarthur had some hidden agenda, some ultimate goal he just wasn't seeing.

The entrance gate rolled aside of its own accord as the Mercedes approached. Redlaw pulled out onto the lane, skidding slightly as he made the turn. There was more power under the Merc's bonnet than he was used to, and more sensitivity in the steering wheel too.

She absolutely detests them.

He had had no inkling of Macarthur's loathing for the Sunless. She'd managed to keep that from him. Disguised it well. Although he had perhaps caught a glimpse of it back there in the observatory, when he'd been bargaining for Illyria's life...

Illyria.

No. Redlaw tamped that thought down. Now was not the time to dwell on Illyria. Focus on Macarthur. He couldn't escape the feeling that he was racing against the clock. Macarthur had embarked on something with the murder of Lambourne, some desperate endgame, the culmination of months of quiet, covert plotting.

Detests them. With a vengeance.

She has the code.

All at once it came to him.

God damn it.

God damn her.

Redlaw switched on the car's sat nav. He wasn't sure of the precise address of his destination but, as it happened, it was already logged into the sat nav's memory. Of course. The Merc must have travelled the route before, countless times.

"Keep going straight on," the computer voice advised, calmly. "You have sixty-one point two miles to go."

CHAPTER
TWENTY-NINE

SOLARVILLE ONE GLEAMED massively ahead, a hill amongst hills, like some mutant outgrowth of the Chiltern range, cancerously black.

As Redlaw drove in along the approach road, a line of SHADE patrol cars passed the other way, officers clocking off and heading home after a busy night. The Mercedes had tinted windows, so he wasn't concerned about being spotted and recognised. The gateway in the perimeter fence, however, guarded by both soldiers and shadies, would be a problem.

He was considering putting his foot down and ramming the barrier, but as he came within twenty metres of it he spotted a row of tyre spikes entrenched in the tarmac, bristling like metal porcupine quills. *Damn*.

Then a wonderful thing happened. Like the Red Sea parting for Moses, the tyre spikes sank into the ground, the barrier lifted of its own accord, and its armed custodians stepped aside. One of them even waved the car through, while another saluted.

Whatever operated the gate to Lambourne's estate also worked its magic here. Redlaw, in spite of everything, couldn't suppress a smile. There was even a parking space near the dome, designated EXCLUSIVE USE OF NATHANIEL LAMBOURNE.

Sitting close by was a solitary SHADE car, in all likelihood the one Macarthur was using to get about. Redlaw placed a palm on the bonnet. Engine still hot. She'd not been here long. Maybe there was still time; he wasn't too late.

He recalled, from the schematic he'd seen in the newspaper, that there was a control bunker onsite where environmental conditions within the dome could be monitored and adjusted, and the Sunless residents kept an eye on. A single-story breezeblock structure near the dome's base, some hundred metres from where he stood, seemed to be the place. Redlaw loped towards it, careful to stay out of line-of-sight from the building's few, meagrely-proportioned windows.

The door required a swipe card and numeric code for entry; Redlaw's only available tactic was the brazen, frontal approach. He rapped firmly and authoritatively on the door, at the same time drawing his Cindermaker. The element of surprise, at least, was on his side. As far as Macarthur knew, he was dead, his body mangled and effaced beyond all recognition. She wouldn't be expecting him.

A SHADE officer opened the door, and as his initial quizzical look turned to one of startlement, Redlaw shoved him inside, putting his gun to the man's head.

There were three other shadies inside the control bunker, and Macarthur. All turned round as Redlaw bundled his hostage towards them. All four looked perplexed, but none as much as the Commodore.

She was standing in front of a computer console, while the other three sat before a bank of TV screens. Images on the screens presented a montage of life within the dome for its recently installed inmates. Sunless were strolling through the streets of Solarville One, many of them shielding their eyes and blinking up towards the sun. Their postures, their body language, conveyed a mixture of trepidation and amazement. They were like space explorers venturing across the surface of an unknown planet, still not quite assured that the alien atmosphere was not going to kill them. A few of the vampires were obeying their age-old, innermost imperative and trying to find shelter from the light, cowering behind walls and the like. The majority, however, appeared to be coming to terms with the idea that the pale glowing disc peeping through the glass panes overhead need not be feared. The sun's radiance was no longer fatal to them.

For now.

"Commodore," said Redlaw. "Please move away from that console."

Macarthur did not budge. There was text on the display behind her, above an empty box with a cursor flashing. The words were too small for Redlaw to make out, but his guess—no, more than a guess, his conviction—was that this was the command to render the dome clear.

She has the code.

Macarthur had called up the emergency failsafe protocol and had been on the verge of eradicating every vampire inside the dome, all one thousand of them.

None of the junior officers would have been aware what she was up to, if she'd gone about it subtly. Nor would any of them have thought to query her actions, because, well, she was the Commodore.

Redlaw had arrived in the very nick of time. Ten seconds later and Macarthur would have pressed Enter and the glass-lightening process would have begun. A mass dusting on an unprecedented scale.

"Move," he said again, "or I shoot this man."

"No," Macarthur replied with confidence. "I don't think you will, John."

"She's trying to wipe them all out," Redlaw informed the other shadies. "The dome's fitted with smart glass. It can be made transparent."

"Preposterous," said Macarthur.

"What are you doing on that computer, then?"

She was, as he knew now to his cost, a smooth liar. "Diagnostic check. Making sure the systems are running efficiently and bug-free."

"Forgive me, but what the hell do *you* know about computer systems? You're sabotaging Solarville."

Redlaw spotted one of the shadies reaching surreptitiously for his Cindermaker.

"Uh-uh," he warned. "Not unless you want this man's death on your conscience."

The hostage whimpered.

"Don't fret, Aaronovitch," Macarthur told the frightened man. "It's a bluff. Redlaw's never killed a human, and he's not about to start now."

"Wrong," said Redlaw. "How come I'm here, still alive? Because I killed Giles Slocock. And now that I've taken one life, another two or three won't make much difference. When you've broken the Sixth

Commandment once, you might as well keep on breaking it. You can't go back, so you might as well go forward."

"Then you've damned yourself."

Redlaw gave a pain-wracked parody of a shrug. "God and I will sort it out between us when the time comes. I think I'll be able to make a convincing case for myself. I doubt you'll be able to do the same, Gail. Not after murdering Nathaniel Lambourne like that."

Consternation filled the room. Macarthur tried to rise above it, dismissing Redlaw's statement with a contemptuous sneer. "So Lambourne's dead, eh? Who's to say you didn't kill him yourself, John, and you're trying to shift the blame? It's all very well bandying accusations about, but unless you have proof—"

"I don't need proof," Redlaw said, overriding her. "He told me exactly who did it, as he lay dying. But your killing him isn't even that important. Good riddance, I say. The world is lighter without Lambourne. What matters is what you're *about* to do, the wholesale slaughter of hundreds of vampires. For the last time: step away from the console. I won't have you doing this. I won't allow it."

Macarthur was debating within herself, he could see. Tallying up all her options. Aaronovitch squirmed in his grasp, but Redlaw put a stop to that by grinding the gun harder into the back of his skull.

Abruptly Macarthur came to a decision and about-faced. Her hands went to the console keyboard. She started to type.

Redlaw swung his Cindermaker away from Aaronovitch and planted a bullet smack dab in the body of the console. Something shattered; sparks flew. The display went blank. Macarthur stabbed Enter, stabbed it again, but the console was dead. There were no sounds, no warning sirens, nothing to indicate that the failsafe command had gone through and the dome was clearing. Redlaw glanced at the TV screens. On none of them was the image growing lighter or a vampire starting to recoil in agony.

"Fuck you." Macarthur turned round with sheer thwarted hatred blazing in her eyes. "Fuck you, John, you *fuck*. What did you have to go and do that for? I was so close. I nearly had them!"

"Gail Macarthur," said Redlaw, "you are under arrest for the attempted unlawful dusting of—"

"You can't arrest anybody," she crowed. "You're not even a shady any more. You're a sad wee nobody, is what you are. Look at the state of you. A half-dead loser who's gone soft on vamps, thanks to that shtriga slut you were fooling around with. At least she's gone now. It was a pleasure to watch the bitch burn."

Her face took on a wheedling, mock-pitying expression.

"Och, did I hurt your feelings there, reminding you of your undead girlie? Tell me, what's it like screwing a vampire? Is that the only way you can get it up, that shrivelled old dick of yours, when the lady's stone-cold and dry as a bone down under?"

"We never—"

But before Redlaw could finish the riposte, Macarthur dived for the SHADE officer nearest her, yanked his Cindermaker out of its holster, and blasted three times at Redlaw. All of the shots missed him but one struck Aaronovitch in the chest, and the impact sent both him and Redlaw crashing to the floor.

In the confusion that followed, as Redlaw lay pinned under Aaronovitch, further shots were fired. There was shouting, screaming, the sound of things breaking. Finally he managed to disentangle himself from the corpse and throw it off him, to discover that another of the SHADE officers was dead, one had a bullet wound to the arm, and the third was crouched behind a chair, face contorted with terror.

There was no sign of Macarthur.

"The Commodore, she's crazy," said the injured shady. "She started blasting away, then ran out." He pointed to a glass-fronted case mounted on the wall. It had been smashed open. "Took that with her."

A fire axe, which had been hanging on spring-clips in the case.

Redlaw launched himself out of the control bunker, spotting Macarthur immediately; she was sprinting towards the foot of the maintenance ladder, which hugged the contour of the dome from base to apex. She leapt onto it and began clambering up, the fire axe dangling from her belt.

It didn't take a genius to work out what she proposed to do. Since she couldn't make the glass panes see-through, the next best thing was simply to smash them individually.

Redlaw ran after her and hauled himself up onto the ladder. The first couple of dozen steps were pretty steep, but thereafter the rising curve shallowed out and the going became easier. It helped that there were safety rails on both sides, affording handholds.

As he climbed, Redlaw noticed switch-boxes positioned at regular intervals along one of the safety rails, each with a green pressure button and a red stop button. The underside of the ladder was fitted with wheels running along grooved tracks encircling the dome. The entire ladder must be able to move, then, swinging around the dome. The switch-boxes enabled maintenance workers to 'drive' it.

Halfway up, a good two hundred and fifty metres above ground level, Macarthur glanced over her shoulder. Looking unsurprised that Redlaw was pursuing her, she pulled the Cindermaker from her waistband and fired twice. Redlaw flattened himself against the steps. Both shots missed, but one ricocheted off the safety rail just inches from his head, hair-raisingly close.

When no further shots followed, Redlaw peered up and saw Macarthur cursing in frustration. Out of bullets. She didn't have a spare clip, so she tossed the Cindermaker away. The gun skittered and clattered down the dome, while Macarthur resumed climbing.

Redlaw followed. He himself had only the one Fraxinus round left. Better make it count.

Within a minute Macarthur was near the summit of Solarville One. The rungs of the ladder were almost level with one another. She tugged the axe out from her belt and leaned over the safety rail. Taking a double-handed grip on the haft, she swung the blade down onto one of the topmost hexagonal panes. The glass was thick and toughened, designed to withstand the worst the elements could bring, and it took her a few blows to penetrate it. Once she did, however, knocking out the rest of the metre-wide pane was relatively easy. She turned her attention to the next pane down and started to repeat the process.

Redlaw had by now made up the gap between them. He halted within a few metres of Macarthur, panting hard. His Cindermaker was out and levelled.

"Enough, Gail," he said. "That's enough. Stop right there."

Macarthur paused, axe poised. "It isn't enough. I won't stop until I've shattered every single pane. Listen. Hear that?"

Faintly, from below, there were screams. Some of the vampires must have been caught in the shaft of sunlight now lancing down from the glassless aperture in the dome. Beneath his feet, Redlaw saw tiny figures scurrying about, panicked as ants when a small boy focuses a sunbeam on them through a magnifying glass.

"You know what that's the sound of?" Macarthur said. "A good start."

"Why?" said Redlaw. "Why do this?"

"Haven't you figured it out?"

"Apparently not. That's the reason I'm asking."

"For her," Macarthur said. "Róisín."

"Leary?"

"How many other bloody Róisíns do we know? They killed her. Bastard vampires killed her. Took her from me, and since I can't get her back, I'm going to get my own back on them. I'm going to dust a thousand of them, because she was worth a thousand of them. Fair exchange."

"But there've been at least a dozen shadies who've died on your watch," said Redlaw. "More. It's an occupational hazard. Yes, Leary was an exceptional officer, but why her in particular? Why's she the one who has to be avenged and not any of the others?"

"I wouldn't expect you to understand, John. It's something called 'love.' It's what happens between people who have feelings and are capable of expressing them. An alien concept to you, of course."

"You... and Leary?"

"Ding! The lightbulb pops on above his head." Sudden tears glistened in Macarthur's eyes. "I loved that woman. She loved me. Of course, we had to keep it secret. Fraternising within the ranks—frowned on. It would've probably cost me my job if anybody had found out, and Róisín's prospects for promotion would have been shot. I think Khalid knew, or maybe he just had an instinct about us, sensed something that offended his religious sensibilities, tweaked his deviance radar. I think a couple of others might have had their suspicions too. But funnily enough, not Leary's best friend. You had no idea."

"I didn't even know she was a..."

"You can say it. Lesbian. What you'll find is, some of us are better at hiding it than others. Some of us have to be. Strict Roman Catholic community like the one Róisín grew up in, it didn't do for a girl to admit she prefers girls. The nuns at her convent school would have tried to flog it out of her if they'd known. So she acted straight, but by God, when we were together, she was anything but. Best sex of my life, John. The love of my life as well.

"We were going to grow old together. Once we'd both done our stint with SHADE and collected our pensions, we were going to buy a cottage near Brighton and become a pair of fat, crotchety old tuppence-lickers with too many cats and a kitchen garden full of veggies. It was all going to be so wonderful."

Macarthur made no move to wipe the tears from her cheeks, but nor did she sob. Her voice remained steely and even as she said, "I miss her every day. Every minute of every day. Undead scumbags stole my future from me. They have to pay for that."

"But then why kill Lambourne? Leary's death had nothing to do with him."

"Use your head. I'm messing with Solarville One, his baby. On the very first day this little money-spinner of his goes into action, I come along and deploy the failsafe—or at least I would have, no thanks to you. How do you think the public would have reacted, knowing this isn't just a place of detention, but has the capacity to be a death camp, a vampire Belsen? Not very favourably, I'd imagine. I doubt he'd have got to build the other fourteen. The PM would have torn up the contract and pretended he never knew and done his best to distance himself from the whole affair."

"So?"

"So, Nathaniel Lambourne is the last person I'd ever want pissed off at me. Look how you've ended up, and you barely cost him a penny with all your shenanigans. Me, I'd be costing him millions. There's nowhere on earth I'd be safe from him. He had to die. The neck wound was a nice touch, don't you think?"

"Police might suspect a Sunless did it?"

"Oh, not for long, but they might to begin with, and that would make them very excited. Cops love a bit of vamp action if they can get it. Best-case scenario, it would throw them off the scent long enough for me to make my play here, then abscond, never to be seen again. The biggest irony of all is, the failsafe was my idea. I convinced Lambourne to put it in. I told him at the very least it could be used to singe the 'Lesses' tailfeathers, if they ever got uppity or out of hand. Just lighten the glass a fraction, for a handful of seconds, to remind them who's boss. It would be an effective method of sanction, as well as a selling point. He came round to it eventually. All my work."

She lofted the fire axe again.

"And now I've just got to go about letting the sunshine in the old-fashioned, manual way."

"No," said Redlaw. "I can't allow you to."

"Shoot, then. Just remember, I'm doing this in memory of a woman we both, in our own ways, thought the world of."

Redlaw took aim. He had no alternative. Like it or not, he was a shtriga now. The vampires in the dome were under his protection. Besides, Leary would surely not have wanted Macarthur to destroy them in her name. The Róisín Leary he remembered was more forgiving than that.

Macarthur brought the axe down, and Redlaw fired.

She'd outsmarted him, though. Instead of chopping into a pane, Macarthur righted the axe at the very last instant and slammed the end of the haft onto the green button on the switch-box just in front of her. The ladder began to roll sideways with a sudden, sharp lurch, throwing Redlaw against the safety rail. His shot went wild, and even if he'd had any more bullets in the magazine, Macarthur wasn't about to give him a chance to use them, as she came bounding down the ladder, swinging the axe at him.

Redlaw threw himself out of the axe's path, lost his footing, and began slithering down the ladder. Macarthur ran after him, hacking frenziedly, the axe blade sparking as it bit steel. Redlaw was obliged to keep propelling himself downwards on his belly to avoid the blows. The empty Cindermaker slipped from his grasp, tumbling to join the other Cindermaker somewhere at the base of the dome.

"Just stay still!" Macarthur snarled. "Just die!"

Redlaw's barely controlled descent was gaining momentum as the steps steepened. The ladder vibrated and juddered beneath him as it moved. Finally, helplessly, he was bounced out over the side. With a flailing hand he grabbed hold of the safety rail, but the ladder continued to sweep slowly round on its axis like the second hand of a giant watch, dragging Redlaw behind it.

Macarthur halted and lined up the axe blade with Redlaw's hand. He let go just as she swung, the axe landing just where his fingers had been.

He was sliding, falling. He managed to catch himself by hooking his hands onto the lip of one of the dome's struts. His feet scrabbled for purchase on another strut below.

Macarthur stepped off the ladder and began working her way carefully across the hexagonal framework towards Redlaw, leaning her body into the dome's curvature for balance.

"Such a pest," she was saying. "You're as bad as one of them. A plague on me, on all of us. You need to be got rid of."

Redlaw had almost nothing left. All his weapons were gone and little strength remained in his limbs. He was some three hundred metres up, clinging to the face of Solarville One for dear life, with an axe-wielding maniac stalking towards him bent on murder.

That was when he felt his crucifix pressing against his chest.

Leary: *"See, the thing is, as with everything where God is concerned, it might not be what you want, but it might just be what you need."*

Redlaw yanked the crucifix over his head, then twined the chain around one hand. Macarthur was now within arm's length of him.

"Going to scare me off with that thing, are you?" she snorted. "You really have lost it, John. I'm not one of *them*."

She lashed out at him clumsily, one-handed, clinging to the side of the dome. Redlaw deflected the axe with his chain-wrapped fist. Then, as Macarthur was drawing her arm back to take another shot, he snapped the crucifix out like a whip. The heavy cross smacked Macarthur full in the nose, with a loud cartilaginous *crack*.

Briefly blinded by pain, Macarthur whirled the axe weakly at him. Redlaw caught the haft and reversed the blow back at her. The haft twisted out of her hand, the axe head dropped, and the blade sank into her thigh.

Macarthur shrieked as blood spurted from the cleaved muscle. The axe pulled itself free and dropped away, spinning end over end. Macarthur slid after it but was able to stop herself. Several panes below Redlaw, her arms braced on two struts, teeth clenched, eyes wild, she hung grimly on.

"John," she said, looking up. Her voice was a trembling croak. "John, I can't hold on. I'm slipping."

Blood poured from her leg. The axe had nicked an artery.

"You can reach me, can't you? Pull me up?"

Redlaw had killed Slocock. Had let Lambourne die.

Three out of three?

"John, I'm sorry. I'm so sorry. For everything. It was all for Róisín. You see that, don't you? All for her."

Redlaw looked at his crucifix, then back down at his former boss.

"Explain it to her yourself," he said. "See if she understands."

The ladder took a full five minutes to circumnavigate the dome. By the time it had completed its circuit, there was only one person left to clamber back on.

CHAPTER THIRTY

REDLAW ABANDONED LAMBOURNE'S Mercedes by the side of a B-road somewhere outside Hitchin.

He walked away from the car, over a stile, into a field. It was a beautiful spring morning. The English countryside was bursting into life, bright green and vigorous. Swallows swooped and larks soared; sheep bleated and cattle lowed.

Redlaw crossed the meadow grass, limping a little, supporting his right arm with his left. He had no clear notion of where he was headed or what he was going to do, but that was okay. There was sun on his face and nothing around him but open farmland, infinite paths and byways.

Halfway across the field, he wrenched the crucifix off his neck and tossed it behind him.

A dozen paces on, he doubled back and retrieved it.

Bending his head, noosing the crucifix back around his neck, accepting its size and weight, Redlaw strode on.

ACKNOWLEDGEMENTS

Clint Langley supplied an awesome cover that made the book look much cooler and made me feel much cooler about the book. David Moore did yet another terrific copy-edit that curbed my writerly excesses and trimmed the manuscript's marbling of fat. Nick Sharps kept me entertained and amused with his comments on my blog. Andy Remic showed by example how far nerve and a screw-you attitude can get you. And all the folks at Solaris – Jonathan Oliver, Ben Smith, Jenni Hill and Michael Molcher, as well as the aforementioned Mr Moore – have been stars.

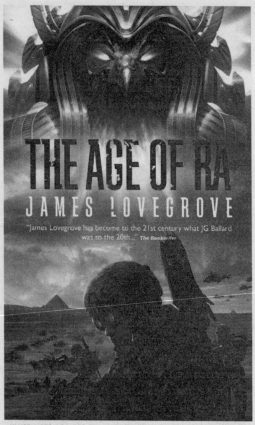

THE AGE OF RA

JAMES LOVEGROVE

"James Lovegrove has become to the 21st century what JG Ballard was to the 20th..." *The Bookseller*

UK ISBN: 978 1 844167 46 3 • US ISBN: 978 1 844167 47 0 • £7.99/$7.99

The Ancient Egyptian gods have defeated all the other pantheons and divided the Earth into warring factions. Lt. David Westwynter, a British soldier, stumbles into Freegypt, the only place to have remained independent of the gods, and encounters the followers of a humanist freedom-fighter known as the Lightbringer. As the world heads towards an apocalyptic battle, there is far more to this leader than it seems...

 WWW.SOLARISBOOKS.COM

Follow us on Twitter! www.twitter.com/solarisbooks

UK ISBN: 978 1 907519 40 6 • US ISBN: 978 1 907519 41 3 • £7.99/$7.99

Gideon Coxall was a good soldier but bad at everything else, until a roadside explosive device leaves him with one deaf ear and a British Army half-pension. The Valhalla Project, recruiting useless soldiers like himself, no questions asked, seems like a dream, but the last thing Gid expects is to find himself fighting alongside ancient Viking gods. It seems Ragnarök — the fabled final conflict of the Sagas — is looming.

THE AGE OF ZEUS

JAMES LOVEGROVE

"James Lovegrove has become to the 21st century what JG Ballard was to the 20th..."
The Bookseller

UK ISBN: 978 1 906735 68 5 • US ISBN: 978 1 906735 69 2 • £7.99/$7.99

The Olympians appeared a decade ago, living incarnations of the Ancient Greek gods, offering order and stability at the cost of placing humanity under the jackboot of divine oppression. Until former London police officer Sam Akehurst receives an invitation to join the Titans, the small band of battlesuited high-tech guerillas squaring off against the Olympians and their mythological monsters in a war they cannot all survive...

 WWW.SOLARISBOOKS.COM

Follow us on Twitter! www.twitter.com/solarisbooks

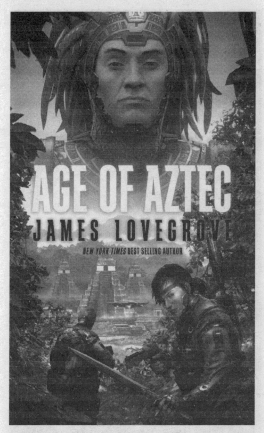

AGE OF AZTEC

JAMES LOVEGROVE

NEW YORK TIMES BEST SELLING AUTHOR

UK ISBN: 978-1-907992-80-3 • US ISBN: 978-1-907992-81-0 • £7.99/$7.99

The date is 4 Jaguar 1 Monkey 1 House – November 25th 2012 by the old reckoning – and the Aztec Empire rules the world. Their reign is one of cruel and ruthless oppression, encompassing regular human sacrifice.

In the jungle-infested city of London, one man defies them: the masked vigilante known as the Conquistador. He is recruited to spearhead an uprising, and discovers a terrible truth. The clock is ticking. Apocalypse looms, unless the Conquistador can help assassinate the mysterious, immortal Aztec emperor, the Great Speaker. But his mission is complicated by Mal Vaughn, a police detective who is on his trail, determined to bring him to justice.

UK ISBN: 978 1 907992 01 8 • US ISBN: 978 1 907992 00 1 • £7.99/$7.99

Carl stumbles across part of a map to an unknown town. He becomes convinced
it represents the city of his dreams, where ice skaters turn quintuple loops and
trumpeters hit impossibly high notes... where Annie Risk will agree to see him
again. But if he ever finds himself in the streets on his map, will they turn out to be
the land of his dreams or the world of his worst nightmares?